EMPEROR OF WRATH

JAGGER COLE

Emperor of Wrath
Jagger Cole © 2024

Cover and interior design by Plan 9 Book Design
Cover Photo: David Wagner
Sensitivity reader: Natalie Tanaka

❀ Created with Vellum

TRIGGER WARNING

Dear Reader,

This book contains darker themes and graphic depictions of past trauma and SA, as well as mentions of somno and free use play.

While these scenes were written to create a more vivid, in-depth story, they may be triggering to some readers. *Please* know your own triggers, and read with that in mind.

Thanks for reading,

Jagger

1

ANNIKA

I'M NOT SUPPOSED to be doing this.

Actually, I'm not supposed to be doing *several* of the things I'm doing right now.

Number one is obvious: attending exclusive, invite-only parties hosted by notorious mobsters *without* an invitation—especially mobsters also infamous for being unhinged psychopaths—is generally considered a bad idea.

Number two might be even worse, though. It's not *just* that I'm crashing Cillian Kildare's birthday celebration for his wife, Una, at their sprawling new estate in the Connecticut countryside just outside New York, which has a veritable who's-who of the mafia world in attendance. I'm not here for the guest list, or the expensive champagne, or the cake.

I'm here to take something that isn't mine.

At least, it's not mine *yet*. But in the world I came of age in, you simply take what you want, and run when those who want it back come looking for you.

It's been like that since I was eighteen and my entire world was yanked out from under me.

"Focus, lady."

I blink at the sudden intrusion to my thoughts, piped into my ear via the skin-toned transmitter half-hidden by a lock of my red hair.

"I *am* focused," I mutter to Freya, turning away from the lawn crowded with mafiosos and pulling a compact from my clutch.

The microphone is in the silver pendant hanging from the delicate chain around my neck. But even if our host this evening is well-known for being a lunatic, and very well *might* talk to himself out loud from time to time, I can't afford to be seen doing so. Sneaking in with a fake invitation is one thing. Doing so with the intention of *stealing* from the psychopathic Irish mobster who lives here is quite another altogether.

Don't break more than one law at a time, right?

I fuss with my hair in the compact's mirror, hiding the movement of my lips with the errant locks.

"Peek-a-boo," Freya snickers into my ear. She can see what I see right now via the little camera in the bridge of the fake glasses I'm wearing, which means she's looking at me pretending to primp in the mirror. "You were focused all right, but it was on that hottie giving 'I'll fuck you 'til you call me Daddy' vibes over at the bar by the pool."

I roll my eyes. "You need help. Or to get laid."

"Is this an either-or thing? I'm not sure we can rule out both."

I snort before I bite my lip to quiet myself.

"The guy giving Daddy vibes would be Ares Drakos, head of the Drakos Greek mafia family. And he's married."

"Hey, you were the one ogling his ass."

"*Therapy*, Frey," I hiss. "Get some. I wasn't ogling anyone. I was being vigilant. In case you've forgotten, we're not exactly supposed to be here."

"What's this *we* shit?" she snickers back. "You're the one crashing Una Kildare's birthday bash. I'm half a mile away quietly minding my own business."

"If I get busted, I hope you know I'm taking you down with me."

Freya laughs. "I've missed this. We should do this more often."

I grin to myself. Freya and I are two peas in a pod. We both come from fucked up backgrounds, and we both had to start over from scratch at a young age.

We also both have a gift for taking things that don't belong to us, which is kind of how we linked up in the first place over ten years ago. Now, we're thick as…

Well, thieves.

I'm the hands-on type: breaking and entering, opening safes, dodging security. It's how I survived when I was first on my own after my old life literally went up in flames. Over time, it went from being about survival to a bankable and highly sought-after skill. Freya, meanwhile, is a computer wizard and can hack her way into pretty much anything.

Like, as a totally arbitrary example, the digital safe hidden in the bookshelf in Cillian Kildare's home office at this very house.

"Yeah, well, we made a promise, Frey," I sigh, my brow furrowing as I glance back at the garden party taking place on the lawn of the Kildare estate. "A promise we're breaking right now."

"Ugh," Freya groans into my ear. "What is this horrible emotion I'm feeling?"

"I think the word you're looking for is *guilt*."

"Hmm..." she ponders. "No, I don't think so. I'm not even sure what that word means."

I grin, but then my smile sours.We really *aren't* supposed to be doing this anymore. And I don't mean the sneaking into private parties bit.

Freya and I were on our own for years. We stole to survive, and then ramped up our skills to do a little better than "survive". And then one day, our band of two became a band of three when I crossed paths with Damian.

Damian, whose uncle Kir Nikolayev runs the Nikolayev Bratva organization, was my and Freya's ticket from the minors into the big leagues. Damian had connections. He had clout in the world of the criminal elite. And he was as much a thrill-seeker as Freya and I were.

That said, our motives for larceny are a bit different. Freya and I steal for money, and because we like the challenge.

Damian likes hurting people when he feels they deserve it.

For a while, the three of us were almost certainly on our way to crossing the wrong person or biting off *way* more than we could chew. That's when Kir stepped in and steered us away from certain prison time or grisly death and gave us all a fresh start.

Handsome, charismatic, and powerful, Kir Nikolayev became essentially our adoptive father, or at the least our cool young uncle. He's the first person who saw me as more than just a cocky thief with something to prove, and the first to view Freya as more than a walking middle finger.

Though the Nikolayev Bratva is *obviously* a criminal organization, it also operates heavily in the legitimate business world. And that's where Freya and I operate too these days. Kir saw my ability to charm, lie, and social engineer my way into places I shouldn't be in order to take things that aren't mine and nudged me in a new direction: corporate takeovers.

That's what I do for him now. I'm the bitch who walks into the negotiating boardroom cocked and loaded and finds whatever weak spot I can to push a deal through. Do I still get my hands dirty? Duh. But I'm not out there breaking into safes or boosting cars like I used to.

Well, mostly not.

And these days, when I *do* get up to my old tricks, there's a certain guilt attached to it. Not for the stealing itself. But for going back on my word to a man who's given me a second chance on life.

So, for those keeping score, I'm, A, crashing a party I'm not invited to. B, fully intending to burglarize said party. And C, breaking my promise to the man who's basically my adopted uncle.

Oh, and if we want to nitpick, I'm wearing white after Labor Day.

"I'm going quiet now," I murmur, tucking away the compact and turning back to the party. I shimmy my hips, pulling at the ultra-tight white cocktail party dress hugging my body.

This is *so* not my style. I barely wear dresses at all, let alone tight little "sexy" numbers like this. I'm more a jeans girl. Or, when I'm dressing to kill at one of Kir's negotiating tables, a classy pencil skirt with a matching jacket. Even then, it's more often a pant suit.

I start to make my way to the huge, sprawling home, gritting my teeth and resisting the urge to reach back and pick my undies out of my ass.

The dress is a necessity for blending in. Unfortunately, it's also tight enough to restrict blood flow to my legs, which means the usual comfy underwear I prefer to wear wasn't an option tonight. Instead, I'm dealing with a thong, which I never fucking wear.

"How's the butt floss?" Freya snickers into my ear, as if reading my thoughts.

I'm moving through the crowd of guests by now, so I can't retort with something snappy and vulgar, but I make a point to brush my hair back with one finger raised in front of my glasses.

The middle one.

Freya laughs. "Fine, fine. No more distractions from my end. Could you just glance one more time at Ares Drakos' *magnificent* ass before I—*goddammit*."

I swiftly remove the glasses, neatly folding them and tucking them into my clutch. I don't *need* to be wearing these until we get to the safe and Freya needs visual guidance to get past the electronic lock.

"Dick," she mutters. "What the fuck am I supposed to do now?"

"I dunno," I mumble under my breath. "Go order another pair of spiked Doc Martens. Or surely you're running low on black eyeliner."

"If you're ever curious why I'm your only friend…" She coughs significantly.

"Okay, *ouch*?" I grunt as I step around a corner of the garden and out of sight and earshot of the guests. "I have friends."

"Name them."

"Hello? Damian? Taylor?"

"Your twin sister doesn't count. She *has* to be your friend."

"Agree to disagree."

"Whatever. I'll allow Damian. That's *one* besides me. Speaking of which, did he ever text you before you walked in there?"

My brows suddenly knit. "No, he didn't."

Damian *always* checks in with me before a job. Especially one that he set up. What we're here to steal is a fifteenth-century "death mask"—a seriously fucked-up little artifact from the Spanish Inquisition made from iron, metal spikes, and *actual human skin*.

I mean… Even for Freya, that's fucked.

But fucked or not, the thing is a must-have for certain collectors. It was stolen from the British Museum in the 1990s, and it's been bouncing around private collections for the last couple of decades. It not technically Cillian's—which does make me feel a little better about taking it tonight. It's on loan to him from a friend of his.

Because of *course* Cillian-the-sociopath wants to borrow a human skin mask and keep it in a safe in his home.

The truly messed-up thing, though, is that this fucking thing is worth close to a million dollars to the right collector—although we're not doing this for the money.

Damian has plenty of that, just like his uncle. And Freya and I...well, we have more than enough. These days, with what Kir pays us for what we do for him, it's enough to live like fucking *queens*. Or at least, enough to keep Freya in eyeliner and one-off collector's edition Doc Martens for the rest of her life.

So, no, we're not doing this for the money. We're doing it because the guy Damian plans on selling it to is going to then owe him a favor, and in our world favors are priceless.

Okay...a favor *plus* we just fucking love doing this, and it's been way too long since Freya, Damian, and I pulled off a good old-fashioned heist. Which, again, makes it odd that Damian never checked in before I walked in here. Still hasn't, actually.

"You?"

Freya exhales. "Nothing. And that's not like him."

"I'm sure he's just preoccupied with seducing someone he shouldn't be, or terrifying small children."

Freya snorts. "That's mean."

"And?"

She giggles. "Probably true."

Between Damian's tall, built physique, high cheekbones and sharp jawline, not to mention the shock of silver-white hair and piercing purplish eyes from a genetic condition, he *can* be pretty frightening.

Or, in the case of women, extremely attractive…if you're not Frey and I and almost his sisters, and if you're into spooky-looking ghost boys, I guess.

"Girl, you need to stop talking to yourself and get in there," Freya mutters into my transmitter.

I bite back a smart response and straighten my back, giving one more uncomfortable wiggle of my hips to try and dislodge the strip of lace riding up my ass.

"How the fuck do you wear these things," I mutter.

My best friend snickers. "How do you *not*? I love them."

It's one of Freya's little quirks. She's basically Rooney Mara in *The Girl with the Dragon Tattoo*: dyed hair, black eyeliner, general goth-techno-punk aesthetic. But her one "girly" indulgence is that under the biker jackets and skinny jeans the chick *loves* expensive, sexy, Dita Von Teese-style lingerie. She owns shitloads of it and wears it all the time.

And she never dates at all.

"Well, you're weird."

"You're the one still talking to yourself, bitch."

"*Fine*," I sigh. "I'm going quiet again. Second floor, east wing, third door on the right?"

"Yeah. Office door key code is six-six-six."

I roll my eyes.

Kinda predicable, Cillian.

Getting back into character, I walk back around the corner of the garden hedge and pluck a glass of champagne from a passing tray, then smile cordially at another redhead who glances my way. When her brows knit, and something between recognition and confusion sweeps over her face, I quickly turn and scurry away into the crowd.

Shit. That was Neve Kildare, Cillian's niece and Ares Drakos' wife.

She's also friendly with my twin sister.

In the shit that went down when I was eighteen and my life went up in smoke, I lost touch with Taylor. We've recently reconnected, which has been amazing, but that's something I never had to worry about before when I was doing heists like this: that there's an identical copy of me out there, and someone could easily mistake me for her, especially now that I've allowed my hair to go back to its natural red after dying it for years to stay under the radar.

Neve knows Taylor because my sister is the hot-shot name managing partner of Crown and Black, one of the most prestigious law firms in New York, who both the Kildare and Drakos families use for legal representation.

I quickly blend into the crowd, hoping Neve doesn't give it another thought. Hey, it's a big crowd, and she looked at me for like two seconds.

It's fine.

It's totally—

Fuck.

My heart leaps into my throat as I duck away from the main living room and scurry into the shadows by a recessed window.

"*Shit*!" I hiss into the mic.

"What?" Freya whispers back.

"Kir's here."

Freya groans. "Are you fucking kidding me?"

I wish. In the past, Kir has mainly bounced between Moscow and London. But recently, there's been more and more Bratva business bringing him to New York—like the growing Yakuza presence in the city, which is slowly eating away at Russian territory.

And *that* is business I have every intention of staying far away from.

Kir's been up my ass worse than this fucking thong about setting up some meetings with Sota Akiyama, head of the Akiyama-kai, to press him on some sort of agreement. Under normal circumstances, I'd be down, even with a dangerous, hardcore Yakuza kingpin like Sota.

Except, it's not *just* Sota I'd be meeting with.

It's *him*.

I'm going to remember you.

In your dreams, sunshine.

No, princess, in yours, *which I'll be fucking haunting.*

I rarely make mistakes, but he was one of them.

Kenzo fucking Mori.

The heir to the Mori-kai Yakuza empire. The top *waka gashira* to Sota Akiyama. The vicious, brutal son of Hideo Mori and a Norwegian socialite, giving him the stunning and terrifying combined physical traits of a samurai and a Viking.

He's huge, dangerous, and powerful. He's also the man who's been hunting me relentlessly for five years like a fucking bloodhound after I stole from him.

So I'm one hundred percent hands-off whatever Kir wants to get into with the Yakuza. Because if I walk into a room with Sota, there is a one *thousand* percent chance that it'll be Kenzo waiting for me.

But that's another problem for another day. The more immediate issue is Kir sipping champagne at the very party I have to sneak through so I can burgle the place. Which is something I've promised him I won't do anymore.

"What the fuck is he doing here?" I hiss.

"Hang on..." I can hear Freya typing madly on her laptop. "Okay, I'm in his phone..."

Yeah, this is what she does. It's perhaps why I have trust issues.

"I've got his schedule." She swears. "He landed in New York a few hours ago. He does have a personal invitation from Cillian. I think they might know each other from London."

"*Wonderful,*" I grunt.

"It looks like he's called you a dozen times since he landed?"

I wince. "I've been ignoring him. He wants to pressure me to get in a room with the Yakuza."

"Yeah, *that's* a hard no because of you-know-who."

"No shit."

"Well, you gotta get past him. Our window closes soon."

Cillian's friend, from whom he's borrowing the creepy death mask, is attending the party tonight. But he's leaving early to fly to Rome in his private jet. When he goes, the mask goes, too.

"It's okay," I breathe. "I've got this. I can—"

"Fuck. Me. Sideways."

My brows knit. "What?"

Freya swallows. "We need to call this."

I scowl. "What?"

"Get out," Freya snaps. "Seriously. This is done."

A chill ripples up my spine. "What's going on, Frey?"

"I'm tapped into the security cameras, and I've got eyes on Kir."

"And?"

She hesitates.

"He's talking with Kenzo Mori."

Every muscle in my body tenses. Every nerve ending spasms. Every hair stands up on end as something cold finger-walks up my spine.

"*Here*?!" I squeak.

"I'm looking right at him," Freya hisses back. "Huge. Scary-looking. Black hair. Yakuza ink. Looks like he might pull out a samurai sword *and* a Viking ax and cut someone in two. Someone like...oh, I dunno...*you*?"

My heart thuds against my chest as my hands tighten to fists, my palms suddenly sweaty.

"*Fuck*," I hiss. I yank out my phone out, wincing at all the missed calls and texts from Kir before bringing up my text thread with Damian and tapping furiously.

ME

Where R U?!?

ME

RED ALERT. Kir is here with fucking KENZO.

ME

CALL ME OR FREY!!

There's nothing. Not even the little dots, like he's typing.

Goddammit, Damian.

I exhale deeply, trying to slow my hammering pulse as I chance a quick peek around the corner. I don't see either of them, but still.

Freya's right. We should walk away from this, now. Kir here is bad enough. But Kenzo Mori is Defcon one, nuclear strike imminent.

If the dangerous devil who promised to haunt my nightmares sees me here, this is going to go very, very badly.

And yet...

Something else spikes in my bloodstream beyond the fight or flight response.

Excitement.

It's why I'm so good at what I do, just like some lunatics go base-jumping or choose to swim with sharks: the very possibility of danger and getting caught makes my blood run hotter and focuses my senses.

I'm not a good thief *despite* the fear of being caught. I'm an amazing thief *because* of it. That fear is a performance-enhancing drug to me.

I swallow the lump in my throat, my pulse quickening again as something electric zips up my spine.

"Where are they?"

Freya is silent for a second.

"You do remember what I literally *just* told you, right? Fucking *Kenzo* is—"

"The favor Damian can get for this would be huge, Freya. For us, for him. For Kir."

"Heard, but can we also agree that getting *caught* by a psycho Yakuza Viking who wants you dead and doesn't seem to understand the concept of 'letting shit go' would be very, *very* bad, yes?"

"I can make it, Frey," I mutter quietly. "Just tell me where they are."

She exhales heavily. "Fuck you, do NOT get caught or I will never forgive you." She pauses, then breathes heavily again. "Okay. Got them. They're in the library downstairs, off the main ballroom. If you go through the foyer and into the second dining room, you can take the back staircase up."

"Perfect, thanks," I say tightly. I glance around the corner, feeling the adrenaline rush explode through my veins like napalm. Steadying myself, I plaster a smile onto my face and march back through the living room and into the main foyer. I thread my way through guests and waitstaff before I slip into the second dining room, then duck out the other doorway.

"I'm at the stairs," I hiss quietly, walking up them as quickly as my heels will allow.

"Glasses on, please."

I nod wordlessly as I get to the upstairs hallway, slipping the glasses out of my clutch and putting them back on. I drift quietly down the hall, find the door, and enter the six-six-six entry code.

The lock opens with a small, satisfying click.

I keep the room dark as I cross to the bookshelves behind Cillian's desk. An ominous and not-at-all-creepy *knife collection* takes up the far wall. But I ignore it as I look for the shelf I know hides the safe.

Sure enough, when I pull on the leather-bound copy of *The Strange Case of Dr. Jekyll and Mr. Hyde,* the shelf pops open on a silent hinge, revealing the state-of-the-art lock behind it.

This is going to be a two-step process. The first involves the little device I have in my clutch. It's how Freya will remotely crack the electronic lock. After that, there's an old-school manual three-digit combination lock.

I pull out the hacking device and magnetically attach it to the keypad of the safe.

"You're up," I mutter.

"Hang on," Freya says, completely focused. "Take it off for a sec and let me see the keypad. I want to make sure I've got the right model."

I do so.

"Okay, I wondered about that. It's a newer version of the Cryo 7000."

My brows tense. "Can you still open it?"

"*Obviously*. But I need you to switch two wires on our device first."

Freya walks me through unplugging a green wire from a red port and plugging it into a yellow one, then reattaching the yellow wire to a red port. I feel like I'm defusing a bomb.

"Put the device back on the keypad."

I watch as the digital numbers on Freya's hacking tool blur and flip. Suddenly, I hear an electronic click.

"We good?"

"Golden, baby," she says, grinning audibly. "Your turn. To quote Ru Paul, don't fuck it up."

I roll my eyes. "Bitch."

I pull out the earpiece out and slip in my electronic headphones so I can have both ears tuned to the clicking. I taught myself this old-school cracking technique long before I met Freya, and fourteen years later, I'm a fucking *pro*...if I do say so myself.

I clamp the stethoscope part of the listening device to the front of the safe, and the whole world goes silent around me. I love this moment, just me and the lock I'm trying to open. I let my pulse slow; let my breathing deepen as I tune into the slight clicking of the dial.

The first number falls into place with a metallic drop. Then the next. I smile to myself as I slowly go back around the dial.

Number three clicks into place.

I'm fucking *in*.

Pulling the headphones off, my pulse heats as I turn the handle and pull the heavy safe door open to claim my prize.

Then my heart drops as I stare into the completely empty safe.

What. The. *Fuck*.

Damian's intel is *never* wrong. Ever. Not once in the years I've worked with him; he's meticulous like that.

I can feel my pulse quickening as I reach for the earpiece again. Even before I bring it to my ear, I can hear the frantic muffled sound of Freya's voice coming out of it.

"—RIGHT FOR YOU!!!"

Her voice screams into my ear.

"Frey!" I hiss. "We have a prob—"

"RUN!!!"

Something cold rips up my spine.

"KENZO IS—"

The breath leaves my body and every muscle I have tenses up as merciless, powerful hands grab me viciously from behind, spin me, and slam me hard into the bookshelf behind me.

The color drains from my face. My mouth falls open in a silent, chilling scream as the floor drops out beneath me.

...As *Kenzo fucking Mori* leers down into my terrified eyes, his face a mask of pure wrath.

"Hello, *princess*," he hisses icily. His coldly beautiful face darkens with rage and fury. His high cheekbones and chiseled, lethal jaw glint in the darkness as the piercing blackness of his eyes eviscerates me.

It's like I'm powerless to move. Even to blink or say a fucking word as his huge hand slowly wraps around my throat. The hand slips around, his fingers never leaving my skin until he's gripping me by the back of the neck, forcing my eyes up to his inky gaze.

"Come, *princess*," he spits. "We don't want to keep them waiting, do we?"

I still can't say a word as he grabs the earpiece from my ear and crushes it in his fist. I watch the pieces crumble like dust to the floor before he snatches the glasses off my face and leers into them.

"Run and fucking hide, *Freya*."

He drops the glasses to the floor and grinds them under his heel. I'm still frozen, and it feels like I'm half tumbling and half shuffling when he suddenly turns and starts to drag me after him by the nape of my neck across the floor, then out the door of the study.

"I—I—"

No other words come to me. I stumble after him down the hall, almost falling down the stairs with my hand scrabbling to hold onto the banister and his iron grip still wrapped around my neck.

"Where—where are we—" I finally blurt as he yanks me through the second dining room. "Where are you—

"Like I said, *princess*," he snarls in a dark, rasping tone, his gruff but posh British accent giving it a clipped edge. "We don't want to keep them waiting."

He storms across the now-empty foyer toward a set of closed double doors which I'm pretty sure leads back into the ballroom.

"Keep who—"

He kicks the doors in, suddenly dropping his menacing grip from my neck to my hand and yanking me after him into the ballroom.

Every. Single. Guest is standing there. Looking at us. Like they were *waiting* for us.

Something is very, very wrong.

My face is white as I pull my gaze around the room. Everyone's smiling at me—beaming and grinning, looking like they're ready to cheer for me.

Everyone except Kir, that is. When I lock eyes with him, all I'm faced with is a cold, dangerous look. Not anger. More like...fear.

And *nothing* scares that man.

I want to run to him and tell him I'm so sorry for being this fucking stupid before asking him what the shit is going on.

But before I can move a muscle, Kenzo's huge hand tightens painfully on mine, as if he's trying to crush it. I turn to him, expecting malice. Rage. Hatred. Hell, even a loaded gun.

Instead, he's fucking *smiling*.

Something is *definitely* wrong.

A waiter brings over two flutes of champagne. Kenzo smiles broadly as he takes his. I almost drop mine when the waiter shoves it into my fingers awkwardly.

"First of all," Kenzo booms, his voice pure silk and honey. Like a statesman greeting his supporters, or a doctor announcing that the life-saving surgery was a success. There's not a single trace of the malice and darkness that I know lurks behind that smile.

"I want to thank our hosts for graciously allowing me to take the spotlight away from the lovely birthday girl for a moment."

He beams as he nods and lifts his glass to Cillian and Una, standing front and center, arm-in-arm, next to Kir.

"A very happy birthday, Mrs. Kildare."

Una smiles, dipping her chin politely as she nods at Kenzo.

What is happening.

What the *fuck* is happen—

"And now, without any further ado..." Kenzo smiles like a dragon as he turns to level his eviscerating gaze at me. "It is my distinct pleasure to introduce you all to Annika Brancovich..."

His eyes turn to daggers, and I swear I feel them slice into me.

"My *fiancée*."

The floor drops out from under me as my lungs seize up and my vision goes black.

What.

The.

FUCK.

2

KENZO

Half an hour ago:

THE SUMMER that I was thirteen, our garden was beset by a plague of rabbits. The furry little fuckers destroyed it, eating every single carrot, every lettuce leaf, every radish...even the flowers my mother loved so much.

For a while there, Tak, Mal, and I—often Hana, too—would join the groundskeeper Mr. Coughlin up on the roof of the gardening cottage with a .22 each, and pick them off whenever we caught sight of them.

I don't hate rabbits. They're cute. They're cuddly. They're dancing and singing in every fucking Disney movie out there. But a thief is a thief, and these little shits were robbing us, not only of vegetables and flowers, but of the happiness those things brought my mother. So we spent hours shooting those goddamn bunnies all day long until the sun went down.

But they kept coming back. They *always* came back.

Then one day, Mr. Coughlin brought in an old army buddy of his, a grizzled, swarthy man we only knew as Rafe.

Rafe didn't come to play.

He came to commit bunny fucking genocide.

I learned more about taking care of business from Rafe in the one week he spent at our estate than I had in the thirteen previous years of my life. First, he set traps outside every damn rabbit hole: huge cages with one-way doors. He baited them and left little trails of bait down into the holes. But the real fuck-you to the rabbits was that Rafe kept pet snakes.

Big, scary, snakes.

Snakes that he'd trained to slither into burrows and either eat or chase out every little furry thief they found. One by one, every burrow got visited by a hungry snake and would then empty out in a rush, straight into one of Rafe's cages.

Then he'd drown them all at once in the pond.

That's how you catch a thief. You bait them. If necessary, you scare them out. Then you trap them and fucking drown them.

Which is precisely why I've to the Kildare estate tonight: to spring the trap I've set.

The first step was reaching out to Cillian, with whom I did some business in England a few years ago before he moved to New York, to wish his wife an early happy birthday. Cillian, in turn, mentioned that he was throwing Una a birthday bash, and would I care to pop by if I was in New York?

Why, abso-fucking-*lutely*. How very kind of you, Cillian.

I already knew about the party. But parties like this require invitations. And there was no fucking *way* I was going to miss this one.

The next step was laying the bait. Ansel Albrecht, a sneaky little shit involved in the German mafia, isn't usually someone I'd wipe shit off my shoe with. But Ansel made the fatal error of coming to owe me a favor once, and this was the perfect time to cash it in.

So I had Ansel reach out to Damian Nikolayev, my particular rabbit's freakish little white-haired friend, and feed him some bullshit about a Spanish Inquisition artifact, and how he'd *owe Damian a favor* should he be able to retrieve it for him. And, wouldn't you know it, that mask just *happened* to be temporarily just outside the city, at Cillian Kildare's Connecticut estate.

How incredible.

It's all lies, of course. The mask belongs to a creepy fucking collector in Austria who has it mounted on the wall of his even creepier sex dungeon. But Damian is a greedy little shit, and he took the bait.

I allow myself a small smile as I snag a flute of champagne from a passing waiter's tray. I survey the garden party as I appreciate Cillian's excellent taste in bubbly, imagining this party is assembled for *me*, not Una Kildare.

Not to celebrate a birthday, but to congratulate me on a successful hunt. On *finally* wrapping my fingers around her fucking throat, looking her in the eye, and knowing as I inhale her fear and defeat that *I've won*.

No one steals from me.

Ever.

If this had simply been about money, maybe I would have tired of this chase by now, and simply hired professionals to bring me the thief's head in a fucking burlap bag.

But not with what Annika stole. And certainly not with *how* she stole it.

I take another sip of champagne, filling my lungs with the clean air of the Connecticut countryside.

I've been spending too much time in New York lately.

It's not that I necessarily dislike it there. It's fun, it's wild, and I know how to bend it to my will. I don't even mind the games we've been slowly playing with the Russian Bratva families, trying to muscle in on their territory ever-so-delicately as Sota expands into New York.

It's come with other perks, too, like slowly getting to know my half-sister, Fumi, not to mention the biological father I spent most of my life believing was dead.

Thirty-five years ago, my mother Astrid, a young aristocratic Norwegian woman, went to study abroad in Kyoto, Japan. There, she fell for—and had a torrid affair with—a man named Hideo Mori.

But Hideo wasn't just her wild college romance; he was the head of the fearsome and powerful Mori-kai Yakuza family. My mother loved him, but she was also scared of him, or at least of the life that would come with him. So when she accidentally became pregnant with me, she ended things with Hideo, left Japan, and returned home to Norway to have me.

She never even told my father that she was pregnant.

But absence, as they say, makes the heart grow fonder. And so few years after I was born my mother *went back* to Japan.

She found Hideo, I suppose with the plan to see if she could woo him away from the Yakuza life, and *then* tell him that he had a son.

Her plan didn't work, and a few weeks later, she came home, certain that Hideo would never in fact leave the Yakuza.

She also came back *pregnant again.*

With *twins.*

A year later, right after my brother Takeshi and my sister Hana were born, Hideo finally found what he never saw with my mother: a way out of the Yakuza. He married a woman named Bella, fathered my half-sister Fumi, and chose to leave the criminal world behind. He changed their name, moved to the US, and until recently, I thought he'd died in Japan ages ago.

I loved my mother, and I understand why she took me away from Kyoto and from a father who lived and breathed the Yakuza.

But you can't change your DNA. I was born of Yakuza blood, and when I was eighteen, against Astrid's wishes, I traveled to Japan to explore that side of my heritage.

That's when I met Sota.

When he heard that a half-Japanese kid raised in England was poking around Kyoto looking for information on a man named Hideo, he sought me out. I'll never forget the day he kicked in the door to my hotel room, yanked up my sleeve, saw the birthmark there in the shape of a crescent moon, and immediately embraced me like a long-lost son.

Sota and my father had been best friends. Like me, Sota thought Hideo had been killed trying to leave the Yakuza years before. So he took me in, and after a single day dipping my toes into the world of the Yakuza, I was hooked.

A few months later, Mal, my adoptive brother from back home, moved out to join me in Japan. Two years later, after our mother died, Takeshi and Hana came out, too.

The rest is history.

Like I said, you can't change your blood. I was *born* into this. It just took me eighteen years to find it.

Through Sota, I learned about the sheer power of the Mori-kai empire, and the weight the name still carried. I joined the ranks of the Akiyama-kai and rose to be one of Sota's most trusted captains.

He even told me that his ultimate goal was to see the rebirth of the Mori-kai, under me, to whom his own empire had once pledged allegiance.

My mood falters as I consider that that day might be coming sooner than expected. Sota has stage three lung cancer.

The miniscule silver lining is that he's been in New York for much of his treatment. But it's still brutal to watch one of the strongest men I've ever known brought to his knees by a cowardly fucking disease like cancer.

But I digress. Tonight is for celebrating, not lamenting.

Because tonight, I will finally catch the little thief who drugged me and stole from me. Tonight, my trap will be sprung, and when I wrap my hand around her throat, I'm going to fucking squeeze. *Hard.*

As if on cue, a flash of red flickers in my peripheral vision. I turn, and the dark, dangerous smile on my jaw widens as my fingers tighten on the stem of the champagne flute.

Just like every time I lay eyes on Annika Brancovich, the swirling, intoxicatingly lethal cocktail of hatred and desire explodes through my veins.

There's a reason she got the drop on me that night five years ago. The drugs she slipped into my drink didn't hurt, of course, but after five years reflecting on what happened, I know it's because *she* got my guard down.

Because as much as I fucking hate Annika...as much as I'd like to tie concrete to her feet and drown her like a warren full of thieving rabbits...there is *zero* denying the fact that whenever I lay eyes on her, my cock has other ideas.

Ideas like *savaging* her. Pinning her to the dirty ground and burying every thick inch of me into every tight little hole she has. Making her scream as her eager little cunt milks my dick. Or watching her moan and drool as I fuck her throat.

My fantasies involving this woman, in case I wasn't clear, do *not* involve making love to her. Or even "having sex" with her.

They involve *dominating her in the fullest extent of the word.* They involve her on her knees, whimpering and begging and submitting to me, with my cum glistening on her skin.

My jaw tightens.

Fucking hell.

I *hate* that this is where my mind goes with this woman. It's not as if I see her often—she has, after all, spent the last five years running from me. But when we do cross paths, even momentarily, or at a distance like this, it's the same thing every time.

There's no denying that Annika is attractive. Half-American, half-Serbian, with high, full breasts and an ass to sink your teeth into. She's also tall for a woman.

I like that.

I'm pushing six and a half feet, which makes me tall in the West and a fucking *giant* in Japan. And smaller women have never appealed to me. They just seem so….

Breakable.

Annika, however, is close to six feet. And although she's on the thin side, probably from her years running and surviving as best she could, she seems…*not* so breakable.

Like I could manhandle her.

Pin her down.

Fuck her *savagely.*

I keep my eyes on my prey as she plucks a flute of champagne from a passing tray and then nods curiously at Neve Kildare, for some strange reason.

Oh. She's trying to fit in.

Play the role all you fucking like, little rabbit, I think darkly.

Soon, you'll be MINE.

Part of me wants to make my move right now. Fuck trying to catch her mid-theft of an item that isn't even in the country. I could do it right here. Scene or not, Cillian and I have old business together. I'm sure he wouldn't begrudge me doing what's necessary to punish someone who's wronged me the way Annika has.

But just as I'm putting the pieces together of what happens *after* I wrap my fingers around Annika's pretty little throat, I feel a presence at my back.

Frowning, I start to turn. Then I go rigid.

"*Sota-san,*" I mutter quietly, bowing in confusion before my eyes lock on those of my mentor. He waves away the two personal guards standing beside him, and I stare at him incredulously.

"What the hell are you doing here?"

Like I said, Sota is both mentor and like a father to me. Family. Around our men, and in public, yes, I will *always* give him the honor and respect that he deserves and is expected within the regimented, ultra-traditional world of the Yakuza. But in private? We can speak a bit more informally.

Sota smiles wryly at me. "I could ask you the same—"

He suddenly coughs violently. I grimace, moving toward him, but he waves me off, hacking up another lung before he wipes his mouth with a piece of silk and tucks it back in his tuxedo.

"Walk with me, my friend," he mutters quietly. For the first time, I notice the lines drawn darker on his face, and uncustomary worry in his eyes.

I frown, nodding as I take his arm. The two of us slowly begin to walk across the manicured lawn, past the garden party and around the side of Cillian's estate.

"I've always told you that a leader does what is necessary, Kenzo. Being a king does not mean you serve yourself. You serve those you are charged with leading. Being a king is not about clinging to power but about earning it every single day and showing those under you why you deserve that power."

I nod my head. "I know."

Again... One day, this will be me. Sota has no children of his own, and even when he thought Hideo was dead, he adhered to the oath he'd made to the Mori-kai decades previously. The Akiyama-kai is an empire in and of itself. But its allegiance, even today, is to the Mori-kai.

Its allegiance is to *me*, and Sota has spent years teaching me and molding me into the king I'll need to be.

I turn to him, smiling gently. "You should be resting back in the city. I'm fairly certain you're not supposed to be up and about in the middle of a treatment cycle."

"This is important, Kenzo."

"Well, you also could have just called—"

"This warrants a face-to-face meeting."

The lines on his face. The haunted sadness in his eyes. The fear...

"Aoki is dead, Kenzo."

Something twists hard in my chest.

Aoki Juro is the head of the Juro-kai, a tribute family to the Akiyama-kai. Aoki and I met about fifteen years ago, when I was new to the Yakuza world, and he was the newly crowned nineteen-year-old king of his late father's empire.

We've been friends almost ever since.

I stare at Sota, understanding the sadness in his eyes. I'm not the only "stray" that Sota has mentored. He's a collector of lost souls. And when, like me, Aoki lost his father, it was Sota who coached him how to step up and be king.

"*What*?!" I hiss.

"There was an altercation in New York two hours ago. Aoki and some of his men crossed paths with some of Kir Nikolayev's men. Guns were drawn. Aoki was killed on the scene…"

"*Fuck*!" I snarl viciously. "Who—"

Sota interrupts me, his voice cold and brittle. "And Damian Nikolayev, Kir's nephew and heir, is on life support."

I go still.

Oh, shit.

Sota looks more worried than I've ever seen him.

"Whether the nephew lives or dies, Kenzo… This is bad," he says quietly. "Very bad. As in, the assassination of Archduke Ferdinand thereby setting off World War One bad."

I grit my teeth, turning away from him, my eyes stabbing through the window beside us and into the house. My gaze lands on a familiar head of red, and my eyes narrow as I watch my prey sashay through the party.

"An agreement has been reached," Sota says, pulling my attention back, "to avoid war with the Bratva."

"Why the fuck are we *avoiding* that?" I snarl.

Sota shoots me a hard look. "War is seldom the answer, Kenzo. And this bullshit between our two families is…untenable. It cannot continue. Aoki was one of our best men. Damian is Kir's fucking *heir*. If this comes to war, it will be bloody, and there will *not* be rules."

I slam back the rest of my champagne as Sota shakes his head sadly.

"War *cannot* happen, Kenzo." I stare at him, livid. "Don't look at me like that," he grunts. "It's not that I'm too old or too weak."

I smile wryly. "That is the very last thing I'm thinking."

"Good," he smiles. "Because I can still best you."

My own smile turns grim as I frown. "So... What's the agreement?"

Sota's jaw sets. "It's going to mean changing your plans for the evening. I know why you're here, Kenzo. I know what you've set up."

My mouth tightens. "I'm sure I don't know what you're—"

"I'm in no mood for games, Kenzo," he sighs. "You're the son I never had. All due respect to Hideo, you're my heir. You'll take both my empire and his and turn them into your own. But that can't happen if there's war."

"Sota—"

"Kir has no sons, which is why his nephew Damian is his heir. He has no *daughters*, either. But like me, Kir took in a stray..."

When it hits me, my whole body tightens. My eyes turn glacial as I stare at him.

"*No*."

Sota nods. "Yes," he says quietly. "I'm asking you to do what is—"

"It's a fucking *no*, Sota."

"While I am still breathing, *Kenzo*," he snarls viciously, "you *will obey* my wishes."

I grit my teeth and bow stiffly. "Of course, Sota-san," I growl.

He exhales a long, stuttering breath. "I am sorry, Kenzo. I truly am."

Slowly, I turn to look through the window, watching as Annika makes her way through the party, her white dress clinging to her every curve, highlighting the modelesque length of her legs.

Watching the swish of her hair as she turns to smile at another guest. The bat of her lashes over her lying eyes. The curl of her poisonous mouth.

"This is the only way we'll avoid war," Sota growls quietly. "You and Annika Brancovich will marry. That's final."

My lips curl dangerously.

Then I think of Rafe.

Straight out attacking didn't work. Baiting helped to draw the rabbits out of their burrow but didn't finish the job.

It took sending a snake inside to truly end things.

My eyes lock on Annika through the window as she blithely sips her champagne.

Hello, little rabbit. My name is Snake. And I am going to eat you fucking ALIVE.

TEN MINUTES LATER, I'm dragging her out of the study, yanking her down the stairs, setting her in front of a crowd of clapping onlookers and announcing to the world that we're engaged.

I have her.

I've trapped her.

So why the fuck do *I* feel like the one who's been caught?

3

ANNIKA

The second I walk into the hospital room, Freya launches herself into my arms.

"*Fuck*," she sobs against my chest.

Really, what else is there to say?

Over her shoulder, my eyes land on Damian, lying motionless in the hospital bed. I *hate* the grotesque plastic tube snaking out of his slack mouth. I hate the machines breathing and pumping his blood for him. I hate the wires and the rhythmic beeping sounds, and the bleachy hospital smell of antiseptic and death.

I hate all of it. But mostly, I hate that I still don't know if I'm about to lose a family member.

I was eighteen when I lost everything. The daughter of a Serbian mafia kingpin and his American wife, I'd already been married off to another crime lord who hated me and the forced marriage as much as I hated him for the same reason.

Right after the wedding, a mafia war broke out and his family was annihilated in an attack on their home. I managed to escape, and one of my father's men, Ruslan, managed to get me home.

But it was too late.

The war had been there first, taking my whole family as well and burning our home to the ground. Ruslan got me as far as Greece before he died from the wounds sustained in the attack on our family. That's the day I lost all that I'd ever known.

I'd lived my entire life as a pampered mafia princess, wanting for nothing. But when it's steal or starve to death because you don't have that wealth anymore, the world of black and white becomes a lot grayer.

I stole because I had to. I stole because I had nothing to eat. I met other people like me—kids and teenagers who lived on the streets of Athens. There were girls like me who found… *other ways*…to keep themselves fed and from dying in a gutter.

I almost did it once myself. I was starving, I was sleeping in an alley, and I had an infected cut that was getting gross.

It was just sex, I rationalized. Insert tab A into slot B. Repeat. Get paid. No big deal, right?

Wrong.

I cleaned myself up as best I could and walked around the square in the seedy section of town with the other girls looking for work. I said yes to the first man who walked up to me with an evil, lustful look on his face, and quoted him the same price I'd heard a girl say to her client ten minutes before.

He brought me to his car. Before anything happened, he opened the back door, punched me in the face, then threw me in.

There are moments in your life that define how the rest of it will play out. That was mine.

I could have let it go. I already had the money, since I saw all the other girls getting paid up front. When he shuffled into the backseat after me and climbed on top of me, I could have just…tuned out.

But while I may have been born into this world a princess, it wasn't without fire and fury in my veins.

So I fought.

I slammed my forehead over and over into his face as he pawed at me, until I heard the crunch of broken bone and his screams of pain. Until I felt the hot drip of blood. When he rolled off me, I kicked him as hard as I could in the balls, over and over, until he threw up and screamed for mercy.

Then I ran and never looked back.

And that was the day I decided I would *take* from this world what I needed and give nothing in return.

I spent the next few years completely on my own. I ignored the world and those around me, took what I needed, and *survived*.

But then one day, in Milan, I saw something I couldn't ignore. Two teenaged boys were dragging a screaming, clawing young girl out from the makeshift tarp shelter she'd set up in the crumbling wreckage of a condemned building. It was obvious they were trying to rip her clothes off, probably to rape her or something heinous. But that's not the only reason the girl was screaming.

It took me a second to realize she was afraid of the sunlight.

In any case, something in me snapped, and the blinders I'd kept on for the last three or four years fell away. I grabbed the first thing I could lay my hands on—a rusty metal pole—and I beat those boys with it over and over until they ran away, screaming and bloodied.

That's how I met Freya.

Like me, she'd been born into one life and then found herself in another, living in alleys and fighting to survive. It was even harder for her because of her condition.

Freya has a rare kind of extreme photosensitivity called xeroderma pigmentosum. Her gothy look isn't just an aesthetic. She's ghostly pale because she literally can't go out in the sun without getting horrific burns on any exposed skin.

After that first day, we became fast friends. Like me, Freya had learned to take what she needed, although she wasn't the type to walk into a store and slip groceries into her hoodie. Her M.O. was to slip a card skimmer onto the checkout machine and then use a library computer to convert the money she'd skimmed into Bitcoin.

We teamed up and started taking on bigger jobs, stealing more than just "what we needed". Eventually, we got in with certain types of people, and started to make connections and a name for ourselves.

Then came the dark years.

The years with...*him*.

I don't like to talk about those years, or even think about that time in my life.

I smile weakly as Frey pulls away, letting me walk over to Damian's bed. I sit in the chair next to it, biting my lip and feeling my breath hitch as I reach out and lay my hand on top of his pallid, unmoving one with the IV snaking out of it.

"Remember his opening line?"

I grin despite the horrible feeling that's settled in my chest, turning to roll my eyes at Freya. "You mean 'Tell me when you're ready to stop wasting your time and start playing in the big leagues'?" I grunt in my best impression of Damian's deep baritone.

And that was when Freya's and my double act became a band of three, after the dark he-who-shall-not-be-named years. The two of us had disguised ourselves as catering staff for an elite dinner party in London being attended by a who's-who of VIPs, state leaders, and a few criminal world kingpins.

We'd made out like fucking bandits. I lifted about a dozen six-figure watches, a *bunch* of jewelry, even a painting from the wall of the venue itself. Freya had been smiling away, pouring cognac and wine, skimming the no-limit credit cards in every pocket in the room.

A few hours later, we were enjoying a few celebratory drinks at a pub down the street when Damian made his dramatic entrance.

What we didn't know until later was that it was *his* pub. Like, he owned the joint. That was how he was able to quietly empty the place of all staff and patrons before making his presence known, which we didn't even notice because we were four drinks in.

Tell me when you're ready to stop wasting your time and start playing in the big leagues.

I will never, *ever* forget seeing Damian for the first time—turning around and feeling surprised through my buzz at the built, six-foot-three, white-haired, frighteningly handsome young man with the purple eyes and the leering devilish grin.

Damian had been a guest at the dinner we'd just robbed. We'd even stolen his Rolex. But he wasn't mad.

He was *intrigued.*

Like I said, Freya and I like taking things for the thrill as much as the money.

Damian likes hurting people he considers his enemies. And if he doesn't want to straight up punch them in the face, hurting them in the wallet is always a good alternative. I guess he thought we could help him there.

I wince as I gaze at his unresponsive body lying in the bed. He's so strong, and a total gym rat. To see him like this is just…*crushing.*

"Anni."

I look up to see Freya staring at me with a haunted expression. We texted briefly earlier, and she knows what happened with Kenzo, but we haven't had a chance to speak about it.

I'm not sure I'm ready for that, especially not here, with everything going on with Damian.

"Not yet," I whisper hoarsely.

She nods.

Then her face crumples, her eyes dragging back to Damian.

"I just don't understand how something like this could happ—"

"Bullets."

We whip around when we hear Kir's voice—the accent a mix of polished Oxford English and grubby Russian prisons—as he steps into the room. He and I didn't speak much on our drive back into the city from Cillian's estate, and even if we had, it's honestly all been a blur since I opened that goddamn safe.

A blur of Kenzo scaring the shit out of me, dragging me downstairs, and telling the whole party that I was his fiancée.

Yeah.

It came up in the silence of the car ride back to New York. Kir had just shaken his head.

"Not now, Anni," he'd murmured quietly, staring out the window in a daze. *"Not yet."*

My heart twists. Damian is like a brother to Frey and me, but he's basically a son to Kir...has been since Kir's sister and her husband passed when Damian was seven.

"Bullets do this," he says quietly. Freya's chest hitches as she runs over and throws her arms around him, hugging him fiercely as he pats her back.

"What'd the surgeon say?"

He exhales. "He's cautiously optimistic. They removed the bullet fragments close to his lungs, so he's in the clear there. The shooter missed his artery by about a millimeter."

"Thank fuck," I croak.

"But he's not out of the woods yet. They're going to keep him in a medically induced coma while they figure out the best way to get the fragments near his heart." Kir's eyes glisten. "I'm bringing the best specialist in the world over from Dubai."

I stand and walk over to them, hugging them both as I twist my head to look at Damian.

This is the ragtag family I've put together since mine was lost. Obviously Taylor, now that we've found each other again, is my other half. But even after reconnecting, and even though she's married to Drazen Krylov of all people, I feel I need to distance her from this side of my life.

Drazen isn't just some street thug. He's arguably one of the most powerful Bratva kingpins in the world, if not *the* most. He's next-level, meaning Taylor is protected in a way I can't even fathom.

But even so, my life is...*messy*, and complicated, and dangerous. And I won't bring that to her door.

She's found a perfect balance. I would bring chaos to that balance.

Chaos like Kenzo Mori.

A shiver ripples up my spine as the words I can never forget replay through my head.

I'm going to remember you.

In your dreams, sunshine.

No, princess, in yours, *which I'll be fucking haunting.*

I'd cringe at the cocky tone I used back then if it wasn't so fucking serious.

In your dreams, sunshine.

I mean I literally said that to the heir to a Yakuza *empire* I'd just drugged as I was robbing him with the taste of his sinful lips still on mine. Who the fuck did I think I was, Anne Hathaway playing Catwoman?

And now it's all coming back to bite me in the ass.

Hard.

Five years ago, Kenzo was an easy mark. A young hotshot in the Yakuza world, flashing money and sports cars all over Kyoto, practically *begging* to be robbed.

But the man I stole from that night was barely a man at all. He was still outrageously hot—dark brooding eyes, lean muscle, Yakuza ink for days. But he wasn't even thirty yet. Still a twenty-something carefree playboy gangster. Emphasis on "boy".

The Kenzo that grabbed me tonight, wrapped his hand around my neck and stared into my very soul is another beast altogether.

Bigger. Stronger. Darker. More sinister and *far* more dangerous. Like a lord of wrath, savaging me with his piercing gaze.

I pull away from Kir and Freya and I turn to look back at Damian as Frey walks over and sits in the chair next to his bed.

"Aoki shot first, if that's important," Kir says bitterly.

The shooting took place at a nightclub that hadn't even opened for the night yet. It's still unclear how it happened, but Damian and some of Kir's men were sitting around talking business when Aoki and four of his men walked right in.

“Words were said, and Aoki pulled his gun,” Kir grunts. “Damian was defending himself and his men.”

Word is that in addition to Aoki Jura, three of the other Jura-kai men were killed, along with two of Kir’s.

I turn to look at Kir, and start to open my mouth, but he shakes his head.

“There’s no other way, Anni,” he mutters. “I don’t like it, and I know you fucking hate it. But we’re past anything else,” he says coldly, pulling his hand from mine to rub both of his up over his tired-looking face. He lets his gaze settle on his nephew, and his jaw tightens as he turns to me. “It isn’t up for discussion.”

“Kir—”

He holds up a hand, silencing Freya when she tries to come to my rescue.

“I’m truly sorry, but this is done, settled. It’s happening.”

He looks at Damian, then at Freya. Then his eyes slide over to lock with mine.

“You’re marrying Kenzo Mori, Annika. And that’s final.”

4

ANNIKA

I NEED to get the fuck outside and away from all of this *right now.*

It's all of it: seeing Damian so helpless. Freya subdued. Kir insisting that I'm marrying the monster who's been chasing me for five fucking years and there's nothing I can do about it.

I storm out through the front doors of the hospital in a fury, wanting to scream until my throat is bloody. Instead, I jam my hand into my clutch and yank out the e-cig I keep there for emergencies.

Yes, it's a shitty habit. A lousy coping mechanism. But there are worse ones, trust me.

I haven't smoked actual cigarettes in almost ten years. I barely even use this stupid thing. But when I feel like I do right now, it's one of the few things that'll bring me back from the edge.

I suck on the nicotine and exhale vapor. It calms my nerves a little, but the pure rage and anger is still there, throbbing beneath my skin and trying to claw free.

I *hate* this.

I've outrun every monster. Every hardship. Every darkness that tried to swallow me whole. And now I'm being gifted to one.

The one.

A stupid fucking necklace.

That's what I took from Kenzo that night in Kyoto five years ago. A stupid. Fucking. Not-even-very-expensive. *Necklace.*

Okay, there was the watch, too. But that was like five grand. Throw in the money in his wallet and we're up to six thousand, tops. I took the necklace because it *looked* expensive. In the end, all I got for it was four thousand from a reputable appraiser.

Ten thousand dollars is a lot of money for a lot of people. But not for a Yakuza *waka gashira* like Kenzo. Certainly not an amount that would warrant chasing someone down for years.

So it's not about the money at all.

Sentimentality isn't something I have in spades, because I had to lose that along the way as dead weight that would have slowed me down. But other people have it, and that makes them dangerous.

With Kenzo, it clearly isn't about the necklace. It's about whatever sentimental value he attached to it. *That's* why he hunted me and why I'm so terrified that I'm being *given* to him now.

I pull on the e-cigarette again, exhaling white vapor as my jaw grinds. I could tell Kir about all of this. I mean he wouldn't be *pleased* that I drugged and stole from a Yakuza lieutenant, especially after he'd officially taken Freya and I in and we'd agreed to stop with the petty larceny. But still, I could tell him what's going on and why I'm so scared of what Kenzo might do to me.

But ultimately, what is that going to achieve?

Best case scenario, Kir talks to Kenzo and warns him not to harm me. Kenzo swears to be a good boy, and once we're married, skins me alive and buries me in a shallow grave anyway.

My brows knit. Or...not.

I'm pretty sure that would end whatever truce our nuptials are supposed to usher in. So maybe he won't kill me.

Maybe he'll just lock me in the basement and keep me barely alive so he can torture me for years.

I take another drag, thinking.

Ultimately, I know I'm not going to say shit to Kir. Because one of the reasons I respect him is that he takes care of things. He simply *gets shit done,* without bitching and moaning. Honestly, I think one of the reasons he likes me is that he knows I'm the same.

So no, I won't be a baby and go crying to Kir that my new husband might be mean to me because I stole from him five years ago.

Which puts me squarely back at square one.

Dammit.

I turn, and my gaze lands on a sporty-looking black and smoke-gray street motorcycle parked near the curb with a blood-red *hannya* mask painted on the gas tank and the kanji for "Mori-kai" written beneath it.

I smile coldly, reach into my clutch, and pull out my little switchblade.

I have no idea why Kenzo is here, but it doesn't matter. That fucker might think he's caught me, but he's going to learn that I come with claws. And he will *rue* the day he ever thought it was a good idea to get into a cage with me.

The air hisses out of the tires in angry gusts as I stab them, smiling smugly.

Take that, fucker.

A mere taste of what's to come. I slip the knife away and take another drag on my e-cigarette.

"That's a disgusting habit."

Kenzo.

Turning, I lock eyes with him as I take another long, deliberate drag and then exhale the vapor directly in his face.

"Okay," I deadpan.

Kenzo's lips curl slightly at the corners. "It's going to *stop* when we—"

"Please don't even finish that sentence."

Kenzo's changed out of the tuxedo he was in earlier. Now he's in black slacks with a fitted black dress shirt, open at the collar, the sleeves rolled up his rippling, veined, tattooed forearms. He folds this arms over his broad chest as he leans against one of the stone pylons that separate the hospital parking lot from the sidewalk.

"Not saying it doesn't make it any less true. And just so we're clear, when you're *my wife...*" He emphasizes the words in that infuriatingly attractive accent. The blend of that tone and those specific words are...not playing nicely together.

Kenzo points at the e-cig. "When you're *my wife*, that's done."

I glare at him. "Are you just here to fucking gloat?"

His brow furrows. "About what?"

"Trapping me."

I gasp as he surges off the pylon and right into me, grabbing me by the throat and looking down into my stunned face. There's a heat emanating from his huge body that tingles against my skin. The clean, woodsy, slightly spicy scent of him invades my senses, and I shiver.

"Believe me, *princess—*"

"Do not call me that."

His lips curl.

"But that's what you *are*, isn't it?" His eyes narrow. "A *princess?*"

I grit my teeth. I know why he's chosen that obnoxious name for me. Because once upon a time, in a life that burned to the ground, that's what I was: a prim and proper, pampered little mafia princess.

But I lost that version of myself years ago.

When I say nothing, Kenzo's jaw clenches and his fingers tighten around my throat.

"I'll call you whatever the fuck I choose," he snarls. "And I didn't want to trap you. I wanted to *exact vengeance* on you."

I fight back a shudder. "Well, you've succeeded."

Something sinister glints in his eyes.

"Not *yet*, I haven't."

The shudder breaks free, rippling down my spine.

"Not even close, Annika."

I jut out my chin at him. "Amazing," I spit back. "Mr. tough Yakuza bad-boy all upset about one stupid little necklace—"

I gasp sharply, whimpering as Kenzo shoves me against the stone pylon behind me. It hits my ass and the small of my back, but he keeps pushing until I'm half bent backward over it, with him looming over me.

"That necklace," he hisses viciously, "belonged to my mother."

I wince, the color draining from my face.

Cocksucking sentimentality.

"So whatever you pawned it for, I can promise it was less than a hundredth of its value to me."

I chew on my lip for a half second before speaking. "So, that's why you set this all up?"

"I thought I was clear a few seconds ago when I emphatically said I *did not* want this," he snarls. "I'd rather marry *anyone else* on Earth before you."

I shoot him a dirty look.

"Uh, *thanks*. Same to you, shithead. Look, if you're also

against this, why don't we work together to get ourselves *out* of—"

"That's not happening, and you know it," he says coldly.

We glare at each other for another few seconds before I bring the vape to my lips and take another pull, blowing it right into his face again.

Kenzo doesn't blink. He doesn't even flinch.

"You never answered my question, jerkwad. If you didn't come here to gloat—"

"Aoki Jura was my friend," he murmurs quietly. "As is the sole survivor from the group that walked into that nightclub earlier." He jerks a thumb over his shoulder at the hospital behind him. "He's in critical condition. That's why I'm here."

"I find that hard to believe."

His brow furrows. "What, that I give a shit about a friend who's lying injured in a hospital bed?"

"I was going to say that you have a heart or a conscience. But yeah, that works too."

He smiles coldly, closing the last half inch between our bodies. His huge, muscled frame pins me against the stone digging into the small of my back as he leers down into my face.

"We're going to be married, princess. Deal with it. And when you're my wife, I will expect..."

His eyes slowly drag from mine, down to my lips. Then further. I shiver, feeling the wrath of his gaze as it slides over my neck with his fingers still wrapped around it, then lower, to the plunging cleavage of this stupid dress I'm wearing.

Without a bra.

It's…a little chilly out.

His lips curl deviously. "*Everything* that comes with that."

Something heated fires through my core before I set my chin.

"Go to hell—"

"*Manners.*"

"Fuck off."

"Obedience."

I try to push him away, but it's like shoving at a brick wall.

"Eat a bag of dicks—"

His other hand jerks up, grabbing my chin while the first one keeps its firm grip on my throat.

"And making *every* part of you *mine.*"

That fucking fire returns with a vengeance, electrifying my core and making my thighs clench.

"In fact," Kenzo murmurs quietly, "we may as well start where we left off the last time."

"Try it and you'll beg for mercy."

The fucker chuckles.

"Here's the thing, Annika. You and your devil-may-care attitude don't scare me. Because you belong to me now."

I laugh right in his face. "You think just because of this arrangement—"

"This arrangement has very little to do with it. Tonight was a trap, you must know that, right?"

He leans closer.

"*My* trap. To catch you. And I did."

"Go fuck your—"

"We've already covered that," he says dryly. "At the end of the day, this is how this is going to play out. You belong to me. *All* of you."

I quickly jerk my hand out from between our bodies and shove it into my clutch. I yank out the little switchblade, flicking it open and bringing the edge to his throat.

Kenzo still doesn't flinch. Or blink. Or even move.

"Touch me, and I'll remove your head," I hiss.

He smiles.

He fucking *smiles.*

"It's adorable that you think knife play doesn't turn me on, Ms. Brancovich. Or should I get used to saying Mrs. Mori?"

His hand leaves my jaw to grab my wrist, pinning the blade against his own neck.

"What other depravities can you tease me with?"

"You will *not*—"

"What? Touch you? That's just the appetizer. When I want to touch you, *I will,*" he growls darkly. "When I want you on your knees with your lips around my cock, I will *put you there*. And when I want to *fuck you,* however I want, *wherever* I want, I goddamn will. *That* is how you repay me."

A shudder ripples through my entire core.

"H—how long," I choke.

Kenzo smiles.

"Excuse me?"

"How long," I spit.

He chuckles quietly. "Well, before, it would only have been until I deemed your debt repaid. But now, you're simply... mine." I tremble as he cups my jaw again, his eyes eviscerating me. "So it's *forever*."

In a blink, he drops his hands from me. He keeps his body pinned tight against me for a second longer, letting his eyes cut into my soul before he slowly takes a step back, taking his heat and that clean, woodsy, spicy scent with him as he starts to walk toward the bike. I allow myself to grin smugly.

"You might want to call a cab," I call after him, my voice sparkling with joy. "Your bike might not be working so well."

He stops, glancing back at me with a puzzled brow. I grin, twirling the switchblade in my hand. *"Oopsie!"* I giggle obnoxiously.

Kenzo arches a brow, turning to look at the flat tires on the motorcycle.

"Oh, that's not mine."

The smile drops from my face.

Shit.

"What the *FUCK* happened to my fucking bike?!"

I cringe at the rough, savage, furious voice behind me. We've never met, but I know who he is the second I turn and face the villainous guy who looks like an even more weaponized version of Kenzo.

Takeshi, his younger brother.

I know all about Kenzo and his siblings.

Know thy enemy, as they say.

"Seriously… What the *fuck*!?" Takeshi roars.

Again, we've never met. But I know his reputation. It's reflected in his nickname in the underground fighting circles he dabbles in: the War Machine.

Fuck.

Kenzo smirks as he lifts a brow in my direction.

"Very diplomatic, princess."

"This was fucking *you*?!" Takeshi bellows like a wild beast as he whirls on me with a fury that terrifies me.

I pale and start to back away as he advances on me.

"I—shit, I'm sorry—"

"You're *sorry*?!" he roars. "What the fuck sort of psycho *bitch*—"

"That's enough," Kenzo growls as Takeshi takes another step toward me, looking like he seriously wants to hurt me.

"I—I'll pay for it—"

"NO FUCKING SHIT!!!"

In that moment, two things happen. Takeshi charges at me like a fucking rhino on steroids. But Kenzo moves as well.

And he's faster.

He springs between his brother and me, his back to me as he plants both palms on Takeshi's broad chest.

"I said *that's enough*!" he snarls coldly.

It's…unexpected.

Hell, I figured he'd *love* to see his animal of a brother tear me apart. Or at least let me squirm a little while longer. I would have lost big money on the "Kenzo steps between you and stops it" bet.

Takeshi glares at me around his brother. But then he rolls his neck and takes a step back. Kenzo turns to level a dark look at me. "You'll pay him back for the bike."

"I—yeah, of course—"

"We're done here…*princess*."

He turns to face me, and steps close. My breath catches as he leans down, letting his lips brush my earlobe again.

"For now."

5

KENZO

For a second, when the door first opens, I'm greeted by a man my height standing in a way that suggests there's a gun hidden behind the door. Then his blue eyes lighten with recognition. Tate smiles as he steps back from the door and opens it a bit wider.

"Mr. Mori," he bows, a little stiffly, and I manage not to laugh.

Tate, my father's full-time nurse, can be a bit of a dork sometimes. Yes, a six-foot-four dork who can probably bench three hundred, but a dork nonetheless. He's big on the formalities, which make sense since he's ex-military—green berets, to be precise—but the way he always bows to me like I'm some ultra-traditional Japanese businessman is almost comical.

"Just Kenzo is fine, Tate. Really," I smile as I step into my father's sprawling apartment, smirking as I catch a quick glimpse of him slipping the gun that definitely *was* hidden behind the door back under his loose jacket.

I spent the early years of my life not knowing anything about my father beyond his first name. None of us ever pressed our mother on it, because it was clear it still pained her to talk about it.

Later, when I went to Japan to learn more about my past and my connection to the Mori name—which my siblings and I later adopted—I thought Hideo had died trying to run away with his family from the world of the Yakuza.

It was only recently that I learned the truth. Hideo *was* attacked while trying to get away, and sadly, his wife, Bella, was killed. But he and their infant daughter, my half-sister Fumi, managed to get out. Hideo got them new identities and new lives, and immigrated to the US as Hideo *Yamaguchi,* leaving behind Mori and everything that came with it.

Hideo and my sister had to start over again from nothing. The fortune he'd built with the Mori empire was gone. But it turns out, my half-sister is a bit of a genius.

Well, after all, she *is* a Mori.

Fumi worked her damn *ass* off, went to college and then law school, and later got hired at Crown and Black, one of the most prestigious law firms in New York.

Coincidentally, that happens to be the firm where Annika's twin sister, Taylor, is a managing name partner: she's the "Crown" in Crown and Black.

Fumi was already doing extremely well for herself, but a year or so back, she fell in love with Gabriel Black, her boss at the time. She married him, and now, that man is Governor of New York.

This is why Hideo now lives in a stunningly gorgeous apartment near Central Park with a full-time nurse-slash-personal-guard.

"How're things, Tate?" I nod at the man as he walks with me through the huge apartment toward the front living room.

"They're good, Mr.—" He clears his throat and shoots me a look. "Kenzo."

"And my father?"

Hideo and I have a complicated relationship. It's not *cold,* but let's say we're still learning who we are to each other.

I could, but don't, blame him for not knowing I existed, just as I don't blame my mother for keeping us from him. She was terrified, and rightly so, of the Yakuza life. And to be fair, he never knew about us.

Still, I know my father feels shame and regret for not having been in my and my siblings' lives. There've been tears shed at the thirty-four years of my life he missed. But there have also been smiles at the time we have now. He might not approve of my heavy involvement in the life and organization he sacrificed so much to escape from, but he respects the fact that my choices have been my own.

He and Sota have even reconnected, too, which I know has made both of them happy.

"Your father is doing great, Kenzo," Tate says with a smile.

Hideo, like Sota, was also formerly battling lung cancer thanks to a lifetime of being the sort of old school Japanese gangster chain-smoking Lucky Strikes. He's on the mend, now. But the lingering health issues are partly why Tate looks after him full-time during the day, with his own apartment directly above.

Hideo's also been turning Tate into a *monster* at *shoji*, Japan's version of chess.

Voices filter in from the living room as I follow Tate down the hall. Before I can ask, he turns to me. "Oh, your sister stopped by about an hour ago. They've been laughing it up ever since."

I smile.

Finding new family can be an interesting thing. It depends on the person. Me, I've enjoyed getting to know my father and half-sister, but I know Takeshi and Hana feel a little differently. There's no *blame* directed at our parents. But it's been hard for them to move past initial meetings and pleasantries with either Hideo or Fumi.

It is what it is. Maybe I had an easier time bringing my half-sister and my father into my life because it was just me and Mom for a couple of years. When Tak and Hana were born, they instantly had both of us, plus of course each other, being twins.

Who knows.

"Hey!" Fumi beams as she scrambles up from the couch and runs over to give me a big hug.

She's had a rough go of it. Being chased by the Yakuza. Losing her mother. Having to adopt a new name and identity, and cross the world to start fresh.

And yet… None of that broke her. None of that took the smile from her face. And I love that for her.

"Madame First Lady," I bow almost as comically deeply as Tate does. "I didn't realize I was going to be in the company of American political aristocracy."

"Oh please, fuck off," she snorts, rolling her eyes.

I grin, giving her another hug before walking over to my father.

"Hey, Dad," I smile as we embrace.

For the first few months when we initially connected, I called him Hideo. Now, it feels weird to call him anything but Dad.

"Heard you guys were getting crazy over here."

Fumi laughs. "Yeah, totally wild. We're going to do sake bombs in a second."

Hideo chuckles, wheezing a little. "Not unless you want to carry me to bed and tuck me into it, we're not."

It looks like Fumi's brought takeout from my dad's favorite Vietnamese place. But when they offer me some *chả giò*, I shake my head.

"No thanks."

"Suit yourself." Fumi shrugs and takes a big bite of fried spring roll. "How's your other dad?"

Hideo wheezes another deep laugh as I shake my head.

"*Sota* is good, thank you."

"And his treatment?"

I smile warmly. "They've got a lot of hope going into this new round of chemo."

"Good, I'm glad," Fumi nods.

"If *I* can deal with that goddamn poison," Hideo chuckles, "then Sota will do it dancing around the room. He was always the best at taking a punch and getting back up again." He pats my arm. "He's a tough son of a bitch."

He understands that his best friend from back home effectively took over as a surrogate father in his absence. And I think that makes him happy.

But that's as far as the conversation goes with him about Sota and my life with the Yakuza. He prefers to not talk about that world at all, considering what it cost him. Fumi's the same way.

So in a sense, I have two lives these days: the Yakuza one, which I talk about with Mal, Tak, Hana, and Sota. And then the other one, that I share with Hideo and Fumi.

Sometimes I like having that dual life. But it's also exhausting.

"How's Gabriel?"

"Oh, you know..." Fumi sighs. "Tons of free time to spend with me. Not a care in the world. Slacker workload."

I smirk. "That rough, huh?"

"Oh my God, it's *endless*. And I thought managing partners put in the hours."

Some might think it an "in" for man like me to have the damn Governor of New York as a brother-in-law. And I'd be lying if I said it hadn't crossed my devious mind.

But nothing funny is ever going to happen, and I have no plans to push for it. I mean, it'd be *nice* to have a "special relationship" with a US governor. But I've also met Gabriel, and that shit *is not* happening.

There's a darkness in that man, definitely. Not the kind that would ever hurt my sister. The kind that would murder for her. It's also clear that darkness doesn't extend to corruption.

"Oh, by the way," Fumi mumbles, her mouth full of *Bún bò Nam Bộ*. "I don't know if she mentioned it, but I grabbed a drink with Hana the other day."

"She didn't, but that's fantastic," I grin.

"She's cool, I like her a lot," Fumi shrugs. "*Great* style. What's new with you?" Fumi asks around another bite of beef noodle soup.

"Oh…" I puff out a breath. "Not much."

I'm just marrying a lying, backstabbing little bitch to stop a war with the Bratva.

"*Really*," Fumi deadpans with a wry look.

Fuck. I have to remember that this woman is one of the best lawyers in the city. She can smell bullshit a mile away.

"I'll fill you in later."

"Better."

We chit-chat for another twenty minutes or so before Fumi announces she has to run to get half an hour with her husband before he's pulled away to yet another governor's function.

I walk her down to her waiting car, hug her, then head back upstairs to my dad. When we're alone, he eyes me coolly with the look of a man who's spent his life reading between the lines.

"You want to talk about what you really came over here to discuss, before you realized Fumi was here?"

I chuckle. "You can take the man out of the Yakuza…"

Hideo smiles wryly. "My sake bomb days are over. But if you wanted to pour two glasses of that scotch over by the window, I'd join you."

I pour us two splashes of the Yamazaki eighteen-year-old, neat, and walk back to my father, taking a seat opposite him and clinking my glass to his.

"*Kanpai,*" he murmurs, taking a sip. "What's on your mind, Kenzo?"

I clear my threat. "I wanted to ask you about marriage."

He chuckles, and then goes still.

"You're serious?"

I nod.

"You've met someone?"

I exhale. "In a sense."

There are certain things that come to mind when Annika enters my thoughts. Things like vengeance and retribution. Things like punishment.

Things too like fucking her hard, and without mercy. Owning her. Dominating and subjugating her. Taking her every way a man can take a woman.

Not once—*ever*—have I imagined *marrying* the fucking woman.

To be fair, it's not a thought or desire I've ever had for anyone else. The darkness in me doesn't allow for anything so normal inside my black veins.

"I didn't know—"

"Neither did I," I growl bitterly, sipping my drink.

My father nods sagely. "Ahh. It's like that."

Yeah, he knows what this is.

"It is," I grunt back. "But my question," I barrel on, "isn't about contractual mafia marriage. It's about marriage itself." I consider how to approach this delicately. "When you met Bella—"

"I just knew."

He says it without a single second of hesitation. Then he quickly frowns.

"I don't mean any disrespect toward your mother. I cared for Astrid, a great deal."

I smile quietly. "I know."

"If she'd told me about you, that second time she came to Japan…" He shakes his head. "I think things might have been different. But I knew I never had *all* of her. I knew she kept some part of herself back. And I think I did the same in response."

"She wasn't your *person*," I mummer. "Bella was."

My father frowns, clearly unsure how to answer that without offending me.

"You won't ever hurt my feelings talking about this, you know," I say quietly. "For what it's worth, I don't think you were her person either. If you were, she would have made it work. She would have stayed and told you about us."

Hideo looks away, nodding and taking another sip of scotch.

"So with Bella…"

"Like I said: I just knew." He smiles to himself before turning to me and allowing it to grow wider. "Instantly. No hesitation. She was it."

"But what if you *didn't* 'just know'," I persist. "What if it wasn't something that made itself instantly apparent."

Hideo looks at me curiously, like he's peering past my walls.

"You're not asking me about true love. You're asking me about cohabitation."

I smile sardonically. "Perhaps."

"And it is an arranged thing by the Yakuza?"

"For the sake of avoiding a war, yes," I growl.

"I see," he nods. "Well, I'll say this. It *always* comes down to cohabitation, even if you do have the love of your life. Believe me. Even Bella and I had our moments."

"And if she's not so much 'a true love' and more 'the enemy'..." I trail off.

Hideo smirks. "Then make it so she isn't."

"I'm not sure that's possible. She's nothing I'd have ever picked for myself in a million years. Reckless. Emotional and quick-tempered. Tempestuous. *Rude.* She cares nothing for traditions, thumbs her nose at any sort of rules. Gives the middle fucking finger to—"

"Point taken, Kenzo," my father chuckles quietly. "But I'll say it again: if you live with the enemy, it'll poison you both. And you, it would seem, *must* do this."

"I do," I mutter.

My father sighs.

“Kenzo, I don’t approve of the life you’ve chosen. You know that. But I *respect you* for following through on your decisions, and doing what you must.” He smiles wryly. “Sota has clearly taught you well.”

“I just don’t think this is the sort of man you wanted me to be.”

“What I want is only a suggestion. *It’s your life,* my son. And this is going to be *your* wife, forever. Make her into someone you can live with. That’s my advice.”

I lift my glass. “Thank you.”

He lifts his. “Congratulations on your engagement, son. *Kanpai.*”

“Kanpai.”

6

"HERE'S THE THING, DICKHEAD," I growl quietly. "You don't get to just tap out. You don't get to leave now and make me and Frey clean this shit up. You got that?"

Damian doesn't respond: unsurprising, since he's still in a medically induced coma. But I'm damn sure he can still hear me and gets the message loud and clear.

It's been a week since the shooting, and he's apparently doing a lot better. Still in the coma, but that's so his body can focus on healing. The specialist from Dubai that Kir flew in says that he and his team are going in one more time to remove a few last fragments of bullet that are still dangerously close to Damian's heart. After that, they say he's going to be better.

He'd fucking better be.

"Anyway, you're missing so much drama while you're napping like a lazy asshole," I mutter at him, squeezing his hand. "I mean, I'm getting married, and you're missing *so* many opportunities for solid A-list jokes at my expense. Let me say that again: *I* am getting married."

I'd half expect Damian to wake up at that.

He doesn't.

"I'm supposed to go wedding dress shopping. But I'm seriously considering just showing up to this stupid fucking thing in a burlap sack. Or maybe a halloween costume just to be hilarious. What do you think?"

The machines surrounding Damian beep and whir in tempo.

"Squeeze my hand once for scary clown; twice for slutty nurse."

I glare at him.

"Well for fucks sake, dude. You gotta pick one."

With a sigh, I smile, lean down and hug him.

"I love you, jackass. Seriously, get better." I bite my lip as I squeeze his hand again. "I don't know if I can do this without you."

I give him a kiss on the forehead before brushing the tiniest bit of moisture away from my eyes and standing. No. Fuck that. I don't cry, ever. And I'm *definitely* not giving Damian the satisfaction or the ammo by doing it over him.

Turning, I march across the room, fling the door open, and stride out—

"*Shit*!"

Right into someone.

I stumble back, an apology on my lips until both of our brows shoot up in surprise as Hana Mori and I regard each other in stunned silence.

"Uh...hi," I blurt awkwardly.

Her brow clears as she recognizes me too. “Hey.”

Again, I know Kenzo’s whole family and his inner circle because that’s what a smart person does if they’re being hunted.

Kenzo has three siblings. Four I guess, if you count Fumi Yamaguchi, aka the First Lady of New York these days. But on the Yakuza side, there are three Mori siblings. Sort of. Mal Ulstad is actually Kenzo’s cousin via his mother. But he’s been living as their sibling since he was like twelve or something.

After that, there are the twins: Takeshi and Hana. And it’s Hana who’s standing in front of me now.

Like her brothers, Hana has this gorgeous blend of both Northern European and Japanese features. She’s taller than average, with long, freakishly straight and perfectly bleached blonde hair, beautiful dark eyes, and soft lips. She *almost* looks like she could fit into Freya’s brand of techno-goth-punk, just more… I don’t know, fashionable? Professional?

No offense, Frey.

She’s dressed all in black, super sleek and stylish, like she’s the CFO of a moon-mining corporation in a sci-fi movie. There’s not a single wrinkle. Not a single—and I do mean *single*—bleached white-blonde hair out of place. And her ever-so-slightly goth makeup is…unff…*chef’s kiss.*

“So, uh…”

“Sister-in-law-to-be, huh?” she says dryly, arching a brow.

“*Guess so,*” I answer awkwardly. “So, um… Who’re you here to see?”

Jesus Christ. The assignment was to be *less* socially awkward, self.

She nods down the hall with her chin. "Okada. He's one of Aoki's men."

I wince.

The *only one* of Aoki's men to have survived the shootout in the nightclub with Damian and his men.

I suppose I should hate Hana for being on "the other side". But there are no winners or losers in a scenario this stupid and senseless.

Everyone loses.

"How's he doing?" I ask hopefully.

Her lips curl a bit, giving me a hint of a smile. "He's… improving, thanks. He's getting out tomorrow."

"That's good," I say quietly.

She frowns as she nods past me to Damian lying in bed. "I'm sorry about your brother."

"Oh, he's not really…" I shake my head. "I don't know why I said that. He basically is my brother. Thank you."

Hana smiles wryly. "Found family is still family. I have a brother-who-isn't-really-my-brother, too."

I glance down at my feet then back up at her. "I'm sorry about Aoki."

She shrugs. "I only met him once or twice. Honestly, by all accounts, he was kind of an asshole. But thanks." She looks past me again at Damian, her lower lip catching between her teeth. "Is he going to be okay?"

I nod. "Yeah. He has another surgery tomorrow. After that, they think they can take him off life support and slowly bring him out of the coma."

Hana flashes me a genuine smile. "That's good." We look at each other with a little less awkwardness and stiffness. "Look, for what it's worth, I'm sorry you have to marry my brother."

I snort. "Oh, so you've met him too."

Hana gives me a look. "To be clear, I love my brother."

Shit.

But Hana flashes me another small smile. "I meant that I'm sorry you have to marry someone you don't want to." She glances at the super cute, *very* expensive looking silver watch on her wrist. "Look, I don't know if this is weird, and you can totally say no, but I was about to go find a dress to wear to the party..." She arches a brow at me. "Wanna come with?"

Wait, what?

Freya was right the other day: I *don't* have many friends, because honestly, I suck at them. Freya and Damian are about it, and I've sort of given up on trying to expand my social circle.

But this feels incredibly friendly, and I'm—embarrassingly—jumping up and down on the inside. Because Kenzo's sister seems *super fucking cool.*

"Uh, yeah," I shrug as casually as humanly possible. "I guess I could do that."

"Cool!" Hana smiles broadly at me as we both turn and head down the hall toward the front lobby.

I furrow my brow. "So, what party is this?"

Hana pulls up short, causing me to stumble to a stop as she turns to raise a brow at me. "Please tell me you're joking. The engagement party, of course."

I bark a loud, sharp laugh, then stop. "Wait...you're serious."

"Um, yes?"

I snort, shaking my head. "Yeah, not happening."

Hana winces. "Yeah, *sort of* non-negotiable, trust me. It's not Kenzo's thing, it's Sota's. And believe me, when that man says something is happening, especially if it's a party, it's not a case of *if*. It's more where, when, and how crazy big is the budget." She grins at me. "Sorry, but you gotta trust me on this one."

I groan as I flop against the wall. "*Shit*."

"Yeah, well..." she shrugs. "It won't be that bad. I mean, maybe you don't want to marry Kenzo—"

"I don't. No offense."

She shrugs. "None taken. And maybe he doesn't want to marry *you*—"

"He one thousand percent doesn't."

Hana smirks. "Well, the feelings of the bride and groom aside, the shitload of people that Sota is inviting are going to spend the entire evening telling you how amazing you look, how lucky you are, and showering you with booze and gifts."

I arch a brow. "Really."

"So, might as well make the best of it, right?"

She slips her arm through mine.

"C'mon. Let's find you a dress."

OKAY, not only am I not much of a "makes friends" type of girl, I'm *really* not much of a shopper. Or a fashionista.

Yet, despite all that, I end up having a *fantastic* time with Hana.

My soon-to-be sister-in-law is a *huge* fashion person and knows every single luxury boutique in Manhattan intimately. Every damn place welcomes her with open arms and champagne and treats us like freaking royalty. And hours and about seven boutiques later, long after nightfall, I've found the *perfect* dress for my engagement party, and I actually love it.

Okay, like it well enough. But for me? With a *dress*? Home run.

After I pay for the dress at the last shop, Hana gives me a hug and swaps numbers with me before saying she's going to stay a little longer, since she and this particular boutique owner are old pals.

I give her another hug, grab my spoils, and pull my phone out as I walk out the door.

Yikes. Nine missed calls from Freya.

I'm about to call her back when suddenly a familiar-looking black Audi screeches to a stop right in front of me. The tinted window rolls down, and Freya smirks at me across the passenger seat.

"Have fun with your new gal pal?"

She nods past me. I turn and see Hana in the window, gabbing away with her friend and sipping bubbly.

"Jealous, Frey?"

"Of her?" Freya snorts. "Um, *yeah.* That bitch is put *together.* She's like me if I had class. I'm the wish dot com version."

I snort another loud laugh and nod at Hana inside the shop. "I bumped into her when I went to see Damian earlier. She's actually pretty fucking cool."

"Seriously. She looks like the coolest person I've ever met." She smiles at me. "I saw Damian last night."

"Night nurses okay with you coming after visiting hours now, or did you sneak in again?"

She grins. "Delores and I are cool now. She told me I remind her of her granddaughter." Her brow furrows. "How'd he look today?"

"Good," I smile as I lean down and plant my arms on the open window ledge of the door. "The doctors told me they're confident they'll be able to bring him out of the coma after this next operation."

It goes without saying that we're both just trying to cheer each other up about all of this.

"Wait, so what are you up to? You weren't picking up my calls."

I squint at her. "Frey… Did you track me here?"

She shrugs. "Like I said: you weren't picking up."

"Okay, we need to work on boundaries again."

She snorts. "I think we're well past that, don't you?"

"What was so fucking important?"

The smile suddenly vanishes from Freya's face. "You might want to get in."

I slip into the car, rolling up the window as Freya turns to me.

"Ulkan isn't letting it go."

An icy skewer pierces my heart. I quickly try to shove it away.

"W-what do you mean?"

"I've been poking around on the dark web, talking to some people I know." Her face pales even more than usual. "Word is, he's putting out serious feelers. He's seriously *pissed* about what happened."

God-fucking-dammit.

Like I said, I rarely make mistakes. But aside from Kenzo, Ulkan Gacaferi was one of them.

It was a few months ago, right as I was being reunited with my sister after so many years apart. I know we shouldn't have, especially for a psycho like Ulkan, but Frey and I took on a job.

Hindsight is a motherfucker. When I look back on this particular job, it had all the red flags I usually walk away from. But I was so focused on the Taylor thing, and the money was *so* stupid good, that I said yes without thinking.

Ulkan Gacaferi, a notorious Albanian crime boss and general psychopath, hired us to steal a car—a brand-spanking-new, neon yellow Lamborghini—from the parking garage of an ultra-exclusive condo building in Midtown.

He was willing to pay *a lot*: three hundred and fifty grand for the car itself, plus another hundred k for our time.

I mean, that's the dumbest, quickest almost-half million you can possibly make. And Freya and I stole *hundreds* of high-end sports cars for buyers in Dubai and China in our day.

So we said yes. There was some concern about the money part, but he paid half up-front and spun us this tale that it was a joke on a friendly rival of his. That they played pranks like this on each other all the time, and everyone would have a big laugh about it later.

So we stole it. It took all of nineteen seconds, and we were on our way to the drop-off point when I thought to check the trunk.

That's when the record scratched and the music stopped.

Inside the trunk, there was what looked like a hundred and fifty pounds of cocaine, maybe two million in cash, and a couple of *very* illegal-looking machine guns.

Unbelievably, that wasn't the worst part.

The worst was that all of it was marked as belonging to *him*.

My devil. My demon. The man who almost killed me and snuffed out a part of me in the process.

The man I'd finally managed to escape, and now we'd just stolen a *fortune* from him.

Valon Leka.

That's when Freya and I made a game-time decision. We ditched the car by the Lincoln Tunnel, wiped it of prints, and *walked the fuck away*.

Obviously, Ulkan's people reached out demanding to know where the car was. We responded using Freya's anonymous messaging service, saying that the job had been presented to us in bad faith and that we weren't interested in stealing from Valon. Ulkan wanted his deposit back, but it was clear he wanted it to come accompanied by our heads in a bag.

So we ditched the burner accounts we'd used to talk to him and put the whole thing behind us.

Or so I thought.

"Shit," I mutter. "How exposed are we?"

Freya makes a face.

"I mean, it's a low number. But I'd like it a whole lot better if it was zero."

My brows knit as I tick off our options. "There's The Broker. But...obviously not."

The Broker is a dark web guy that specializes in setting up jobs like this. He's the one that reached out to us with the job offer from Ulkan. But he's incorruptible. I mean *incorruptible.*

"There's the guard." Frey's face is worried.

I shake my head. "No. He didn't see me."

It was the one thing we couldn't plan for: a security guard in the parking garage who lingered on one floor too long to smoke a cigarette, throwing off his rotation. It meant he saw me crouched next to the car as I was getting the door open.

When he yelled, I launched into my "bimbo looking for clues that her boyfriend is cheating on her" routine, and when he got close, I pulled out my emergency gas can and sprayed him in the face, knocking him out.

Not my proudest moment.

"Anni..."

"We talked about this, Freya. Anyone who gets dosed with that gas loses their memory for the thirty seconds before it hits their system."

"But you don't know how long he was looking at you *before* he yelled at you and you got close enough to gas him."

I shake my head. "No. No chance."

"He might remember your face, Annika. I'm just saying, we should have—"

"I'm not a killer, Frey." I turn to see her looking sheepishly at her hands. "Neither are you, for that matter."

She exhales. "I know. But, that's our weak link. Just saying."

"He'll never place us."

"Better hope not," she mutters. Freya clears her throat and nods at the bag in my hand, changing the subject. "That looks suspiciously like a dress."

"Brace yourself."

She grins. "Seriously? For what?"

"My engagement party."

She snorts loudly. I just shake my head.

"Laugh all you like, you're coming too."

"Not a *chance*."

"Oh, come on. You know how Kir gets with tradition and fancy events, and it would mean *so* much to him if you came, what with Damian—"

"You're an asshole," she grumps.

"And you love me in spite of it. So…yeah…*any*way," I laugh. "If you're looking for a dress, I highly recommend this place." I turn and nod at the shop I just left. "Just…" I roll my eyes. "Never mind."

Freya frowns. "No, what?"

"I was going to say stay away from green because that's what I'm wearing."

"And then you remembered who you're talking to?" she snickers. "All black, bitch. Maybe I'll get some extra eyebrow piercings, since it's your *special daaaay*," she coos, laying on the sarcasm.

"Now who's the asshole."

7

KENZO

"I'LL STOP you right there before you get going," I mutter, eyeing Mal coolly over the rim of my Old Fashioned.

"No idea what you're talking about," he says mildly, a rare hint of a smile on his jaw as he lifts an amused brow and a glass to his lips.

"The million and one jokes. Let's just *not*, please?"

Around us, the engagement party is in full swing. Heads of tribute families to the Akiyama-kai. Friends of Sota. Kir and his contingent from the Nikolayev Bratva, and heads of *their* tribute families.

The event is taking place at the house Sota bought in the West Village after it became clear he was going to be spending more time in New York for his treatments. On the one hand, Sota is one of the most hardened, deadly, and cold-blooded Yakuza kingpins to have ever lived.

On the other, the guy is really kind of a housecat.

Yes, he could easily stay in top-of-the-line hotels whenever he came to New York. But Sota doesn't want individually wrapped soaps and room service. He wants a familiar mattress. He wants a kitchen to make his own tea in, and a garden to look at while sipping it.

Hana played a huge part in redesigning the older West Village brownstone into a stunning palace fit for a dark shogun. It's modern in a distinctly contemporary Japanese way, but also has plenty of nods to the older culture that I know Sota gravitates to.

Tonight, it's ground zero for my and Annika's "engagement" party.

Whatever.

Beside me, my brother takes a heavy swig of his drink as he glances around the room. It's funny: Mal and I *are* related through my mother's side, though he's technically my cousin, not my brother. But when his mother—my aunt—passed away, Mom took him in, and he came to live with us at our estate in England. Mal was twelve at the time, and he's been by my side pretty much ever since.

If that doesn't make someone your brother, I don't really know what does.

The funny part, of course, is watching other people try and wrap their minds around the word "brother" when they look at the two of us. Obviously we share half of our lineage, since our mothers were sisters. But where he's basically full-blooded Viking with his father also being Norwegian, I've got Hideo's Japanese ancestry as well.

It's precisely that blended background of mine that makes me cling so tightly to those who I call family, and why I've hardened myself against the world after a lifetime of not "fitting in".

In the snooty, old-money circles that my mother came from, I had "just enough" Asian in me to stick out, and a lot of those fuckers never let me forget it. Then, when I fell in with Sota and the Yakuza, I was "not *quite* Asian enough" for a lot of their friends.

Sota himself didn't give a fuck. And he had no tolerance for anyone else calling me *gaijin.*

"He's not a foreigner," he'd snap. "He just took his time making his way back home."

Mal knocks back the rest of his cocktail. Just as he swallows, his jaw tightens and a frown creases his brow.

"Who the *fuck* is that?" he mutters quietly.

I turn to follow his piercing gaze across the room. Freya Holm has just walked in.

I grimace, grinding my teeth. "Annika's friend," I mutter. I frown at her attire. I mean, it's a formal occasion with a formal presumed dress code. And sure, black *would* be acceptable.

...But Freya's hardly wearing a little black dress. It's more like something Morticia fucking Addams would wear to a goddamn funeral. Black velvet falling to the floor, long bell sleeves, and a dramatically plunging neckline half filled with fucking *fishnet.*

And she's paired it with glossy black combat boots and has a goddamn *spiked choker* around her neck.

On top of that, she's playing up her normally ghostly appearance with shades of white, purple, and black for makeup, and her dark hair is twisted up into something that would make Helena Bonham Carter smile with pride.

This is only the engagement party. What the fuck is she going to wear to the actual wedding, a *Scream* mask and a funeral shroud?

My attention is yanked back to Mal as he knocks back his empty glass, taking the last of the ice cube into his mouth and crunching down on it harshly.

"What's her *name*," he hisses.

"It's Freya—sorry, *what* is this about?" I growl, peering at him.

"Nothing."

"Mal..."

He shakes his head and blinks as Freya haunts her way into the crowd and disappears. Mal clears his throat and his shoulders visibly relax. "Nothing," he grunts with more conviction this time. "Thought she was someone else."

"Who?"

He turns, his eyes dropping to my empty glass. "Let's get you a drink."

Well, that's the end of that conversation, I guess.

For now.

The two of us head over to the bar running along the side of Sota's enormous living room.

"So," Mal smirks, completely back to his usual self. "Where's your blushing bride-to-be?"

"Plotting my demise, probably."

He smirks again. "I have to ask. Do you have to..." His grin widens. "*Consummate* this thing?" He lifts a shoulder. "I mean, don't take this the wrong way, but arranged or not, and disliking her or not, she *is* pretty hot—"

"Thanks, Mal."

"I mean, the fucking *ass* on—"

"Yeah, I got it," I hiss.

"Those lips? Wrapped around—"

"*Shut the fuck up*," I snap.

Mal looks amused.

"What I'm *actually* concerned about," he remarks casually, "is her cutting your dick off, not you fucking her with it."

"That won't be happening."

"You know, they make some great lightweight body armor these days. It could feel just like a pair of extra thick boxers—"

"No, I mean the..." I sigh. "I'm not going to be fucking her."

"*Why*, exactly?"

"We have..." I eye him coldly. "We have history," I finally grunt.

"Oh, really?" Mal chuckles. "How *salacious*."

"It's *not* what you're thinking," I mutter. "That night a few years ago, when I was robbed at the Clover Club in Kyoto? When I lost mom's necklace?"

He frowns. "Wait, the night—" His eyes go wide. "Get the *fuck* out," he almost wheezes, holding in a loud laugh. "That was her?! You're marrying a fucking *animal*! I mean...holy shit." He snickers, shaking his head.

"I'm well aware," I growl back.

Just then, in my peripheral vision, the crowd parts a little. I turn, and my breath hitches as my eyes land on Annika.

Shit.

Annika doesn't walk into the room so much as *glides*. I've seen her in a dress before—twice. Once was just the other day at Cillian's party. The other time was Kyoto. But that was five years ago, and it was dark.

And I'd been drugged. By her.

From my research into her, I'm well aware that she's not generally a dress type of girl. But when she walks in, and the whole room sucks in its collective breath and turns to stare at her a fraction of a second longer than I'm guessing anyone intended...

It's enough to make you wonder why the fuck she *doesn't* wear them more often. My simmering distaste for and anger toward Annika aside, the woman looks like a fucking *dream*.

She floats into the room in green satin; a single-strap, floor-length gown that angles diagonally across her chest, giving just the tiniest hint of cleavage. The bias-cut satin hugs every goddamn curve on her tall, slender frame, cinching in at the waist a little before flaring out over her hips and the curve of her ass. A slit cuts up dramatically high on her thigh, giving a teasing glimpse of her long legs and the strappy gold and pearl heels on her feet.

Her hair is where the shockingly out-of-character elegance falls short: it's pulled up in a no-nonsense ponytail with a few stray locks framing her face. As if someone else had been in charge of dressing her, but Annika was firmly in the driver's seat for everything else that came with getting ready for the evening.

Still. Fuck me. She looks *stunning*.

I can feel my blood burning a little hotter, and I'm fully aware of my dick swelling and thickening in my suit pants as I drink her in.

As if sensing my eyes on her, Annika turns toward me. Our gazes lock across the room, and I tilt my head as I give her a soft nod of my chin…

And then Annika lifts her hand and flips me off before walking away in another direction.

"God, this wedding is going to be *incredible*," Mal laughs next to me. "Not even joking—someone needs to pat that woman down for weapons before the string quartet launches into Pachelbel's *Canon in D minor*."

I shoot him a dirty glare. "Do me a favor?"

"Yeah?"

"Go bother someone else."

He chuckles. "I'll go look for Tak. I haven't seen him in a hot minute, which at events like this usually means he's getting into trouble."

He's not wrong. I haven't seen our younger brother for a solid half an hour either, which history would suggest that means he's either A, engaged in an aggressive drinking contest with the staff, B, fighting someone somewhere, or C, is balls-deep in someone else's wife.

"Yeah, that's…" I frown. "Probably a good idea."

"Good luck with..." Mal turns to nod his chin to where Annika is disappearing into the crowd. "Well...everything." He snorts, shaking his head as he wanders off to go find our brother.

I'm taking a much-needed sip of my drink when I catch a glimpse of Hana making her way toward me. Thank God. I was steeling myself for small talk with a bunch of Sota's elderly Yakuza buddies, wanting to congratulate me or trying to curry favor for that day I take over the whole empire.

My sister looks her usual elegant and gorgeously put-together self in a shimmering silvery gown that ties at the back of the neck and cuts at a sharp angle from hip to opposite ankle. There's the tiniest little hint of lavender to the silver, which has a way of highlighting her dramatic dyed blonde hair, which is pulled into an elaborate up-do.

I swear to God, in another reality, Hana is the no-bullshit CEO of a major innovative tech company in the 23rd century.

"I hope no one's told you how beautiful you look tonight."

She shoots me a pissed look. "Excuse me?"

"I'd hate to break anyone's face at my own engagement party."

Hana rolls her eyes. "You need to work on your bizarre compliment delivery before you get married. It's...off-putting."

I grin, shrugging.

"For your information, maybe someone *has* told me I look great tonight."

"Who?" I frown.

"Yeah, let me just go ahead and tell you so that you, Mal, and Tak can go into crazy overly protective brother mode and kill somebody. Not happening." She shoots me a look. "Did you notice who *else* is looking pretty amazing tonight?"

My jaw sets. "I think you need to elaborate on who you mean."

"Oh, I don't think so." She smirks. "She cleans up pretty nice, gotta say."

"It's…not a terrible dress."

Hana snorts. "Gee, thanks. I picked it out for her."

I frown. "You two went dress shopping?"

"Yes. And?"

"Hana…" I scowl and shake my head. "She's not your friend."

"Says who?"

"Me."

Hana barks a laugh. "Well, in that case, *your highness*," she snickers. "Have you considered that she has about as much interest in marrying you as you do her? Possibly *less*?"

"Considered. Filed away. No shits given. She's a peace treaty, Hana. A necessary evil."

Before I can say another word, I see one of the older Yakuza guys I was hoping to avoid talking to heading my way. Even worse, it's Matsui Aki.

Matsui and the Aki-kai are a smaller Yakuza family that long ago swore allegiance to my father's Mori-kai. In the absence of the Mori-kai being a thing for the past few decades,

Matsui has pledged allegiance to Sota. But since I've begun rebuilding my empire, Sota has insisted that families like Matsui's honor their original vows to the Mori-kai. Ergo, Matsui now reports directly to me as his *oyabun*.

Which would be great, except for the fact that Matsui is a sneaky, selfish little shit whose only real allegiance is to himself and his bank account. Worse, he has lately taken to all but hurling his daughter, Nishi, at me.

"Oh, shit, I almost forgot…gotta run."

Hana starts to walk away, but I grab her arm.

"For?" I growl.

"A…a thing…" She gives me a stricken look before glancing at Matsui as he moves toward us. "Fine. He gives me the creeps. *Please* can I go?"

I sigh. "Sure. See if you can help Mal make sure Takeshi isn't up to his usual bullshit."

"Good luck," she mutters as she drifts away, just as Matsui sidles up to me.

"Ahh!" He beams broadly. "Congratulations to the prince!"

The lack of *any* sort of smile in his eyes lets me know he's probably one of the least pleased people in the room about my engagement, third only behind Annika and I. After all, this means I won't be entertaining his less-than-subtle attempts to get me to marry his daughter.

Nishi, who's standing right next to him dressed in—I have to say—a *stunning* red gown that leaves little to the imagination, smiles at me as she moves closer.

"Congratulations, Kenzo," she purrs. Her tongue slips out to wet her lips with just a hint of provocativeness, her eyes locking with mine. "She's a very lucky girl."

"*Arigato,* Matsui-san," I say, bowing formally to him before turning and giving a briefer nod to Nishi. "And thank you." I turn back to her father. "And, Matsui, I need to talk to you to iron out the...*delays* in the new guidelines I've laid out for our organization."

As I've slowly been rebuilding the Mori-kai and establishing more of a presence in Kyoto, I've recently issued a decree to all the family heads who report to me. I'm making a few changes, and one of the bigger ones is that our organization will *not* be dealing in prostitution going forward.

Sota has no patience or stomach for the trade either, and has similarly banned it from his organization top to bottom for decades. But there are a few families who have snuck through the cracks. The Aki-kai is one.

Matsui's organization was one of the ones who went out on their own as mini empires when my father left and the Mori-Kai empire folded. For a while, he set his own rules, did whatever business he wanted, and answered to no one. When other, larger families started encroaching on his small empire, Matsui was forced to join up with Sota, and to pledge him his allegiance. In a case like that, it was harder to get him to get on board with how Sota does business. Which is why Matsui has continued to run girls and brothels.

That's ending, now. I won't have it. The problem is, Matsui makes a lot of money from his girls, so he's been purposefully stalling in giving me his response to the decree.

"Ahh, yes! Of course, of course." Matsui smiles at me like we're old pals.

"Now, Matsui."

"Soon, yes."

My jaw tightens. "I don't think you heard me. I need you to give me your pledge *now* that you will stop—"

"You know, my poor Nishi was so sad when she heard you were engaged."

God fucking dammit. It's the same damn script every time with this fucker.

"Matsui—"

"I must go congratulate Sota," he smiles at me, pulling away. "Why don't you and Nishi talk?"

Nishi smiles seductively at me as her father dives into the crowd. She sidles close, her tongue wetting her lips and her eyelids batting as she runs one scarlet-painted nail up my arm.

"I *was* so sad, Kenzo."

"Nishi, no disrespect, I don't think you and I would have ever worked out. But I'm *sure* there's a young man out there who would give his left arm to have you at his side."

I frown when she ignores me and pulls even closer, her finger trailing over my chest. Then, over her shoulder, I realize we're being watched.

By *Annika*.

She's not really so much "watching" as "glaring death". Her brow is furrowed deeply, her blue eyes spark with something wicked and fierce, and her lips are pursed as she stares dangerously at Nishi pulling closer to me.

Interesting.

She's got a jealous streak as green as her dress that comes out sometimes. Even if she hates me and this situation, it seems Annika doesn't like being fucked with.

She might be lowkey wishing a piano would fall through the ceiling and crush me this evening. But she doesn't like being slighted by anyone. And that includes Nishi trying to breathe down my neck and trace my fucking nipple through my suit at my own engagement dinner.

"You know, Kenzo…" Nishi purrs into my ear. "You might be getting married, but we're from the same world. I know we understand what this marriage really is."

"I don't need you to explain it to me, Nishi," I growl, planting my hands on her arms to gently push her away from me.

She doesn't budge.

"I can offer you a…*different* sort of arrangement, you know."

"Take your hands *off* me, Nishi," I mutter.

"My father just wants me to be happy, Kenzo. When I'm happy, he's happy. And when *he's* happy, he does whatever you ask him. So, you might have to be married to the cold *gaijin* who looks like she wants you to fall down a flight of stairs…"

Frighteningly accurate.

"But *I* could warm your bed." Nishi's voice lowers to a whisper as she leans even closer. *"You could fuck me however you want. Do whatever—"*

She gasps as I shove her away from me.

"My advice to you, Nishi," I hiss, "is to find some self-respect. And while you're doing that, stay the fuck away from me. Are we clear?"

Her face heats as her lips purse. She nods quickly, the sultriness vanishing as she turns and quickly hurries into the crowd.

Christ, I need a drink.

I turn to hit the bar, and find myself walking almost directly into a tsunami of ginger and green. I halt quickly, my brow arching as Annika glares at me with a cold expression on her face.

"Enjoying the party?" she hisses.

I smirk. "Spying on me, princess?"

"It doesn't take James Bond to see you all but fucking that woman in the middle of your own engagement party—engagement to *me,* I might add."

I chuckle. "Jealous?"

"*Annoyed,*" she counters. "I'd like you to stop acting like you're the only one getting screwed with this arrangement."

"I'm pretty sure the issue is that I'm *not* going to be getting screwed with this arrangement." I arch a brow. "Unless…?"

Annika flushes deep red. "Unless you go fuck yourself. Get used to it."

"So, you *don't* want to fuck me…"

"Not in a million fucking years," she says sweetly.

"But the idea of *Nishi* fucking me—"

"It's you disrespecting me in the middle of this party," she snaps. "We don't have to like each other, but some basic regard would go a long way."

"That's a strange way to say 'Kenzo, you talking to that girl makes me jealous'."

"Oh my *God*, you're a fucking child." She glares at me. "I'm *not* jealous."

I shrug. "If you say so."

She rolls her eyes and spins to walk away.

"For what it's worth, princess," I growl, halting her. "Ultimately, her offer was a business one. Her father reports to me, but he's been stalling on agreeing to new terms for our organization."

"What the fuck was her offer?" Annika spits. "You let her suck your dick and her father signs off on your royal decrees?"

"I mean..." I lift a shoulder, grinning. "Essentially."

"You're a fucking pig."

I sigh. "I didn't *agree* to it."

"How noble!" she gushes dramatically. "Would you like a medal?"

"Your mouth would suffice."

Her eyes bulge, but then just as quickly as she gets flustered she swallows it back, smoothing a calm, no-fucks-given expression over her face.

"Here's the thing, Kenzo," she says with an artificial smile, stepping closer and leaning into me. "I don't rattle so easily.

I'm not one of your fawning little Yakuza fangirls. I'm not a cabaret girl massaging your ego and topping off your drink for a buck. Okay?" Her lips thin to a line. "I'm stuck with you, but *you're* equally stuck with *me*." She leans even closer. *"I can be your worst fucking nightmare."*

Annika is all smiles again as she pulls back, her hand patting my chest patronizingly before it drops away.

"Okay?"

My lips curl. *"Listen,* princess. We—"

"Kenzo!"

Motherfucker.

Just as I'm seriously contemplating dragging Annika off somewhere to remind her of her place by spanking her bare ass, Matsui barges back into my personal space.

"Kenzo, what did you say to my Nishi?" he growls, ridiculously over-the-top fury plastered on his face.

"Matsui, I suggest you walk away," I snarl. "Perhaps we can have this conversation another—"

"I won't have my daughter disrespected!" Matsui spits back. "What the hell happened—"

"What *happened,*" Annika hisses, butting in abruptly, "is that your daughter—"

"Excuse me," he snaps. "Kenzo and I were—"

"Matsui," I murmur quietly through clenched teeth. "Allow me to introduce *my fiancée,* Annika."

His face pales, his eyes bulging as they quickly dart to Annika. It's glorious to see.

"Oh—yes," he stammers. "Yes. I mean no disrespect, Ms. Brancovich, of course."

"Of course," she parrots back in a bored tone. "Mr. Aki, let me tell you what *is* disrespectful. When your daughter approaches my fiancé at our engagement party, and offers to be his *whore*—"

"*Excuse me*?!" Matsui blurts indignantly. "How dare—"

"*Do not* interrupt me again," Annika snaps coldly.

My brow arches.

Well, *this* is interesting. And unexpected.

"When your daughter approaches my husband-to-be and offers him sexual favors in exchange for getting *you* to agree to his business propositions, I find that *extremely* disrespectful. To me, naturally, but also to my fiancé. *Certainly* to Sota-san... Wouldn't you agree?"

Matsui scowls, and you can almost hear the wheels turning in his mind as he tries to come up with a response. Before he replies, Annika suddenly smiles at him with a strange expression on her face.

"Mr. Aki, do you like Paris?"

He frowns, glancing at me before looking back to Annika. "Pardon?"

"Paris, Mr. Aki. The city. Do you enjoy visiting?"

He clears his throat, glancing around nervously. "I'm, uh, afraid I've never been."

"Oh, come now!" She smiles broadly as she fixes her gaze on him. "That's not true at all!" she laughs.

Matsui coughs awkwardly. "Ms. Brancovich, I can assure you, I've never—"

"You're not a fan of the city? Of Rue Véron, in particular?"

The color drains from Matsui's face so quickly it's as if someone's pulled the drain in a tub. His eyes widen, his mouth dropping open as horror washes over his face.

And Annika just *smiles*.

"Well… Maybe I'm mistaken," she says, shrugging casually. Her eyes lock with Matsui's as she steps forward. "Either way, I think you should agree to my fiancé's new business terms right now. Wouldn't you agree?"

Matsui says nothing, his jaw still on the floor. He turns to me, utterly pale, and finally manages to pull himself together and swallow.

"Yes…yes, I think…" He swallows again as he glances at me. "I think that's a wise decision for everybody."

"I couldn't agree more," Annika says brightly.

Matsui turns to me, awkwardly clearing his throat and not meeting my eyes before bowing stiffly.

"I agree to all new terms laid out by you, Kenzo-san. I will stop running my girls immediately."

"Thank you, Matsui," I growl. "I look forward to our continued fruitful business dealings together."

"Of course, Kenzo-san," he mumbles, bowing low again before glancing fearfully at Annika and then scurrying off into the crowd.

I turn to level a look at Annika. "What the *fuck* was that?"

"*Thank you,* Annika!" she sing-songs. "You're so *good* at what you do, Annika. I don't think I could have done that *without* you, Annika!"

I glare at her. "You finished?"

She grins, pats my chest, and turns to walk away. "Stick with me, Kenzo," she tosses over her shoulder. "You might learn something."

8

ANNIKA

*S*UCK IT, *Kenzo.*

There's a famous scene in *The Watchmen* where one of the characters, a vigilante named Rorschach, gets put in prison. At first, the other prisoners think he's an easy target, being a loner and on the smaller side. Then he beats the hell out of a huge prisoner.

After that, Rorschach turns to the other prisoners and tells them that he isn't locked in with *them. They're* locked in with *him.*

That's how I think about my upcoming wedding to Kenzo. We might be forced together. But it's not *me* who's trapped with him. It's going to be *him* trapped with *me.*

And trust me, he's going to regret ever letting this go this far.

I sip on some bubbles, smug in the double whammy of both snubbing Kenzo *and* making something happen for him, business-wise, that he wasn't able to pull off himself.

I *knew* I recognized Matsui when I saw him in here, it just took me a minute to place where and how I did. Maybe a year ago, I was looking into dirt on the CEO of a company Kir was...*aggressively* pursuing. It's part of my gig: if negotiations stall or flame out, I find other, "creative" ways of motivating someone to sell or agree to terms.

Aka blackmail.

I tailed this particular CEO to Paris, and then to a gorgeous older home in Rue Veron, in the Pigalle district near Montmartre.

The CEO was married, to a woman, and very much monogamously. And yet the house he was visiting was an elegant, high-end brothel of sorts with a specialty dealing in very young, very pretty *men*.

Needless to say, after watching him visit this place four times in five days, I got *exactly* what I wanted out of negotiations. But I also have a fairly photographic memory. And over the course of that five-day stakeout, there were a few other exceptionally important looking men who visited that house.

One of them was Matsui Aki.

Yes, I just gave Kenzo a win. But it was at the cost of losing to me. And that's where it matters.

I'm leaning against the bar, feeling quite pleased with myself, when suddenly, the rug gets yanked out from under me.

Two words spoken in his horrible, bone-chilling voice are all it takes to turn my skin numb and deaden me inside. To push me right back into that deep, dark hole he kept me in for so many years.

"Hello, puppet."

The world goes cold. Numbness and a rabid desire to block it all out and run away screaming suffuses every corner of my being. But I can't run. Can't scream. Can't breathe.

Can't *escape*.

Slowly, I turn. My heart twists violently, and a shudder ripples down my spine as my eyes lock with Valon's.

Instantly, I'm plunged right back into the darkness.

I was twenty-two when Valon Leka first crossed my path. I'd just met Freya, and we hadn't yet hit our stride in making money, or even surviving very well. We were living job-to-job, mostly just stealing to eat and have a place to sleep inside.

That's when we met Valon, the head of The Brotherhood, an Albanian crime syndicate with cult-like tendencies. Valon hired us for a job—our biggest one yet. When we pulled it off, he heaped us—me, mostly—with praise, and even let us keep *half* of what we'd stolen instead of the agreed-upon ten percent.

We did another job, and it was the same thing. The third one, he let us keep almost the *entire* take, and heaped us with even more praise. Then came the gifts and favors. The clothes, and fancy dinners, and fun cars.

Looking back, I know now that what that was is called grooming. I was twenty-two, had no family or place to call home, and I'd been running for years.

Valon, meanwhile, was forty-five. He was charming, good-looking, powerful, and promised to take care of me. When you've had to take care of yourself for years and years, letting someone else take the reins is really hard to say no to.

So I didn't say no. Not to the gifts, or favors, or Valon taking me out to dinner or the ballet or to fancy clubs, just the two of us. I didn't say no to him bringing me back to his house, and then to his bedroom.

I didn't say anything at all, actually. He did what he wanted, heedless of my thoughts on the matter.

And I let it all happen, even when I hated it to the point of holding back tears, because I felt like this was the best I could do. I had nothing, and Valon gave me *something*. I never once tried to tell myself it was love. But in my shattered, hastily glued-back-together state, I figured whatever he was giving me was as close to romantic love as I'd ever get.

I stayed with him for three cold, miserable, dark years. Years I don't really remember, because I've blocked them out. Years that Freya and I don't talk about. Years where I was alive, but not really.

And he called me his puppet.

I suppose it was meant to be a cutesy pet name, but to me, it was a reminder that someone else was pulling my strings and making me do things I didn't want to.

One day, Valon had to leave his base in Milan and spend a few weeks in Istanbul as his empire expanded. By then, even though I was mostly kept in the dark, I knew that The Brotherhood was no longer a low-level mafia organization that dealt in gambling, smuggling, and some counterfeiting. They were a full-blown drug organization working with the Sicilian and Turkish mafias in the cocaine, meth, and heroin trade.

Valon was going to be gone for two weeks. It would be the longest I'd ever been "without" him. The truly fucked up thing is, I never once thought about leaving. Not because I *loved* him, or even liked him, but because I was scared of him, and of going back to that life of having to steal to eat, never knowing where I would sleep that evening.

I'll never forget the night Freya came to my room with two packed bags and put a gun to her own temple. She told me we were leaving, now, and never coming back. If not, she'd be pulling the trigger, because she couldn't stand to watch me live this horrible life a minute longer.

That was eight years ago, and I've avoided my former jailer ever since.

Until tonight.

Valon's older now, and the lines on his face are deeper. But he's still got that slightly charming, slightly demented, dark look in his eye as he casually sips a drink and lets his gaze sweep over me.

"I hear you're getting married, puppet," Valon purrs, smirking darkly at me. "How *nice*."

My insides turn to ash, my gaze stabbing into the floor between my feet as I hug myself and wish I was anywhere but here.

"What *isn't* nice, though," he mutters quietly, "is taking things that don't belong to you."

A shudder slices through my body, and cold terror sneaks in after it.

He's talking about the Lamborghini I stole for Ulkan—the one Freya and I abandoned outside the Lincoln Tunnel after figuring out it was full of Valon's drugs and money.

"Wouldn't you agree?" Valon says chattily. "After everything I did for you, and all that I gave you… First you run away without so much as a thank you, and then you steal from me?"

"I—" the word rasps like powdered bone and dust in my throat. "I didn't realize…"

"I imagine Ulkan wasn't very happy with services rendered, was he?"

An icy talon scrapes up my spine.

"You know, before the police found the car, someone *else* did, and emptied the trunk."

I shudder violently. "I didn't know it was yours—"

"I don't care."

His words are sharp now. Cold. Merciless. That's how it always went. First, it was all smiles and soothing tones. Next came the slap to the face, or emotionally freezing me out. Gaslighting me. Negging me. Telling me I was unlovable or calling me a whore. Then he'd flip flop, and we'd be back to smiles, presents, and favors.

I shiver again, still unable to meet his eyes.

God, I hate the power this monster has over me. Even now.

"I'm…" I shake my head. "I'm sorry."

Valon chuckles quietly. "Well, there's that." He clears his throat. "You know, I'm not an unforgiving man, puppet."

Yes you are.

"So maybe I could look past this."

I flinch as his hand slips into my vision, holding a black plastic keycard for a hotel room between my eyes and the floor.

"Why don't you come over for a drink later. We can find a way you can make me"...he coughs delicately..."*happy* again. For old times' sake."

It takes everything I have to hold back the vomit that surges up my throat, burning like acid. My blood turns to ice as his hand touches my hair. I flinch, shuddering and shaking as he pushes it behind my ear and leans down.

"Congratulations again on your engagement, *puppet.*" He pushes the keycard in between two of my numb fingers. "If you're smart, I'll be seeing you soon...my little whore."

He turns and walks away. My body curls in on itself, my heart thudding loudly and my skin crawling. I whirl, breathless, my vision swimming, and stagger back to the bar.

"Shot," I whisper to the bartender, throwing the card aside.

His brow furrows. "What sort of—"

"Literally anything. Now, please."

It turns out to be vodka.

I slam it back, hissing as I tap the bar with the empty glass. "Another," I croak. "A double this time."

"Miss—"

"Please and thank you," I blurt, staring at him haggardly.

The guy nods, looking worried as he pours a huge splash of vodka into the glass. I lift it, nod to him and knock the full contents down my throat at once, my brain still screaming and my skin still crawling.

Fire burns in my gut as I slam the glass back to the bar and turn wildly. My eyes land on Valon's back and shoulders as he walks away through the crowd toward the door.

Then my gaze lurches to the buffet.

…And the catering staff member cutting wagyu steak into little strips with a razor-sharp chef's knife.

My eyes rip back to Valon.

I'm going to kill him.

I have to.

Fuck the consequences.

I only make it one step to the buffet table before a powerful hand is suddenly grabbing my wrist. I gasp as Kenzo shoves my arm behind my back, yanking me against his hard, unyielding chest, glaring maliciously down into my eyes. His black hair hang and fans around his face as if he's a dark avenging angel of death.

Or the prince of Hell.

"What the fuck was that?" he snarls coldly.

My mouth opens, but no sound comes out.

"*Answer me,*" he snaps viciously. "Who the fuck was that?"

The room starts to spin. "I—no one," I mumble.

Kenzo's lips curl as he leans closer. "I don't give a *fuck* how much you hate this, Annika," he growls. "I don't even give a fuck if you hate me. But we *are* getting married. And as my wife, you *will* play the role."

He looms closer.

"Which means no other man talks to you like that, or touches you, or gets close to you like that motherfucker just did." His snarling tone is so serious and heated that it startles me. "Is. That. Fucking. Clear."

I could answer rationally. Or even just nod. But the walls I've worked so hard to erect to block out certain parts of myself are beginning to crumble. Memories I've desperately tried to purge from my system rear up, angry and vengeful at being silenced for so long.

And I do what I always do when I feel cornered or vulnerable: I lash out.

"Your jealousy is pathetic," I spit at him.

Instantly, his hand on my wrist tightens, pinning it to the small of my back. A cold shiver ripples down my spine when his other hand grabs the back of my neck possessively, angling my face up to his.

"This is politics, Annika," he growls. "This needs to be sold. And it doesn't *get sold* if you're schmoozing with some other fucking guy, letting him touch you, getting cozy with him—"

I'm spiraling. The pain and shame of those years are smashing against the walls and barriers inside. The screams I held back and the horrors my body and soul endured in shuddering silence begin to wail and rise up as the room spins and my vision goes dark.

It feels like I'm about to drown under the weight and the pain of it all. And so I reach out for the one rock I can grab hold of.

I do the only thing I can to silence the agony and drown out the horrific memories of a monster surging up inside.

In one motion, I grab Kenzo's tie, yank him down, and crush my mouth to his, kissing him.

And the whole damn world goes *still.*

It escalates quickly. One second, I'm holding his tie and pressing my lips to his. The next, it's like Kenzo comes alive. His hand tightens on my wrist, pulling me hard against him. His mouth opens, his tongue dancing over my lips and then plunging between them.

His dark, masculine groans rumble through my body and turn my core to molten lava as the spicy clean scent of him consumes me.

His hand on the back of my neck slides up, his fingers threading into my hair and gripping me possessively as he kisses me. Around us, partygoers begin to laugh and smile, clapping and taking pictures as I melt against Kenzo's chest in the single most powerful, gravity-shifting kiss of my entire life.

...And for the first time in longer than I can remember, the screaming in my head goes utterly and completely *silent.*

I don't know how long it lasts. But I do know when he finally pulls back, his teeth raking across my bottom lip, my legs are shaking and I've stepped into a different reality.

A ragged breath leaves my swollen lips as I stare up at him. My mouth curls a little at the edges, my pulse roaring as Kenzo locks eyes with me.

He turns to flash the crowd a smile as I stand there still staring up at him like a fool.

Slowly, he turns back to me. But there's no confusion or even happiness in his eyes. There's no charming grin, no eager lips.

Just wrath and malice lurking under the surface as he leans down, his lips brushing my ear so that only I can hear.

"Don't think for a second I don't know what you just did," he hisses quietly.

His hand slides back to the nape of my neck, gripping it firmly and making me wince.

"Don't ever fucking take me for a fool again, Annika," he snarls. "And don't take me for a man who'll take another's scraps, either. When I do more than kiss you, princess—and I *will*—you'll be thinking of me and only me. Is that fucking clear?"

I'm trembling, but I nod quickly, swallowing the lump in my throat. "*Yes.*"

"Good girl," he growls.

His hands drop from me.

"Now, let's go sign this fucking contract and get it over with."

He turns and walks away.

9

KENZO

THERE'S a fury roaring through my veins I don't quite understand as I walk away from a woman I'm not entirely sure I *want* to be walking away from.

Such is my confusion when it comes to Annika.

I want to be rid of her, yet I want her wrapped up in me. I want to hate her, yet I want to possess her completely. I want to punish her...and, well, I want to punish her.

Angrily, I duck into Sota's home office and stride across the elegantly tasteful room decorated with priceless Edo-era Japanese artifacts to Sota's bar cart. I pour a heavy splash of the good scotch I know he keeps in here, bringing it to my lips. My eyes stab out of the fourth-floor window looking across the West Village.

What the *fuck* is this fury inside me? This raging wrath? I mean, obviously I'm not *jealous*. But it's still completely fucking *not okay* for her to be getting so close and chummy with whoever that motherfucker was.

I swallow a gulp of scotch, trying to place him. Older, well-dressed but a little sleazy. I didn't get a good look at his face, but given that he got into the party, he's someone important that either Kir or Sota knows.

I file that away as a clue, so I can track him down and...

What, exactly?

Hit him? Tell him to stay away from my fake wife that I don't even like?

Maybe.

Or maybe just break his fucking face, and casually mention staying away from Annika afterward? Yeah. Better.

I grumble to myself as I finish my scotch, pour a second one, and walk back to the party before I'm missed.

But beyond the anger at Annika for talking to that fuck, and at *him* for getting so fucking close to her and goddamn *touching* her, there's something else nagging at me.

A darkness. A hunger. A desire I should not have.

That kiss shouldn't have happened.

I'm not exactly sure *what* drove her to grab me and fucking kiss me like that. I mean, it sure as hell wasn't about "selling" the marriage. A, it's clear Annika gives even less of a shit about this whole thing than I do. And B, there was something seriously weird in her eyes right before it happened. Like she was drowning in something. Almost like she was disassociating.

Which, to my fucked-up tastes at least, is more than slightly arousing: the idea of her being awake but *not*. Her body being mine while her mind has checked out.

What? We can't choose our kinks. I didn't *pick* an extreme free-use kink like somnophilia as the "thing" that gets me hard.

Sleep sex. The idea of taking a woman in her sleep. Or in Annika's case, of fucking her mercilessly while she disassociates and "tunes out".

I adjust my slacks, trying to hide the throbbing bulge between my thighs.

I digress. Again, that *shouldn't have happened*. I shouldn't have allowed it to *keep* happening, and I absolutely should *not* have kissed her back. Hungrily.

Because I'm not a fucking idiot, and that's hardly the first time a woman has decided to "get over" some other man, or get some kind of "payback" for her man slighting her, by trying to hook up with me.

I mean, I'm six foot six, I work out daily, and I won the genetic lottery. I'm hyper-aware of the way women look at me, especially when the ink on my arms makes it clear how dangerous I really am.

That fucking said, I've *never* been a fan of being someone's "wild story" or their fucking payback. And I sure as *fuck* won't allow my own goddamn wife to play that way.

I'm still stewing when I spot Mal across the room. Mercifully, he's got our agent of chaos brother, Takeshi, with him. Good.

In an hour or so, Tak can go off and terrorize Manhattan with his usual brands of forbidden trouble all he likes. Before that, I need all my family present when Annika and I sign the blood marker which will bind us to this fucking marriage.

I make my way over, joining them near the windows overlooking Sota's back garden and koi pond.

"Staying out of trouble, I hope?" I growl, eyeing Takeshi darkly.

He grins, pushing his long hair back from his face and turning to eye the room. "At present...mostly."

"Think you can resist the urge to sow chaos and disorder for the next hour or so?"

"For you, brother, I'll certainly try."

I roll my eyes as he smirks at me, then claps me on the shoulder.

"I'm not the one anybody needs to worry about," he shrugs. "*You're* the one making out with your fake fiancée in the middle of your fake engagement party. That's a cry for help if I ever saw one."

"Or, shocker, he just wanted to kiss her." Hana joins us, a glass of red wine in her hand. "I know real interpersonal connections are a mystery to you, Tak..."

He rolls his eyes at his twin. "As if we're not all painfully aware of my many, *many*—"

"I mean of the real, emotional kind," Hana sighs heavily, giving him a stink look. "Like the romantic kind?"

"Whoa. That what that was, bro?" Tak smirks, glancing sidelong at me.

"*Hardly*," I mutter. "Just selling it."

"Well, you're a hell of a salesman, then," Hana mutters dryly, grinning as I flip her off.

"Let's not forget Mal over here, mooning over that goth chick with the fucking collar," Takeshi snickers.

"Who, Freya?" Hana asks.

"Wait, is there more than one goth chick with a spiked collar at this party?" Tak laughs. "Because now I'm interested."

Hana ignores him as she turns to Mal. "Got a thing for Freya?"

"Not at all," he growls. "Tak just likes making shit up and stirring the pot."

The usual sibling bickering that I secretly love fades into the background and a dark scowl crosses my face as I spot something across the room.

Not something. Some*one*.

"Anyone know who the fuck that is?" I grunt, nodding my chin at the same motherfucker Annika was talking closely with before. The fucker who seems to have *not* made the enlightened decision to leave yet.

"Guy in the charcoal gray suit?" Hana asks. I nod. "Valon Leka." Her brow creases. "Head of The Brotherhood, an Armenian crime syndicate. They do a lot of intermediary work on the smuggling pipeline between Italy and Turkey. Meth…coke…heroin too, I think." She shakes her head. "By all accounts, not a nice guy."

My eyes narrow.

What the actual *fuck* is Annika doing talking to an Armenian drug smuggler?

"How the fuck did he even get in?" I mutter.

Takeshi snorts. "Wait, are you serious?"

I eye him. "Yes?"

My brother grins. "Fucking hell, I *love* it when I know shit you don't."

"Stop being an asshole and just tell me."

He scoffs. "Sota is in talks with him about contracting out some work to his organization."

I stare at him. "Christ, *that's* the smuggler he's been speaking to?"

"Yup," Mal grunts. "Do us all a favor and see if you can get Sota to back off there. Leka has a seriously bad rep. I mean, he's offering a sweet deal, but that's because Sota would be his first business with the Yakuza, and he wants that in." Mal shakes his head. "Dude is a fucking psychopath, though, at least so I've heard."

"Noted," I growl. "Why the fuck is he even entertaining the idea of working with someone like that?"

Hana rolls her eyes. "Take a guess."

Shit.

"Tengan."

"Bingo," my sister mutters.

Tengan is Sota's business manager. He's also a thorn in my side, and to say we don't see eye to eye on most things is like calling World War Two a "disagreement". Mercifully, I have almost no interaction with him. Hana, unfortunately, doesn't have that same luxury.

"Seriously," Hana says quietly. She turns to me. "Sota really should stay away from this guy."

And so the fuck should my fiancée...

"Kenzo," Mal says, elbowing me and tapping his wristwatch. "That time, brother."

"Shit."

Hana turns and smiles at me. "Hey, chin up. Like I keep trying to tell you, she's pretty cool."

Tak grins at me, clapping me on the shoulder. "Cool or not, you're about to commit yourself to this in blood. No backing out now, bro."

Traditionally, blood markers aren't a thing in Japan. But as the Yakuza world moved into the twentieth and twenty-first centuries and started doing more global business with criminal organizations of the West and Middle East, they've become more common.

They're exactly what they sound like: mafia contracts signed in the literal blood of those involved in said contract. Each signatory places their thumbprint next to their name, too, also in blood. They are absolutely, unquestionably iron clad. To break one is tantamount to excommunicating yourself and your entire organization from the criminal world.

In other words, they're sort of a big deal.

When the four of us step out onto the rooftop deck of Sota's brownstone, he, Kir, and Kir's number two Isaak are already waiting for us.

So are Annika and Freya, off to the side.

I turn, frowning when I see Mal's gaze stabbing across the roof garden into Annika's friend. I elbow him sharply.

"Either tell me what the fuck this is, or let it go *now*."

He turns to me instantly with his full attention.

"Nothing to let go."

He nods his squared jaw as we both turn to bow to Sota, who walks over and hugs me close, patting my back before he pulls away.

"I'm proud of you, Kenzo," he says quietly. "And in his own way, I know your father is, too."

"Well," Kir says, gesturing to the table laid out next to him. "Shall we?"

On it is the contract that binds Annika to me, and me to her. We'll still be legally married a bit later. But this cements the engagement and ensures the wedding will happen. Next to it is the little metal medallion with a pin sticking out of it: the instrument with which we'll prick our thumbs and sign in blood.

There's no fanfare. No grand, drawn-out speeches. We both read over the contract, and then without any further ado, Annika is pushing past me to grab the medallion. She winces just a little as she stabs her thumb and squeezes, then dips the old-school fountain pen into the little well that now holds some of her blood.

Her hand moves quickly as she signs her name in rust, then abruptly she stabs her thumb onto the paper next to it.

"Done," she mutters, like she's just aced a pop quiz.

She doesn't look at me as I take the medallion and the pen from her, doing the same routine, signing my name and making a thumbprint next to hers.

It's official.

I'm turning to Annika to say—what? I'm not even sure yet—when my gaze snaps to the little red dot on her chest, hovering over her heart.

Oh fuck.

The dot slides up to her forehead, and I roar.

"GET DOWN!"

I slam into her, plowing her into the table and sending it, the contract, and us crashing to the ground. The sound is muffled, but there's no mistaking the distinct *pop pop* sound of rifle fire as it slams into the wood of the patio. Glass shatters as Mal grabs Sota, and Tak grabs our sister, everyone hitting the deck as more shots ring out.

I whirl, my eyes darting first to Sota. Mal nods curtly, giving me a thumbs up before he yanks a gun out of his suit jacket. Takeshi does the same as I glance at him. It's only then that I'm aware of the fists pounding on my arms and chest.

"Get the fuck off—!"

"*Stay down*!!!" I hiss at Annika as she fights to get me off her. She hits me again, and I grimace as I grab her wrist and pin it above her head. I turn my head, my eyes stabbing into the darkness and across the street to a building one story higher than this one.

...And the shadowy figure quickly springing along the edge to crouch down for a better vantage point.

"FAR ROOF!" I roar.

Keeping Annika pinned down with one hand, I bring up my gun and squeeze off three shots. Tak and Mal do the same, jumping up to aim better. Isaak and Kir both have their guns out too, and the shadowy figure quickly drops back.

I snarl, finally letting Annika go as I jump to my feet. I can *just* see over the lip of the far roof. The guy is trying to break his rifle down quickly.

He's going to run.

And I'm sure as fuck going to give chase.

"Stay with Sota!" I roar at Hana, who nods curtly. Kir hangs back, too, though not out of cowardice. The man is the head of the Nikolayev Bratva. With his only heir on life support in the hospital, he doesn't have the luxury of jumping across rooftops chasing down a shooter.

But we do.

Mal, Takeshi, Isaak, and I sprint across the roof and make a wild jump to the private roof deck of the building next door. From there, we spring to the *next* building, which is still under construction and has a crane attached to the side of it to lift heavy materials to the top floor.

The crane sticks out over the street, forming a bridge to the other side…if you're fucking crazy enough.

Turns out the four of us are.

Isaak hits the roof last, and we take off back in the direction we came. We move silently—Tak, Mal, and me because stealth is something hammered into you in the Yakuza. But I have to say, I'm impressed with Isaak's speed and silence as Kir's tall, built number two keeps pace with us.

"Down!"

Mal tackles me, dropping me to the ground just as a piece of the brick wall behind me explodes. Up ahead, we catch sight of the sniper as he quickly breaks his rifle down again. But this time, we're much, much closer.

He's fucking *ours*.

"Head right!" I hiss at my brothers. The two of them nod and take off to the neighboring roof, moving to flank the shooter. I glance at Isaak, and he gives me a stern nod.

"You on me?"

"Ten years special forces?" he grunts back. "Yeah."

That'll do.

"Go!"

We both take off toward the shooter as he drops to one knee and brings his rifle to bear. Then he flinches and ducks as Takeshi and Mal make a run at him from the side. He never saw them coming.

Got you, you fucker.

"Drop your weapon!" I yell as we charge at him.

He does so. Then, he does something completely unexpected.

He drops his rifle, stands, whirls, and then sprints to the edge of the five-story building.

"Wait—!"

He hurtles over head-first, arms to the side. I rush to the edge and look over, grimacing as I catch sight of him hitting the pavement below and his skull splattering like a melon.

"What the *fuck*?!" Tak grunts, also peering over the edge, his face twisted. "Why the hell would he do that?"

"Didn't want to get caught," Isaak grunts, shrugging as he calmly holsters his weapon.

"Yeah, but...*seriously*?" Takeshi mutters.

Isaak shrugs again. "What? He didn't get caught."

WHEN WE GET BACK to Sota's building, he's who I go to first. His breathing is fucked up, but just from the adrenaline hit. He's not wounded, and Hana and three of Sota's men have already gotten his oxygen tank to him, allowing him to breathe easier.

Then I turn, and my eyes lock with Annika's. Wordlessly, I cross the roof deck to her.

"You okay?"

She nods. She looks shaken, but not overly so.

It hits me: this isn't the first time she's been shot at.

Why does that bother me so much?

"You're not hurt...?"

"She's fine," Freya mutters, shooting me a look.

"She can answer for herself, Morticia," I throw back.

Freya's eyes narrow, and then she grins. "I know you're *trying* to be a dick, but I actually take that as a compli—"

"Great. Take it however you want," I mutter, pulling away

from her to frown down into Annika's face. "You're really not hurt?"

She arches a brow. "Oh my God, how many times do you want me to say it?"

"Once, audibly, would be nice," I grunt.

She rolls her eyes. "I'm fine. You can stop pretending to give a shit now, okay?"

She gets up, pushing past me to go over and talk with Kir, Isaak and Freya. I just keep staring after her.

The thing is…

I'm realizing how very urgently I asked her if she was okay, and that *none* of it was for show, to pretend that I gave a shit.

Which begs the question: why the fuck was it so important to me to make sure my fake wife, who I don't even like, was okay?

The answer rustles against my ankles. I scowl, reaching down to pick up the blood marker before it blows right off the roof. My eyes stab into our names written on it.

I give a shit, because like it or not, duty or not, *this woman is my fucking wife.*

The marriage will come. It was pledged it in blood. It was cemented in violence.

And there's no going back now.

10

ANNIKA

For the two weeks following the attack at Sota Akiyama's brownstone, we're basically on total lockdown. Since moving to New York a few months ago, I've been living in Taylor's amazing apartment, seeing as she now lives with Drazen at his *ludicrously* luxe place on billionaire's row on Central Park South. Freya, meanwhile, has been living her best rock star life at various luxury hotels.

After the shooting, though, Kir shuts all that down. Frey and I move into the two-level penthouse he purchased about a year ago while he himself heads to London on business.

We're safe there: the penthouse is a fortress, guarded by a small army of his men. But we're basically prisoners. No going outside, aside from Kir's patio. Even then, we're only supposed to be out there if we notify Kir's guards first, so they can be on extra alert.

Honestly, it's a pain in the ass. But at least I've got Freya with me, and after about a week, I'm on her mostly nocturnal schedule, which I don't really mind.

Finally, after two weeks of captivity, Kir gives the all-clear.

The sniper who shot at us hasn't been identified. But it's clear that he was a hired professional. The gun and the ammo were untraceable, the guy had his fingerprints *chemically burned off*, and even had all his real teeth replaced with implants.

In our world, those are all *very* clear signs of a professional hitman. A seriously expensive one, too. Him choosing suicide over being caught underscores that even further.

But honestly, Sota has plenty of enemies who could've wanted him—or any of us—dead. Kir probably has twice as many. So with the shooter dead, there's sort of no other option but to go on with our lives.

That's just the Bratva world we live in. Danger is always just...there, lurking around the corner. You just have to learn to be quick enough to see it coming before it gets you.

I haven't told Taylor about the shooting and the subsequent lockdown, because, like I said, I want to separate my messy world from her organized one. She does, however, know I'm marrying Kenzo.

We've had some chats about it, and as Drazen's wife she gets it, even if she's not thrilled that her sister is marrying into the Yakuza to stop a war.

After the lockdown, though, and as the wedding looms closer, Taylor tells me that she's taking me out for a bachelorette dinner.

Not "asks if I want her to". Tells.

Gotta love her.

The night of my reluctant bachelorette party for a wedding I don't want actually ends up being pretty great. Taylor, as managing name partner of Crown and Black, carries some weight around this city.

She somehow gets us reservations at an incredible two Michelin star restaurant. When we enter, we're escorted to a private VIP dining room adjacent to the kitchen itself, with a window so we can watch the chefs prepare everything in the pristine, gorgeous kitchen.

As an extra surprise, as soon as we sit down, Fumi, Kenzo's half-sister and Taylor's best friend, sashays in and gives me a big hug.

"What the hell are you doing here?" I blurt incredulously. I mean, she's become a friend, but the wife of the Governor showing up to a bachelorette dinner for a mob wedding seems…iffy…in terms of optics.

Fumi snorts a laugh. "Uh, celebrating you?"

My face darkens. "Sorry, that came out wrong. I just mean…*should you* be here? Like, being the governor's wife and all?"

"Oh." Fumi wrinkles her nose and waves me off. "Yeah, fuck that. I can definitely be here."

"I am *here* for First Ladies who say 'fuck that'!" Freya laughs as the champagne that Taylor ordered arrives.

After it's poured, Freya makes a quite eloquent toast to me, surprisingly almost devoid of any vulgarity and swears. Fumi makes another one, which is *extremely* well worded, touching on finding feelings where you don't expect to find them, discovering your other half where you least expect to…

Blah blah blah.

I mean it's a beautiful toast, and I walk around the table to give her a hug after she finishes it. But…c'mon.

I'm not "finding feelings where I don't expect them" with her grumpy, power-hungry dick-bag of a half-brother. Sorry, not sorry.

After the second toast, I glance at my sister, expecting one from her. She just eyes me with one of her "looks".

"Okay, say it," I sigh.

She shakes her head. "You know what I'm going to say."

"That you don't want me to marry a Yakuza asshole to stop a war?" I glance at Fumi. "No offense."

Fumi laughs. "None taken. Kenzo is"…she clears her throat delicately…"an interesting character. We're getting to know each other. But I mean…" She waggles her brows. "I get it, lady. He's intense."

"Yeah, spelled d-i-c-k-h-e-a-d," I mutter, turning back to Taylor. "So, was that the gist of it?"

She rolls her eyes. "Words to that effect, yes."

"Says the lady who is herself married to a mobster. I mean, pot…kettle."

Fumi and Freya laugh as my twin gives me another look before smiling and reaching over to take my hand. "Just… Please don't think you only have one parachute. I've got you, always. You know that, right?"

I do. But I've also spent my life with certain personal mantras. And one of the big ones, *especially* after he-who-will-not-be-named, is that I pay my own way.

And my own debts.

I'm sure that Taylor could get me out of this marriage by asking Drazen. He sits at the Iron Table—a sort of collective of super powerful Bratva families—along with Kir.

But this is what I have to do. I don't like it, but Kir's been there for me for half my adult life. He gave me a home, and a life beyond just stealing from one gig to the next. If doing this stops a war and keeps he and his people from getting embroiled in a bloodbath, then so be it.

That's a price I'm willing to pay.

At one point, I stand to go to the ladies' room, and Freya comes with me. I can already tell from the look in her eye and from the way she's been uncharacteristically quiet all night that she's got something on her mind.

"Okay, out with it," I sigh as the door closes behind us.

She shoots me a look before she quickly glances under the stall doors to make sure we're alone. Then she turns to me.

"Look, I didn't want to talk about it at Kir's place, because I'm sure it's bugged to hell."

My brow knits. "Okay?"

Freya swallows nervously. "The shooting..."

"Frey, it could be—"

"Are we gonna talk about he-who-shall-not-be-named being at that party at some point or not?"

I go still.

"Sorry," she says quietly, touching my arm. "I just... It's been two weeks, and you still haven't mentioned him being at that party to me. But I saw him."

"It's fine," I mutter.

She swallows, her eyes searching mine. "It's *not*," she blurts. "Like…not at all."

"Look, I don't know why he was there, okay?" I say testily. "But obviously he knows Sota, or else how could he have even gotten in?"

"What'd he want?"

"Nothing," I snap. "Okay? Can we drop this?"

Her mouth twists.

Guess that's a no.

"Does he know about—"

"The car?" I mutter. "Yeah."

"*Shit*," she blurts, twisting her hands together anxiously. "Fuck, Annika, that's…" She looks away. "Do you think it was him behind it? The shooter, I mean."

I shudder. "I don't… I don't know."

"C'mon, Anni," she says quietly. "It *has* to be."

"We don't know that."

She exhales, leaning against the vanity. "Think it might be time to tell Kir about all this?"

My head shakes violently. "Fuck no. *No*."

This has always been Freya's and my creed: don't include found family in any bullshit arising from *our* shenanigans.

That fucking car with Ulkan and he-who-will-not-be-named is *squarely* in "don't involve Kir" territory.

"Then tell your soon-to-be-husband?" she whispers.

"No. Way."

"Why the fuck not?"

I smile wryly, pulling my friend into a hug. "Because he'll use it, Frey."

She scowls. "Fuck. You're probably right."

"And besides, we don't *know* it was he-who-shall-not-be-named. It could have been someone gunning for Kenzo, for all we know. I mean…" I shudder.

It *would* be weird for him to come proposition me at the party and then have some hired gun try to shoot me from a rooftop thirty minutes later.

"Could be Ulkan?"

Shit. I hadn't even considered that.

The two of us exhale quietly in the silence of the bathroom.

"Fuck," Freya moans. "I'm making this the worst bachelorette party ever, aren't I?"

"Hey, it could be worse."

"How, exactly?"

I grin as I pat her on the shoulder and open the restroom door. "Could be *you* marrying the fucker."

Again, in the end, we have an amazing time. The food is amazing, the wine is phenomenal, the company is lovely. It even turns out that the chef is a personal friend of Taylor's, so he comes out to serve us a specially created dessert himself and talk to us about the food sourcing.

It's an incredible night, and by the time we walk out, I'm happy enough to ignore the fact that I'm marrying Kenzo soon.

But even the amazing evening doesn't make me forget that I kissed him.

Worse, that he kissed me back.

Double worse, the fact that when he did, *I liked it.*

A lot.

I don't know what came over me that night. I mean, yes, I was drowning in the darkness that being near that motherfucker Valon always brings. And yes, Kenzo was so close to me, and I guess I just felt he was the only lifeline I could cling to, to prevent me from drowning.

But then? I don't know. It's been two weeks, and I *still* can't figure out why I kissed him like that.

...And then spent the next two weeks dreaming about it, every night.

Wetly.

Shamefully.

Taylor and Fumi have to jet after dinner, since they've got important depositions in the morning. When it's just the two of us outside the restaurant, Freya turns to me and shrugs.

"Well? What sort of trouble are we getting into now?"

"Whatever it is, can I tag along?"

We both turn at the sound of her voice, and I smile widely when I see Hana standing there. I'd invited her to dinner tonight, but she'd politely declined. And yet, here she is.

She inclines her head gracefully, as if reading my mind. "Still getting used to the whole 'I have a half-sister' thing," she shrugs. "I'm better with Fumi if we're just one-on-one. You know?"

"Well, you're just in time for the fun part," Freya grins. "We're trying to figure out what trouble to get up to now."

Kenzo's sister grins. "I might have an idea." She clears her throat and turns to me. "I don't know you," she says frankly. "I mean, no offense, and dress shopping was fun and all, but I don't. Not really."

I shrug. "Fair."

"Well." She grins slyly. "I always say there's only one *real* way to get to know someone."

Freya frowns. "Which is…?"

Hana grins. "Karaoke."

Freya snorts a laugh. I arch a brow. "Think we can bring our shadows?" I mutter darkly, nodding my chin at the black SUV parked a half block away. Kir's never *mentioned* having people tail us post-lockdown. But, come on. I'm not an idiot.

Hana shrugs. "We could." She winks at us. "*Or* we could…lose them?"

OBVIOUSLY, we end up going with option B. And *obviously,* it's a resounding success.

An hour later, with Kir's men successfully ditched, the three of us are at an insane Karaoke bar in K-town. I'm not *drunk*-drunk, because I like to hit a certain point and stop there, but I've had a nice buzz going since dinner, and I have to say, though I've never previously been a big karaoke fan, I'm having a blast.

Hana is truly *amazing*. Frey has gotten over her hilarious girl-crush on her, and the two of them are getting along famously as we head downstairs to the main bar and lounge area for another round of drinks.

We're waiting for the bartender, when Freya—who *is* fairly tipsy—turns to us with a grin.

"Let's play secret talents."

Hana arches a brow. "What?"

I groan. "Frey and I play this game all the time. But it's a little dumb because we already *know* each other's secret talents."

Hana laughs and then shakes her head. "I envy you guys. I don't have many friends, especially not girlfriends." She makes a face. "*Way* too many psycho brothers."

"Well, here's your invitation to play," Freya giggles. "Spill. What's your secret talent?"

Hana blushes as she hides her face in her hands. "Okay, it's... dumb. And embarrassing..."

Freya hoots. "All the more reason to share, lady!"

I grin at her. "C'mon."

Hana sighs. "Fine, fine. Okay. So... I can do a shot without using my hands."

Freya and I erupt in laughter and calls of "prove it!"

Hana groans, hiding her face again as the bartender comes back over with our drinks. "Actually, can I get a shot of tequila with that?"

The bartender nods, grabs a shot glass, pours the tequila, and slides it in front of Hana. She glances at us, her face flushed as she cringes with embarrassment. "Okay, buckle up."

She pulls her blonde hair back with both hands and leans forward. Freya and I watch stunned as her lips wrap around the rim of the shot glass in—not gonna lie—a pretty suggestive way. She holds back her grin as she lifts her head, jerks it back, and downs the shot, her throat working to swallow with her lips still wrapped firmly around the glass. Then she lowers the empty glass, still with just her mouth, before popping back up with a fanfare.

"Ta-da!"

Freya and I hoot and holler.

"Holy shit!" Frey laughs.

"Okay, that was—"

"Shit, baby!" A guy next to us at the bar interrupts me, turning around to leer drunkenly at Hana. "That was *hot*."

"Great, thanks," Hana says curtly, ignoring him and turning back to us.

"I got something else you can hold your hair back and wrap your lips around," the guy slurs.

"Not interested, you can fuck off now, thanks!" she says brightly, giving him the finger over her shoulder. "Okay, so that was embarrassing. Now it's one of your—"

She jumps as the guy lurches off his bar stool and grabs her hips, yanking her ass against his crotch and grinding into her. Freya and I are both about to drop his ass, when Hana herself whirls. In the blink of an eye, she's got him on his knees, with one hand twisted awkwardly behind his back and a look of terror on his face as he screams in pain.

"Fuck you!" he blurts. "Psycho fucking bitch—"

Hana's knee jerks, slamming into his stomach and knocking the wind out of him. She yanks his arm again, jerking him to his feet before suddenly dumping him back onto his ass on the floor. Then she drops suddenly, slamming the side of her hand into his face.

The guy screams as he gets to his feet, blood streaming from his nose, and stumbles off somewhere.

"Dude, *what*," Freya blurts, staring at Hana in awe.

I've got the same shocked look on my face as she nonchalantly hands us our drinks.

"Second secret talent: I've done jiu-jitsu since I was five."

"Hell to the fucking *yes*, girl," Freya grins. "That was awesome!"

Hana shrugs, still blushing a little, which is extra hilarious seeing as she's usually so put together and in charge. She takes a sip of her cocktail before she turns to Freya.

"Okay, you're up."

"Deal." Freya turns to grin at me, and I already know which party trick she's going to pull out. "I can get into an iPhone and steal money."

Hana frowns dubiously. "Sorry, calling bullshit. No one can crack an iPhone. The *FBI* has to issue a summons to Apple when they want to get into one."

Freya grins wider. "Watch and learn, new friend."

She turns to scan the crowd, her eyes narrowing and a grin spreading across her lips. "Him. That guy. That's the mark," she says casually, pointing to a total finance bro with a three-hundred-dollar haircut and a gleaming, huge Rolex on his wrist.

Hana giggles. "It can't be done. I'm telling you."

"Well, then you get to say I told you so," Freya smirks.

I watch, shaking my head as my friend hikes her dress up into a scandalously short skirt. She loosens the straps, letting them fall seductively off her shoulders and letting her tits almost spill out.

Yeah, Freya can be a serious femme fatale on the rare occasions she's not cosplaying *Girl with the Dragon Tattoo*.

"How the fuck is she going to pull this off?"

Freya stalks off toward her mark. "Just watch," I murmur.

So we do, sipping our drinks as Freya sweet-talks the guy across the lounge. She pulls out all the stops, fawning over the guy, touching his shoulder and his chest, whispering in his ear.

In less than a fucking minute, he's completely wrapped around her finger.

That's when she strikes.

He hands her his phone, unlocked, presumably so she can

give him her number. The guy turns to grin at his buddies while Freya smiles and taps away on his phone.

Immediately, her phone, which she's left on the bar next to us, dings. Hana and I glance over, and I crack up when I see a Venmo notification that "Jack Myers" has just sent Freya *five grand*.

Hana explodes with laughter, covering her mouth as Freya slips the phone back into the guy's hand, blows him a kiss, and sashays back to us.

"What the actual *fuck*," Hana blurts as Freya rejoins us. "That was insane!"

"Okay, I don't have to actually hack the iPhone," Freya grins. She taps her head. "Just social engineering, baby."

"I stand corrected," Hana laughs. "You did tell me so."

Freya winks. "Drink up, ladies. We should probably get out of here, seeing how I just committed a felony."

We spill out into the streets of K-town laughing our asses off. I'm still just pleasantly buzzed, but the other two are definitely well into drunk territory, and it's hilarious.

"Wait-wait-wait," Hana says, shaking her head. "We didn't do your special talent!"

I wave her off, shaking my head. "Nah, I'm...whatever."

"*Bullshit*," Freya snickers. "She's a master thief."

Hana eyes me. "So I've heard, to be honest. Like...*how* master are we talking?"

"The best!" Freya shrieks. "Absolutely the best."

I roll my eyes. "Stop. Let's get a cab."

They ignore me.

"Like jewelry and shit?" Hana asks.

"And paintings, and *cars*," Freya giggles.

"Prove it."

The three of us go quiet. Hana smiles coyly as she glances at me. "C'mon, master thief. Prove it."

I shake my head. "Come on. Let's go find food somewhere—"

"Prove it, Anni," Freya giggles, egging me on.

God damn, she knows how to push my buttons.

Fuck it.

I'm just buzzed enough to decide bad ideas are *okay* ideas. So when I turn and my eyes land on the Bugatti parked down the street, my lips curl dangerously.

Hana sees where I'm looking and goes still.

"No fucking way," she grins, a little nervously, turning back to me.

I just arch my brows as I glance at them, my pulse racing with the thrill of the impending take. "In or out?"

"Oh *shiiit*," Hana laughs. "You don't fuck around, do you?"

"I'm just saying out loud that this is a super bad idea," Freya giggles. "But fuck yeah, I'm in. Ride or die, bitch."

I turn to grin at Kenzo's sister. "Hana?"

She smirks as she arches a perfect brow at me. "I'm going to enjoy being related to you, aren't I?"

"If I don't get you killed? Probably."

She grins. "Let's fucking do this."

It takes me eighty-two seconds to get the Bugatti unlocked and the engine purring.

Damn, I'm rusty.

Ten seconds later, the music is blaring, we're all losing our shit, and I'm gunning the sports car through the streets of Lower Manhattan.

I turn and groan as Freya lights a joint next to me.

"Are you fucking serious right now?"

She grins at me. "What? I have a medical card, and anyway, it's legal now."

"Not while you're in a car, it's not. Ever heard of just breaking one law at a time?"

"Nope. Hana?" Freya passes the joint into the backseat, and Hana takes a puff.

That's when we hear the sirens, and see the flashing lights hit the back of our car.

...The stolen car, with someone smoking weed in it. Plus, I'm not drunk or anything, but the legal limit in New York is like half a drink, so I'm definitely over.

"*Shit,*" Freya hisses next to me, sobering up a bit pretty instantly.

"Fuck!" Hana blurts.

I glance at Freya, she glances at me. And I'm reminded why it is we've been best friends for the last eleven years through all sorts of shit.

"How far are we willing to take this?" I say tersely to the whole car.

Hana stares at me in the rear-view window. "What the fuck does that even mean?"

"Well, it's probably best if we don't get pulled over in a stolen car. How far—"

"Ride or die," Freya mutters next to me, her throat working. "As far as it takes."

Hana looks grim as she reaches into her bag and pulls out a freaking *gun*.

"Yeah, so, Kenzo likes me to carry this, but I don't exactly have a permit for it. So..."

"So that just made our decision *much* easier," I announce, my hand tightening on the wheel as I reach for the shifter. I glance back at Hana through the mirror again. "Your brother is *not* going to be happy with me, though."

I slam the pedal down. All three of us suck in our breath as the car speeds forward into the night.

11

KENZO

Where the FUCK is she.

I glare angrily at my watch as I pace the sidewalk outside the church in Brooklyn—the venue for this evening's fucking wedding.

At least, it's *supposed* to be. Except this shitshow is due to start in half an hour and no one's seen or heard from my blushing bride-to-be in almost twenty-four hours.

Or my sister, for that matter.

I can easily see Annika going AWOL on purpose, just to give me and this entire situation the finger like the petulant child she is. But it's not like my sister to go radio silent like this.

Black thoughts circle and swirl through my head.

It's been two weeks since the shooting on the roof of Sota's building. He and Kir have agreed that there's no telling who might have sent the guy. They're both powerful men with *lots* of enemies. Given the fact that the shooter was a clear pro, with his fingerprints burned off and no dental records... yeah. Could have been anyone.

Yet I can't shake one little detail from that night that I've kept to myself: the laser dot was on *Annika*. And an assassin of that caliber doesn't aim at the wrong person or let his scope wander.

Yes, killing Annika could have been an attempt to hurt me, but I was *right there*. So was Sota and the rest of my family. And it's obvious Annika is a new addition and clearly not someone I'm in a real relationship with. If they wanted to hurt me, shooting Hana or Sota would have done far more damage.

So why the fuck was he aiming at her?

I glance at my watch yet again.

And where the ever-loving *fuck* is she?

I've had teams of people combing the city since this morning, looking for Hana. I even contacted a high-end hacker I know to try and trace her phone to its last known cell-tower ping, since it's clearly turned off. And I know Kir's had people looking for Annika and Freya, though when I touched base with him two hours ago, he didn't seem all that concerned.

Yeah, because he's dealt with her bullshit for *years*. Or maybe he just has the patience for it. I sure as fuck don't.

The church door opens behind me. I glance back to see Takeshi walking out and loosening his tie.

"So," he grunts. "When are we calling this?"

"We're not," I shoot back.

"Well, if this thing drags out any longer, people are going to start asking awkward questions." He jerks a thumb back over his shoulder at the church. "Not gonna lie, bro. It's already tense in there. Our guys are mean-eying Kir's guys, and vice versa. If the word starts to get around that your dear wifey is a no-show, shit's going to hit the fan."

Obviously, we've only told a select few that Annika's missing. But Tak is right. This whole thing is a fucking powder keg, and every minute she doesn't show up is basically her chucking lit matches at it.

"She's the one that pushed for a nighttime ceremony, yeah?"

I nod. "It's for Freya. She's got this skin thing with sunlight."

Takeshi snorts. "Wait. Seriously?"

I nod.

"So it's *not* just a goth thing?"

"Guess not."

I don't know why him reminding me of that little tidbit annoys me even more. Annika *did* push to have the wedding after dark so that Freya could attend comfortably without dressing in a space suit or anything.

Maybe because it proves that Annika's not just a spoiled Bratva princess with a perpetually raised middle finger. She's compassionate, too. Which means she's made a conscious decision to go MIA the day of our goddamn wedding. She's *chosen* to let me pace in front of the church like a pathetic dickhead about to get stood up for prom.

She's not here yet, half an hour before our fucking wedding, because she *wants* me to think she's skipped out. She wants me to worry.

Because that's Annika's style: she does what she wants, fuck the world, and let everyone else deal with the wreckage and the consequences.

Well, there *will* be consequences for this.

Consequences like putting her over my knee and spanking that bratty attitude right out of her.

I scowl as that particularly dick-twitching thought enters my head. Then I shove it back down.

Get your shit together.

"Kenzo."

I glance at Tak, and then follow his gaze to where the black SUV with an Uber sticker is pulling up to the curb. The back door opens, and my eyes pull to slits as an *extremely* disheveled Hana slides out, obviously still in the "going out" clothes from the night before.

"You're fucking kidding me," Takeshi mutters, voicing the words I don't even trust myself to say out loud.

I storm over and grab my sister by the bicep.

"What the *fuck?!*" I snap.

She scowls back at me. It's *rare* that my sister doesn't look completely put together without a hair out of place. Right now, she literally looks like she slept in the damn Uber.

I drag her away from the car, looming over her and glaring down into her face. "Are you fucking serious right now?! Where—" I close my eyes, sucking in air through my nose to try and calm the sirens in my head.

Just as my pulse is about to creep down from thermonuclear

levels, it spikes again as someone else slides their bedraggled ass out of the SUV, some dress bags over her arm.

Annika.

"Get the fuck inside," I snap coldly at Hana. "I'll deal with you later."

Hana gives me a sheepish look, grabs the dress bags from Annika, and scurries into the church. Just as I turn to read my bride the riot act, Tak beats me to it.

"Where the *fuck* did you take my fucking sister!?" he roars in Annika's face. She backs away from him against the side of the SUV as he cages her in with his hands against the windows on either side of her. Suddenly, he reaches out and grabs her arm roughly. "You *fucking* bitch—"

"That's enough!"

Before I even realize what I'm doing, I've crossed the distance between us, grabbed my brother by the back of his collar, and yanked him away from her. Takeshi goes stumbling backward, almost falling onto his ass on the sidewalk.

He shoots me a dark glance, but before he can chew me out for getting on his ass instead of Annika's, I march over to him and jam a finger in his face.

"Don't you *ever* lay a hand on her again. Understood?"

Takeshi's eyes bulge in disbelief. A vein on his forehead starts throbbing as pure violence churns through him like diesel in an engine.

"I said," I snarl. "*Is that fucking understood,* Takeshi."

He grinds his teeth, but nods.

"Fine…fuck," he growls. His eyes swivel past me to Freya getting out of the car. "What about *this* little psycho."

"Oh, she's fair game," I grunt. "Do your worst—"

"You lay a finger on her, and I'll fucking cut it off."

My brow furrows darkly as I turn. Annika is glaring daggers at me as the SUV behind her wisely gets the fuck out of Dodge.

"What did you say?"

"I said if you touch her," she hisses, indicating Freya, "I'll cut your fucking finger off." She clears her throat. "Now, if you don't mind, I have this bullshit wedding to star in?"

She and Freya march past us, and I sure as shit don't miss the smug little looks on their faces.

"Are you seriously going to let her talk to you like—"

"Why don't you let *me* worry about how my wife speaks to me, Tak," I growl at him. "Get inside. Get everyone ready. Tell Kir his little fucking princess has deigned to make an appearance at her own party."

"Can I say it like that?"

"Write it on his face in fucking Sharpie for all I care," I mutter, stalking off in Annika's and Freya's direction.

Inside the church, an usher smiles weakly at me and points me in the direction of a small room at the back of the church. I pause for a second to try and talk myself down from "livid" to just plain "furious" as I pause outside the door.

Then I'm barging in.

Annika startles a little, glancing up at me from where she's plugging in her phone next to a table laden with makeup, hair products, and roses. One of the dress bags is hanging from a hook on the wall.

"Where the *hell* have you been?!" I snap coldly, slamming the door shut.

Annika gives me an *infuriatingly* cheeky grin. "Miss me?"

The smug smile drops in a heartbeat when I surge across the room into her, forcing her against the wall behind her.

"Is this a game to you? A fucking *joke*?"

She swallows and slips past me, walking over to the table and picking up a bottle of water. "Not a game," she shrugs, cracking the bottle and chugging half of it before shoving her hair back from her face. "A joke?" She shrugs again. "I mean, yeah, kind of—"

She gasps sharply as I grab her wrist, knocking the water bottle from her hand as I yank her back to me, spin her around, and slam her against the wall, looming over her. All the sass and color fades from her face as she stares up at me.

"Um, *excuse me?*"

Her hair is a mess. Her makeup from the night before is smudged and faded. There are bags under her eyes, and I'm pretty sure I can still smell the alcohol on her.

But Jesus *Christ* she's hot.

It's inexplicable and undefinable, and way more than just looks, too. It's like there's a power radiating off her. Maybe pheromones or some shit. Or... Who knows.

Regardless, my pulse is racing from more than just anger. My skin is throbbing, as if the few inches between us is too great a distance.

It's making my dick hard as fucking steel, too.

"What's the matter, Kenzo?" she purrs, batting her eyes exaggeratedly. "Were you worried?"

"I'm going to take the bait and say yes."

She makes a puppy-dog face. "*Awww,* how—"

"*Not for you,* princess," I growl. "For my sister. For what today means to a lot of other people *besides fucking you.*"

She exhales slowly, looking away as she tries to smooth her gingery red hair.

"We…got carried away last night."

"Where the fuck were you? We've had people looking all over the city since last night."

She winces. "Our phones died."

"*Where. Were. You.*"

Her full bottom lip retreats between her teeth.

"Goddammit, Annika, I am *not* in the mood. Where—"

"Montreal."

At first, I'm *sure* I misheard her. But as the silence lengthens and the heat spreads over her cheeks, I realize I did *not.*

I stare at her. "I'm not sure I was clear about the not joking—"

"I'm…" She swallows. "Not joking."

"Excuse me??"

"There may have been a...misunderstanding."

"With?"

She smiles weakly. "The cops?"

My jaw drops. *"ABOUT*?!"

"A car."

She flashes another sheepish smile as the steam curls out of my fucking ears.

"Whose fucking car?!"

That fucking sheepish grin comes out to play again, and my teeth grind.

"You're fucking joking," I hiss. "You stole a fucking car, with my sister, and drove to fucking *Canada*?!"

Annika winces. "I know it looks bad—"

"NO. SHIT."

She shivers as I roar.

"The plan wasn't Canada, it was just—"

She whimpers as I grab her jaw.

"Please," I snarl quietly. "Don't omit a single fun little detail."

Annika shivers. "The cops were following us, and—"

"Chasing," I snap. "They were *chasing you*."

"Okay, okay." She looks away. "Yes, the cops were chasing us. But, it's not like it's my first time being chased by the—"

"For my fucking sister it was."

"Well," Annika attempts a grin. "Thanks to me, she's not in jail?"

"She was only in that mess to begin with thanks to you!" I roar. "*CANADA*?! Are you fucking serious?!"

"Well, once we were out of the city, there were State Troopers on the highway, and *they* started following—"

"Chasing!"

"FINE!" she yells back. "They were *chasing* us too, and to get out of all of that, we went up I-87. We lost them—*you're welcome*—but then realized we were only like two hours from the border."

I stare at the woman to whom I'm about to commit my life in awe and terror.

She's insane. She's legitimately fucking *insane*.

"So you made the logical decision to go to fucking Montreal? What, were your drunk asses craving poutine?"

"Is...that a trick question?

My face turns crimson as she shrugs.

"I mean... It *was* my bachelorette party."

I shake my head. "Whose idea was this?"

"Mine," she blurts, just a *bit* too quickly.

I'll find you in a fucking second, Hana.

"Now," Annika mutters, shooting me a dirty look. "If this interrogation is over—"

My eyes widen. "You actually think this is the end of this?" I scoff, shaking my head. "You're fucking unbelievable."

"You don't *have* to marry me, you know."

"Unfortunately," I grunt. "We both know I do. But make no mistake…"

I relish the way Annika gasps as I surge into her, grabbing her by the chin again and leering down into her face.

"Marrying you doesn't mean I've forgotten this, or it just goes away."

She rolls her eyes. "What are you going to do? Punish me?"

The second she says it, the room goes quiet. Because for some bizarre reason, that seemingly innocent little phrase "punish me" doesn't feel quite so innocent when it's hovering between us, alone in a room together, with our pulses racing.

Fuck me.

My cock twitches as soon as she says it. And within seconds, I'm tenting the front of my slacks.

I picture her on her knees, tits and tongue out, thighs spread. Maybe a plug in her ass and a collar around her throat as she looks up at me and begs for it.

Please punish me, sir?

I grit my teeth, willing my cock to calm the fuck down as I shake those intoxicating thoughts away.

"Get ready," I mutter coldly. "We don't have much time."

"Well, *you're* the one keeping me."

Forty seconds later, I'm barging in on Hana in another little room just as she's struggling to zip up the back of her dress.

"Hey, hi, have we heard of knocking?" she mutters. She

shoots me a look in the mirror in front of her. "Actually, can you get this?"

I nod, storming over and yanking the zipper up the rest of the way.

"Thanks," she mumbles.

Our eyes meet in the mirror. Outside may have been a rare moment of Hana looking disheveled. But it's taken her no time at all to morph back into her customary utterly put together self. Her makeup is flawless. Her hair is combed out to its usual thick, glossy straightness, the blonde streaks perfect and neatly in place.

"What the *fuck,* Hana," I growl at my sister.

"I'm not *really* in the mood, Kenzo," she sighs, futzing with her hair in the mirror as I glare at her.

"That fucking woman," I snarl, jabbing a finger at nowhere in particular, "is—"

"About to be your wife, brother," Hana says dryly.

I roll my eyes. "Well, she's trouble."

My sister snorts. "Sure is." She laughs to herself as she reapplies lipstick. "But, I gotta say, she kept up."

My brow furrows. "With?"

"With me," Hana shrugs. "She's cool. I like her."

"Because she took you to fucking Canada?"

She frowns. "No. Because she wouldn't back down no matter how far I pushed things. And she didn't 'take me to Canada'," she shrugs. "That was my idea. Fuck, I never thought she'd actually do it."

I turn to stare at her, thunderstruck. "You stole a car—"

"Technically, your *fiancée* stole a car."

"What in God's name would possess her to do that at her bachelorette party?"

Hana grins sheepishly.

"*What,* Hana," I grunt.

"Because… I dared her to?"

I groan. "Fucking *hell.*"

"Please," my sister sighs. "What are we, clergy? You do realize you're about to be a *king,* right, Kenzo? I mean, live a little."

"There's living a little, and then there's recklessness. Learn the difference, Hana."

"Oh, like going after a woman for years just because she stole a *necklace* from you?"

My eyes narrow. "You *know* what that necklace—"

"You've got a lot of Mom's things, Kenzo," she says tersely. "I do, too. So I'm wondering if it was the necklace, the girl, or the fact that someone *beat you* that had you all angry and riled up for five fucking years."

My brows knit. I don't actually know how to answer that. For the millionth time, I'm reminded how smart my younger sister is.

"Better get ready, Kenzo," Hana says quietly. "It's almost showtime."

From my place standing by the altar, my eyes scan the crowd as the string quartet begins to play. I nod to Sota, who nods back. My father isn't here, but that's okay. I saw him last night, and we shared food and a couple of drinks, and he talked to me about married life and being a man and all that.

He doesn't need to be here for the actual ceremony. Especially since he's long since left the mafia world.

Takeshi gives me a thumbs up, and Mal next to him gives me a firm nod. A few rows back, I can see Drazen Krylov settling into his seat next to Annika's twin sister, Taylor. Fumi, my half-sister, is another one who couldn't be here today. She called me earlier to congratulate me, of course, but the First Lady of New York State can't exactly be seen attending mafia weddings. I get it.

The doors at the back of the church open. Everyone turns to watch Kir walk Annika down the aisle.

And my heart stops.

Not because this is suddenly all so very, very real. Not because I'm about to chain myself to a batshit crazy little fucking thief.

No. My heart stills for a moment because when she walks in, all I can see is how fucking *beautiful* she looks.

I mean...*fuck*.

I half-expected her to walk down the aisle in a Halloween costume, just to fuck with me. But here she is in floor-length white satin and tulle, with pearls sewn into elaborate little floral designs up one side, and dainty leaves made of silky lace scattered across the deep neckline and plunging back.

Christ, she looks incredible.

Kir has to cough to yank my attention back when they reach me at the altar. He puts her hand in mine, and then gives me a hard look as he leans close.

"This woman is a daughter to me," he says so quietly that only I can hear. "And I already have a bullet with your name quite literally on it. If you hurt her..."

"I won't."

"I'll be making sure."

He pats my forearm before he turns to kiss Annika on the cheek.

I won't lie: even that gets my blood heated and my teeth grinding in ways I'm not quite ready to dissect just yet.

Annika and I face each other as the priest says the words. I slip a ring onto her finger, and she does the same to me before we utter our vows.

"And now, by the power vested in me by God and the State of New York, I pronounce you man and wife. You may kiss your bride."

Annika half turns to smile at the assembled guests and the cameras, already moving as if she's about to walk back up the aisle.

I can't honestly say what makes me do it. Tradition, maybe. Sticking to the script, or "selling" this to anyone present who's too stupid to understand that this marriage is a peace treaty, not a declaration of love.

Whatever the reason, I'm moving before I realize it. In one motion, I've grabbed Annika around the waist, turned her around with a gasp on her lips, and yanked her against my body.

Her brows furrow in confusion as she looks up at me.

"What the fuck are you—"

"This."

My mouth slams to hers. Our lips sear together as my hand cups her jaw and draws her in. My tongue dives into her mouth and captures hers.

And everything around us just…fades.

Just as I'm about to try and stop myself, or at least decide what the fuck just came over me, an ear-splitting crash explodes through the church.

We whirl along with the rest of the crowd, and then I'm roaring and jumping in front of Annika as the van comes crashing through the doors of the church in a hail of splintered wood. Guests and their guards lurch out of the way and screams fill the air as the van plows into two pews and then whines to a stop, smoke billowing from its wrecked front grill and its windshield spiderwebbed.

"MAL!" I roar. He, and Tak, and a bunch of our guys are already whipping guns out and approaching the sides of the van. Kir's men are doing the same. I glance over and spot Drazen keeping Taylor behind him, his gun drawn as they back away toward a side door, surrounded by his guards.

I turn to Hana, but she's already with Sota and his guys, also moving toward the side door.

"OUT OF THE VAN!" Mal roars. "Now!!"

When there's no response, he edges closer. The whole fucking church is on edge, like we're teetering on our toes on the precipice of a cliff.

"OUT!" Mal doesn't hesitate this time. He charges the driver's side door, yanking it open and jamming his gun inside. I see the wild look on his face before he even turns back to me. "It's empty!"

Oh fuck.

"GET BACK!" I roar, shoving Annika back toward the door leading to the vestry and then running to the van as the whole damn church descends into chaos. "GET BACK! *Mal*! Get the fuck away from—"

The air turns to fire as I'm punched backward off my feet from the force of the car bomb that shatters the night.

12

ANNIKA

The alcohol is strong and fierce and it rolls down my throat like fire. I don't normally chuck booze straight like this, but given the events of the last two hours?

Yeah. I think this is necessary.

I pause, letting the first massive gulp of vodka settle in my stomach before I tip the glass back and swallow the rest of it. I inhale deeply, wincing as I set the glass down before reaching for the bottle again.

Like I said: *necessary*. Plus, I *am* half Serbian.

Drinking vodka like water is in my DNA.

Mercifully, there've been minimal casualties from the car bomb that ripped through the church earlier—and miraculously, no fatalities. Kenzo's brother Mal has a nasty gash across the temple from shrapnel, and seven other Mori and Akiyama men have various minor injuries from the blast.

Lev, one of Kir's guys, is in the worst shape after taking a piece of van in the stomach like a machete. But even he's going to be okay. So are the four other Nikolayev men who took shrapnel.

No one else was hurt.

My first fear in that terrifying moment after the explosion rocked the church was for my sister, of course. But by the time the van came crashing through the front wall, Drazen was already hustling her out through the side door, and they were outside when the bomb went off. They're both fine.

Kir was apparently similarly dragging Freya out before the bomb even blew, and Sota Akiyama and Hana were also already outside as well.

But even knowing all that…and even though I grew up in the mafia, and went through what happened to my family, and then spent so many years living with danger… I'm still shaken by what just happened.

Hence the drinking.

I pour another hefty glass and bring it to my lips. It stings a little less this time, with the first shot already numbing my body a little, and settles inside to warm my core.

"Keep him there, Mal," Kenzo growls into his phone across the room.

We're in the penthouse apartment he keeps in Manhattan; a stunning spot high above Central Park East with huge double-story walls of glass that look out over the city. The penthouse is sparsely decorated and furnished, since he doesn't spend much time here, and even when he *is* in New York, he's mostly at Sota's place.

Kenzo explained all of this in a few words when we first walked in.

"I don't give a fuck that he's angry," Kenzo hisses, turning his back to me perched on the couch as he paces near the windows. "We're *all* angry. His fucking job right now is to sit his ass down and guard Sota and Hana, not run around the city looking for a fight. Tell Takeshi I'm pulling rank and that's a goddamn order."

I glance back at my phone as I keep swigging vodka.

FREYA

You're SURE ur good??

ME

Yeah. Tons of security. Five of Kenzo's guys watching the lobby plus three of Kir's.

My brow knits.

ME

Are YOU okay?

After the explosion, Kenzo insisted on bringing me here, which he claims is one of the safest places in the city. Freya, meanwhile, went with Kir to his place. I'm not worried about her safety there, because I know Kir's place is impenetrable. But I *am* worried about the fact that we both just experienced a fucking bombing.

FREYA

I'm good. Kinda shaken. Like WTF

FREYA

We thinking Kenzo's enemies, or ours?

It's impossible to know yet. All anyone *does* know is that the van was driven into the church and detonated via remote. It was a rental, too, and I'd bet my ass that the rental was done using a fake ID. No one would be stupid enough to bomb a mafia wedding and leave any *possible* trail back to themselves unless they wanted to die with their genitals stuffed down their throats.

ME

No idea, honestly. It DOES seem more like a Bratva move than Yakuza?

Not that the Yakuza don't have open conflicts, too. But with firearms being so controlled in Japan, the Yakuza tends to wage war quietly. Swords, poison, that sort of thing. It's the Russians who like to go barreling in with guns blazing and blowing shit up like a bunch of fucking cowboys.

I shiver as I glance back at my phone.

ME

Kir sent guys to watch Damian, yeah?

Damian's last surgery was a huge success. But they're giving him a few extra days in the induced coma after all, to help him heal a little more before they bring him out of it. The thought of him just lying there helpless in the hospital, easy pickings, sends a shiver up my spine.

FREYA

As if that wasn't my first thought?

FREYA

Or Kir's?

ME

Sorry. Kinda freaked out

FREYA

Same. I'm just giving you a hard time. Yeah, there's like ten guys at the hospital right now.

I exhale slowly. Thank God.

After I tell Frey to stay safe and to text again later, I pour myself yet another glass of vodka and knock half of it back. Then I check in with Taylor. Obviously, she's holed up safe and sound in Drazen's luxury tower penthouse, probably surrounded by like a thousand guards and fucking air support, knowing her husband.

It's also pretty clear neither Drazen nor my sister was the target of the attack today.

ME

How r u?

TAYLOR

We're good. I mean Drazen is ready to level the whole city right now. But once I calm him down, he'll be good

I grin, happy that my twin is as safe as she can possibly be. At the same time, I *hate* that this happened with her there—that the messiness of my life almost got *her* hurt.

When I'm finally off my phone, I polish off the glass sitting next to me and pour…fuck. I've officially lost count. But I've stopped shaking, so there's that?

Across the room, Kenzo is speaking quietly in Japanese. I don't really know any, but I can vaguely guess from his tone that he's probably talking to Sota.

I sip my drink, feeling warm and fuzzy as I watch him.

My husband.

I groan, scrunching up my face.

Fuck that feels weird to say, even inside my head.

I never once—and I truly mean that—pictured myself getting married. When I was younger and on the run, romance or even talking to a man never even crossed my mind. It's hard to date, or even flirt, when you're struggling to survive.

Later, of course, there was *him*. But….

I shudder as I bring the glass to my lips and drink deeply.

That was something else. That was hell. A prison. And even in the depths of my most pathetic moments with he-who-will-not-be-named, I never *once* thought it would end in marriage.

And after the horrors he put me through were behind me, I could barely look at another man. Much less date one. Or fall for one. Or even *touch* one…

A warm feeling spreads through me as my eyes drag across the dimly lit penthouse. Rain falls softly outside, pattering against the tall glass wall as I watch Kenzo. He's still on the phone, but as I stare at him, his back to me, he shrugs off his jacket and gets rid of his tie. He holds the phone against his broad shoulder as he unbuttons his dress shirt and peels it away.

My lip slips between my teeth.

The vodka feels *real* nice in my core right now.

My eyes drag slowly over Kenzo's broad, muscled, lean back. The *irezumi* style Yakuza ink that spreads across his skin ripples as his corded muscles clench.

Down, girl.

Kenzo says a last few words in Japanese, nodding stiffly before he ends the call and slips the phone into his pocket. He keeps his back to me as he sighs heavily, and for the first time, it hits me that he's more than just this smug, steely-eyed Yakuza prince.

The man…*cares*. A lot. At least, about his own family. In this moment, you can almost see the weight of his future empire pressing down on his shoulders, and his back almost bowing under the heaviness of it.

I flinch slightly as he suddenly turns. His eyes stab across the penthouse right into mine. His chiseled jaw ripples a little, and when he rolls his neck, his pectorals flex.

Fuck me, the man is *shredded*.

Hard, lean muscle curves down his ribs and bands across his abdomen. The clearly defined eight-pack of his abs clenches as he starts to walk toward me, the ink on his chest and arms rippling with each step.

My eyes drop to the sinfully defined v-lines that cut down his hips into the waist of his dress pants, like warning signs on a dark road.

Caution. Turn back. Danger ahead. Step the fuck away, Annika.

"Let me take a look at that."

His low, growling voice yanks my eyes from his body to his face. Then I glance down, following his gaze to the blood seeping through my wedding dress over my thigh.

I checked it out in the bathroom when we first got here. It's not a bad cut at all. From the tear in the satin itself, I'm guessing it was a piece of church pew, or maybe the van, that blew past me.

Well, not *quite* past me.

"I'm fine," I shrug, picking up my glass and draining it. "It's nothing. I already bandaged it up in the bathroom when we got here."

His dark brows furrow. "I'm only going to ask this once," he growls, moving closer to me.

He plucks the bottle of vodka from the table, looking right at me as he brings it to his lips and takes a long, drawn-out gulp. Then a second one. When he sets it back on the table, he rubs his jaw with one hand.

"Okay: who's trying to kill you?"

I frown. "Who says anyone's trying to kill me? *You're* the up-and-coming—"

"I am well aware of all the people who want me dead. I'm even somewhat aware of the people who might want *Kir* dead. And that wasn't any of them."

I roll my eyes. "What are you, Sherlock Holmes? How the fuck could you possibly know that?"

"Because I've taught myself to be observant," he growls. "And mindful of my surroundings. Unlike some people."

I flip him off. "If you feel compelled to talk about how great you are, there's a mirror in the bathroom that might be a better conversationalist."

"Funny," he mutters. "The shooter the other day was aiming at *you*."

Do you think it was him behind it? The shooter, I mean.

I flinch as the face of he-who-shall-not-be-named emerges from the blackness in my mind.

But no. It can't have been him.

He wouldn't hide in the shadows when he tried to kill me.

"Today's the second time in as many weeks that someone's tried to kill me or my family, and I generally like to limit that to once a month. I want answers. Now."

His abs clench as he reaches for the bottle again, towering over me, and brings it to his lips. I just glare at him.

"I don't *have* answers, because I have no more fucking idea who might be behind today than you do."

"Bullshit. Annika—"

"What are you going to do?" I spit angrily, grabbing the bottle as soon as he sets it down and taking a heavy swig. "Torture me until I give you a name?"

"No. But I believe there was mention of punishing you."

My face explodes with heat, and I can feel my lip shrinking back between my teeth as I look away.

"Let me see that wound."

"I'm fine," I mutter quietly.

"The hell you are." He starts to reach for the hem of the wedding dress. Before his hand gets there, I slap it away in a clumsy, vodka-slowed motion.

"Leave me alone."

Kenzo rolls his eyes. "Are you always this goddamn stubborn?"

"Things you would have known if we'd spoken for more than nine seconds before getting engaged."

His eyes narrow. "I think we've done more than speak for nine seconds."

"Really? I've forgotten," I say, casually shrugging.

"Some of us *didn't* forget you *drugging and robbing them,*" he growls tightly. "Now *stop* being a pain in the ass and let me see your wound."

"You're bleeding, too."

He glances down at his wrist, frowning, as if noticing the red on his skin for the first time.

"It's not my blood," he grunts, and wipes it off on his pants.

"*Oh.*"

"Now are you going to show me the wound, or am I going to cut this dress off you to see it?"

Without waiting for an answer, Kenzo drops to his knees right in front of me. I watch him almost in a daze as he takes the hem of my wedding gown in his hands and gently pushes it up over my knees. His big, veined hands slip easily around the back of my knee and thigh without any sort of care about invading my personal space. He lifts my leg a little, causing the dress to ride up higher on that side.

My face throbs as he leans closer, his brow furrowing.

"Where the fuck did you learn to dress a wound, TikTok?" he grunts, scowling at the admittedly half-assed job I did in the bathroom with three Band-Aids and some old wrap tape.

"It's *fine,*" I mumble.

"It's a fucking infection waiting to happen. Don't move."

Kenzo walks away, disappearing into the darkness outside the dim glow of the living room. He returns a few minutes later with a first aid kit.

Still shirtless.

Distractingly shirtless.

My head floats a little, the alcohol burning in my veins. Kenzo says nothing as he drops to his knees again in front of me. Once more, he pushes my knee to the side.

My breath catches sharply as his hand skims up my inner thigh to a few inches past my knee. His long, strong fingers grip the edge of the tape and the Band-Aids, and without any warning, he yanks my crappy bandage off.

"*Shit*!" I wince, hissing as my leg jerks back. "What the fuck!"

"Hold *still*," he mutters without looking up at me. He grabs hold of my leg again, a little roughly—honestly, right now, I don't mind—peers at the cut, then reaches down and brings up a wet antiseptic wipe. I hiss sharply as he dabs it on the small gash on my thigh.

"*Fuck*!" I blurt, my leg jerking again.

"Calm the fuck down."

I roll my eyes. "Your bedside manner is *shit*, for the record —*ow!*"

I glare at him as he roughly dabs the cut again.

"Oh…*sorry*," he says, without a trace of apology in his voice.

Smiling. He's fucking *smiling*.

Asshole.

I purse my lips, refusing to whimper as he finishes cleaning the cut. Then he tapes a bandage over it, pressing down on the edges and dimpling my skin as he makes it stick fast.

"There," he grunts, nodding his chin at his handiwork. "Much better."

Admittedly, his work *does* look like I went to a doctor. Mine looked like a stoned raccoon did it.

"Wonderful," I mutter. "Are we done now?"

"Almost."

It happens quickly. And yet, it also feels like the moment is drawn out for hours. I watch, my eyes slowly widening and my mouth falling open as Kenzo leans down, brushing the bandage gently with his thumb.

Slowly, he lowers his mouth. His lips press to the white gauze in a brief, soft kiss.

For a moment, we both freeze. His lips hover a half inch above my bandage, his warm breath teasing over my bare skin. I can feel my pulse thudding in my ears his fingers grip my thigh tighter, the raw power of his strength pulsing off his fingertips and into me.

I shiver when he leans back down, his lips brushing my bandage once again. My breathing becomes quiet little staccato gasps as his dark eyes slowly lift to mine. He holds my gaze unflinchingly and mercilessly as he slowly moves his mouth an inch higher.

This time, it's bare skin that his lips touch. A zap of something electric throbs in my core, tingling and teasing every extremity with nervous, buzzing energy. Kenzo's strong hands on my thigh push a little bit higher, sliding the dress up with them.

His mouth follows, dropping another teasing, soft, electrifying kiss on my tingling skin.

Oh fuck.

We're both utterly silent as he pushes the wedding dress even higher, letting it slide almost all the way up to my panties. My breath catches sharply as his mouth drops to land another soft, wet kiss against my skin—though this time, it's a little harder.

More insistent.

Less fluttery.

Demanding.

I bite back the involuntary whimper that forms in my throat as his hands slide boldly up my thigh, pushing on my leg. He pushes the dress up to my waist, and a heat flushes scorchingly through my body and over my face as he lewdly spreads my legs wide.

His eyes never leave mine as he moves his mouth higher. This time, when his lips brush against my skin, it's followed by a sharp—and I do mean sharp—bite of his teeth on my bare inner thigh that makes me gasp.

"*Fuck...*" I choke in a breathless whimper, my throat closing in on itself as my eyes widen.

Then he does it again, marking me again with his teeth in the same fucking spot. I wince, a raw, erotic pain throbbing through my skin, electrifying me and making my thighs tremble. I can feel my core clench and my nipples tighten as his tongue swipes at the bite he's just given me.

"*Kenzo*," I mumble quietly. "What..."

"I did warn you, princess," he rumbles darkly, his eyes sweeping up to mine before he lowers his mouth again. I cry out when his teeth rake over my skin, followed by a slow, wet swipe of his tongue.

His gaze drops between my legs, and I watch the raw, black fire in his eyes pulse with something vicious as they lock onto the apex of my thighs, covered only by a thin strip of lace.

"When you're my wife, it'll be in every sense of the word."

He roughly pushes my legs wider apart, spreading me open.

"You..." I choke on my words as his strong hand pushes up my thigh. "You can't just—"

"Watch me."

I try to close my legs, but he slaps my thigh, pushing them apart again, making me whimper. His lips brush my skin once more, and I cry out when his teeth come out to play again. The sting of them sinking into my flesh sends a raw throb through my core, and I'm still shuddering from the bite when his hand boldly slides up between my legs.

Oh, FUCK.

Kenzo's huge hand cups my swollen pussy through my wet panties. My face burns with heat. My eyes hood as I stare at where his hand is resting, watching, biting back a moan as he drags one finger up my lips through the slick lace.

My breathing becomes heavy and rasping, my skin tingling everywhere as my nipples tease against the inside of my dress.

Our eyes lock—

And I hiccup.

Mother. *Fucker.*

Kenzo's brow furrows, and his hand starts to pull back.

"What are you doing?" I blurt.

His hand stays where it is, his palm against my needy sex. But his finger isn't moving anymore. His eyes lock with mine.

"You're drunk," he growls quietly.

"No, I'm *noooot.*"

Fucking fuck. Even I can hear the slurring of my words as they slide from my lips. My eyes drift to the side table, landing on the empty glass and the bottle of vodka with the *sizable* dent in it.

Okay, maybe all the vodka is catching up to me.

With a vengeance.

"I'm really *noooot—*"

"Yes," he growls. "You are."

I hate how disappointed I get when his hand moves away.

"What," I mumble. "You won't touch a drunk girl?"

Kenzo says nothing as he starts to stand.

I snort loudly. "Wowwww. And here I thought you were this big tough Yakuza badass."

"And that necessitates sexual assault?"

"Can't rape the willing."

The *nanosecond* those words leave my mouth, it's like I sober up instantly. My hand slams over my mouth as heat explodes across my face.

What is *wrong* with me?

That's not the only thing that happens when those words fly out into the universe. Kenzo freezes as if turned to stone. His eyes change from their usual intense dark fire into this breath-arresting darkness throbbing with wrath and malice.

Slowly, those eyes lock with mine, and a flame ripples through my core.

"*Say that again,*" he rasps, his voice rippling with a dark energy that both terrifies and electrifies me.

I shiver as he moves up, crouching between my lewdly spread thighs with my wedding dress bunched up around my hips, looming over me. He reaches down, and I whimper as his powerful fingers wrap like a vice around my throat.

"I *said,*" he growls savagely. "*Say that again.*"

I tremble but shake my head. "No."

Kenzo's lips curl monstrously.

"*Careful,* princess," he murmurs. I bite back a whimper as he leans down into me, his body spreading my thighs wide as his mouth brushes my neck and my earlobe. "*I might just get used to that word and like it a bit too much.*"

I shudder, a heady mix of fear and raw lust exploding, raining liquid fire through my core and my veins.

"*I—*"

"You want my hands on you?" he snarls.

I cry out as his hand roughly pushes between my legs, cupping my throbbing pussy through my panties. A whimper falls from my lips as his fingers slip underneath the edge. His arm jerks, his muscled forearm rippling, and *rips* the fucking lace away from me.

That's just the start of it.

Suddenly, without any warning, I feel two thick fingers push between my needy lips. A raw, aching groan is torn from my throat as he roughly sinks them into me, shoving them deep.

"*FUCK*…." I choke, shuddering as my hands instinctively reach for and grab hold of his muscled forearm.

"How about *now*, princess," he snarls dangerously. His fingers start to slide out, only to instantly ram right back in, curling up against my g-spot.

"*Oh*..." I whimper, shivering and shuddering as he starts to stroke his fingers in and out of my aching, wet pussy.

Then he cranks it up and starts to finger me even harder and more roughly.

"And *now*?" he purrs darkly.

"*Yes*…" I choke pathetically, clinging to him as the waves of dark pleasure begin to swell and crash against my insides.

I can still feel the alcohol surging through my veins. I'm drunk—*very* drunk—but all it does is throw fuel on the fire surging in my core. The room spins and my senses swirl and pulse. The slow descent into inebriation walks hand in hand with the dark pleasure he's wringing from my body, and all I want to do is ride this wave for fucking ever.

"Who knew my wife was such a desperate, needy little *slut*," Kenzo hisses in my ear.

I moan, loudly.

"*More*," I whimper desperately, feeling myself tighten around him.

He chuckles darkly. "*More*?" he growls. "What a *greedy* little slut."

He suddenly adds a third finger. My eyes fly open, my mouth gaping wide as I'm suddenly filled like I never have been before.

"*Shiiiiit...*" I moan.

I'd meant more filthy talk.

But this is....

Fuck.

It's unreal. Untethering. Unearthly. The sensation of his huge fingers stretching my pussy wide and filling me to my limit is even more intoxicating than the vodka—an aching adrenaline rush mixed with the desperate need for pleasure.

His mouth drops to my neck, and I cry out as he bites down hard. His fingers curl tighter around my throat, pinching off my blood flow and my oxygen just enough to take the swirling sensation of the alcohol in my veins to an otherworldly level.

Everything blurs and turns to liquid fire. My skin comes alive, and I beg him for more, more, *more* as he roughly savages my neck with his teeth and fingers me into oblivion.

"Why don't you be a good little fuck-toy and fucking come for me like the greedy little slut you are, *wife*," he snarls viciously into my ear. His thumb starts to rub my clit as his three huge fingers keep ramming into me. "Come on my fucking hand, *now*, like a good girl."

Sweet. Fucking. Jesus.

When I explode, it's like reality itself blurs around me. Like the world I know blips out of focus for a second, sending me spiraling in a freefall into blank space. I cry out, my hands clutching his forearm as tight as I can, feeling the tendons and muscles under his tattooed skin ripple as his fingers curl deep inside of me.

He bites me one last time, dragging a moaning shriek from my trembling lips. Then his fingers slip out from between my legs. His mouth and hand pull away from my neck and throat.

Shit.

My head is spinning, and while the orgasm is part of it, it's also obviously the several shots of vodka I had all starting to creep up on me at once. I bite my teeth together and cling to the chair as the room starts to spin a little.

Suddenly, I'm being lifted. I drag my loopy gaze up and then feel a fuzzy smile spreading over my face as I look up into Kenzo's eyes.

He's carrying me somewhere, one arm under my knees, the other under my back, like I'm a baby.

"Where..." I mumble, my words slurring badly. "Where're we going?"

"To bed," he growls curtly.

Heat throbs through my core.

"Are yooouu gonna fuhck-me noooow?"

I *hate* how disappointed I get when he scowls and shakes his head.

"No."

My lips twist petulantly. "Whyyy?" I whine, sagging against his strong arms as he carries me through the penthouse. "Cause I'm not Matsui Aki's bimbo daughter?"

He smirks when I say it. I hate that too, dammit.

We walk into a huge, dimly lit, very masculine bedroom. I gasp a little too dramatically as he drops me onto a huge, insanely soft bed. I grin as I feel my body snuggle into it.

"I'm not going to fuck you while you're passed out," Kenzo growls, pulling a blanket up over me as my eyes begin to drift closed.

"You could."

I freeze instantly. So does he, the blanket halfway over me.

"What did you just say?"

There's a lethal, dangerous edge to his voice. I open my eyes to see him leaning close to me, his black eyes boring into mine and sending little pulses of nervous heat tingling through every nerve in my body.

"I...nothing—"

His hand wraps around my throat again.

"What did you just say," he growls.

"I...I said *you could,*" I whisper breathlessly.

My eyes drop closed again. My mouth goes slack as the comforting embrace of the bed begins to swallow me whole.

"Fuck me..."

The blanket is pulled up over me.

"Get some sleep, princess."

Then I'm out.

13

KENZO

"Come on in."

Mal strolls into the penthouse, closing the door behind him.

"Casual Friday?" he quips, eying me. I'm still shirtless from earlier.

"I'm sorry, should I have put on something nicer for you?"

He smirks and rolls his eyes. "Is your new bride as casually attired at the moment?"

Something heated flashes in my chest as I whirl on him. "How about you stop that imagination of yours right the fuck now," I snarl quietly.

Mal arches a brow, but doesn't say a word.

He doesn't need to. I'm already thinking it.

What the fuck was that?

It's the same gut response I had to Takeshi getting in Annika's face earlier this evening, before the wedding. This protective—one might say *overly* protective—instinct when it comes to her.

I understand it about as much as I understand my actions earlier, when I put my hands on her and didn't *stop* putting my hands on her until I'd wrung that shattering orgasm from her body.

You could.

Something black, deviant, and monstrous roars awake inside me.

I've never been ashamed of anything I've done: killing, maiming, extorting. Ruining lives and taking countless others. I've lost exactly zero minutes of sleep to the vicious things I've done. I *have* to do them, in my world.

That lack of shame extends to my more…*personal* tastes, and sexual proclivities.

Free use.

Somnophilia.

Taking total control, perhaps when a partner is incapacitated in some way…*or asleep.*

Again, I categorically don't feel ashamed for wanting to fuck like that. But a tiny part of me knows that perhaps I *should.*

And those words coming from her mouth, after I'd just had my fingers inside her, the taste of her skin still on my lips… After she'd just shattered for me, and was falling into an alcohol-driven oblivion…

God fucking help me, I almost did.

I stood in that bedroom for another ten minutes watching her sleep.

I took off her dress.

I *may* have spread her legs and stroked my cock, feasting my eyes on her little pink cunt.

But that was as far as it went. Now she's under the bedsheets, away from my monstrous stares and desires.

"Drink?" I grunt to Mal.

He nods as I walk over to the bar cart and pour us both a splash of Yamazaki 18.

"At the risk getting my head bitten off for merely mentioning her name," he smirks, "how's Annika? I mean with what happened earlier."

I hand him the glass. "She's fine. She's sleeping now."

"That was fucked, Kenzo," he growls quietly. "And I know we both know what this marriage is, but still. I'm sorry that it happened at your own fucking wedding."

"Hey, it beats having to stand there afterward and shake everyone's hand while they all pretend I'm actually in love with my new bride."

He chuckles, and when he takes a sip of the Japanese whiskey, his eyes close for a second.

"Fuck, tastes like home."

I smile wryly. "Missing Kyoto?"

He nods. "I don't mind New York. It's not the same, though."

"I sometimes feel like that too—" My brow furrows as Mal turns into the light a little more, and I see a dark mark on the side of his neck, like he got hit by a chain or something. I scowl. "Is that from the explosion?"

"What?"

I nod my chin. "Your neck."

He frowns and his hand comes up to touch the spot. Something flashes across his face I can't quite place. Before I can dwell on it any longer, the look fades and he shakes it away.

"No idea. Probably." He clears his throat.

I nod to the bandage on his forehead. "And how's the noggin?"

"I'll live, Kenzo," he sighs. "Anyway, I've been flipping over stones to see if anything crawls out regarding that fucking bomb."

"And?"

He shakes his head. "Nothing. Whoever it was, the attack wasn't specifically on us or Sota. Not directly. I even went looking for trouble myself and met up with Nam Dae-Hyun."

My brow raises sharply. "Are you fucking serious?"

Dae-Hyun runs a mid-level *kkangpae*—a Korean crime syndicate—here in New York. I wouldn't say we're exactly "at war" with them. But let's just say Nam wouldn't brake very fast if he saw me or a family member crossing the street in front of his car.

Mal grins. "I interrupted him while he was trying to cop a happy ending at a massage parlor. He wasn't thrilled."

I shake my head. "That was reckless."

"But hilarious," he snickers. "Anyway, I pressed him pretty hard about what happened. Like, gave him every opportunity to take ownership of the attack, or even just lie about it. That guy would walk over nails or sell his own mother just to *claim* he drew blood from us."

"Nothing?"

He shakes his head. "Nope. It wasn't him. It wasn't anyone he even *knows*. Which crosses the last names off my list of potentials." He takes a heavy drink from his glass. "Whoever that was, they weren't gunning for us."

"You're *sure*?"

Mal clears his throat. "You want to double-check my math? Nam decided to be an idiot and tried to jump me as I was leaving his interrupted hand-job session."

I scowl. "You good?"

"*I'm* fine," he shrugs. "But if you want to ask him yourself about his involvement in tonight, I could make that happen. Quickly."

Mal grins.

"He may or may not be downstairs in the trunk of my car if you want to take a little drive."

I raise a brow. "But you don't think he was involved."

"No. He did, however, express a fairly strong hope that whoever it was tries again and doesn't miss you or your new wife next time."

That black, molten lava surges through my chest again.

I trust Mal's judgement. If he says so, then I'll believe that Nam didn't have anything to do with the bombing.

He's still an asshole, though.

Senseless violence is usually more Takeshi's line. But what can I say? It's been *a night*.

"Why don't we go…double-check with Nam," I growl quietly.

AN HOUR LATER, I'm back in my penthouse. Mal is back at Sota's.

Nam Dae-Hyun is at Mt. Sinai, presumably getting his jaw wired shut and his broken arm put in a cast.

Hopefully, they can inject him with some manners while he's there.

I pad quietly back into my bedroom, shedding my shirt and pants along the way. I stand at the foot of the bed, watching Annika sleep, illuminated by the neon lights of New York.

Mal was right. We weren't the target of tonight's attack.

My jaw tightens as my gaze sweeps over the woman I just married.

I'm still confused why considering that *she* might have been the target tonight fills me with such rage.

Fury.

Wrath, and the unbreakable need to make *sure* that does not happen.

14

ANNIKA

CONFUSION WRAPS around me like a thick fog as I slowly open my eyes. It's dark, the only light the slight glow of the city coming in through the shades. For a minute, I'm unclear where I am as my eyes slowly adjust and take in the unfamiliar bedroom. Then as consciousness slowly sinks its claws into me, and the pain of the vodka comes back swinging, it all begins to fall slowly into place.

Kenzo's bedroom. That's where I am. That's where he...

I groan.

That's where he *carried me,* after I'd drank way too much way too fast. After—

Oh God.

My face heats as it all slams back.

After I told him to fuck me even if I was drunk and out cold.

I wince, and my head starts to throb. So does the body against my back.

Wait...what?

I tense, my eyes going wide as I feel warm skin and hard, grooved muscles pressed tight to me.

It's him. *Kenzo* is sleeping next to me, with his arm slung over me. He's all sharp edges, heated skin, strong muscles, and...

My eyes bulge even wider as I shift against him.

Holy fuck.

He's...*hard.* Like, extremely so. And extremely *big.* A shiver ripples up my spine as I feel the hot weight of his throbbing erection against my ass. It's only then that I realize I'm naked. But even though that brings up all *sorts* of questions, none of them seems to matter right now.

All I can think about is the electric heat where his thick cock is twitching against me.

Part of me thinks I should get out of this bed right now. Yeah, I still have questions about what's going on, and why he's here with me. But, I mean, it *is* his bed.

There's a perfectly good couch out there in the main living room I could adjourn to for the remainder of the night.

But I don't move.

I don't want to.

My bottom lip dips between my teeth. Heat floods my face, and I push back a little.

Fuck, is he big. His swollen dick is pressed lengthwise to the crease of my ass, and it feels like there's a fucking *forearm* back there.

I arch my back a little, my breath becoming ragged and gasping as I push back. Then I do it again, feeling his length slide up and down my ass crack as my cheeks part a little more.

Holy fuck.

My breath catches as his thick shaft slides between them. I grind again, shuddering when I feel the hot underside of him gliding back and forth over my asshole.

An electric zap tingles through me. My nipples tighten to hard points. My core clenches.

My thighs turn slick.

I need to get out of this bed. I need to stop this madness. But I can't. My eyes flutter closed, and my breathing becomes even more ragged as I push back again, grinding my ass on his fat cock.

"Such an eager little slut."

JESUS.

My eyes fly open as my body jolts and spasms, as if to lunge away from him. But before I can, the arm over me wraps tight around my body, pinning me hard against his thick cock. I squirm, my pulse jangling as I try to escape.

Kenzo doesn't *budge.*

"Did you find something you wanted to play with, princess?" he mutters, his arm tightening around my squirming body as his lips find my ear. I whimper and then gasp sharply as he nibs at my earlobe, biting me again.

I mean, is he part wolf? What the fuck is with the biting?

Not, mind you, that I'm complaining.

"*I—*"

He rolls his hips against me, sliding his cock up and down the cleft of my ass. My eyes roll back, my breath coming in staccato gasps as his shaft rubs back and forth against my back hole.

"Where…" I swallow. "Where are my clothes?"

"I removed them."

"You can't—" My words choke off as he pulls his hips back further, making my body ripple with forbidden need as his swollen head bumps against my puckered hole before his entire shaft glides back up between my ass cheeks. "You can't do this when I'm asleep—"

"I didn't do anything while you were asleep," he rumbles against my shoulder. "Though maybe I *should have,* since you begged me to."

Shame and heat flood my face even as an aching need pulses in my core.

"*Can't rape the willing,* isn't that right, princess?"

His big cock rubs back and forth against me.

"Is this where you wanted me to take you first, princess?"

I bite down on my lip as he grabs my ass with his big palms and spreads me a little more. He angles the throbbing, swollen head of his huge dick against my asshole and my eyes widen.

"Did you want me to fuck your ass like a filthy, dirty little cock slut while you were asleep? Although I don't think you'd stay that way for very long," he growls.

His hand slides around to my front and cups one of my bare breasts. I whimper when he roughly rolls and pinches my swollen nipple.

"I very much doubt that even drunk you'd sleep through my hungry cock pushing into this tight, hot, *needy* little hole for the first time."

There's *always* a dark aura around Kenzo. But right now, it's at a level I've never seen before. It's like a being of pure malice and supernatural malevolence is at my back, rendering me helpless.

"No, princess," he murmurs, shifting his hips. "Not yet. Tonight, it being our *wedding night*, it's only fitting that I claim and ruin another of your greedy little holes."

His cock slips away from my ass. Suddenly, my eyes are starting from my head as I feel the heavy, swollen shaft slip between my thighs. His fat cock pushes over my slick, velvety lips, parting them around his girth as the crown glides over my sex.

Holy fucking hell.

His fingers mercilessly tease and pinch my nipples until they're on fire and my breasts feel deliciously bruised by his touch. His hips roll, guiding his fat cock back and forth over my pussy, spreading my wetness all over my thighs and his shaft as I whimper and try to stop from moaning.

"I wanted you awake for this, princess," he murmurs darkly, letting his head slip between my lips and rest against my opening for a second.

My breath quickens.

"I almost fucked you while you *weren't,*" he rasps into my ear. "But this first time, I want you *thinking of me* when I fuck you."

The thing is, *I was.*

When I awoke just now, it was from a vivid dream—the kind that leaves your body tingling with dampness between your thighs.

In the dream, he was already taking me.

Now, he's really going to.

Kenzo grinds his thick cock back and forth across my lips again and again, the bulging head rubbing over my clit and driving me wild as I grab a fistful of the sheets and squirm against him. He's just so *big* all over—his muscles, his height, his shoulder width.

His *cock.*

I'm not a small woman—I mean, I'm five foot ten. But even I feel *dwarfed* by his massive size.

His hand slides from my breasts to my throat. Even in the dim light, I spot something that gives me pause for a second.

"You're...bleeding," I choke hoarsely.

"It's not mine."

He wraps his fingers around my throat.

"Remember this moment, princess," he growls, centering his swollen head against my opening as my lips spread around him. "Because this is the moment I make you *mine.*"

Oh FUCK.

My jaw goes slack, my eyes widening in a stunned, gasping flinch as Kenzo's huge cock begins to sink into me.

"Wait—"

"No."

I moan as he drives another fat inch into me, arresting my breath as my pulse skyrockets.

"No, I mean…" I choke back another whimper. "Do you have a condom?"

"No."

With a low, masculine groan, Kenzo feeds another inch of his massive cock into my eager, swollen pussy.

"But…shit," I gasp, whimpering as he starts to push deeper and deeper into me. "I'm not on—"

"I don't care."

One hand tightens on my hip. The other one wraps like iron around my throat as his teeth rake down my shoulder. Then suddenly, two things happen simultaneously.

Kenzo bites down *hard* on my shoulder—hard enough that I'm sure he breaks the skin. Just as he does so, and the pain spikes through my system, he rams into me, burying every single thick inch of his fat cock deep in my eager pussy.

The combination is like a rush of blood to the head. I cry out, writhing and moaning as my back arches and my toes curl and kick at the sheets.

FUCK, that's good.

It's pure ecstasy. My body melts against his as his arm tightens around me, his fingers splayed out on my neck digging into my throat as he rolls his muscled hips back. I can feel every thick inch of his huge cock sliding out of me, and my lips clinging to it as if I don't want to let him go.

He keeps pulling out until just the head is spreading me open, teasing against me.

Then he drives right back in.

"*There's* my good little fuck toy," he growls darkly into my ear as our bodies begin to grind together. He starts to fuck me harder, ramming his cock into my slickness as I whine and whimper eagerly. "Such a greedy little cunt I've found here. So fucking *desperate* for my cock."

I moan deeply, almost unable to move from the powerful way he's gripping me and pinning me to his huge body. His hips thrust forward, slapping my ass sharply as his thick cock is buried to the hilt inside me.

"My *wife*," Kenzo rasps against my neck. "In *every*"—he rams in again—"single"—I cry out as he fucks me deep and hard—"sense"—slam—"of the word."

His hand on my ass winds up and spanks it, hard. I whimper and sob in pleasure, writhing against him as he does it again and again. He grabs my leg, lifting it to give him more access, pushing that enormous dick even deeper into me.

I can feel his abs pounding against my ass with each vicious stroke. His heavy balls slap my clit, and the fingers on my neck *squeeze*, dimming my vision.

My eyes roll back in my head as his teeth rake savagely down my skin. As his fingers dig into me. As he half rolls me over, pinning me to the bed as he starts to fuck the living *shit* out of me with his hand around my throat.

It is, unquestionably, the most savage, wild, and brutal way I have *ever* been fucked before. It's like nothing I've ever even imagined or fantasized about.

It's even better.

Rougher. Harder. More aggressive and animalistic. The feel of his massive body pinning me helplessly to the bed as he takes his pleasure from me throws me into the stratosphere, sending me reeling, ecstasy exploding through my core.

"Now be a good girl," he hisses into my ear, "and stop holding back. Don't make me spank the orgasm out of you, princess. Be a good little cum slut and come all over my fat cock. Let me feel your greedy little pussy gush all over me. Show me how fucking *mine* you are, *wife*."

His swollen cock rams deep as my body wrenches and spasms. My breath catches and my vision goes black.

And then I'm coming harder than I've ever come in my *life*.

It's like detaching from reality. Like my body is blowing into a million pieces as he fucks me to my release. I scream into the bed, clawing at the sheets, clenching them in my fists, biting them with my teeth. My eyes squeeze shut, my legs kicking out behind me as the spasming, shuddering tidal wave of my orgasm explodes through my core.

"*There's* a good girl," Kenzo groans low in my ear, not even slowing, fucking me right through my orgasm. "There's my good little slut. I can feel your greedy cunt squeezing every inch of my cock, desperate for me to fill it with my cum—"

My eyes fly open.

"*Wait*!" I yelp as he fucks into me hard and mercilessly, his swollen cock spreading me wide and utterly claiming me. "Wait, you can't come in—"

"Yes I can and yes I will."

Holy. FUCK.

It's the demanding tone in his words that shoves me over the edge all over again. I explode, screaming into and biting the sheets as I come undone. Kenzo groans, burying his fat cock balls-deep in me as I feel him swell and surge. He grunts, and I whimper when I feel the hot flood of his cum spill into me.

...And I know that nothing is ever going to be the same again.

15

ANNIKA

It's light out the second time I wake up.

Alone.

I blink myself out of the haze of sleep. Feeling nobody at my back, I roll over, almost expecting him to be there. But it's just me in the bed as the morning sunlight peeks through the shades and into Kenzo's bedroom.

I close my eyes, sinking into the pillows again.

Holy. *Hell.*

Whatever last night was, it was...beyond intense. Beyond comprehension and anything I've ever even dared myself to fantasize about.

It was fucking *good.*

My head hurts a little; a lingering gift from the obscene amount of vodka I downed in twenty minutes flat last night. And I know I was still less than sober when what happened...happened.

But I have *zero* regrets.

Yes, Kenzo might be an arrogant, walking asshole with control issues. We might not even *like* each other very much. But if I'm going to be legitimately married to someone—especially someone with a flair for possessiveness who I'd guess is the last man on Earth to be okay with me "seeking it elsewhere"—than I suppose it's pretty fucking great that we seem to have fantastic physical chemistry.

Silver lining to every cloud, and all that.

I sit up in bed, wincing as another throb of the hangover stabs into my temples. Then I tense up as I spread my legs a little gingerly.

Fuck, am I sore. Like...everywhere, but especially between my legs. I open them wider, holding the sheets away from my naked body to glance down at myself.

What the actual shit...

It looks like I went nine rounds in a cage match with a prize fighter. Or maybe a goddamn tiger.

There are *claw marks* on me, for fuck's sake. Bruises cover my breasts, my hips, my ass and my thighs, and when I bring my hand up to the soreness ringing my neck, I feel more bruises there. I grit my teeth as I glance over my shoulder, making a face at the fucking *bite* mark there.

Okay, last night was *crazy* good. But I don't know if I'll survive another session like that with him again.

I consider that I don't actually have any clothes as I swing my legs out of bed. There's my wedding dress, but I don't see it anywhere. Who knows what Kenzo did with it after he took it off me last night.

While I was sleeping.

Something wicked, dark and illicit sparks inside me as I let that sink in. The man *stripped me naked* while I was asleep.

He could have done *anything*.

Part of me wonders if he did, even though he said he didn't.

...And an even more fucked-up part of me gets excited at the prospect that he might have.

You need fucking help, self.

I get out of bed and start to wrap the comforter around myself. Then I spot the pile of folded clothes on the end of the bed, which I'm guessing are for me: sweatpants and a hoodie. I can already tell just by looking at them that I'm going to be *swimming* in them.

Still, better than walking out there naked.

Nothing he hasn't seen, but again, I'm not sure I'd survive if he decided to have a round two this morning.

As good as that honestly sounds...

I chase the thought away as I venture into Kenzo's bathroom and turn on the shower. The water stings at first as it cascades over my bruised body, and forget facing the spray—my nipples say hell-to-the-fuck-no to *that*. But as the warm steam envelops me, the aches and soreness slowly melt a little.

Three aspirins and a quick towel-dry later, I'm slipping into the crazy oversized sweatpants and hoodie that I'm sure are his. On the plus side, the enormous hood acts as a giant baggy turtleneck, hiding the vicious bruises around my throat.

Although... Something tells me he'd *like* to see those. Like a beast likes to smell its scent on a trail. Or a conquering king likes to place his flag on the enemy's palace.

The smell of sweet, merciful coffee hits me when I walk out of Kenzo's bedroom. I start to walk toward it, but I suddenly jump as a tall, dark figure steps menacingly out of the doorway to what looks like a study of some kind.

Takeshi glares down at me, jutting out his chin at me.

"Good...morning?" I mumble, frowning up at him.

Kenzo's brother doesn't have the highest opinion of me. And I can't imagine me slashing his tires when I thought they were Kenzo's did much to improve that sentiment.

"Morning," he grunts, his brow furrowing deeper. "I got an email earlier to schedule the delivery of a motorcycle I didn't buy."

I resist the urge to grin.

"Yeah?"

I mean, Takeshi might not like me, but my beef is with his brother, not him. And since Hana has turned out to be so freaking cool, and Takeshi *is* her twin...

Let's just say that while we were in Montreal, before my phone died, I *may* have made a little purchase as a peace offering.

"Yeah," Takeshi scowls. "A Kawasaki ZX10R."

"Wow." I nod thoughtfully. "That's a pretty sweet ride."

I didn't just replace his tires.

I bought him a whole new bike. Go big or go home, right?

Takeshi eyes me, his muscled arms folded over his broad chest. "Your adoptive daddy foot the bill for that?"

"Did yours, for *your* last bike?"

"I pay my own way, *witch*," he snaps coldly.

"Funny. So do I."

His mouth twists. "Don't try to buy loyalty from me."

I sigh. "I wasn't buying shit. It was an apology." I lift a shoulder. "I shouldn't have fucked with your bike. I was mad."

"And?"

God, is nothing easy with *any* of the Mori brothers?

"And I'm sorry. Truly. It was shitty of me."

Takeshi glares at me a moment longer. I nod at the phone in his hand.

"You see it's coming with the new Akrapovič exhaust mount?"

Takeshi cocks a brow. For one second, his usual mask of violence and bloodlust slips a little, and I *might* have even caught a glimpse of something approaching "impressed."

"You know bikes?"

I nod. "Yup."

"Why, because you fucking steal them?"

"Yup."

He smirks.

"I mean, partly."

"What's the other part?" Takeshi growls.

"That I don't get *caught* when I steal them because I know how to ride, too."

Takeshi's lips curl up a little at the corners. "What were you mad about. At the hospital."

I stay silent.

"My brother?"

I glance away and he chuckles. "Yeah, he's good at that," he smirks. Then he exhales. "Okay, it's a pretty fucking sweet bike."

"You're welcome."

"I wasn't thanking you. Though, it would've been nice to have it delivered to Kyoto instead of here."

"Oh, are you going back to Kyoto?"

Takeshi grins widely as his brows shoot up. "*Shit*. This is going to be *good*."

"I'M FUCKING SORRY!?" I snap coldly as I barge into the kitchen.

Kenzo looks up from where he's sitting at the counter with a cup of coffee and scowls at me. "Yes? Can I *help you?*"

"*Kyoto*?! I'm not moving to fucking Kyoto."

He exhales slowly. "Well, *I am,* and you're my wife. Soooo..."

"So go fuck yourself," I hurl back. "I'm not going."

"You can come or you can be *brought*. Which is to say, you can accompany me willingly or I can *make you*."

"Like you *made me* last night?"

Okay, that's a cheap shot. And a shitty thing to say when we were both so clearly into what transpired last night, *including* the use of force, and him pinning me down, and continuing even when I said no.

"Excuse me?" Kenzo growls, a warning note in his voice. I ignore it.

"I was blind drunk, and you knew it," I snap. "The phrase 'taken advantage of' comes to mind, wouldn't you agree?"

"Certainly not," he snarls coldly, rising from his chair in a way that sends a bolt of lightning through my core. "And I do not take kindly to being accused of something like *that*."

I swallow in embarrassment. Yeah, I've overstepped bigtime.

"Well—"

"Well *nothing*," he spits, storming over to me and looming down into my face. "You were wide awake."

"And you just helped yourself to my bed."

"Technically"...he grabs my wrist..."it's *my* bed, and married people tend to share them."

I tug at my arm. "Let go of me."

"No. Not until you admit that you came like a greedy little slut all over my cock last night. *Several* times."

I look down, my face throbbing.

"Well?"

I shrug.

"I'm waiting."

"*Fine*," I mutter, blushing fiercely. "Fine. It was…good."

"That's not what I asked."

"Okay, I—"

"You will look at me when you're talking to me, princess."

I fume, my teeth grinding as I drag my gaze up to his. The minute I lock eyes with his gorgeous black ones, all the fiery sass in me snuffs out.

"*Fine*, okay," I mumble.

"Fine, okay *what*."

Oh my God, he's going to make me say it to his face.

Asshole.

I draw in a breath, squaring my shoulders. "Fine, *okay*," I breathe. "I *came*, okay?"

"Like?"

Kenzo just smiles, raising a brow.

"Any time, princess."

"Like…like a…"

"Starts with a G, rhymes with needy little slut…"

I shoot him a withering glare.

"I *came*," I mutter darkly. "Like a greedy little slut."

His brow cocks expectantly, and I sigh.

"*Several times*."

"Good girl."

He lets go of my wrist and I yank it back, trying to squash down the tingling, needy feeling I get from being called that.

Kenzo turns and walks back to his coffee.

"You didn't use a condom."

He sips from his mug, not looking at me. "I did not."

"Well?!"

"Well, what?"

I stare at him open-mouthed. "*Well,* pregnancy is a thing!" I snap. "And who the fuck knows what I could have caught from you!"

He glares at me. "Right back at you."

I glare back. "I do *not* have any STDs. Ass."

"Well, *I* don't know that."

"I do!" I blurt. "As for *you,* who knows where you've been sticking that thing."

"'That thing' doesn't like to be called *that thing,*" he frowns.

"I honestly couldn't give less of a shit. And please don't tell me you've named your dick."

"I haven't," he mutters. "That includes 'that thing.'"

I roll my eyes. "What I'm saying is, who the hell knows where you've been."

"I do," he hisses. "And it's nowhere bad."

I wrinkle my nose. "I really don't want to talk about it."

Kenzo snorts. "No, you know what? I think we should. How about you? Where have *you* been?"

I fix him with a withering look. "You're an asshole."

"And you're avoiding the question."

"*Trust me*," I mutter. "I don't have any STDs. Okay?"

Kinda easy to be sure of that when you've only slept with *one* person ever, and tested clean after you managed to escape them.

Kenzo rolls his eyes. "What, are you actually trying to sell me on you being a thirty-three-year-old virgin?"

"Fuck off," I mutter, turning away from him.

"Give me a list."

I whirl back. "*Excuse me*?"

"A list."

"*Of*?"

His face darkens. "All the men you've been with."

My jaw drops as I stare at him with fury in my eyes.

"Are you even fucking for real right now?"

"Do I look like I'm joking, princess?"

I spin to leave. Suddenly, I'm yanked backward and around as he grabs my arm.

"The fuck you are. Let's not forget that there are two things going on here. You're my *wife* to stop a war—"

"I—"

"But you'll be whatever else I want you to be," he hisses quietly. "As your *punishment*."

"For what?" I spit. "Having a freaking sex life before you?"

His jaw grinds. “No. For fucking *drugging* me and stealing from me.”

I shiver at the sheer malevolence in his eyes, leveled at mine.

“W-what does that entail?” I mumble.

Kenzo’s lips curl. I tremble as he leans down and whispers in my ear. “Whatever I want.”

I try and fail to ignore the needy throb that pulses in my core.

“So, what, you want to fuck me again? Is that what this is going to be?”

He chuckles quietly to himself, pulling away, shaking his head and fixing me with an amused look.

“So greedy and *eager*.”

My face flushes with heat. “That was meant as an insult.”

“It came off as desperate and needy, but okay.”

“Fuck. You,” I snap. “How about this: hard pass.”

“To?”

I smile smugly. “Sex. I’ll be your wife in public, but that’s it. Enjoy your blue balls because you’ll be getting nothing from—”

He yanks me into him, spinning us and pinning the small of my back to the kitchen island behind me. My thighs squeeze tight as he looms over me and cups my jaw, lifting my face to his in this outrageously possessive, dominant way that…

Does things to me.

"Here's what's going to happen," he growls quietly. "You're going to say it again."

I gulp. "Say what, exactly?"

His smile says it all. I shake my head.

"Not happening."

"It is. Admit that you came like a greedy little slut all over my cock last night. Several times."

I glare up at him. He smirks right back. The tension crackles between us until finally I can't take the fierceness of his gaze any longer.

"*Okay,* fine," I mumble. "Whatever. Yes, I orgasmed."

"Once again, that was not my question." My breath stutters as he leans down into me, his eyes slicing me in two. "*Say it.*"

My face flushes as something unignorable twists and pulls at my center.

"I..." My blush spreads and darkens. "I...came a lot last night," I mumble.

"Like...?"

I try to look away, but his grip on my chin tightens, pulling my eyes right back to his.

"*Like a greedy little slut,*" I whisper hoarsely.

"Where."

Oh my God, he can't be serious.

"*Where,* princess?"

I wet my lips, my breath coming faster.

"All over your cock."

Just saying it has my core melting and heat pooling between my thighs. Kenzo smirks, a supremely arrogant look of triumph on his face. But he doesn't pull away. His hand doesn't leave my chin as he holds it fast.

"Good girl."

Sweet fucking hell.

I was wet before.

Now I'm *soaked.*

"I'll bet this pretty little pussy is nice and fucking messy for me now, isn't it."

I'm already shaking; when I feel his other hand slide over my hip, my skin pebbles to goosebumps. His fingers deftly slip under the hem of my baggy hoodie, teasing across bare skin as he slowly circles to my front, dancing his fingertips over my stomach.

He leans down to my ear. My breath involuntarily sucks in as I feel his hand slip into the waistband of the sweatpants.

"Let's. Find. Out."

His warm palm presses to my skin as his big hand pushes down into the sweats. My entire body trembles, and I bite back a whimper as his touch moves lower and lower. Slowly, his thick finger rolls over my swollen clit and sinks between my lips.

My world blurs at the edges, and I moan as I cling to the counter behind me. My hips begin to move on their own, pushing forward as his finger runs up and down my lips in a teasing motion.

"What a fucking *messy* pussy."

I groan, sucking in air through clenched teeth as he suddenly sinks a finger into me. It's not the three from last night. And it's nowhere near the size of his cock.

But it's still *so fucking good.*

Kenzo curls his finger inside, stroking against my g-spot as I start to writhe between him and the counter. My breath turns halting and haggard, my core clenching, my eyes rolling back.

"You want me to fuck you again, princess?" Kenzo breathes into my ear.

His teeth come out to play, biting sharply on my earlobe before his mouth drops to my neck. I'm still so fucking sore there, but I don't care. I *crave* the pain when he bites down, putting bruises on top of bruises as his finger strokes in and out of me.

"That's what you want, isn't it? You want me to spread your legs and ram my thick cock deep into your pretty, pink pussy until you're coming all over me like a greedy little slut. You want me to empty my fucking balls inside you again."

I'm hanging onto the counter for dear life as my whole world begins to shatter. I can feel my walls gripping his finger tightly and my core clenching as the wave begins to crest over me.

"You want me to make this slutty little pussy come, my good girl?"

My whole face scrunches up, and my mouth falls open as I prepare to fall over the edge.

Abruptly, Kenzo's finger slips out of me. He yanks his hand

out of my sweats as my eyes fly open in confusion and protest.

What—!

Kenzo is smiling coldly at me, his eyes full of gloating smugness as he leans close to my ear again.

"Hard. Pass."

I choke and sputter.

"Enjoy the blue balls, *princess*."

Without another word, he turns and walks out of the kitchen, leaving me shaking and clinging to the counter, with a mortifying and now uncomfortable wetness dripping down my thighs.

Asshole.

16

ANNIKA

Even though I've been here about a zillion times, I'm always struck by the sheer opulence of Kir's mansion whenever I step inside. Or even drive through the grand front gates, past the guards that watch as you make your way up the curved white-stone driveway to the massive front door beneath the portico.

I mean, the place is *gorgeous*.

Kir keeps an apartment in Manhattan, but he's had this house up in the Bronx for years. It's an older home that was once owned by the Vanderbilts—yeah, *those* Vanderbilts—during the Gilded Age, complete with gold inlay *everything*, white and rose marble, soaring vaulted ceilings, and priceless impressionist and modern art on the walls. The grounds are gorgeous, with roses, fountains and perfectly manicured hedges, and it even boasts an underground garage large enough for Kir's—and Damian's—vast collection of classic cars.

I remember almost being put off by the display of wealth at first. I mean, I grew up with money—Taylor and I lived *extremely* well in Serbia, in a mansion bigger than this one, with sprawling, fairytale grounds—but there's an added...*something* to Kir's estate that gives it an edge.

Maybe it's the fact that this is only one of *seven* homes he owns, all equally breathtaking.

For a long time, when I was out on my own, money like that didn't make you powerful to me; it made you a *mark*. I also equated wealth with lousy character. The people I'd encountered who had that sort of money were almost always insufferable, arrogant shitheads.

But Kir changed my thoughts on that as he moved from someone I did business with to essentially family. Because he really is different. He came from nothing, bled, fought, and almost died on the streets, and then built an empire from scratch. Now, he's a literal billionaire who runs one of the most powerful Bratva families on the planet, and even sits at the Iron Table.

There's no arrogance or shitty character. Just steely resolve and unwavering strength.

And, okay, a little dash of violence. That's the Bratva for you.

I find him in his office, pacing the room with a scowl on his face and his phone glued to his ear. He catches sight of me but doesn't smile, just shoots me a look and holds up a finger up before whirling to bark into the phone in Russian.

I used to think it was odd that Kir never married, or even dated. For a while, Freya and I nurtured a pet theory that he was gay but closeted because he had decided that having a boyfriend wasn't a good look for him as head of a major Bratva family. Which is a stupid idea, but who knows.

As time went on, though, we ditched that theory. It's not that Kir prefers the company of men. He's just married to his empire.

A little over forty, the man has the physique of a professional athlete half his age, outrageous good looks, a full head of hair, and piercing blue eyes.

And, for real. The guy needs some female company in his life *besides* Frey and me. Like, *that kind* of female company.

I wait until he's done tearing someone a new one in Russian. When he's done with the call, he rolls his neck and cracks his knuckles before turning back to me.

"*You*," he grunts, as in "Your turn to get chewed out."

I frown. "What? I wanted to talk to you about this insane idea that I'm moving to fucking Japan—"

"Sit."

The fuck? Kir never addresses me like this, or commands me.

"Excuse me?"

His Paul Newman blue eyes glint dangerously.

"I said *sit*, Annika."

My brow furrows even deeper. There's something about this tone—at least, this tone being used on *me*—that's unnerving.

I walk over and sit on one of the sofas near the large black marble fireplace set into the bookshelves of his office.

Kir remains standing as he leans against the mantel and folds his arms over his broad chest.

"What's going—"

"You got involved with *Ulkan Gacaferi*?!"

Oh, fuck me.

I clear my throat. "What? No—"

"Goddammit, Annika," Kir hisses. "Do *not* lie to my fucking face."

I grimace, my shoulders sagging.

"Who told you?"

"You, just now," he spits.

Double fuck me.

"But I had a hunch before you just confirmed it."

I grit my teeth and look away. "A hunch, or Isaak had a snoop into my personal business?"

Kir snorts. "The second you and Freya decided to work with that psychopath, you damn well made it my business, too." He levels a withering look at me and jabs a finger my way. "That was fucking him the other night at Sota's, wasn't it?"

I shake my head. "I—"

"I swear to God, Annika, if you lie to my face twice in one day, there will be consequences."

"I honestly don't know," I say miserably. "Truthfully."

"Full story. Now."

I take a slow, deep breath.

Here goes nothing.

When I'm done telling Kir about the job we took for Ulkan stealing the Lambo, he stares at me like I'm insane.

I mean, he's not far off.

"*Valon Leka*?" he snarls.

I resist the urge to flinch when I hear the actual name spoken aloud.

"You stole from *Valon*." He swears viciously in Russian as he whirls and shoves his fingers through his hair. "*Fuck*, Anni," he hisses. "You know we're in talks to go into business with him!"

I look away, my teeth sinking into the flesh inside my mouth.

I decided a long time ago that when the man who hurt me, abused me, and gaslit me went from having a name to being exclusively referred to as "he who shall not be named" by Freya and I, he became a part of my past, buried in a locked box, with the key thrown into the ocean.

Then, not so long ago, Kir casually mentioned—to my horror—that he might be going into business with the fucker.

I could have told him. I *should* have told him. I could tell him right now, and there's no doubt in my mind that Kir would immediately go put a bullet in the bastard's head.

But the man standing in front of me has given me *so fucking much*: Purpose. Power. A new start in life.

Protection, family and love.

It's sort of the same as how I keep my messy life separate from Taylor's tidy one. Kir has built this empire from nothing and been kind enough to bring me and Freya along for the ride.

He doesn't deserve the chaos I bring with me stemming from my own bad choices.

That's why I never have, and never will, tell him the truth about my history with that fuck.

"Does he know?"

I flinch at the sound of Kir's voice.

"Sorry, what?"

"Valon," he says, totally unaware of the anxiety that name spoken out loud brings me. "Does he know it was you who took the damn car?"

I hate lying to Kir, so I rarely do. Today, I'm making an exception.

"No," I shake my head. "Not a chance."

He exhales slowly, his shoulders unclenching with relief. "Good," he breathes. "Good."

I clear my throat. "So, Kyoto—"

"You're going."

I stare at him. "*What??*"

"Annika, someone *shot* at you the other night," he hisses tightly. "Then a bomb drove into your wedding."

I swallow. "Look, we both know any violence this early in the treaty with Sota could destroy—"

"You think I give a fuck about the treaty?" he murmurs quietly, his brow furrowing deeply. "Anni, I give a fuck about *you*."

He looks at me with genuine pain and concern.

"I'm sending you to Japan because *I'm worried sick about you!*" he hisses. "You're family to me, Annika. I will *not* sit by idly while any harm comes to you."

I shake my head. "Kir, you have men here in New York. I'm completely—"

"And Kenzo has a fortress and an *army*," he growls. "In Kyoto."

I stare at him. "Kir—"

"This isn't a discussion, Annika," he growls.

"Fuck that!" I hiss, lurching to my feet. "I'm *not*—"

His phone dings loudly, cutting me off. Kir yanks it angrily from his jacket pocket and glares at it.

"Hey! I'm still talking!" I spit at him. "I'm a grown fucking woman, and I am *not* going to just be sent—"

"Annika."

Kir's smiling as he looks up at me from the screen.

"Damian is awake."

"FUCK ME."

I sigh, grinning as I roll my eyes.

"First of all, I'm flattered, but I just don't think of you that way?"

The doctors are only letting us in one at a time to see Damian. Kir pulled rank and went in first. Freya and I played rock-paper-scissors for second, and I lost. But here I am, finally seeing him.

He looks…well, like he's been shot. He's a little gaunter than usual, having been lying in a hospital bed for a few weeks instead of spending half of each day at the gym. But he still looks like the Damian I love.

Plus, *he's alive.*

He grimaces and shoots me a look. "Don't be gross, Anni."

I grin. "Well, and I don't know if you've heard, but I'm a married woman these days."

A shadow crosses Damian's face, his lavender eyes darkening.

"I fucking *hate* that you had to do that because of me."

I scowl as I punch him playfully in the arm. "Shut the fuck up."

"Okay, *ow*?" He rubs his arm. "Remember the part where I got fucking shot?"

"Sorry," I quip. "I'll hold back on the punching."

"Yeah, could you?" he mutters, a small smile on his lips. He exhales and reaches up to run his fingers through his white hair. "Fucking hell. I wake up from one goddamn fight to find you married to *Kenzo*?"

I smile wryly, looking away.

I refuse to let my mind drift to the events of last night.

Or this morning.

"It's not your fault, Damian."

He shakes his head. "I… Fuck, I don't know, Anni. I mean, Aoki drew first, I'll say that."

"Damian—"

"But maybe if I'd just winged him instead of killing him?" He grits his teeth. "Or if I hadn't even been *at* the club for that meeting—"

"*Damian,*" I hiss sharply. "It is what it is, okay? You know me and dwelling on the past."

He smiles wryly. "What's done is done."

"Exactly."

He grimaces. "I still fucking hate that you had to get married and I wasn't even there to cause a scene and tell Kenzo to go eat a bag of dicks."

"No time like the present…"

He chuckles and then winces, bringing his hand to the bandage covering his healing wound on his side.

"So. Kyoto," he grunts.

I roll my eyes. "Kir's orders."

"He's not wrong, you know," Damian growls. "I mean he filled me in on all the shit I've missed. New York is too fucking hot right now. When you don't know where your enemy is coming from, or even who the fuck they are, you don't stand your ground and risk getting shot in the back. You retreat and regroup."

"That's not my style."

He rolls his eyes. "Go to Kyoto, Anni. Seriously. I may not like Kenzo, but I respect him. He's a prick, but he's a man of his word. And this truce means as much to him and Sota as it does to us. He won't let someone take you out and potentially destroy that fragile peace."

I scowl and look down at my hands.

"But *also*," he grunts. "The second they spring me from here, I'm flying to Kyoto so I can keep an eye on the fucker who's decided to play house with you."

I grin at him. "For real?"

"Not even a question," he mutters.

I smile as I reach over and squeeze his hand. "Okay. *Fine*. I'll go. But do me a favor?"

"Anything."

"Resist your urge to fuck things up and just focus on healing?"

Damian grins. "I think I can do that."

"Good. If you don't, I'll shoot you again myself."

LATER, I stop by Taylor and Drazen's to talk to my sister about what's going on.

"You shouldn't have been there and been put in danger like that—"

"Anni." Taylor smiles quietly as she takes my hand. "I know you say your life is messy and complicated. But, I mean..." She turns and nods across her and Drazen's ridiculous palace of an apartment, where her husband is standing on one of the balconies high above Central Park on a business call.

"I married *into* messy and complicated. And danger." She turns back to me. "You don't have to worry about me, ever. With him?" She smiles as she looks at Drazen again with this look of sheer...

Love.

Joy.

Contentment.

A synchronicity with another human that I've never felt.

"I'm always safe with him. *And,*" she eyes me, "I want *you* to be safe, too. If that means going to Kyoto until things cool down here?" She shrugs. "Then I think you should go enjoy a little well-earned vacation in Japan."

"It's just..." My face scrunches up. "I just feel like we only just found each other."

She smiles as she pulls me close and hugs me tight.

"Me too," she whispers. "But if it's all right with you, I'd like to *continue having* what we only just got back to. And that requires you remaining alive."

I hug her fiercely. Drazen comes back inside and I hug him, too, and make him promise to keep my twin safer than safe.

Then it's home to pack.

And *then*, it's off into the unknown yet again.

17

ANNIKA

I'VE BEEN on private jets before. Kir owns one that's as stunning as his eight homes, and I'm not gonna lie, that thing is one *sweet* ride.

But flying on Sota's massive 747 is next level. There are two floors, complete with a main cabin, individual bedrooms, an office and conference room, a dining area with a freaking sushi chef, a bar, and a gym.

Yes. On a *plane*.

A few hours into the flight, I've already watched *Air Force One* and *Snakes On A Plane*. Call me crazy, but it felt like appropriate viewing material for being taken to Japan on a jet against my will.

Eventually, my legs need stretching, and I take a little tour. I wind up at the sushi counter, where the chef greets me with a smile and begins to prepare the first course of an *omakase* tasting menu.

"I hope you don't mind if I join you?"

Startled, I turn to see Sota.

"Not at all. I mean," I smile wryly, "it's your plane."

The older man chuckles as he takes a seat at the counter next to me. The chef bows to his boss, quickly pours a carafe of sake, and slides it over.

"Sake?" Sota asks, turning to me.

"I'm actually taking a small break from drinking."

He arches a brow, not looking away.

"I mean… Yeah, sure, why not," I shrug.

Sota chuckles as the chef delivers two little sake cups before bowing again and going back to preparing the sushi.

"Jiro doesn't know any English," Sota says in his beautifully accented voice, nodding to the chef. "Feel free to speak freely."

He pours the sake as Jiro slides a plate in front of each of us with a stunningly arranged slice of hamachi over a light seaweed salad with what looks like sliced yuzu.

"*Kanpai*," the older Yakuza boss says gruffly, raising his glass.

"*Kanpai*."

"To a fruitful marriage," he says quietly. When he clocks the look I can't quite hide quickly enough, he smiles. "It may not have love," he continues. "But may it at least have peace, respect, and kindness."

Well, *that* was beautiful.

I take a sip of sake and pick up the chopsticks to taste my delicious first course. When I glance over at Sota, I notice something I never have before. My gaze drags down his forearm, over the *irezumi* ink, until it lands on his right hand.

…and the pinky finger that's missing the top half.

"When I was young," Sota says, catching me looking, and holding his hand up with a wry smile, "I was a bit like Takeshi. Headstrong, impulsive, wild." He chuckles. "Like Kenzo, too, although he at least keeps a level head."

"What happened?" I ask, frowning at his finger.

"I disrespected my *oyabun*," he says matter-of-factly. "In the Yakuza, respect is everything. Luckily, my *oyabun* was a wise man who saw potential in an otherwise headstrong youth. He could have asked for my heart. Instead, it was only *yubitsume*."

I stare wide-eyed at his pinky again.

"He cut your finger off?"

Sota chuckles and shakes his head as he turns back to his hamachi.

"No." He takes a sip of sake. "*I* did."

Holy *fuck*.

I mean the Bratva is serious, and it frequently wanders deep into the hardcore part of the forest. But cutting off *your own finger* over a slight to your boss is *way* past that.

Sota sighs, glancing at me as we both finish our first plate. "Now you think the Yakuza is savage and merciless."

I could lie to him, but something about Sota makes you want to speak honestly.

"It's...a little extreme to me. Granted, that's just my opinion, not being from that world..."

"True," he nods. "But the Bratva is extreme in its own way, is it not?"

Good point.

"And though you were young and much of it may have been hidden from you, your father's empire was fairly *extreme* in certain ways as well."

I frown curiously. Sota smiles.

"I met him once. Your father."

Shock spreads over my face. "Seriously?"

He nods. "Not for business. We were both in Monaco and played poker together at a table. He was good," he chuckles ruefully. "He took a lot of money from me that night."

I smile privately. I don't think of my parents very often. But every once in a while I allow myself to, like a little treat.

"Yes, the Yakuza can be savage and extreme," Sota says as Jiro puts another plate, uni this time, in front of us. "But it's what saved me as a young man. I think it's what saved Kenzo's father Hideo, too. He was my best friend, you know. And I understand that at a certain point, he wanted out, for his family. But to me, the Yakuza *is* my family. It's my greatest love," he says fiercely, turning to me. "I believe it's what saved Kenzo, too."

"From?"

He shrugs. "Blandness. From wandering through life unsure of what he was and who he should be. He could easily have stayed in England with his mother, God rest her soul. He could have lived his life on the periphery of the aristocracy, never *quite* being accepted into their ranks. But blood speaks, and his blood brought him back to Japan. Back to the Yakuza. It's through that savageness and extremism that he's found himself. And now?" He turns to raise his glass to me, smiling. "It's how he's found *you*."

I smile back as I touch my cup to his. "*Kanpai*, Sota-san."

He grins. "*Kanpai*, Annika."

AFTER A *LOVELY* DINNER WITH SOTA, I meander toward the back of the plane, to the office and conference room area. It's unclear how long I'm going to be in Kyoto. But I've been prepping for an acquisition for Kir, and we're planning to make our move in the next three months. That means getting Kir's army of corporate lawyers and finance nerds all on the same page.

Hey, this is the job.

I'm on a video call on my laptop, sitting at the desk facing the rest of the conference room. Suddenly, the door to the room opens, and my face flushes a little as Kenzo walks in. I drag my eyes back to the screen, nodding at something someone's just said into my earbud. Then I'm aware of Kenzo walking right over to me.

"Excuse me one second," I say politely. I tap a button, muting my mic and turning off my camera as Kenzo leans against the desk right next to my monitor. "Can I *help you*," I mutter.

"Maybe," he growls, a spark of something dangerous in his eyes.

My core flutters and my face heats. But I swallow it back as I glare at him. "I'm on a video call."

He smirks. "Just what do you think I want that can't be done on a video call?"

My cheeks throb. "If you don't mind, some of us have work to do." I push at his hip, nudging him off the edge of the desk until he's out of view of the camera. "Excuse me," I say brusquely, turning back to the monitor and pushing the button to turn the camera and the mic back on.

One of Kir's lawyers is going over some contractual stuff. My focus is suddenly broken by movement past the monitor. I glance up, and my eyes bulge when I see Kenzo standing by the conference table, unbuttoning his black dress shirt and peeling it off his muscled, tattooed shoulders.

My lip catches between my teeth as I watch him drape it neatly over the back of a conference table chair.

His hands drop to his belt and start to undo it. That's when I hit the mute and camera off button again.

"What the fuck are you doing?"

He pulls off his pants, hanging them neatly over the chair next to his shirt. Then he turns to me, and I suck in a breath of air as I drink in his freaking *insane* body.

I mean, the man looks fucking photoshopped.

"Hello?" I hiss. "What the fuck?"

Kenzo shrugs. "It's another good few hours to Japan. I'm getting comfortable."

"Well, can you please do that somewhere else?"

Someone is calling my name in my ear.

Shit.

I quickly swing back to the monitor and unmute myself again, turning the camera back on.

"My apologies, the Wi-fi isn't great. I'm actually flying to Japan at the moment—"

I almost fall out of my chair when my eyes snap to the scene unfolding in front of me. Kenzo has walked right up to the desk, casually standing next to it just out of view of the camera, running a hand over his chiseled jaw.

He's completely naked.

My mouth falls open. I can't help it: my eyes drop *straight* to his dick. I mean for fuck's sake, it's *right there.* He's not even hard, but the freaking thing is still huge, and thick, and looks heavy as it hangs between his thighs.

"Excuse me, don't you have a video call to attend to?"

How can I? My full attention is embarrassingly fixated on Kenzo's cock.

How the actual *fuck* did that fit inside me? Like, within the boundaries of biology? I want to reiterate that he's *not even hard* right now.

"Annika?"

I rip my attention back to Kir's lawyer on the screen, blushing furiously.

"I apologize, Sean. There's a serious delay with this connection. Can you go ahead and email me the rest of the contract, so I can look it over? I'll set up a follow-up call once I've landed and settled in, and we can circle back to these points.

I want them set in stone before we walk into that conference room looking for blood."

"Sounds good, Annika," Sean smiles. "Enjoy the flight. We'll talk later."

I end the call and turn to glare daggers at Kenzo. He's already walking away, giving me an eyeful of his—I hate to admit it —*absurdly* sculpted, perfect ass.

"I'm sorry, is there something *wrong* with you?"

He half turns, arching a brow as he smirks at me from across the room, pulling on gray sweatpants and a black t-shirt that fits snug around his biceps. "I wouldn't have pegged you as a 'circle back to these points' kind of girl."

"Is there a legitimate reason you came in here? Or is it just fun for you to bother me?"

He smirks. "We should discuss our needs."

My brow furrows. "Excuse me?"

"Our needs. Sexually, I mean."

I roll my eyes, but my face pulses with heat as my every brain cell fixates on last night.

His hands on me. His possessive power and dominance over me.

The filthy way he talked to me, and touched me, and *fucked me* like I've never even imagined.

I swallow. "I don't know why we need to—"

"Every human has them," Kenzo says evenly. "We're married, so we should discuss them." His lips curl up coyly. "What, for example, are your kinks."

I stammer, flustered. "Kinks? I—I don't…" I catch my breath. "I don't have any."

Kenzo snorts. "Everyone does. Do you enjoy sex?"

My face tingles.

"It would appear you do," he purrs. "But I'd like to make sure."

I mean, I do *now*. I didn't, for the years I was under *his* control. After that, I just…didn't have it. Ever.

Until I did, with this man standing in front of me.

I could guess," Kenzo goes on. "And you could just tell me yes or no. Or even just give a thumbs up or thumbs down—"

"Jesus, are we seriously doing this?" I blurt, standing and crossing to the far side of the conference room.

"We're married, princess," he growls quietly as he takes a seat at one of the conference table chairs. "We should know where the boundaries lie." His lips turn up in a wicked smile. "Or indeed if there *are* any boundaries."

I shiver as his dark eyes stab into me.

"You *did* mention something about not being able to rape the willing…"

My eyes widen as fire erupts across my face. "That—"

"So maybe it's a rape kink," he growls.

Forbidden heat creeps up my spine and throbs in my core.

"*Consensual non-consent*, as they're calling it these days."

When I don't answer—because I don't trust myself to speak —he just smiles.

"I'll take that as a maybe. How about bondage."

"I don't want to talk about—"

"Ah, also a maybe," he says calmly.

I glare at him. "I didn't say that."

"You didn't say *no*, either."

My lips purse. "Okay, *no*. No bondage," I mumble, completely unconvincingly.

"Final answer?"

I bite my lip. Kenzo smirks.

"Staying on the maybe list, then."

"What about you?" I snap back. "What gets you going? Mommy issues?"

He looks amused. "Low blow, but *no*."

"Fisting?" I blurt, going for the weirdest shit I can think of. "Pissing on people?"

Kenzo's brows arch, an amused look on his face. "No, but if that's *your* thing, I'm sure I can be convinced to give it a try."

"Absolutely *not*."

"Which one?"

My face throbs. "*Both*."

"Are you sure about that?"

I roll my eyes. "Will you just tell me whatever weird thing you're into so I can tell you it's not happening and we can move on?"

He shrugs. "Gladly." His eyes fix on me. "Bondage," he growls.

Oh.

Yeah, that's not a "maybe" for me.

...It might be a *yes*.

But like most things sexual, it's been tainted for me. It's been weaponized and used to control me by a man I *loathe*. Still, to say I've never fantasized about being tied down...or otherwise immobilized...and *used* would be a lie.

Kenzo stands and slowly crosses the room to the corner I've retreated to, until he's standing right in front of me.

"*Control*," he murmurs quietly.

He reaches up, and I shudder when the back of his finger lightly brushes my throat.

"Free use."

My face blooms with forbidden heat as my thighs tighten. Kenzo smirks.

"I'll take it from that you know what that is."

"I..." I swallow, my breath coming faster. "*Yes*."

"Anytime, anywhere," he growls darkly. "I have control over you."

"Just you over me?" I toss back, in a vain attempt to keep myself on some semblance of an equal footing.

"Or we can make it go both ways."

I roll my eyes. "*How* generous. And if I say no?"

"Are you?" he murmurs, his finger slowly stroking up and down the side of my throat. "Saying no?"

I swallow hard, but say nothing.

"Hm...another *maybe*," Kenzo purrs. "My, this is getting interesting."

He drops his hand and turns, walking calmly to one of the chairs at the conference table behind him and sitting.

"Come here."

It's not just the soft but commanding tone. It's not the stupidly hot British accent.

It's the way he crooks his finger at me in that "come hither" way. It just...*does something* to me.

Before I can second guess myself, or put up any sort of defense against the traitorous feelings inside me, I'm moving toward him. I go to sit in the chair next to him, but Kenzo shakes his head.

"Here," he murmurs, patting his lap.

"What?" I choke.

"Come. *Here*," he growls softly, crooking his fingers again and pointing at his thighs.

My face erupts with heat as I sit on his lap. Then I shiver and gasp as he turns me around and boldly yanks me over his legs, face down.

"*Kenzo*!"

My eyes bulge and my breath chokes off as he grabs hold of the back of my yoga pants and yanks them down over my ass to mid-thigh with a strong jerk of his arm.

"What the *fuck*—!"

I yelp as he grabs my panties, pulling them down as well. My whole world explodes, my face tingling and my body throbbing not only with shame but also a vicious need for something *more.*

Something dark.

I tremble, feeling intensely exposed and vulnerable.

I've felt like this before. But this time is different. This time, it's not a weapon being used against me, to torture me and to keep me in place.

This time, there's something weirdly freeing about what he's doing. What he's allowing to blossom inside me.

What he's unlocking from deep in my psyche.

He-who-will-not-be-named was a monster. His intentions were vile and corrupt. Kenzo might be a dick, maybe even a little psychotic. We might be enemies.

But he's *not* a monster.

So when his hand slides up the back of my thigh and over my ass, I don't flinch or crawl in on myself. I don't block it out or retreat.

I embrace it.

I breathe it in.

I let the heat of his touch and the scorch of his gaze melt into my skin and set me ablaze.

Kenzo's big hand grabs one of my ass cheeks. My face throbs with embarrassment when he spreads me wide open, and I feel cool air against the slickness between my thighs.

"What…" My voice is shaky. "What are you—"

"Whatever I want, princess," he growls. "Don't forget, you're *my wife*. You're *mine*—all of you. Including," he murmurs, "this pretty little pussy."

His hand slides between my thighs, and I bite back a moan when one of his fingers teasingly drags up my lips.

"Isn't that right," he says quietly.

"I—I—"

"Say it."

I defiantly shake my head.

"*SAY* it," he growls.

I pause. "I-it's yours," I finally mumble, heat pulsing in my face.

Kenzo chuckles darkly. "*What* is."

"My…" I swallow. "My…vagina."

He sighs heavily. "Princess, princess. You can do better than that."

I yelp as he casually swats my ass, making the skin erupt with fire and heat. He does it again to the other cheek, making me simmer and squirm with desire. I feel him reach for something in his pocket. Then his hand slips back between my slightly spread thighs, teasing over my wetness.

"What are you—"

I whimper, biting my lip as I feel something hard and rubbery slide into me. My eyes roll back in pleasure as it sinks deep, and it's only then that I realize that it's U-shaped. One end rests inside against my g-spot, the other end of the U sitting against my clit.

My whole body begins to tremble.

I hear the click of a button being pushed.

Oh FUCK…

The toy starts sending vibrations radiating through my core like tidal waves. It's almost *too* intense, but just shy of being unbearable. I try and bite back the moan, but there's no stopping the audible cry of pleasure as the throbbing rumbling against my clit and my g-spot send me hurtling into an abyss.

"Now," Kenzo murmurs darkly over the vibrating hum turning me into a puddle on his lap. "Let's try that again, shall we?" His palm spanks my ass, hard, making me yelp as I sob in pleasure. "Say it."

"It's...yours!" I choke, clinging to his muscled thighs and squirming against them.

"What is? Try harder."

My world melts as my mouth goes slack. "M-my…*pussy*!" I whimper.

"Is?"

"*Yours*!" I whine loudly as the waves crash over me.

I can't believe I'm saying or doing this. I don't "submit". I *never* submit, to anyone. But right now, I'm craving it. Desperate for it.

The pulsing of the toy is my entire world. The pleasure is all I know. His thumb slips into my mouth, fucking my lips shallowly as I moan around it.

"So nice and wet, princess," he growls.

His thumb slips out with a soft pop. Then I can feel him slowly moving his hand back…

His thumb teases against my ass.

Jesus…

"Kenzo, I'm not—"

"I don't remember asking for your opinion or permission, princess," he murmurs.

I moan deeply as his wet thumb circles the rim of my tight hole, before suddenly he's slipping it inside.

Holy fuck…

I feel something else push against my lips. For a minute, I think it's his other thumb. But when I take it inside, I realize it's another rubber toy, although it's shaped differently from the one pulsing against my clit and g-spot.

"I'd get this *really* nice and wet, if I were you…"

I whimper, moaning as I tongue the toy, coating it in my spit. He slips it from my mouth as his thumb sinks deeper into my ass and then gently slips out.

The toy teases my back hole, and my eyes widen.

"Kenzo..."

Without warning, without asking, and without any preamble, he pushes the little toy into my ass.

FUCK.

I grunt, my legs shaking and my toes curling in the air. The butt plug sinks into me, widening to such a point that I choke on a whine before it suddenly narrows again to a flared base that rests against my ring.

It was just in my mouth. I know that it's fairly small. But holy fuck, it feels *huge* back there.

"Interesting," Kenzo murmurs.

A choked moan tumbles from my mouth. "Wh—what?"

"You've never had anyone here, have you."

He's right.

"No," I whimper. I groan as he grabs both toys by the parts outside me, gently pushing them in and out as if fucking both my holes at the same time. My eyes roll back and my mouth goes slack. My nails dig into his firm, muscled thighs as I cling to him and moan in pleasure

"I'll enjoy stretching this little hole some day," Kenzo growls. "But first, *on your knees."*

"Wh—what?"

He leans down, his lips near my ear.

"You're going to get on your knees and swallow every inch of my cock like a good little whore."

It's like someone dumped ice water over my head and utterly doused the fire that was threatening to consume me.

You're such a good little whore, Annika. MY little whore.

Instantly—and I do mean *instantly*—whatever fierce desire I had is extinguished as memories of the shame, the darkness, and the abuse surge to the forefront of my thoughts.

I lurch away from Kenzo, scrambling off his lap and yanking my panties and pants up quickly.

He frowns, and starts to speak. I beat him to it.

"I'm not a *whore,"* I snarl coldly. I step back from him, my arms reflexively crossing over my chest as I look away. "I'm *not."*

He says nothing. Slowly, I glance back to him to see an impassive look on his face as he tilts his head and eyes me.

"I didn't—"

"You *literally just did*," I hiss.

He studies me thoughtfully.

"We're not done here," he finally growls.

"Trust me, *we are*."

I whirl, storming across the conference room and out the door. I march in a cold, angry haze back up to the main cabin and plop down in a seat next to Hana. She frowns, pulling out her earbuds and turning away from whatever she was watching to look at me with concern.

"You okay?"

"Yeah," I mumble. "I'm—"

Then my eyes bulge, and I have to slam a hand over my own mouth to stop from gasping aloud.

In my haste to escape the memories that were crowding forward, I've managed to storm back here with Kenzo's fucking toys *still inside me*.

...And they just started to rumble and move.

Both of them.

I squirm in my seat, clutching the armrest in one hand and twisting my head away to bite the heel of my other hand.

"Jesus, Annika," Hana blurts. "Are you—"

"*I-I'm fine*," I choke. "I just have to—"

Just as I'm about to get out of my chair and *run* to the bathroom to get these fucking things out of me, a firm, powerful hand lands heavily on my shoulder.

"Easy there, *wife*," he growls evenly.

I stare at him with a mix of "fuck you" and "are you crazy" as he smirks right in my face, reaches down, and clips my seatbelt in place. He tightens it against my stomach as I squirm and fight back the urge to moan.

"The captain just told me we're about to experience some turbulence."

He shoots me a slight grin that only I can see.

Lying sack of—

I gasp sharply as the plane jolts. Kenzo's smirk turns downright smug as he sits in the seat facing me.

He buckles up as the plain lurches again. Then he pulls his phone out of his pocket and smiles coolly at me as he holds it up and cocks a brow significantly.

Oh you FUCKER...

He taps the screen, open to the app or whatever that controls the fucking toys inside me. The buzzing, throbbing, and pulsing all ramp up a notch as I cling to the seat, a horrified look on my face even as the pleasure intensifies.

My eyes lock with his as his mouth curls dangerously.

"Strap in, *wife*," he grins. "It might be a *very* bumpy flight..."

18

KENZO

IT'S BEEN clear from the get-go that Annika and I are...*different*. Opposites.

At odds.

She's chaos, and I'm control. She's fire, I'm ice. She's fluidity, I'm order.

But the longer we're together, concrete examples of us being opposites get thrust in my face more and more.

For instance, I *hate* long flights. Even on a plane as sumptuous as Sota's, I feel trapped, like my life is on pause while the rest of the world keeps going. Annika, however, seems to enjoy them, at least this one.

She watched movies, took a tour of the facilities, had sake and sushi with Sota in the dining area, and then conducted a business meeting.

My favorite example of our differences so far might be what we find *entertaining*. For instance, *I* was happy to watch Annika squirm, bite her lip, grip her seat, and squeeze her mouth and eyes shut as I forced her to orgasm somewhere in the vicinity of four times via the remote control toys, while trapped in her seat due to the turbulence.

Annika, it would seem, *was not* as amused by that.

Imagining how much less amused she would be to know that the "turbulence" was actually just the pilots fucking around at my request is even *more* entertaining to me.

Eventually, once we leveled off, Annika basically levitated to the bathroom. She walked out ten minutes later looking furious, flustered and *very* worn out before she shoved the toys into my hands, wrapped in a wad of paper towels, and told me to "fucking choke on them."

Yeah, she hasn't seen the last of those.

We ride in silence as the car winds from the airport through old Kyoto to the mansion I've recently taken over.

Until recently, it belonged to the man that I thought had killed my father.

This city has been my home since I was eighteen and came to Japan to discover the Yakuza side of me. Everyone knew who I was—the *gaijin* that Sota had taken in like a stray. But they didn't know who I *was*. That I was heir to the Mori throne, I mean.

That's how I was able to infiltrate the Ito-kai: a rival Yakuza family led by Orochi Ito and his shit-bag nephew, Takato. Both "men"—I use the word loosely—completely without honor.

When my father tried to leave the world of the Yakuza, it was Orochi who turned on him and made moves to take over my father's empire before he'd even left. It ended in the car crash that killed Hideo's wife—Fumi's mother. I thought the crash had killed *Hideo*, as well.

Sota alone knew I was Hideo Mori's son. Meanwhile, Orochi was a stupid, vain man. So when I told him I was "tired of Sota's leadership" and "looking for a stronger, more powerful *oyabun*", the fool bought it hook, line, and sinker and welcomed me to his inner circle.

I spent a year "undercover" in the Ito-kai before the night I cut them off at the knees. Though it was *Fumi* who ended up dealing the final blow that ended their empire.

Since then, I've stepped out of the shadows. I'm still fiercely loyal to Sota, and I always will be. But after that night, the Yakuza world learned that the Mori-kai was on the way back to its former glory.

I took what I wanted from the wreckage of Orochi's organization: his warehouses, his connections, his politicians, his businesses.

I also took his fucking house.

I turn and watch with smug satisfaction as Annika realizes the stunning home sitting high on the cliffs overlooking Lake Biwa on the outskirts of Kyoto is our destination.

"*This* is where you live?" she whispers, her brows arching.

The mansion is a mix of contemporary and old-world Japan—soaring balconies, distinctly Japanese *kirizuma* gabled roofs, lush gardens. But it's also got walls of contemporary glass windows and all the modern luxuries.

It's also a fucking fortress.

High walls with electrified fencing at the top surround the grounds, which are patrolled by some of my most elite, highly trained guards. The front gate could hold off an army, and cameras cover almost every square inch of the place. Yet you'd never know most of these security measures and fortifications were in place unless you were looking for them. A person never feels like they're living in a prison while they're here.

I fucking love the place. So do my siblings, which is why they live here, too.

God knows it's big enough.

I allow the smug feeling at Annika's shocked expression to simmer inside me as I shrug.

"Do you like it?"

She tips her head, not looking at me. "It's...fine, I guess."

I roll my eyes.

The guards wave us through the front gates and onto the grounds. The driveway curves up from the lakeside road, winding through gardens, past staggered koi ponds, and under huge Japanese red maples until we get to the house itself.

I step out and smile.

Fuck, it's good to be home.

Hana is exhausted from the trip, and after giving Annika a hug and me a perfunctory nod, she heads off to the wing of the house she's sort of claimed as hers. Mal heads to one of the out-buildings on the property that he's adopted, and Takeshi grunts something about "seeing if the ladies missed him" before he saunters off to the huge garage that houses the car collection I "inherited" from Orochi, as well as a bunch of motorcycles.

Those would be Takeshi's "ladies".

An apartment over the garage is where he lives when he's here, because of course it is.

Sota's already back at *his* home in Minami Ward in central Kyoto. So after my siblings take off, it's just Annika and I standing by the front doors.

She glances my way. Go figure, she hasn't been able to meet my eyes fully since I made her orgasm four times on the plane.

"What, you don't have servants or whatever to show us to our rooms?"

I lift a brow. "How elitist of you."

She purses her lips. "I mean I'm *surprised* you don't have servants. Or slaves, or whatever."

"You have quite the low opinion of me, don't you?"

"I'm sure there's room for it to go lower, don't you worry."

I chuckle to myself as I open the front doors and step inside. Annika follows, and when I glance back, I grin at her failure to hide her stunned expression.

"I'm assuming Sota gave you this place?"

"What makes you think I didn't buy it myself?"

She eyes me doubtfully. "Did you?"

"No."

She rolls her eyes and makes her way slowly through the double-height front entryway.

"I stole it, actually." I grin at her shocked expression, then walk past her into the house. "Hungry?"

She shakes her head, still mostly avoiding my eyes.

It pisses me off. Because it's not *just* since I made her come on the plane. It started earlier, in the conference room, when I called her a whore.

The thing is, I wasn't literally calling her a whore. Not like *that*. I meant it as in "you're *my* little whore."

"Bad girl" and "slut" seemed to turn her into a fucking puddle when I called her those. But the W word was too much.

Violently so. Alarmingly so.

Tellingly so.

And that's what's pissing me off. Not that she's refusing to look me in the eye. But that there's something in that word that holds a dark, painful power over her. And I fucking want to know what it is.

"Not hungry at all?"

She shakes her head. "Honestly, I'm just tired."

"I'll show you to the bedroom."

Annika follows me through the house, gawking at the gorgeous views of Lake Biwa. You can even see the ruins of the 16th century Sakamoto Castle.

Upstairs, I lead her to the master suite. Her brow furrows.

"*All* of this is my bedroom?"

I smile. "*Our* bedroom."

Her eyes snap to mine and her jaw sets as her face heats. "Um, what? Hey—!"

My hand reaches up to cup her chin, lifting her defiant eyes to mine.

"You're still not really grasping this whole 'marriage' thing, are you?"

"Oh, I grasp it just fine," she mutters. "I just like my privacy."

"What's mine is yours, princess," I quip. "In sickness and in health—"

"Try and touch me again, and we'll get to 'til death do us part' sooner than you might like," she says evenly, an icy smile on her face.

"We've already consummated the marriage," I growl, smiling darkly at her. "I think it's been well established that what's yours is *emphatically* mine."

"Enjoy the memories," she mutters, her face dark as she looks away. "Because it's *not* happening again."

"Really," I smirk.

"Really."

"All because I called you the wrong bedroom name?"

Something I can't quite place flashes across her face. Something...supremely complicated. But after it passes, she shoots me one of her trademark defiant looks, saying nothing.

"I'm not a mind-reader, Annika," I grunt.

"It's not about that," she shrugs.

Bullshit.

"It's about you lacking any respect for my boundaries."

"I thought I'd made it clear that there'll *be* no boundaries between us," I grunt.

She swallows, and I relish the blush on her face.

"You walked into a meeting I was in and took out your fucking dick!" she spits. "I mean are you kidding me?"

Okay, that's fair. And I'm about to say as much...before she *keeps running her fucking mouth.*

"How the fuck would *you* like it if I walked into one of your business meetings and yanked my pants down and bent over?"

She clearly regrets saying it the nanosecond it flies out of her mouth.

"Okay, that—"

"I'd quite enjoy it, actually," I grin wolfishly. "And I'm willing to bet you would, too. You'd have my cock fucking that pretty little cunt of yours before your panties even hit the floor."

Annika's cheeks turn bright red as she stumbles over her words.

"Y-you're a pig."

I grin.

"You also"...the blush on her face turns crimson as she leans closer..."made me *orgasm*," she hisses.

"You're welcome?"

She shoots me a vicious look. "On the plane! In front of your fucking family!"

"Yes, and I was very impressed by your ability to completely shatter for me without anyone else having the slightest—"

"*Enough*, Kenzo," she sighs, glaring at me. "It's been a long day, and I need to sleep."

I gesture past her to the huge bed. "All yours."

"Really?" she questions, giving me a significant look. "Or will I be sharing it?"

"Is that an invitation?"

She flushes. "I *just said* I'm going to be sleeping."

"Same question, but now I'm even more curious to hear your answer."

She looks away and her brow worries.

"Are we…" She swallows, and when she turns back to me, her face is full of concern. "Are we safe here?"

"This house is a fortress, and I have a small army guarding it."

"But I mean, if anyone were to slip by, and get past all your men to the house…"

"They won't."

"But *if they did*," she insists.

I shake my head. "In the impossible situation where that occurs, this room is also impenetrable."

"How?"

I walk over to the bedside table and push a button. There's a click as the wall of windows all lock.

"That's blast and bullet-proof glass," I say. "The locks are the same as the ones the US uses in their embassies in hostile countries."

She chews on her lip. "And the door?"

"It's got the same lock as the glass."

Annika raises her worried blue eyes to mine. "Show me?"

"Of course."

I walk over to the door with her.

"Here." I point to the lock on the inside knob. "This button locks it, and the panel back near the bedside table will secure it with steel bolt locks around all four sides. You couldn't blow through with a tank."

She smiles quietly, relieved, and her eyes lift to mine. "Thank you."

It takes a lot to catch me off-guard. But when Annika stands up on her tip toes and kisses me softly on the lips?

Add that to the list.

Her lips are soft against mine, and there's a quiet moan in the back of her throat as her hands go to my chest.

Suddenly, it all goes wrong.

I lose my footing as she leans into me, quickly. I don't realize I'm being pushed until I step backward, past the door frame.

Shit.

I see Annika's smug grin for just a second before the door slams and locks in my face.

Goddammit.

19

ANNIKA

The triumphant feeling I get from locking Kenzo out of his own bedroom is short lived, because I forgot the golden rule of siege warfare: *have enough provisions to outlast the enemy.*

Eventually, the next afternoon, it's hunger that has me coming out of my fortress. When I do, though, I'm met with a surprise.

Kenzo *isn't* waiting for me so that he can grab me and yell at me for locking him out. In fact, he's nowhere to be seen.

I looked, and yes, the house is *huge,* but no matter how many rooms I poke my head into, I'm finally forced to acknowledge that my husband is not here.

I don't take as much glee in that as I should.

I end up finding Hana doing some work sitting outside in one of the many gorgeous gardens. When she explains what it is she does for Kenzo and Sota, I laugh, because it turns out we have similar roles, albeit different styles. She's not so much the scary bitch that walks into negotiations and sets the place on fire, like me, but her cool, laser-focused precision makes her a force to be reckoned with as the head of business acquisitions for the Mori and Akiyama families.

Other than her, though, the house really does appear to be empty. No Mal. No Takeshi. No *Kenzo*.

And no staff. Hana explains that there's a housekeeper and a cleaner who come twice a week. Other than that, there's just Jiro, the chef from the plane—who works for Kenzo, not Sota, as I would have guessed.

I make myself some coffee and a snack in the huge modern kitchen. Then I find a tranquil spot next to a koi pond outside and get to work. Hours later, there still seems to be nobody around.

I close my laptop and take a walk around the grounds. A few guards spot me, but they seem to know who I am and barely look at me, giving me only quick, perfunctory nods before continuing on their patrols.

High, wire-topped fences surround Kenzo's property. I make my way to the imposing front *torii* gate that we drove through when we first arrived. Then I follow the main drive back up to the house, and keep going, past it.

Evening is starting to fall when I stumble across the massive garage. I gawk as I step inside and take in the rows and rows of gorgeous vintage cars and motorcycles. The sound of what might be a power drill draws me past the Corvettes, Mustangs, Porches, and a *beautiful* old Ferrari, and I walk through another doorway into a mechanic's bay.

Takeshi is crouched over a bike frame, welding some bits together. When he sees me approach in his peripheral vision, he kills the power and lifts the welder's mask, painted to resemble a ferocious *hannya* mask.

"Looking for your boyfriend?"

"Not particularly, no."

"He and Mal are out on a business thing."

I shrug. "Okay."

"Heard you made him sleep on the couch."

I turn to Takeshi. "I didn't *make him* sleep anywhere. It didn't have to be the couch. I just pressed my advantage and locked him out of the bedroom so I could have it to myself."

Takeshi smirks. "So is this the newlywed honeymoon phase I hear so much about?"

I roll my eyes. "Beats me."

I'm just starting to stroll around the workshop, eyeing a few other serious looking sports bikes, when Hana walks in through the open bay door.

"I was wondering if I'd find you here." Her mouth twists. "Kenzo just called me. He wants you to be ready to go to some cocktail party thing tonight. He wants to be leaving here by ten-thirty."

"How *lovely*," I deadpan.

Hana smirks. "He's just…."

"Kenzo," Takeshi sighs. "He's just Kenzo. Though I doubt he'd be pissed if we just started calling him Dad."

Hana snorts a laugh as I grin at them both. "What's that about?"

Takeshi shrugs. "He's been playing dad to all of us since we were kids. I mean with Hideo not around and Mom…" He frowns and shakes his head, like this is something he doesn't really want to discuss.

I get it. I'm not a fan of talking about my parents, either. It's too painful, even now.

He eyes the Kawasaki Ninja bike that I'm standing next to, then drags his gaze to me.

"Do you really ride?"

I nod. "I mean…well enough."

He glances at Hana, then back to me. "Define *well enough*."

"Tak…" his twin says, a warning note in her voice.

"What, I'm just asking."

I cock a brow. "What do *you* mean by well enough?"

His manic, wolfish smile widens, like he's half feral. "I'm asking if you ride well enough to keep up with *me*."

"Goddammit," Hana sighs.

Takeshi grins. "Hana has issues with saying no to a challenge." His eyes flash dangerously. "Which is why I'm issuing one."

"You're an asshole," Hana grumbles, turning to grin at me before glancing back to her brother. "Fine. What's the challenge."

"Race-time, baby."

Hana frowns. "What, you versus me?"

I can already see the craziness sparking in Takeshi's eyes before he corrects her. Yeah, a simple race isn't enough for someone like him.

"Nah," he grins. "All three of us."

Her nose wrinkles. "Tak, no. She can't ride like—"

"Who says I can't ride?"

Hana turns to shoot me a look. "I'm not asking if you can ride a motorcycle. I'm asking if you can ride one of Tak's mostly not street-legal crotch-rockets on steroids."

"That *was* you in the back of the stolen Bugatti I drove to Canada, right?"

She grins widely. "Fair."

"Hell *yeah,* let's do this," Takeshi says gleefully, a manic look all over his face. "Here to Kiyamachi Street. Loser buys two rounds at Club Lotus."

Hana frowns. "Tak, she doesn't know Kyoto. She has no idea where that is."

Takeshi strokes his chin. "Okay, let's do this. You two are on a team versus me. So you can follow Hana. *But,*" he grunts, turning to his sister, "you *both* have to beat me to win."

Hana sucks on her teeth as she turns to me. I shrug, grinning. "I'm game if you are."

Takeshi throws me a helmet.

"If you were shitting me about your ability to ride earlier, now would be a good time to say so."

My only answer is to yank the helmet over my head and flick

open the visor. "Just so you know, Takeshi. I like my martinis dry with a twist. Vodka."

Hana hoots as she hands me a set of keys and points to a neon pink, purple and black bike, while she climbs onto an all-white one with a slash of red down the side like a sword cut.

"Just keep as close to me as you can, yeah?"

I nod, my adrenaline thrumming as I climb onto my bike, watching Takeshi settle astride a matte black beast with a golden dragon curling down the side and an engine that looks like it powered a fighter jet in its previous life.

"Let's fucking *go*."

I *MAY* HAVE OVERSOLD my motorcycle abilities. I mean, I know how to ride, but I haven't been on one in like five years.

Just the same, when it comes to sink or swim situations, I generally only ever see one option.

...I mean who the hell wants to sit at the bottom of the pool?

Hana and I *do* end up losing to Takeshi, probably because we both place at least *some* value on our lives, which he clearly doesn't. But it's still close. I buy the drinks at Club Lotus, because I'm sure Hana held back just a little so I wouldn't be totally lost trying to find our destination.

Two and a half hours later, the three of us pull back into the garage and kill the engines.

Takeshi eyes me coolly as he kicks his stand down and pulls off his helmet. His long dark hair is wild around his face, only adding to that feral vibe he's got going on. "Not bad," he nods, sliding off his bike.

"*Not bad?*" Hana rolls her eyes as she alights. "We were right on your ass the whole way there and back."

I'm breathless, my face hot and my body tingling from the breakneck ride back to the house. There's also an energy surging through me that I'm loving: the rush I always get from something and someplace new.

"Have fun?" Takeshi smirks.

"Holy *shit*!" I gush as I peel off my sweaty helmet, my hair sticking to my forehead. "That was incredible!"

"I'm glad you had such a good time."

The energy dies instantly as we turn to see Kenzo leaning against the open bay door, his arms folded over his chest. He's wearing a full suit, his hair nicely slicked back.

My eyes dart to the wall clock.

Shit.

Ten-fifteen.

"Kenzo, we—"

He turns, shooting his sister a withering look.

"C'mon, man. We just had to blow off some steam. You know, shake the dust off after that fucking plane ride—"

"I'll speak with my wife now," Kenzo growls. "*Alone.*"

Hana and Takeshi glance nervously at each other, then at me. I smile back weakly, shrugging like it's nothing,

Like I'm not *absolutely* scared of the wrathful, dark way Kenzo's energy is sucking the very *light* out of the garage.

When it's just the two of us, I lift my eyes to his.

"I can get ready fast—"

"Amid all your bitching and moaning about being stuck with *me*," he growls, "has it ever once occurred to you that I'm not exactly thrilled to be stuck with *you*?"

"I—"

"This cocktail party tonight is important, Annika. Maybe not for you personally. But it is for me, and for my future. Which, though it pains me to say it, you're now a part of."

Okay, *ouch*?

"Important people expecting to meet with me are there tonight. People I might be going into business with."

"So *go*!" I fire back. "If I'm such a burden to drag around, *don't*. Just go without—"

"That's not what's expected of—"

"Who cares?"

"*I do!!*" he roars, making me gasp as he surges into me. "I fucking do. These things *matter* to me, Annika."

I wince a little, backing up against the bike behind me.

"Okay, okay," I mumble, suddenly feeling shitty about all but blowing off the event tonight to go joyriding.

This isn't Kenzo being a jerk, or bossing me around. He's right. It's not just the Yakuza where it would be expected for someone to bring their new bride to an important event like tonight's. It would be fully expected in the Bratva, too.

He's not the asshole here.

I am.

"Look, I'm..." I clear my throat. "I'm sorry. I mean it."

He grunts, still frowning.

"I really can get ready super fast."

"Let's find out."

Kenzo all but drags me after him by the wrist as he storms out of the garage and across the grounds to the main house. I follow him upstairs to our room and into the huge, attached dressing room.

I stumble to a stop and stare at the wall of women's clothes on one side of the room. I unpacked my two suitcases earlier. The contents took up an eighth of this space. Now, the rest of it is *filled* with gowns, dresses, skirts, tops, shoes, jackets, and more.

Kenzo walks over to the wall and plucks a garment bag off one of the racks. He turns and hangs it on a hook next to a full-length mirror and unzips it, revealing an *extremely* revealing but still elegant midnight blue gown with the faintest sparkle of sequins.

It's floor length. But above the waist, it's literally just two palm-width strips of fabric that cover the breasts and tie at the back of the neck.

"What is this?" I ask, my lips thin.

"*This* is what you should have had on an hour ago."

I glance at him, raising a brow. "You're joking."

"I am not. Put it on. Time's a-wasting."

"No way!" I balk. "It's…trashy."

"It's *Versace*," he says through clenched teeth. "And you're putting it on, or I'll do it for you."

"I'd like to see another option—*hey*!"

I shiver as he moves in on me, grabbing me firmly and spinning me around. I whimper when he pins me to the wall, one hand clutching a fistful of my hair as the other grabs the back of my leggings. In one yank, he tugs them and my panties down to my knees. My hoodie comes off next, my pulse thudding as he shoves it up over my back and pulls it off my head.

My bra follows. Then my core tightens and my breath catches as he drops to his knees behind me, yanking my leggings and underwear off first one foot and then the other.

He stands, and without warning, his palm spanks me with a sharp crack.

"*That's* for being a pain in my ass."

Fire spreads through my core as he spanks the other cheek.

"And *that's* for making us late."

My pulse jangles as he spins me back to him and cups my jaw. He lifts my chin and slowly lets his gaze rake down over my nudity, then back up to my eyes.

"Put on the fucking dress," he growls.

Fucking hell. That tone…that accent…that velvety way he demands it… It's not playing fair.

Kenzo steps back, watching me closely as I take the dress off the hanger and slip it on. I reach back to tie it, but he stops me, turning me around and doing it himself. I shiver as I feel the heat of his fingers brush the nape of my neck.

When he's done, I look at myself in the mirror.

Oh.

I'm not, generally, a dress girl. But I've just changed my opinion on *this* one.

It's not trashy.

I look good.

Really, *really* good.

The fit is perfect. Yes, it shows off *a lot* of cleavage, even some side-boob if I turn that way. But it's not in a skanky, overdone and too-revealing way. It's like...classy sexy.

I twist my hair up into a tight knot, tucking in all the stray bits before I slip the hair tie off my wrist and use it to keep it all up there. I pull one tendril free, letting it hang down the side of my face before I meet his eyes in the mirror.

"Eh?"

Kenzo's eyes bore into mine, a fire in them I can't quite decipher.

"Yeah," he growls. "That works."

I nod. Then my brow furrows. "I'm not going commando."

"No, you're damn well not," he growls.

He walks over to some of the drawers set into the wall and opens one, revealing an *insane* collection of sexy, lacy lingerie.

"I have my own underwear, thanks."

"Your Tuesday everything-else-is-in-the-laundry period panties aren't going to work with this."

"I have nice underwear, jerk."

"Trust me—you don't."

He turns, dangling a skimpy little black thong off the end of his finger.

"*This* is nice underwear."

I balk. "I am *not* wearing that."

Kenzo just smiles.

"I'm not—*hey*!"

One second we're standing a foot apart from each other. The next, he's dropping to one knee in front of me, grabbing my ankle.

"What the hell—"

Kenzo slips the thong over my foot, sliding it up my calf.

"Kenzo—"

He drops that foot and grabs the other one, planting it on his thigh. He grips my calf, sliding the thong onto that leg. I stay frozen as he slides the panties up my legs, pushing my dress with it. My face heats but all I can do is stare, my mouth agape as he pushes the gown all the way up until my bare pussy is right in front of his face.

Heat floods my face. Slowly, Kenzo slides the lacy, sheer panties up until they're snug against my sex.

"There."

"I don't wear thongs."

"Tonight, you do."

"I don't like how they feel."

"Time to change that."

He leans closer, his breath hot on my inner thighs. My pulse jumps into the stratosphere as he presses his mouth right against my pussy through the thin fabric. Heat hums against my lips as he groans against me. I can feel his tongue swipe up, dragging through the lace, and my jaw goes slack.

Oh fuck...

Kenzo's eyes slide up to mine, kneeling in front of me, his mouth still on me. His hand skims up my thigh. His fingers slip under the edge of my panties, and I whimper as he pulls them aside before his mouth moves back into position.

Shit...

I moan, choking on the sound as his tongue drags slowly up my seam, rolling over my clit. His lips fasten around the throbbing nub, and when his tongue dances over it, my legs buckle and I almost fall.

Kenzo doesn't blink. He doesn't stop tonguing my clit as he reaches up and pulls my hands down to his hair.

My pulse hammers in my ears as I slide my fingers through his black locks, clinging to him for dear life as he starts to lick me a little faster. His hands skim over my ass, and one slips between my legs. I moan again when I feel his fingers center against my opening. He pushes two up into my pussy, stroking them in and out as he sucks on my clit.

My body ripples before going slack. I choke back a gasping breath, sagging against his mouth as my fingers tighten in his hair. He's merciless and insistent as his mouth demands the orgasm from my body. I moan when his two fingers sink deep inside me, stroking and curling against my g-spot as his tongue and lips feast on my throbbing clit.

Fucking hell, I'm going to come already.

My face crumples as I moan deeply, shamelessly gripping his hair and pulling him tighter to my pussy.

"Oh my God..."

"*My husband* works just fine," Kenzo growls into my folds. "Credit where credit is due, princess. It's not *God* making this messy little cunt come. It's me."

I gasp as he sinks a third finger into me, stretching me to my limit as he sucks hard on my clit. With a spasm and a wrenching cry, my hips buck forward. My legs almost give out as the orgasm explodes through my core, his other hand sliding up to grip my ass firmly, keeping me pressed to his mouth.

I'm still shaking and my vision is still swimming when he pulls back. He tugs the thong back into place, sending an electric sensation buzzing through my body as the silky lace teases against my sensitive, swollen pussy.

He stands, cupping my chin and leaning into my ear, letting the gown fall back into place.

"The thing about thongs, princess," he growls. "Is that they fit a bit better when they're nice and *wet*. Now," he purrs darkly, rolling his shoulders as he pulls back from me. He pushes his messed-up hair back, shifting into his customary utterly put-together, utterly ridiculously handsome self as he straightens his tie. "We should be going."

I nod, barely able to make words as my face pulses with heat. I swallow, still shaking as I turn to walk out of the dressing room.

"Aren't you forgetting something, princess?"

I stop halfway to the door. When I turn back to him and see what's in his hands, fresh heat blooms in my face and across my chest.

It's the toys from the plane: the little black rubber U-shaped one with a gold band around the middle, and the small black butt plug with the gold hilt.

"I—"

He doesn't say a word. He just raises his hand and crooks two fingers at me.

A tingling sensation ripples through my core as I move toward him in a trance.

"Open your mouth."

He slips the plug between my lips.

"Keep it there."

He lifts my gown. I tremble when he slips his fingers into the top of my panties, pulling them away from my glistening sex and slipping the toy down into them. I moan quietly as he curls the toy into me, sinking it against my g-spot with the outside part of it resting against my still-throbbing clit.

He reaches up and slips the second toy from between my wet lips.

"Turn around."

I do so, willingly, eagerly.

I bite back a whimper as he lifts my gown again. His fingers tug the tiny back strip of the thong aside, and when I feel the rubber plug push against my tight puckered ring, I wince and my breath catches.

"Breathe, princess," he growls, nipping my ear. "My cock will feel *much* bigger than this…"

The adrenaline rush of his touch, combined with his dark promise, have my body shivering and pulsing. I whimper as the toy pushes against my tight hole, slowly opening me up. It sinks into me, making my core flutter as I feel my ass tighten again just below the flared base.

"*Now* we can go," he growls.

20

KENZO

The death of Orochi Ito and his nephew shook up the Kyoto underworld. At first, everyone expected there to be a massive bloodbath in the ensuing power vacuum.

But that never happened. Because *I* filled that vacuum.

I might still be the new guy in town. But the old guard of the various Yakuza families in Kyoto accord me a measure of respect due both to my last name, and the fact that I'm essentially Sota's heir.

Unfortunately, hand in hand with respect and becoming one of the kings of the city comes having to play the tired old guard games. Like enduring insufferably boring sit-downs where everyone just glad-hands each other and bull-shits about how powerful they are, or the never-ending social calendar of weddings, engagement galas, or *omiya-mairi* ceremonies celebrating the birth of one heir or another.

Tonight is yet another of these asinine social gatherings. Worse, it's *my own* asinine social gathering.

Tonight's shindig has been organized by Sota to celebrate my marriage to Annika, and the peace and prosperity between our family and the Bratva that that brings.

Just shoot me.

Sota's not oblivious to my thoughts about this whole thing. And he's not being an asshole and forcing me to celebrate it. This is just what's expected. It would be disrespectful to the other Yakuza families in Kyoto *not* to throw something like this.

Still, it's me that has to suffer through the bullshit of a bunch of chain-smoking old guys ogling waitstaff and sipping expensive sake and whiskey while they make deals to make themselves even richer.

And yet...

When I turn to glance at Annika sitting next to me in the back of the black Range Rover, with the streetlights and the neon of the city washing over her in waves, I'm not sure the word "suffer" is accurate.

It's an insult to *actual* suffering to characterize sitting next to a woman as beautiful as she or walking into an event with her on my arm as my wife as such.

There was a reason I fell for Annika's bullshit five years ago. Sure, I was drunk, and high on my own successes. I was younger, and reckless, and probably looking for trouble.

But when trouble walked in looking like *her*? I was fucked.

She wore a blonde bob wig over her long red locks that night, but the disguise did nothing to hide her beauty. Her raw sensuality. Her tantalizing promise of recklessness and bad decisions.

I bought her a drink, then another. She asked if we could go somewhere "just the two of us"...and my dick took over.

I woke up eighteen hours later, vaguely remembering the drink she poured me back at my place tasting funny. With faint memories of putting on a record and asking her to dance to Al Green with me. I distinctly remember wanting to punch myself in the dick the next day at my sappiness regarding *that* move.

But most of all, I remembered *her*.

The feel of her body swaying against mine as *So Tired of Being Alone* crooned over my stereo system. The scent of her skin, a mix of jasmine, orange blossom, and the sea.

The taste of her soft lips when I kissed her, taking her by surprise.

I'm pretty sure my next maneuver would have involved less romance and more "ripping her clothes off and fucking her into the mattress until she saw God". But we never made it that far before the drug she slipped me took hold and sent me reeling to the floor.

"I'm going to remember you," I growl as the darkness closes in. I stare at her face, memorizing every detail.

Remembering.

The blonde flashes me a cocky smirk as she pulls my wallet from my jacket pocket. "In your dreams, sunshine."

"No, princess." I grab her by the wrist with the last of my strength as reality fades. "In yours, *which I'll be fucking haunting."*

Hana wasn't that far off when she asked me if it was "the necklace, the girl, or the fact that someone beat you that had you all angry and riled up for five fucking years." I already know the answer to that.

Spoiler: it's not the necklace.

It might not even be that someone got one over on me.

And that leaves the girl.

Annika turns to look at me as the flickering lights from the club signs outside illuminate her soft features and her full lips. Her big, seductive eyes. She arches a questioning brow, curious why I'm staring at her.

I don't have an answer to that. At least not one I'm prepared to voice, even just to myself inside my own head.

When we pull up outside the lounge where the event is being held, I get out first. Some of the press is waiting—pictures of the Yakuza sell as well as photos of movie stars in Japan—and I turn away from the flash of cameras to open the door and help Annika out.

I'm sure people will have plenty to say about the half-*gaijin* Yakuza prince marrying a European girl. But I don't give a fuck. I don't care if I'm not "Japanese enough" in their eyes.

I know where I came from. I know who I am. My family's blood is soaked deep into the streets of this city.

I'm no *gaijin* outsider.

I'm Yakuza, through and through. And the woman at my side is my fucking queen.

"WELL NOW, if it isn't the guest of honor," Mal says sarcastically.

I tap the rim of my scotch glass to his. "And if it isn't the one Mori kid who wasn't fast enough to weasel his way out of this trainwreck."

Takeshi and Hana were both quick to come up with "legitimate" reasons for Sota why they couldn't come to this thing tonight.

Mal's excuse, if he even tried one, wasn't solid enough. I mean, it's not like Sota would *order* him or anything. But that thing parents do...where they're not "mad", just "disappointed"...fucking *works*. And Sota is a master at it.

"Touche," Mal grunts, sipping his drink.

We turn to survey the crowd at the Nijo Empire, the exclusive VIP club named after some local castle ruins, where tonight's festivities are being held.

"Where's your bride?"

"Nakahara Turo's wife found her and dragged her in with the other wives."

Mal grimaces. "Brutal. You just threw her to the wolves like that?"

"She can handle herself."

He smirks, eying me. "Well, she seems to be handling *you* just fine. That's no mean feat."

I'm about to reply with something biting when Mal scowls, his gaze shifting past me to the front of the club.

"Fuck me, look at Tamura."

Tamura Yoshito's father was a mid-level enforcer who held allegiance to my father, and was by all accounts, a loyal, well-respected man.

His son, however, is a fucking dipshit.

The kid walks around like he's cosplaying some blend of *Fast and the Furious* and whatever Japanese gangster movies he's been watching too much of lately. Honestly, if he was *just* reckless, cocky, and hungry, he'd be fine, and he'd fit right in with most of the other guys in the Yakuza his age.

But Tamura is also *unbelievably* fucking stupid.

For instance, he's been skimming a little off the top of his collections before handing the money over to my mid-level guys.

You don't have to be in the Yakuza to understand that *stealing* from them is a bad idea.

Normally, I'd have already had him dangled off a tenth-story railing, or even removed one of his hands. But I can't pull shit like that without hard evidence, unless I want to sow leadership doubt in my ranks.

And I don't have hard evidence.

"I say take him to the cliffs near the ruins of Sakamoto Castle and dangle him by his fucking balls until he confesses."

"I'm sorry, until who confesses to what?"

I can't help but grin widely as I turn to see Annika standing there.

Looking stunning.

Fuck-me-that's-my-wife.

Mal frowns. "Nothing," he grunts.

"Oh, so just a *casual* conversation about hanging someone by their balls over a cliff. Got it." She shrugs with a sly grin.

I exhale, turning to nod my chin at Tamura, who's currently trying and failing to hit on one of the waitresses.

"One of our guys is skimming, we just can't prove it."

"*That dweeb* is skimming from you?" she says incredulously.

"I'd almost be impressed, if it didn't make me want to cut his head off," Mal mutters.

"And you need proof."

I nod.

"Okay, so what would prove he's skimming so you can make a move on him?"

"Evidence?" Mal says sarcastically.

She rolls her eyes. "Thank you, Dr. Watson, that's *most* helpful. I meant where could one *find* such evidence."

"On his phone, probably," I mutter. "He's always on it, does *all* of his business that way. It never leaves his side."

"So take it *away* from his side."

I roll my eyes. "Shockingly, that idea *has* crossed my mind. But it's not like we can hack into a fucking iPhone."

"Not with that attitude, you can't."

I eye her, finding myself both amused and aroused by the look in her eyes as she glances over to Tamura.

"What are you scheming?"

She turns to bat her eyes at me. "Who, me?"

"Annika—"

"You *know* he's skimming?"

"Yes."

"And the evidence is probably on his phone?"

"Again, yes. But before you go stealing it, you *can't* hack into an—"

"Why don't you let the professional handle this, okay?"

In the blink of an eye, she turns, leans up on her toes, and kisses my cheek.

We both blink in shock, like neither of us saw that coming.

She blushes and quickly looks away. "I'll be back," she blurts, melting into the crowd.

Mal waits a whole three seconds before clearing his throat.

"We, uh, gonna talk about what just—"

"Nope."

He tilts his head, taking a large sip of his drink. "Okay then."

"Kenzo. Mal."

We turn at the sound of Sota's voice, both of us bowing, as we're around the kind of guys who like to see that sort of behavior. When I straighten up again, I realize he's not alone.

My jaw sets as I stare at Valon Leka, the Albanian smuggler Annika was getting *far* too cozy with at our engagement party.

My eyes narrow a little as I size him up. Never mind what Hana said about him being a psychopath: I don't fucking like the look of him. He's not an unattractive guy, but there's something unsavory about him. Like he's wearing a suitably handsome mask to hide the rot underneath.

I don't necessarily buy into all that auras and energy and woo-woo crystal shit. But if I *did*?

This fucker's got bad vibes coming out of his *ass*.

"Kenzo," Sota says. "Allow me to introduce you to Mr. Leka."

Valon puts his hand out to shake mine. I almost don't take it, but that would be as insulting to Sota as it would be to this prick. So I grip his hand, maybe a *little* more forcefully than necessary.

Leka looks at me with a strange glint in his eyes that I brush off as the psycho thing Hana was mentioning.

"Pleasure to meet you, Mr. Mori," he purrs in his Eastern European accent.

"As you know, Kenzo, I've been speaking with Mr. Leka about going into business together. He—"

Valon coughs delicately. "I get things from one place to another, Mr. Mori," he growls. "It's been suggested that you and I could work together."

I glance at Sota. He smiles and steps closer to me, leaning in.

"*This is all yours*," he murmurs in Japanese, patting my hand. "Your deal to make or not. The decision, terms, and execution are all up to you."

I arch a brow at him. "Do *you* want this?"

Sota turns to smile broadly at Leka, who very clearly has no idea what we're saying, not understanding Japanese.

"I think he's a slimy little snake," Sota says, still grinning pleasantly.

Mal coughs to cover his snort of laughter.

"I think he'd sell his own *mother* if he got a good price. But..." Sota shrugs. "He's apparently one of the best. Either way, it's your call, Kenzo."

He turns back to Leka and switches to English.

"Kenzo and you can work out the details. He has my blessing to speak for both his organization and mine."

Sota and Mal exchange a look, glance back at me, then head over to the bar.

"He speaks highly of you, Mr. Mori," Leka smiles at me.

"Sota-san is a good man."

"And I want to congratulate you on your marriage."

I nod. "Thank you."

"She's a *lovely girl,* that Annika."

My smile hardens. "Yes, she is."

"I won't keep you." He flashes a shark-like smile at me. "But let's talk soon—"

"Mr. Leka, I'll be blunt."

I've already decided. I don't like this fucker. I don't like the way he talks, or the way he schmoozes, and I *really* don't like the way he calls my wife a *lovely girl.*

I fix him with a flat, businesslike smile.

"I'm not really looking to bring on more people right now. I'm happy with our current network. Nothing personal, of course."

His jaw sets, and a flash of malice crosses his face.

"Mr. Mori, I think if we could sit down and speak, I could show you—"

"No need. My mind is made up. Again, nothing personal."

His face darkens. "Perhaps we should invite your *wife* into this conversation."

Something vicious snarls and claws inside of me.

"Perhaps, Mr. Leka," I growl, stepping closer, "you should keep my wife out of this conversation, and *utterly* out of your thoughts. Because that, I can promise you, I *will* take personally."

Valon scowls. Then he clears his throat, pasting on a smile.

Yeah, he gets it. He might be hot shit back in his little fiefdom or when he's running drugs for the Cosa Nostra or the Turkish Mafia. But here?

Here, I'm a fucking *Emperor*. Here, he bows to *me*.

"Of course. My apologies, Mr. Mori. I hope that if you ever revisit the question, you'll keep me in mind."

Eat shit.

I smile politely as I nod my chin. "Of course. Thank you for coming all the way to Kyoto to meet—"

"Oh, I had other business here as well."

I don't give a fuck.

"Then I hope it's fruitful, Mr. Leka. And I hope you're able to spend some time in Kyoto enjoying yourself."

"Maybe I will," he says with a lackluster smile.

I nod, turning and making my way through the crowd to find Sota and Mal. On the way, I bump into Annika. I'm unable to stop the grin from spreading over my face.

For her part, she beams smugly as she holds up an iPhone in an X-rated manga case.

"Uh…what the fuck is that?"

She winks. "Tamura's phone. You're welcome."

I snort, but then I shake my head. "Nice pull. It doesn't change the fact that we can't crack an iPhone."

"You men, always thinking there has to be brute force involved."

"I'm not sure I've heard much complaint from you about my brute force."

Her face heats, her lip catching between her teeth, but then Annika clears her throat. "No need for brute force when you have the password."

My jaw drops as she calmly types it in, unlocking the phone.

"How the *fuck* did you get that?"

She grins. "I saw him type it in. All I had to do was bat my eyes, show a little cleavage, ask if he wanted my number…"

I growl savagely and grab her arm, making her gasp sharply. Annika's big blue eyes snap to mine, a shiver of something heated crossing them.

"*Jealous much*?" she teases, her voice husky and breathy.

"Maybe I just don't like my wife flirting with other men," I mutter.

"It was to get the *phone*," she murmurs softly.

"I don't *care*."

Her lips curl into a grin. "You know, they have a name for that."

"Yeah? What's that?"

"*Jealousy*."

I roll my eyes as she giggles. She drops her gaze to Tamura's phone, tapping on the screen and making a face.

"Okay, *lotta* anime porn on here. Jesus." She frowns. "But also…spreadsheets." I watch as she scrolls. "Oh, yeah, right here." She turns the phone toward me. "Yeah, he's skimming."

She passes me the phone and pats my chest.

"I'm going to go grab a drink. You're welcome."

I watch her as she slips away. I'm not thinking about the damn phone, or even Tamura.

I'm still thinking about her lips.

21

KENZO

"You're a terrible husband."

I chuckle, turning to flip Mal off as he shakes his head.

"Nakahara Turo's wife just stole Annika again."

"Like I said," I shrug, "she can handle herself."

He smirks, eyeing me.

"What?"

"Nothing." He shakes his head again, looking away into the crowd.

"Don't make me choke-hold it out of you."

He chuckles. "I was just going to say... I like her."

"Good. She's going to be around for a while."

He rolls his eyes. "I meant I like her *for you.* I like what she does to you."

"What, drive me crazy?"

"Keep telling yourself that all you want. If you actually believe it, you're a fucking idiot."

I smile to myself as I turn back to survey the crowd, sipping my drink.

"So," I grin, side-eying him. "Is it true what they say?"

"About?"

"Absence making the heart growing fonder?"

He frowns as he turns to me. "What the fuck are you talking about?"

"Like, do you guys *text*, or FaceTime, or is it a snail-mail kind of thing. I bet she'd think that was very romantic."

"Kenzo, I have no idea—"

"It's all good," I grin. "She's coming out this way soon. She and Annika were talking yesterday, setting it up."

His brow furrows. "What in the ever-loving fuck are you—"

Then his eyes narrow on me.

I chuckle. "*There's* the light bulb fading on."

"Freya," he growls quietly. "You're talking about Freya."

"Obviously."

"You don't know what the fuck you're talking about, Kenzo," he growls coldly.

"Really? I think I'm talking about someone's little *crush*—"

"Drop. It."

Whoa. There's a viciousness on Mal's face that I rarely see, unless we're in the middle of a goddamn gunfight.

"The fuck is going on, Mal?"

He slams back the rest of his drink and the anger melts off his face.

"Nothing. I'm going to go get some air."

I frown, watching him disappear into the crowd.

What the *hell* was that?

I'm about to go get myself one last drink, but when I see Mrs. Turo and her gaggle of Yakuza wives giggle their way past me—*sans* Annika—something darker catches my interest.

Fuck the drink.

I'm grinning to myself as I prowl the crowd, looking for her. I had a taste earlier at home, when I made her come on my tongue. But I've been savoring the taste of her cunt all fucking night, and now my dick is *exceedingly* jealous of my mouth.

I think back to our conversation on the plane about free use kinks.

I groan to myself, my eyes stabbing around the club as I picture finding her, taking her to the nearest bathroom, closet, or dark corner, bending her over, and fucking her until she can't walk straight. Or putting her on her knees and fucking her mouth until I empty my swollen balls down her throat.

I just have to fucking *find her* first.

I'm headed to the curtained-off hallway that leads to the

restrooms to check there when I hear a voice I recognize on the other side of them.

"*Get me* this deal, puppet."

Valon fuckhead Leka.

I grit my teeth, stopping to listen to him talk to, I assume, one of his goons—over the phone, since I don't hear any reply.

"Get me what I want," he snaps coldly. "Or I'll tell your new husband what a little *whore* his wife used to be—"

"Don't fucking *touch me*!"

My whole field of vision bleeds red. My world turns to fire.

He's talking to *Annika*.

I see nothing but rage and feel nothing but fury surging inside me as I rip the curtain aside and storm forward like Death on his pale horse. Valon's holding a shaking, terrified, almost catatonic Annika by the wrists. When he sees me, his eyes go wide and he backs away.

"Kenzo, whatever you heard—"

I hit him so hard I feel it all the way down to my fucking *feet*.

I feel his teeth crunch through his lips under my fist. Leka isn't a small man, but still he half-falls, half-stumbles back, mewling in pain as I bash his face again.

He doubles over, choking and spitting up blood and vomit before I slam my knee into him as hard as I can, hearing his ribs break. My knee crashes into his face next, splitting his mouth open, sending his head jerking back.

Valon stumbles into the door to the ladies' room. I crash into him, breathing pure hate and vengeance in his face as we both go splintering through the door and crashing onto the tiled floor.

He's bleating and sobbing, holding up his hands, begging me to spare him.

I hear nothing. I see nothing expect the unacceptable fact that he's still breathing.

I drag him by the throat over to one of the stalls, kicking the door open and shoving him forward. I use my foot to stomp his head into the toilet bowl. Then I drop to my knees and grab him by the neck, shoving his face deeper into the water.

I hold him there as his feet and hands kick and flail.

Kick and flail.

And start to slow...

"Kenzo!"

I'm dimly aware that strong arms, maybe belonging to Mal, are trying to drag me away. But it's Sota's sharp, cold voice that finally breaks the spell. I turn, blinking, shoving my hair back and reentering reality.

It *is* Mal trying to pull me off Leka. Sota is standing in the ruined doorway, surrounded by his guards. Behind them all, I see her.

Annika.

She's got her arms wrapped around herself and she's ghostly pale, that frozen, catatonic look still on her face. And she's shaking.

My hands drop from Valon, allowing the shithead to drag himself sputtering and gasping from the toilet.

I don't say a word when I stand. I don't look at any of them.

I just storm past them and grab her arm.

"We're leaving," I snarl. "*Now.*"

22

ANNIKA

IT FEELS like I'm frozen in ice: numb everywhere, seeing the world through a frosty window I can't quite clear.

I see nothing as we drive in utter silence. If Kenzo is even saying anything to me, I don't hear it. But I also know he's doing no such thing.

Since he took one of his men's cars, buckled me into the passenger's seat and hit the gas, we haven't spoken a word.

He hasn't even looked at me. Or maybe he has, but I've been too busy drowning in the pain and shame of my past to notice.

A cold, creeping sensation walks up my spine. I feel dirty. Gross. Untouchable and undesirable. It's like whatever mask I've managed to hold up in front of my face has finally been yanked away, letting Kenzo see the ugly monster beneath.

I shudder, blinking out of my haze a little as the car screeches to a stop and the engine switches off. I glance dully out the side window, only then realizing that we're back at Kenzo's mansion.

He storms away from the car, shoving his fingers through his hair. I step out, following at a distance, my eyes downcast, a horrible, disgusting feeling of self-loathing souring inside of me.

Just before he reaches the front door, he whirls on me with a fury that sucks all the air from my lungs. His face curdles into a mask of anger, pain, and jealousy that stabs me like a blade as he looms over me.

"*This*," he snarls, "is why I wanted that fucking list."

My brow furrows, a shiver rippling down my spine as I stare at him. "*List*?" I choke. "What—"

My face falls as it clicks.

I know what list he means.

"*Fuck you*," I hurl at him, my voice hoarse. "FUCK. YOU."

"Yakuza, Bratva, Mafia…" He shakes his head. "This is a *small* fucking world we exist in, *wife*. Tell me—who else am I going to walk into a goddamn meeting with, to talk business with, only to find out later that *they fucked you*!"

He roars the last part with so much anger and pain that I flinch.

"That is *none* of your business!" I choke, my eyes filling with tears.

"The *fuck* it isn't!" he snarls back. He jabs a finger into the night. "You fucked Leka, what, once? *More* than once?"

Tears roll down my cheeks as the black walls inside me start to crack and crumble.

"Fuck you," I spit, shaking. "You don't know—"

"How many are on the list, Annika—"

"Besides you?! *ONE*!" I spit venomously, my hands clenched to fists as my entire body shakes. *"One,* you fucking *asshole*!"

Kenzo's face is incredulous as his jaw clenches. *"What?"*

I turn to walk away. "This conversation is over—"

"The fuck it is."

I jolt when he grabs my arm and yanks me around to face him. "Were you in a fucking *relationship* with that fucking—"

"I was in PURGATORY with him!" I scream into his face, blasting away his furious expression and turning it to one of worry. "It was *hell*! You want to know if I was in a fucking *relationship* with him!?"

I'm screaming, but I don't care. I'm shaking, but I feel nothing.

"Let's review, Kenzo! I was twenty-two, homeless, and broke. He was in his forties, rich, and had all the power. I didn't know what the words grooming or gaslighting meant, meanwhile he *traded* in them! I was told it was love and romance when I had bruises and bled. I was told what I felt didn't matter, nor my consent!"

The tears start to stream down my face.

"I still make myself throw up in the shower sometimes to try and purge the memories. I still scrub my skin so hard it bleeds. Maybe it wasn't three years of rape because technically I never said no," I roar in his face as the world blurs, "but it was pretty fucking close!! You tell me, Kenzo!! Does that sound like a *relationship* to you!? Does that sound like that fuck was my fucking *boyfriend,* you arrogant, *privileged* piece of—"

Suddenly, it's like everything shatters. The walls inside crumble in a thunderous explosion. My heart wrenches.

...And Kenzo wraps me in his arms and pulls me tight to his chest.

"Princess," he whispers hoarsely.

I break in two and melt against him. I cling to his shirt, sobbing into his chest as it all comes out. All the shame, all the self-loathing. All the ways I've called myself ugly and unlovable.

It all comes out as the walls come crashing down.

"I'm so fucking sorry, Annika," he chokes into the top of my head, holding me so tightly that the air squeezes from my lungs.

But I want that. I need it. I need the raw power and the unmovable force squeezing the life out of me, because I need it all gone.

"I'm right here," he hisses, holding me even tighter. "I'm right fucking here, and I'm not going anywhere, ever," he chokes. "I'm here, and I'll be whatever you need. Whatever it is, *tell me,"* he groans, burying his face in my hair and surrounding me with his strength and power.

"Just hold me," I whisper against his chest. "Hold me and don't ever let go."

"I can do that," he whispers back, squeezing me against him.

We stand like that in the moonlight outside his front door for... I'm not sure. It might be hours, or it might be just a few minutes. But in that blind strength and raw power, and in that immovable force, I find a peace I've been seeking for years.

Kenzo shakes his head. "I'm so fucking sorry, princess. *Forgive me.*"

I squeeze him tight, crying softly into his chest.

"There's nothing to f—"

"Yes," he growls, pulling back a little. He cups my chin in his hands, tilting my gaze up to his. "Yes, there is."

I smile wryly, wiping my eyes with the back of my hand. "I forgive you."

His face twists with pain. "Annika, what did he—"

"It's in the past."

His grip tightens on me. When I glance back at him, I shiver as I see the raw fury on his face as his jaw ripples.

"*Fuck that,*" he snarls.

"Kenzo, I *really* don't want to talk about—"

"I need to—"

"I am *done* digging up my past!" I spit, my voice breaking.

His face softens as he leans down, cupping my face again as his eyes lock with mine.

"You misunderstand, princess," he murmurs quietly. "I don't want to dig up your past."

Something malicious flickers in his eyes.

"I want to fucking *bury it.*"

In the blink of an eye, he's crushing his mouth to mine. I whimper softly, tears still falling down my cheeks and over his fingers as his lips bruise mine in a cleansing, avenging kiss unlike anything I've ever known.

I'm shaking a little, my heart racing, as he pulls away. His eyes lock with mine.

"I'll be back."

I blink, my pulse jangling as he turns and starts to march toward the garage.

"Wait!" I cry. "Wait, where are you—"

"To put your past in a hole in the fucking ground."

23

KENZO

I'VE KNOWN BLINDING anger before in my life. When my mother died, the fury I felt toward the world, karma, God, and whoever was unlucky enough to cross my path almost killed me.

But it didn't touch what I'm feeling right now.

It's *not* some macho chest-thumping ego thing, either. This isn't anger that Leka "got what's mine" or anything juvenile like that.

Annika and I are both adults in our thirties. We've both obviously had lives before we met each other. Again, that's *not* what this is, and it's not my fucking ego.

It's that against my better judgement, and despite every attempt to sabotage it, somewhere along the way, I caught feelings.

No. More than feelings.

Somewhere along the way, this "fake" thing with Annika has become very, very real. I'm not sure if I have a word for it yet, or maybe I know the word just fine but the fact that I've never used that word before scares the fuck out of me.

She matters to me.

A fucking *lot.*

She's an addition to the thing beating inside my chest that I wasn't looking for, because I never knew that part of my heart was missing.

As much as she pisses me off sometimes, *damned* if that woman isn't the first thing I think of when I wake up, and the last thing I think of before I fall asleep.

That's why I'm beyond fucking angry. It has nothing to do with her past experiences before me.

It's about *him.*

Valon.

And the fact that that piece of shit hurt her.

Abused her.

Gaslit and groomed her. Used her desperation and her pain of losing her whole family to get what he wanted, and to hell with her opinion on the matter.

He *hurt my fucking wife.*

Tonight, he's going to die for it.

I grab a helmet off the wall and snag the keys to my all-black BMW bike with the thin, silver etching of a screaming *hannya* mask on the gas tank. I have a small arsenal in a storage locker under the house, but Japan's strict firearms laws make it *very* hard to go into a place shooting without the goddamn army coming down on your head.

Instead, I go to a locker against the far wall, key in the passcode, and pull out an exquisitely crafted, old-school samurai sword.

This was my grandfather's—given to Sota by my father when he was leaving Japan.

Now it's mine.

I want to use this *far* more than any crude gun, anyhow. I slide it into a scabbard slung across my back as I throw a leg over the bike.

"Off to commit violence, brother?"

I pause, turning to look at Takeshi as he walks into the garage. His lips curl dangerously.

"You know that's my *favorite* hobby," he growls menacingly.

I shake my head. "This is just me, Tak."

"What's this about, Kenzo?" When I don't reply, his brow furrows deeply. "Annika?"

I'm frozen for a second. Then I dip my chin curtly.

Takeshi's jaw grinds.

"In case you've forgotten, brother, your wife is my *sister*."

Without saying anything more, he grabs his helmet and keys, then pulls a second, *non*-heirloom sword out of the locker.

Honestly, if Takeshi had his way, he'd *always* use swords.

"Who are we raining mayhem and pain down on?" he grunts as he gets astride his bike.

"We're not fucking anyone up tonight," I hiss. "We're burying them."

"*Excellent*," he smiles, pulling on his helmet. "Let's go."

IT'S quiet out when Tak and I roll to a stop a few blocks away from the vast home Valon is renting in the luxurious Kamigyo Ward. We leave our helmets with the bikes and move in silence, two noiseless, shadowy angels of death.

Common sense would say to call for backup and wait until I have a small army of men at my disposal before surrounding the house, and only *then* going in to drag Valon out by the balls.

But fuck that.

The wrathful monster inside me isn't waiting for anything right now.

Tak and I keep to the shadows as we slip along the wall surrounding Valon's rental property. Avoiding the front gates, we keep going until we find an old, gnarled tree which gives access.

Seconds later, we've climbed the tree and dropping down into the darkness inside the walls. I allow myself a dangerous smile as I slowly unsheathe the lethal blade at my back. Takeshi does the same and we move in silence toward the back door, ready to strike down anyone who gets in our way.

No one does. And that's…odd.

When we get to the back door, Takeshi taps me on the shoulder. I turn to see him frowning deeply. He gestures with his chin to where he's looking. When I follow his gaze, my eyes widen.

It's almost unnoticeable, but there's a small splatter of red against the white stones of the Zen garden beside the back door.

I glance back at my brother. He nods.

The hunt is still on.

The back door opens noiselessly. We creep in on silent feet, blades ready, eyes scanning the darkness inside. We move through a sitting room and into a lounge area that looks out over the city.

We both freeze as our eyes drop to the same thing—more blood, splattered across the wall and one of the white sofas.

I glance at my brother again. He frowns, as if to say "something is fucked." He's not wrong. I'm also not leaving here without Valon's fucking head.

We push on.

In the kitchen, the refrigerator door is ajar, a bullet hole in the side of it and more blood dripping down the wall next to it. Bloody footsteps lead to a dining area, but they end there without a body.

Just as I'm about to admit that there's no one still here, we both freeze when we hear a quiet groan of pain. Takeshi and I move quickly, sweeping through the house until we step outside.

A man lies curled up in the fetal position in the middle of the dark, moonlit inner courtyard. Blood pools around him as he groans in pain.

God damn.

It's fucking *Valon*.

Takeshi and I run over. The piece of shit cries out pathetically as I yank him over, turning him face up and leering down into his stricken face.

"Good," I growl quietly. "You survived. Now it's *my turn—*"

I whirl at the grunt of pain next to me, just in time to see Takeshi slump to the ground. Then blinding pain explodes in the back of my skull. Gravity goes sideways as I tumble to the ground next to him, my vision swimming before it all goes dark.

"Do you hunt, Mr. Mori?"

I blink back into reality. Someone is tying my hands behind my back against one of the porch pillars.

Takeshi—

I snap my head left and right, looking for my brother, almost expecting to see him being tied up too. When I don't see him at all, my fury surges. I hiss violently, yanking at the ropes behind my back trying to break free. But they hold fast, and I grunt when the man behind me kicks me swiftly in the ribs.

A dark, rasping chuckle rumbles beside me. I turn and narrow my eyes at a stocky, bearded man with dark eyes and a shaved head as he steps into my field of vision.

"Where the fuck is my brother?" I spit.

He raises a brow and glances significantly at the spot where Tak and I just got jumped. My skin crawls as I realize the blood I'm looking at isn't just from Valon.

"*Where* the *fuck—*"

"He'll be found soon, don't you worry, Mr. Mori," he growls quietly. "Either by my men or, judging from his wounds, by death."

Tak got away.

I level a vicious glare at the man. "Who the fuck are you?"

He smiles coolly at me, turning my sword in his hands.

"My name is Gacaferi, Mr. Mori. Ulkan Gacaferi."

The name makes me pause, my brain searching the memory banks for how I know this fuck. Then it hits me: Ulkan's a mid-level Albanian strongman who runs a B-list crime outfit. He also lives in *New York,* so why the fuck is he standing over me in Kyoto?

"What the fuck is this," I snap coldly at him, pulling at my binds. I nod my chin at Valon as he lies bleeding and moaning on the ground. "If you're here for him, we're on the same side. But he's *mine,*" I snarl.

Ulkan smiles, examining my sword again and running his thumb up the side of the blade.

"Put that down," I growl quietly.

His eyes lift to mine. "I'll ask you again, Mr. Mori. Do you hunt?"

It starts to filter into my consciousness that Ulkan is known to be a complete psychopath.

"I do," I growl.

"Have you ever gone trapping?"

"Bunnies," I hiss. "I've trapped bunnies."

His smile grows as he circles me slowly, thumbing the edge of my blade.

"Ahh yes, rabbits. You must bait a cage for rabbits, yes?"

"What the *fuck* do you want, Mr. Gacaferi?"

His head swivels to me, his eyes glinting in the moonlight. "I want what I'm owed, Mr. Mori. Our honor is the one thing we have in this world, no? And to lose it, or have it taken from you, is a terrible thing. I think men like you and I can agree on that."

"I don't even fucking *know* you," I snarl. "What the fuck do you think I took—"

"Ahh, I apologize. You misunderstand, Mr. Mori," Ulkan sighs, hefting my sword in his hand as he slowly walks over to where Valon is lying on the ground. He gestures to the fucker lying in his own blood, pointing at him with my sword.

"*That* isn't my bait, Mr. Mori. Because it is not *you* I am hunting."

He twirls the blade thoughtfully as he turns. His eyes land on me as he slowly walks toward me, smiling cruelly.

"No, *you* are my bait, Mr. Mori."

My jaw clenches as I glare up into his face. "And what the fuck are you hunting?"

He leers at me as he squats down in front of me, running his thumb up the side of my sword, looking me dead in the eye.

"Your wife, Mr. Mori. I'm hunting *your wife.*"

24

ANNIKA

HANA and I sit together in silence. She doesn't ask why I've been crying, or why Kenzo and I were screaming at each other. She doesn't question why I'm still shaking a little, or inquire where her brother flew off to.

She just sits beside me in the garden with an arm around my shoulders and her hand stroking my hair.

As if I needed a reminder why I like her so much.

I feel her move, and I turn to follow where her gaze has just shifted. Mal walks out from the living room, his brow furrowed.

"What do you need, Annika?" He growls. "Tea?"

"I think something stronger and more Scottish might be better."

His chuckles wryly and nods. Just as he turns to head back inside, we whirl at the sound of an engine roaring up the driveway. Tires squeal, and the crunching sound of metal has us all scrambling to our feet and bolting around the side of the house toward the driveway.

Shit.

Takeshi, who I saw ride off with Kenzo earlier, is staggering to his feet from the crashed bike. His helmet is missing, and even before he drops to his knees, I can see blood dripping down the side of his face and from the arm he's cradling against his chest.

"TAK!" Hana screams as the three of us run over to him.

"What the fuck happened?!" Mal hisses, crouching next to his brother. I wince when I see the gash on the side of Takeshi's face and the pain in his eyes as he grimaces. His eyes are blurry, but when they find mine, they come into focus.

"*Kenzo*?" I breathe.

His throat bobs. "They took him," he grunts, wincing in pain.

"*Who* did?" Mal growls.

"Some fucking…Albanian, I think," Takeshi mutters through grit teeth. "Pretty sure that's what I heard him speaking to his men."

"What happened?" I blurt.

"We went to Leka's house," he mutters, wincing again. "But it was empty, and there was blood all over the place when we got there. We found Leka all cut up, but then we got jumped by this fucker and his men." He shakes his head. "Big motherfucker with a shaved head and a beard. Eastern European, for sure. His guys were calling him Gaza, or Gaza-something—"

"*Gacaferi*."

My heart drops, my face going white as the name falls from my lips.

"Yeah," he grunts. "That was it."

Oh fuck.

"They knocked Kenzo out. I got one of them, but there were like a dozen more. I..." His voice chokes as he looks away. "I...I *left him*—"

"No, you *got out*, Tak," Mal hisses quietly, shaking his head and grabbing his brother's hand. "Getting yourself killed fighting a dozen guys doesn't save Kenzo. Getting out and getting backup might. You got that?"

Tak nods grimly.

I'm already standing and marching away.

"Woah, hang on, cowboy," Mal grunts.

I ignore him, my face stony and my heart thudding as I storm toward the garage. Inside, I grab a helmet and the keys to the same bike I rode the other night. Mal storms in behind me as I pause in front of the open locker on the wall.

"What the fuck are you—"

He puts his hands up, stepping back as I whirl at him with a sword in my hand, pointed straight at him.

"I'm going after Kenzo," I hiss. "What the fuck are *you* doing?"

His eyes flare as he tilts his head to the side. "It's a trap, Annika," he mutters. "You think they just *let* Tak run off? Gacaferi wants—"

"He wants *me* to come to him," I snap. "And he's going to get his wish."

Mal frowns.

"We have...history," I hiss. "A business deal gone wrong. If this is how he wants to settle it..." I glance at the blade in my hand. "I *know* it's a trap, Mal. But he's got *my husband*."

"And my brother," he growls, turning and grabbing another set of keys and a helmet. He pushes past me, pulling a sword from the locker. "C'mon. We're wasting time."

My heart lurches as we step into the courtyard of Valon's rental house.

That's a *lot* of blood.

Like, a *lot*.

"Not Kenzo's," Mal growls quietly. His brow is furrowed as he stoops down, running his fingers over scuff marks on the stone patio. "Kenzo got dragged over...here," he murmurs, moving quickly to one of the porches that ring the courtyard. He squats next to a post, pointing to some scuff marks on it. "He was tied up here. There's a little blood, see?" He points a little higher up on the post. "Tak said they hit Kenzo in the back of the head. That's what this blood is. It's not..." He turns to nod his chin at the huge stain in the middle of the courtyard.

"Valon," I hiss venomously through clenched teeth.

Mal nods. "Yeah, I think that was him." He frowns. "Shit. That's...a lot of blood."

The stain becomes a wet looking drag mark, like a body being pulled away to one side. We follow the trail, my heart thumping at the prospect of walking around the corner and finding the monster cut in half. When we hit a wall with bloody scrabble marks streaked up and over it, my brow darkens.

He got out too.

I glance at Mal, who is nodding.

"My guess is, they left Leka for dead. After he was alone, he made it over here and got away over this wall."

I swallow thickly, twice. A second later, I glance over at Mal to see him looking at me curiously.

"I want him dead," I hiss coldly.

He nods. "I think you probably already got your wish. That's a crazy amount of blood on the ground. He might've managed to get over the wall, but he didn't get far." He peers at me closely. "Leka's *gotta* be dead, Annika. He might've made it down the street, or across the road on the other side of this wall to hide in a ditch. But he has to have bled out by now."

A burning desire to go find the body and cut out the heart consumes me. But there's something else I crave even more than that.

I need to find Kenzo.

I can't think about Valon right now, or my revenge if he *is* somehow still clinging to life nearby.

Right now, I have to find my husband.

"They're not far."

Mal is crouched down, pointing to a cigarette butt in the white stones of the Zen garden. It's still glowing faintly.

The bastards who took Kenzo are still close.

Which means he is too.

A searing pain I've rarely felt before stabs into me. It's the pain I felt the night my family died. The night I thought I'd lost Taylor. It's the pain I felt not so long ago, when she was in harm's way and I almost lost her all over again.

The realization hits me like a slap.

I know what this pain is.

It's the fear of losing love: real, genuine love. The sort of love I've tried to shield myself from since I was eighteen. The sort of love I now feel deep in my bones and in my soul for Kenzo.

I am not going to lose that.

I'm not going to lose *him*.

"How tight are you with the local authorities?"

Mal nods, reading my mind. "Tight. I'll call our guys at the local station. There's only so many roads in and out of Kyoto. They can set up some bullshit drunk driver roadblocks and scan for Gacaferi and his men."

I nod brusquely and yank out my phone. "Thank you," I mumble as I tap on the contact name and bring the phone to my ear.

"What is it, two in the fucking morning there?" Freya grumbles. It's around one in the afternoon back in New York, which means she's probably just getting up.

"I need you to hack into the Kyoto municipal CCTV system," I blurt.

"Oh, is *that* all," she mumbles.

"*NOW*, Frey!"

Her sarcasm drops. "On it. Hang on," she says quickly, sensing the urgency in my voice. "Gimme a minute."

I can hear her keyboard clicking.

"Okay, I'm finding a back door right now. Shouldn't be too…*there* we go," she grunts. "I'm in. What am I looking for?"

"Ulkan."

Freya sucks in her breath sharply.

"He's *there*?" she hisses.

"Yes. And he has Kenzo."

There's a pause.

"Did you hear me?" I mutter. "He—"

"Yeah, no, I heard," Freya responds, typing away. "I guess sentiments have…changed?" she asks, her voice lifting in surprise.

I nod, my heart wrenching. "They have," I whisper. "Please. Find him, Frey."

"Gimme a starting point."

I rattle off the address for Valon's rental house.

"Back up the footage maybe forty-five minutes or so."

"Just a sec." Her fingers clack on the keyboard of her laptop. "*Okaaaay,* here we are." She swears. "Yeah, there's Ulkan. Looks like his guys offed the guards at the house and dragged them inside…" She types some more. "Fast-forwarding—got it. Yeah, they're dragging someone off the property..."

My chest clenches when her breath sucks in again.

"It's Kenzo. They shoved him into a van and drove off."

"Is he hurt?" I whisper, staring into the middle distance as Mal eyes me with concern.

"*Yeah,* Anni," Freya says quietly. "He's hurt."

Fuck.

I glance up, my eyes locking with Mal's as his jaw grinds grimly.

"I got the van," Freya blurts into my ear.

I start to run back to the bikes with Mal hot on my heels.

"Guide me."

25

KENZO

"In my opinion, marriage is *vastly* overrated."

I raise my head. My right eye is fairly swollen, but I can still glare at Ulkan anyway, despite the pain…well, all over.

Everything hurts. Before we left Valon's house, two of Ulkan's goons went to work on me with fists and the same rubber club they used to knock me out earlier—while I was still tied to that fucking post, I might add.

But I'm not focused on the pain or on Ulkan's ramblings. Instead, I'm trying to gauge how badly off the rails this psycho's original plans have gone.

I glance over at the terrified mother huddled in the corner of the kitchen, keeping her two small kids well behind her.

Yeah, whatever Ulkan had in mind, it wasn't this.

"Everything is going to be okay," I murmur quietly in Japanese to the woman.

Her face is pale and stricken, her eyes wide with fear for her children as she shields them behind her back.

"Do you know who I am?" I ask her.

She nods quickly.

"Then you know I will take care of this. I am sorry to have bothered your family—"

I grunt as Ulkan backhands me across the mouth.

"It's *rude* to speak a foreign language in front of those who don't know it, Mr. Mori," he snaps coldly. He turns to nod his chin at the woman. "What the fuck were you saying to her, eh? Telling her to rush me?"

He pulls out a vicious-looking knife and starts to advance on her.

"Ulkan!" I roar at his back, stopping him. "It's me you want, not them," I growl. "She's scared. Her *kids* are scared. I was just calming her and telling her it was going to be okay."

He slowly turns to look back at me with a manic grin. But just as he twirls the knife in his hand, one of his men barges into the kitchen and starts to jabber to his boss in what I think is Albanian.

Ulkan either misses or chooses not to acknowledge the irony as he barks something back in the same language. Then he whirls on me, his face clouded and angry.

I smirk. "What's the matter, Gacaferi? Things not going as planned?"

It's obvious that Takeshi getting away was no accident. None of Ulkan's men seems to have followed him, and no one looked that concerned about it on our drive.

They *wanted* him to "escape". They knew he would run back to my family and tell them what happened, so they'd come looking for me.

So *Annika* would come looking for me.

But this low-income apartment block is clearly not where Ulkan meant for us to lie in wait. Something spooked them while we were driving, and we diverted here to this unlucky woman's home right off the highway.

He whirls to me, his eyes narrowing. "There are checkpoints set up on every highway out of the city," he mutters darkly. "The cops work for you?"

I smile.

Yeah, *that* tells me Tak made it home. It also means Hana's already called the people she knows in the police department. They don't "work" for any one Yakuza family. But the whole system is built on favors and debts, and there's always someone at the top you can do a favor for and bank it until you need something later.

"Whatever you've planned," I spit at Ulkan, "it's gone to shit." I laugh coldly, coughing as the pain in my ribs slices into me. I turn and spit blood onto the floor before turning to level a withering look at the Albanian. "You think I'm just some random Yakuza muscle?"

I turn to look at the poor woman in the corner.

"Do you speak any English?" I ask in Japanese.

She nods. "*A little*," she chokes back.

"Can you please tell this fool who I am?"

She nods, turning fearfully to Ulkan and pointing a shaking finger at me. "*King*," she blurts. "*Kyoto King*."

An uncertain look crosses Ulkan's face as I smile coldly at him.

"I *am* the Yakuza in this city, you dumb fuck," I growl. "Your only hope was to get out before the roads closed." I shake my head. "You won't leave Kyoto alive now, I promise you."

One of Ulkan's men's phones rings. He barks into it, nods curtly, then hangs up and tells his boss something. Ulkan's lips curl as he turns back to me.

"It would seem, Mr. *King*," he snickers, "that your people have found us."

I smile darkly. "Here's my offer. Let this woman and her children walk out of here. Untie me and lay down your weapons. Offer no resistance. If you do all of that, I will grant you a clean, painless death. The alternative, believe me, will be *quite* the opposite."

Ulkan just grins at me. "Please forgive my imperfect English, Mr. Mori. I meant *one* of your people, not several of them."

Shit.

"Tell me, Kenzo," he drawls. "Which of your friends rides a pink, purple and black bike? Because I'm about to kill them in front of you."

I try to think. Takeshi has a half dozen bikes he tinkers with, but he mostly rides the black one with the gold dragon. Hana's go-to is the white Yamaha with the red slash, and Mal likes the black and neon green Ninja—

It hits me like a cold stab of ice to the heart.

...*Annika* was on a pink, purple, and black bike when she, Tak, and Hana went on their joyride.

Oh God...

Before I can get control of my emotions, Ulkan begins to chuckle. "Oh, *please* tell me I'm not that lucky," he wheezes. "Did your bitch wife come to save you, Kenzo? Is *she* the one who—"

"The next time you speak about my wife like that," I growl evenly, "I will cut out your tongue."

He smirks. "I'm terrified, Mr. Mori," he mutters sarcastically. His eyes gleam. "You see, it's not even the money she owes me that I'm concerned about anymore. As I said, it is our *honor* that is most precious in this world. To be wronged like she wronged me requires"...he levels a cold gaze at me..."an *equal* response. She stole some of my honor. So when she charges in here to save you, Mr. Mori, I'll be taking some of *hers...*"

I stiffen as he leans down close to my ear.

"Out of her *ass*, in front of you. In fact, I think I'll let *all* my men have a turn at that hole."

He laughs as I roar at him, thrashing in the chair I'm tied to.

"Stay as angry as you like, Mr. Mori," he chuckles, turning to bark orders at his men as the sound of a motorcycle rumbles up outside the apartment block. "It matters not to me."

Of the original dozen men Ulkan had at Valon's rental, there are only six here now. The rest took off in other cars, and I'm guessing they're the ones scouting ahead who called to let him know about the roadblocks.

But that's still six fucking guys here. And they might not have guns, but they're still hefting sizable knives, clubs, and in one case, two hatchets.

"ANNIKA!" I roar at the top of my lungs. "GET OUT! LEAVE! IT'S A TR—"

I grunt as Ulkan backhands me across the mouth again, scrambling my vision as blood sprays from my lips. The woman and her children in the corner flinch and turn away as Ulkan storms over, grabs a dishrag off the counter next to them, and comes back to gag me with it.

The engine turns off outside. Ulkan nods at his men, muttering something in Albanian.

No.

I roar into the dishrag, bucking and slamming against the chair back as if to smash it and get free. But it's hopeless, and my roars aren't loud enough. She's going to walk right into this trap.

Outside, I hear the sharp yells of Ulkan's men as they go charging out the front door. Annika herself doesn't scream. All I hear is the clang of steel on steel. Again and again, and then the sound of a man groaning in agony.

More clashes of metal on metal. The wet gurgling sound of death taking another man.

A wrenching cry of pain as yet another goes down screaming.

What the *fuck*. That's *three* she's taken out now.

My eyes dart to Ulkan. His face is lined, worry creasing his brow as he pulls a mean-looking machete out of his belt. He edges toward the front door of the apartment, gripping the machete tightly as a fourth man screams outside, dying.

A hand wraps around my mouth from behind. A scent I know so very well fills my nostrils just as I flinch.

"Stay still."

Annika's voice whispered in my ear removes all the pain. It sends a rush of fresh adrenaline coursing through my veins as she cuts the rope around my wrists, freeing them.

I glance at Ulkan, but his back is to us in the other room. I turn back to Annika.

She grins at me, her eyes bright and her bottom lip caught between her teeth.

There's so much I want to do right now. I want to kiss her. I want to wrap her in my arms and never let go.

I want to tell her I love her.

But there's no time for any of that.

"Get them out of here," I hiss quietly, nodding my chin at the woman and her children.

Annika's brow furrows as her gaze slides over me. *"You're hurt—"*

"Please," I shake my head. *"Get them out."*

She nods quickly, turning to smile warmly at the terrified mother and the two little ones. She beckons and the woman approaches, quickly ushering her children after Annika. They go to an open window on the other side of the small kitchen and tiptoe out onto the fire escape one at a time.

"You little *bitch*!!"

I whip my head around just as Ulkan comes charging in from the living room, his machete brandished at Annika who is helping the woman step onto the fire escape.

Instantly I'm on my feet, grabbing the chair I was just tied to and whipping it around, flinging it in Ulkan's face. He bleats in pain as it smashes into him, knocking him on his ass as blood sprays from his mouth.

"Kenzo!"

I turn as Annika grabs my grandfather's sword which has been leaning against the wall. She throws it, I catch it, and I spin around as I yank it free of its scabbard.

Ulkan comes charging at me, his machete held high aloft and a manic look of fury on his face.

My blade stabs forward evenly with practiced ease. Ulkan chokes, gurgling on the blood that froths in his mouth as my sword sinks deep into his chest. His eyes bulge, the machete dropping to the floor.

I yank the blade free and Ulkan drops heavily to his knees, air wheezing out of the hole in his chest as blood pours from his mouth.

"Tell her to look away, princess," I growl quietly, turning to lock eyes with Annika, still standing by the window to the fire escape. "That woman doesn't need to see—"

"KENZO!"

I grunt as something hard slams into me, knocking me off my feet in a hail of splintered wood.

Fuck me, it's the chair I threw at Ulkan.

I hit the ground hard, blinking black spots and stars as a whining sound fills my ears.

Get up.

Get the fuck up.

Annika screams.

The pure adrenaline exploding through my veins has me on my feet and staggering toward them. Ulkan's got Annika pinned to the wall, roaring in her face as his blood spurts all over her front. He's got that fucking machete again, and Annika screams again as he winds his arm back as if to bring it down on top of her head.

He doesn't get the chance.

I grab my grandfather's sword off the ground as I rush Ulkan. The steel flashes, and his lifted arm suddenly drops to the floor, severed clean from his shoulder, the hand still clutching the machete.

Annika shrieks as I grab Ulkan and send him crashing to the floor. I whirl on him as he stares blankly at the gushing stump of his shoulder where his arm was a second ago. His eyes bulge as his gaze swims up to me.

"I told you what would happen if you ever called my wife that again," I mutter.

He tries to say something. But my blade stabs forward with a flash, sliding into his mouth, severing his tongue, and emerging wetly out the back of his neck.

The light flicks off in his eyes as I yank the blade out again and he topples over into a heap on the ground.

"Kenzo..."

Annika runs to my side, catching me before I collapse. I turn to her, groaning as I pull her tight against me.

The front door kicks in. Wincing, I force myself to turn, sword raised.

Mal slides to a stop halfway through the doorway, his blood-soaked blade ready. His eyes lock with mine as my legs start to give out.

"Easy there, brother," he grunts, darting forward and catching me alongside Annika before the two of them wrap their arms around me and walk me out the front door.

"The woman who lives here," I choke when I catch sight of her hiding with some neighbors who've come out to see what the fuck is going on. I bow my head to her and then glance at my brother. "See that she and her children are taken care of. Get them a new house; a nice one. And give her whatever she needs for life money-wise, plus enough so her kids can go to school."

He frowns. "Okay, but how about we get you home first—"

"Get it *done,* Mal."

He nods firmly. "All right, it's done, you have my word. I know how you feel about Yakuza shit disrupting the lives of civilians."

"And *now* can we *please* get you home?" Annika mutters as she hugs me close.

26

ANNIKA

Blood.

So much blood.

I stand under the warm spray of the shower, my hair slicked across my face and my arms crossed over my chest.

Pink water trickles down my body. Red swirls at my feet and spirals down the drain. But there's still so much of it.

So much fucking blood.

The image of Ulkan roaring in my face and trying to grab me while his lifeblood gushed out of his chest plays on a loop, making me flinch and shudder. I squeeze my eyes shut, breathing in steam as I try to shake away the memory.

A hand touches my side. I flinch, whirling with a scream in my throat before my eyes lock with Kenzo. Naked, his own wounds still bleeding, he steps under the water with me.

Wordlessly, his eyes lock with mine. And that's when I worry that I'll see it: the *look*.

Like I'm broken. Faulty.

Damaged goods.

He knows everything now. He knows the worst part of me, my disgusting history with Valon.

Kenzo reaches for me. But I flinch again and retreat against the tiled wall at my back.

His brow furrows.

"*Why*," he growls quietly.

"I'm...dirty," I whisper.

He turns to reach for the body wash. "I'll get the spots you missed—"

"No, Kenzo," I choke, pulling back as his hand reaches for me. "I..."

I avert my eyes again. He stills for a moment, but then suddenly his hands grab my hips, pulling me close. I stiffen, trying to pull away again. But he holds me fast and tight, reaching up to cup my face and lift my eyes to his.

Water streams over his gorgeous face and dark hair. His piercing eyes hold mine.

"*Kenzo...*"

"What was done to you was evil, Annika," he says quietly. "That in no way taints you in any way. It doesn't change the way I see you."

His one hand slips into my hair. The other tightens on my hip.

"*None* of that changes the way I feel about you..."

He backs me against the wall, chest to chest, heart to heart.

"The way I'd *kill* for you..."

My pulse skips as he brushes the hair back from my face and leans closer, our eyes never even blinking under the spray of the shower.

"Or the way I love you."

He cups my face as his mouth descends, his lips crushing mine as I melt against him. I moan, clinging to him desperately, like I'm being tossed in a hurricane and he's my only grounding point. I whimper hungrily into the kiss, holding him tightly as he lifts me into his arms, shuts off the water, and carries me out of the shower.

The air hitting my wet skin is a reality check. I stiffen against him and pull back from his lips with a shudder.

"He..." I swallow. "He's still out there," I breathe. "He got—"

"Leka's dead, Annika," Kenzo says quietly. "The police found a body not far from the rental house—cut to hell, but matching his description." His eyes harden. "They say he bled out *slowly*." Kenzo grits his teeth. "I couldn't bury the past for you, princess," he mutters quietly. "I'm sorry—"

"Yes, you did," I whisper back, cupping his face and resting my forehead on his. I kiss him softly as my heart thuds against his chest. *"You just did."*

I melt into his lips again as he turns and carries me out of the bathroom.

27

KENZO

I WATCH the gentle rise and fall of her back as she sleeps next to me. Personally, I've always been a "back" sleeper. Recently, though, with her here, I've found myself sleeping on my side, because *not* sleeping with my arms around this woman has become intolerable to me.

Annika, however, can sleep in any position. And she does. On her side, half draped over my chest. Sprawled on her back. But frequently, when I'm still awake watching her sleep, she's on her front. Like tonight.

I reach out quietly and gently brush some errant red locks away from her face, letting the moonlight illuminate her.

God, she's beautiful.

And *fuck*, do I love her.

I know that now. No doubt or hesitation. No reservations. No self-reflection. It's as true as the fact that I'm alive. As true as the fact that I'd go to war with the entire world for this woman.

I'd burn the whole thing to the ground, if it was necessary to keep her by my side.

Annika fell directly asleep after I carried her in here after the shower. For the last hour, I've been downstairs with my siblings and some of my and Sota's top *waka gashira* planning what comes next.

Bluntly, we're going to be wiping our enemies off the face of the Earth.

With Ulkan and most of his men dead, his organization is basically toast anyway. But there's no harm in making sure it's completely razed to the ground and the fields sown with salt. The rest of his men, the ones who were driving around Kyoto, have been found and are currently sitting in the bomb shelter sub-basement of a warehouse that Sota uses for this sort of thing.

I don't give a fuck if they were only following orders. They had a hand in the kidnapping of the woman I love. Tomorrow, I will *remove* those hands for the offense. Followed by their heads.

Plans are also in place to go after whatever is left of Ulkan's operations in New York. I've reached out to Kir and am allowing *him* to "eliminate" whatever is left of the man who stole Annika.

He seemed quite pleased at the prospect.

Valon Leka is another matter, though. Yes, his empire will also be razed to the ground and then pissed on. But the tricky thing there is that apparently one of Valon's clients was the White Queen herself: Yelizaveta Solovyova, head of the Solovyova Bratva. She also sits at the Iron Table and is Kir's cousin.

She's also *very* powerful and does *not* like her business interests to be fucked with. It's going to be a slightly easier conversation to have, since I didn't personally kill that asshole Valon. But it's still going to be...tricky.

Right now, though, all that can go fuck itself.

Right now, all I want to do is watch Annika sleep.

I let my finger trail down her hair, brush over her shoulder, and slip under the sheet. I slowly pull it off her shoulder and slide it slowly down the soft skin of her back.

My eyes drift over the swell of her breasts beneath her. The ridges of her ribs, and the dimples at the small of her back, right above her ass.

Something needy and hungry sparks in me as I peel the sheet down further.

Okay, watching her sleep isn't the *only* thing I want to do right now.

I pull the sheet completely off her. My eyes hungrily drag down her bare body, my gaze roaming over the tight globes of her ass and the swell of her hips. Down her long, toned legs...

My dick begins to swell. My blood flows hotter, making my skin tingle as my cock thickens and lengthens, bulging obscenely under the sheet before I pull it away from myself as well.

Annika doesn't move as I get onto my knees beside her. I let my gaze slide over her gorgeous, naked form, drinking in every fucking inch of her as I wrap my hand around my cock and start stroking slowly.

I can't shake the possessiveness. This woman was just almost taken from me. Threatened. Now that I have her back, and in my bed, the need to take her and prove to the world just how *mine* she is, is almost overwhelming.

And *fuck*, am I hard.

Annika only stirs a little as I sit astride the backs of her thighs. I run one hand over her bare hip, gripping her ass softly and feeling the flesh beneath my fingers as I stroke my fat cock with the other hand. My dick hangs heavy and pulsing above her ass, the veins bulging, the head swollen with need.

A drop of thick, clear precum beads at the tip before dripping onto Annika's soft skin and trickling down between the tight globes of her cheeks.

A dark beast stretches awake inside me.

I let go of my cock and put my hands on both her cheeks. I groan when I spread her open, my hungry gaze dipping between her thighs to roam freely over the pretty pink flush of her cunt. My dick jumps and twitches with a mind of its own as I open her up even more. Her pink lips spread so fucking gorgeously and invitingly, glistening, like she's already dreaming of me taking her. Her tight little back hole flexes, feeling the air teasing over her most private place.

I stroke my hand down between her thighs, parting them just a little more as my knees spread wider. I run my fingers up over her pussy, opening her petal-soft lips and dragging the slickness I find there up and down.

Annika mewls sleepily.

Her ass pushes back against my fingers just a little bit.

Good girl.

I run my fingers up and down her seam again. She's getting wetter by the second, her arousal coating my fingers and dripping down to her clit. My fingers follow, rubbing and toying with her throbbing little button as she whines softly again.

I center a finger at her opening and slowly push into her. Annika moans quietly, obviously still asleep as I start to stoke my finger in and out of her greedy, messy little cunt.

Fuck, I need her.

I fucking *need* her sweet little pussy wrapped around my cock, *now*.

Her walls cling eagerly to my finger, trying to suck it back inside every time I draw it out. I slowly sink it deep into her again, stroking her g-spot as her hips begin to rock.

Fuck. I'm so fucking hard it almost hurts. The need to bury my swollen dick in her hot little pussy is almost overwhelming. This is a kink I've had for *years*, since I was a teenager, but obviously it takes a high level of trust and intimacy to do something like this—to *fuck* someone while they're asleep and vulnerable.

While they're *unable* to give something like consent.

A dark part of me acknowledges that *this* is probably part of the reason I'm so drawn to this kink.

However, while I've been with women before, I've never once had anything even approaching a relationship.

I don't *do* intimacy with women. I've let no one in.

But Annika is new. Real. Important to me.

She's my fucking *wife*.

I slide my finger out of her pussy and rub her slick arousal over the head of my cock, mixing it with my sticky wet precum. My quads flex, my knees on either side of her thighs as I grip her ass and spread her wide open to my hungry gaze.

I roll my hips forward, letting the swollen, eager head of my cock slip between her thighs and nudge against her pretty, pink cunt.

Annika mewls again, her face twisting a little and her lip catching in her teeth as she continues to sleep. I drag my cock up and down her pussy lips, watching them open for me and part around my thick head. Precum and her own drippy arousal coat our skin, making lewd wet sounds as I slide up and down her slit.

My balls throb with need, swollen with cum as I groan and watch the veins of my cock throb hungrily.

Pushing forward, my teeth gritted and my eyes hooded with lust, I watch as her pussy opens for me. Her lips begin to stretch lewdly around my fat cock as I begin to slide into her, careful not to wake her.

Not *yet*, at least.

I stare, transfixed at the stunning vision laid out before me: Annika on her front, her legs together and her arms pillowed under her sleeping head. Her ass spread lewdly wide with my fat dick slowly pushing into her tight little pussy.

I groan as I sink in another inch. *Christ*, she's so fucking tight, and her lips are stretched so pink and wet around my swollen cock. I ease in another inch or two, watching as her ass flexes and her back arches just a little.

Her face crumples in pleasure as I drive another thick inch into her greedy little hole. My abs flex as I push, driving my dick deeper and deeper into her slippery, heavenly heat. I wet my thumb and bring it down, stroking gently over her back hole as I grind my cock deeper into her pussy. Annika moans, her body coiling and shifting. I groan and push the rest of the way in, sinking the rest of my thick cock into her hot little pussy until my heavy balls are resting right against her lips.

"Kenzo…" she whimpers in her sleep.

I grin savagely, grabbing her ass and rubbing her puckered hole as I slowly draw out. I let the head stay in, savoring the way her lips cling to me and try to coax me back inside.

I'm all too happy to oblige.

I drive back in, a little harder and faster this time. Her body jolts, her ass jiggling seductively as I fuck into her. I pull out again, groaning a little louder when I thrust back in.

Annika is moaning softly now. Her hips lift as if to give me easier access. Her mouth falls open and her brow caves.

Her pussy clenches around me, dripping all over my balls as I plunge into her again.

"Kenzo..." she murmurs sleepily. *"Kenzo…"*

She's breathing my name with every exhalation. Moaning for more as I ram my cock into her hard.

"Kenzo!"

Her eyes fly open. Shock explodes over her face, and on instinct, she squirms and writhes as if to shove me away from her.

That's obviously not happening.

I growl as I grab a fistful of her hair near the nape of her neck in one hand, and her hip with the other. She whines and writhes as I pin her roughly to the bed and ram into her hard. My hand tightens in her hair, twisting her face to the side so that one eye can see me claiming her.

"*Oh fuuuck*," she cries, shuddering as I ram my fat cock into her greedy little pussy. "*Yeah, fuck me, baby*," she whimpers.

"*So fucking eager*," I snarl as I lean over her to bite her shoulder hard. She squeals and squirms again as I thrust savagely. "Such a greedy little slut, going to bed with no panties on so that just anyone could come and fuck her needy little cunt."

Annika moans wildly, twisting and writhing beneath me.

"*Noooo*," she whines, gasping in pleasure as I thrust into her over and over.

"No?" I hiss, fucking her hard as my thumb circles her asshole. "That's *not* what you were doing, like the bad little slut you are?"

She moans louder, trying to thrust back to meet my hips as they bounce off her ass.

"Not...just...anyone," Annika chokes, shuddering as I start to fuck her even harder, making her whole body shake.

"*Only youuu*!" she whines.

I groan as my cock throbs even harder, my blood sparking and rippling like liquid fire as I thrust into her.

"*Whose fucking pussy is this*?" I snarl.

"*Yours*!" my wife moans and gasps. "All fucking yours!!"

She cries out, a guttural, deep moan as I add my thumb to the mix, sinking it wetly into her tight little ass. She squeals and whimpers, her legs kicking and her toes curling into the sheets as I fuck my swollen dick into her pussy over and over.

"And whose *ass* is this?" I rasp.

"*Yours*!" she sobs in pleasure. "My ass is all yours, too!"

I groan as I feel my balls being to swell. "From now on, princess," I growl, "you will not *touch* this fucking bed with any panties on. Do you understand?"

She moans, her mouth slack and drooling onto the sheets as she clings to them and my swollen cock rams into her over and over, fucking her within an inch of her life.

"You will wear *nothing* below the waist when you enter this bed. And I *will* take you and fuck you in any hole I fucking want, *whenever* I want," I groan.

"Even when I'm asleep?" she whimpers eagerly.

"*Especially* when you're asleep," I groan.

"What if I say..." Her breath catches as I pound into her. "*What if I say no*?" she chokes breathlessly.

Annika whimpers as I lean over her, roughly yanking her head to the side by the fistful of her hair and letting my teeth rake over her earlobe.

"You never say no to me, princess," I rasp. "But if you did?"

My thumb slides out of her tight little ring, only to be replaced by two thick fingers. I push them into her ass, making her hot little pussy stretch even tighter around my cock.

"If you say no, *I'll only fuck you harder.*"

"Oh FUCK!"

Without warning, Annika suddenly spasms and writhes underneath me. She screams into the sheets, sobbing in pleasure as I thrust into her over and over. Her body explodes around me, her pussy clenching and gripping my fat dick like it's trying to strangle it.

I keep fucking her, thrusting into her right through her orgasm, not stopping at all. My fingers and my cock fuck her tight holes, claiming her as mine as I ram her into the bed.

"Kenzo!" she whines, shuddering under me. "I—I—"

"Be a good girl for me, princess..."

"I'm gonna fucking come again! Oh shit! Oh SHIT!" She chokes. "I'm—OH *GOD!!"*

This time, when I feel her pussy clench and grip my cock as she explodes around me, there's no holding back. I groan, my vision swimming as black stars dance in front of my eyes. I sink my swollen cock into her, grinding as deep as I can as my balls throb and explode.

My cock jumps and erupts like a volcano, my hot cum spilling into her slick, eager pussy as she claws at the sheets and writhes beneath me.

I pump into her again and again, her tight pussy wringing every drop of cum from me until I sink against her.

Slowly, I slide out of her perfect, *perfect* pussy and collapse onto my side. She's gasping for air as she rolls into me, snuggling back against my body as I wrap my arms around her.

She's trembling as she takes my hand and lifts it to her lips, kissing my knuckles softly.

"I love you," she whispers, so quietly I almost don't hear it.

But I do.

And I fucking *grin.*

"I love you, too," I murmur as my arms wrap tighter around her and her body melds to mine.

28

KENZO

"Do you have the *slightest* idea what you've done, Kenzo?"

Tengan glares over the rim of his glasses at me as he, unbelievably, manages to stop his frantic pacing for *a single fucking second*.

"Kenzo?"

My face still hurts. My body still hurts, too.

My *dick* hurts as well, now that I think about it, but that's in a good way. That particular part of me is sore because I spent the entirety of last night tangled up in bed with Annika, pumping her so full of my cum that she'll be feeling me drip into her panties for a week.

And as soon as this absurd "high priority meeting" that Tengan insisted on is over, I'll be finding Annika wherever she is and dragging her back to bed for round...fuck, I've lost count.

Sota's business manager glares at me over his glass again, as if I'm some naughty schoolboy.

"*Do you?*" he hisses shrilly.

"First, you will lower your voice and calm your tone when you're speaking to me," I growl. I catch the hidden smirk on Sota's face before he tucks it behind his customary "business Sota" mask of indifference.

"Second, I didn't *do shit*. Ulkan Gacaferi killed Leka, not me."

If Ulkan were still alive, I still haven't decided if I'd send him a gift for killing that fuck or kill him myself for robbing *me* of that honor.

It's probably the second one.

"Yes, but you gave the order last night to declare open war on Leka's people, not to mention seize his assets and businesses."

"His *people* are a bunch of drug smugglers who've been dipping their toes into human trafficking. I sincerely doubt anyone in the world will mourn their passing," I snarl. "This, I should add, is why I was never going to go into business with him."

And that was even *before* I learned that he'd hurt Annika.

"The *issue*, Kenzo," Tengan mutters snippily, "is that by declaring open season on Leka's interests, you've made it clear in just about every circle that you're glad he's dead."

"Which I *am*," I growl.

"It makes it look like you could have had a hand in his death."

"Tengan," I mutter tiredly. "I still fail to see the downside—"

"Leka was in long-term business deals with Yelizaveta Solovyova."

I shrug. "Yes, I'm *aware*. I spoke with Kir last night, and he's going to smooth—"

"That hasn't gone quite as planned," Tengan spits at me. He turns to shake his head at Sota. "Sota-san," he whines. "The White Queen is *not* pleased. My people—"

"Who exactly are *your people*, Tengan?" I grunt. "Surely you mean *Sota*'s people, no?"

The little twerp shoots me a look before he turns back to Sota.

"Of course, Sota-san, I mean your people—"

"It's fine, Tengan," Sota says mildly. "Go on."

"Yelizaveta is not at all pleased with how this was handled." He whirls back to me before I can open my mouth. "Before you say anything, yes, we can all agree that Valon Leka was not a good man. But that's really not her concern considering the amount of business she did with him, and the value of the product that he transported for her."

I sigh. "I'll get in touch with Ms. Solovyova and give her the full—"

"Leka still has people, you know," Tengan spits shrewishly. "In fact, his brother Basor, with whom he started the business, is interested in taking over. He's currently in prison in Bulgaria, but he reached out to me this morning—"

"I'm sorry, *what?*" I snarl, lurching to my feet. Tengan scuttles back when I jab a finger at his face. "Exactly *who* do you work for, Tengan—"

"Kenzo." Sota raises a finger. "Let him finish. Tengan's loyalty is not up for debate."

I glare at Sota's business manager, but then nod respectfully to Sota and sit down again.

Tengan straightens his tie fastidiously. "Of course I work for Sota-san, Kenzo," he mutters. "But it's my job to make sure business flows as it should. So, yes, Basor contacted me this morning from prison via a smuggled phone. He wants the death of his brother to settle whatever disagreement you had with him…."

Disagreement?!

I could strangle the little fuck. But I keep myself in check.

"And as *he* will be taking Valon's place as head of the organization, he wants to talk about doing business as planned and going ahead with the original contract that was discussed."

I shake my head. "Not happening in a million years. No. *Fuck* no."

Tengan's face darkens as he glances at Sota.

"*Sota-san,* if you could kindly talk sense into your—"

"Give us a moment, Tengan," Sota says quietly.

Tengan glares at me, then he turns and bows stiffly to his boss. "Of course."

After he's gone, I shake my head and point to the door that Tengan just retreated through.

"He's a big problem," I growl.

Sota smiles, nodding amicably. "He would be, if he wasn't so loyal to me."

I exhale slowly. "I just can't okay doing business with Leka's successor, even if the bastard himself is dead. Besides, I've heard of Basor. He's supposed to be even more of a piece of shit than Valon was."

Sota nods. "You understand what Tengan is saying though, yes? If we were to go into business with Basor, it would reassure Yelizaveta that the feud was with one man, not an entire organization with whom she does significant business." He sighs. "I know it might not be what you want, but you had to know there would be fallout from everything that happened last night."

I nod. "I know, and I'll face it, Sota. Look, I made a choice. And I'm sticking to that choice. I'll deal with whatever comes of it."

A small smile creeps over his face. "Good," he says quietly. "If that's the way you feel, then you're ready."

My brow furrows. "For?"

"In eight weeks, I'm going to be going to Italy for a few months. I'm not sure exactly how long. But I've always wanted to visit the vineyards of Tuscany and Piedmont, and I can't think of a better time to go."

I stare. "Sota, in eight weeks you have to be in New York for your next round of treatment—"

"I won't be going to New York for another round of treatment, Kenzo," he says quietly.

Something breaks inside me. My face falls, my pulse skipping as I stare at my second father, every emotion roaring to the surface.

No.

I'm not ready yet. I'm not ready for this man to leave this world. Not now, and definitely not like this.

"Sota," I choke. "Whatever they said, there are other options. There's a doctor in China right now doing some amazing breakthrough stuff with mRNA—"

"I'm not going back to treatment, Kenzo," Sota says with a small smile, "because I'm in remission."

The world freezes. I stare at him, shocked and stunned, watching the grin creep across his face.

"*Goddammit,*" I groan, lurching to my feet and striding around the desk. "You're serious?"

Sota stands, laughing as I hug him fiercely.

"Completely," he smiles warmly. "Full remission after my last blood test."

I grin, shaking my head at him. "You scared the shit out of me, you know."

He grins, shrugging. "Let an old man have his theatrics."

I exhale heavily, shaking my head again. "That wasn't even the littlest bit funny. Do me a favor, don't pull that crap with Hana. It'll break her."

Then, suddenly, I frown.

"What did you mean by me being ready?"

He smiles as he takes my hand and pats it. "I understand your father now. I *understand* the need for something different and more peaceful than the Yakuza. In two months, Kenzo, I'm done. I'm going to Italy without a return ticket, and I plan on eating good pasta, drinking fine wine, and kissing beautiful Italian women. And when I do…"

I tense up as it hits me.

"Sota—"

"You're ready, Kenzo," he says quietly. "To be King."

29

ANNIKA

SEEING Freya again feels like a homecoming, even though it's *her* who came to me. The original plan was for us just to meet up at the Mori estate. But I nixed that plan and insisted instead on going to the airport with Kenzo's people so I could meet my best friend on the tarmac.

As an added surprise, Kir's come along too, which is fantastic. He's also brought Isaak, which makes me realize how much I had missed the big grump. I hug them all fiercely the second they get off the private plane. Then Kir is smart enough to step back and let Freya and I freak out together and scream and yell and do all the insane asylum shit we usually do when we've been apart for a while.

When we're done alarming Kenzo's security guys and finally get into the cars, Kir Facetimes with Damian, who's completely on the mend and walking around just fine, thank you—just not quite well enough to be flying to Japan.

Back at the house, the anarchy gets right into full swing.

Adding someone like Freya into the mix of me, Hana, and Takeshi is a bit like hurling some fireworks into a bonfire.

"A toast!" Kir smiles as he taps the side of his glass of vodka with a chopstick.

We've all just finished eating dinner in one of Kenzo's gorgeous gardens, and we're keeping the festive mood going with an impromptu party. Everyone's here: Kenzo and I, Hana, Takeshi, Kir, Isaak, Sota, and a number of both Sota and Kenzo's people are all smiling around the table in the garden, drinking and having a blast.

Well, almost everyone. Mal is missing, without much of an explanation aside from a text to Kenzo that he had "business" to attend to.

Party pooper.

Kir taps his glass again as everyone goes quiet. "I know we're long past the wedding. But any marriage worth its salt is always worth celebrating." He turns to where I'm standing next to Kenzo, my husband's arm firmly around my waist and his hand possessively on my hip. "To the daughter I never thought I'd have, who I've been lucky enough to call family. And to her husband." He nods his chin at Kenzo. "It takes a brave man to weather our Annika. And it takes a truly remarkable one to steal her heart."

I grin widely as Kenzo pulls me tighter to him and Freya turns around to waggle her brows at us.

"To Annika and Kenzo," Kir growls.

"Annika and Kenzo!" various voices cheer.

"To you, wife," Kenzo purrs quietly, turning me in his arms and pulling me close as the party music turns back on.

"To *us*," I murmur, grinning as he leans down to kiss me softly.

Just then, I yelp as a grinning Freya pulls me away from him. "Sorry, I know you're married. But technically I'm the *first* marriage, so, you know...deal with it."

Kenzo chuckles as Freya and Hana pull me toward the impromptu dance party that's broken out next to the speakers. Takeshi turns out to have *great* moves. Kir's effort is admirable, and even Isaak makes a stoic attempt at "dancing", if you can call it that.

Hana, Freya, and I get another round of drinks and head back to the dance floor, laughing and having a great time. It feels like I'm drinking straight happiness as I turn to lock eyes with Kenzo across the party before I'm pulled right back into the mayhem.

"How does it feel to know you're singlehandedly destroying an empire that has endured for over three generations."

I startle as I turn and come face to face with Tengan. He glares at me, swaying slightly and splashing the drink in his hand on his own shoe. The scent of sake wafts over me strongly.

"Excuse me?" I say curiously as the music and the party rages on around us.

"You've ruined everything," he slurs. "*Everything.*"

I frown at him. "Tengan, I think you've had a bit too much—"

"Just because of some fucking *lover's quarrel,*" he continues. "Because you couldn't *stand* seeing your fake husband doing business with the man you used to *fuck—*"

It happens so quickly I almost can't comprehend it. One second, I'm about to smash my glass of wine into the side of Tengan's face. The next, a huge shape is barreling into him like a freight train and slamming him back five feet into the side of the house with a roar.

The music goes silent. And suddenly, we're all staring in shock as Kenzo grips Tengan by the throat, holding the tip of a naked blade to his jugular.

"Do you know what happened to the last man who spoke to my wife like that?" he seethes.

Tengan looks terrified as he stabs his gaze past Kenzo, scanning the crowd.

"Don't look for Sota," Kenzo growls. "He won't help you here."

Tengan's throat bobs against Kenzo's hand.

"The last man who spoke to her like that got his arm removed. Then his tongue. Then his *head*," Kenzo hisses, pressing the edge of the knife against Tengan's throat. "Now, I'm celebrating tonight...and arms and heads leave a lot of blood...so why don't we start with the *tongue* and see where the evening takes us—"

"Kenzo."

It's not Sota who stops him.

It's me.

When he feels my touch on his shoulder, it's like the granite his body had hardened into melts a little. He turns, his expression softening as our eyes lock.

"He's not worth it."

"Princess—"

"*Please*," I say softly. "No more blood over me."

His jaw grits. But he slowly nods his head, and pulls the knife away from Tengan's throat.

Sota's business manager gasps deeply, choking for air as he drops to the ground. Then he's instantly lurching to his feet again and snarling at Kenzo.

"The fucking *gaijin* prince, choosing a *whore* over an empire—"

He goes still as the edge of a sword swishes to a frozen stop a fraction of an inch from his jugular.

...*Sota's* sword.

The older man levels a cold, withering look at Tengan .

"It is only at my daughter-in-law's request that I'm staying my hand. But you will find that that is the extent of my generosity this evening." He pulls the sword away. "Your services to me and the Yakuza are no longer required. You have one minute to leave this property, and twelve hours to leave this city. If I ever see you in Kyoto again, I will let Kenzo do whatever he wishes to you. Is that understood?"

Tengan balks, his face falling. "*Sota-san*!"

"Your one minute has already begun."

Tengan shoots a helpless, glaring look at Kenzo. Then another at me. Finally, he turns tail and runs into the dark gardens in the direction of the front gates.

"Well, that's that," Sota clears his throat, smiling as he puts his sword away. "I think we need more music, and more sake."

Everyone cheers as the music comes back on. Kenzo turns to peer down into my face.

"Are you okay?"

"Yeah. It's nothing," I exhale, waving a hand.

"Annika..."

"I'm serious, Kenzo," I say quietly. "I really am fine."

His hands slide possessively over my hips and draw me close to him.

The heat of his body throbs against me. The scent of his skin which I now know so well wraps around me like an embrace. His dark eyes pierce into mine, and suddenly, I flush as something pulses in my core.

Jesus, he's *hard*.

"What you are, princess," he murmurs thickly, "is *mine*."

He grabs my hand.

"And I'm going to show just you how mine you are right now."

30

ANNIKA

The millisecond the door to the bedroom shuts behind us, we explode.

I moan, shuddering and gasping as Kenzo drags me against his body. His hands are all over me, gripping and squeezing, ripping away clothes. I tremble as I do the same, feverishly tugging at his shirt and yanking on his belt.

His mouth falls to my neck, biting sharply and making me cry out, sending a bolt of adrenaline through my core.

I drop to my knees and pull open his pants. He reaches into his black boxer briefs, his thumb stretching the waistband down as he wraps his hand around himself and pulls his cock out.

Fuck.

I bite my lip, my thighs squeezing together as my gaze drifts over the v-line grooves of his hips. I stare at his heavy, thick cock as he slowly strokes it in front of my face before my own hand comes up to push his away.

I shiver as I stroke him, feeling the weight of the shaft and the pulsing of the thick veins under the silky skin. My eyes lift to his, our gazes locking as I lean forward and wet my lips with my tongue. When I kiss his swollen head, Kenzo sucks in his breath, his abs clenching as his jaw grinds.

"*Fuck*, princess," he groans.

My own pulse throbs as I kiss the head again, stroking him. I lift his heavy cock, kissing the underside and swiping at it with my tongue.

Kenzo's fingers thread through my hair, wrapping it in a fist, sending an electric jolt through my core. My lips part, and when I slide them over his throbbing crown, he groans deeply.

I moan around him, the sheer size of him stretching my lips wide. My tongue swirls around the underside as I try and take him even deeper. He grunts, his grip on my hair tightening as he pushes into my small mouth. His fat cock hits the back of my throat, sending a shivering thrill through me as I whimper around him.

Our eyes lock as he grips my hair more tightly, slowly sliding his glistening cock out of my mouth before pushing back in. I moan as I stroke his shaft and let my fingertips tease over his heavy balls, my gaze never leaving his.

"Such a greedy little slut," he growls thickly. "You look so fucking pretty with my cock filling your slutty little mouth."

I moan deeply, opening my throat and gagging as I try and swallow him down. Kenzo hisses in pleasure as I choke on his cock, spit dripping from the corners of my mouth as my head spins with lust and need.

There's something so fucking hot about choosing *him* over oxygen.

Choosing his pleasure and his gorgeous dick over my own ability even to breathe.

The adrenaline spikes in my core as I force his cock as deep as it can possibly get. My eyes water and tear up, and my lungs burn as I take him into the very back of my throat.

I'm fucking *soaked.*

Kenzo hisses again sharply, throwing his head back as he grabs my hair and fucks my mouth. I moan around him, stroking and teasing as I gag on his dick, wanting to feel him explode down my throat.

He's got other plans.

I whine in protest when he groans and pulls me off him. Then he's yanking me to my feet, grabbing my jaw, and kissing me brutally. I shiver as he shoves my dress off my shoulders and rips it down my body until it puddles at my feet. My bra follows before he lifts me and carries me across the room, making me shriek.

My pulse spikes as he tosses me onto the bed. Kenzo drops to his knees at the foot of it, dragging me to the edge and slipping his fingers into my panties. They're yanked down my legs and tossed aside, and before I know what is happening, he's draping my legs over his shoulders, and diving between my thighs.

"Oh fuck, Kenzo..."

I cry out as his skilled tongue delves between my lips, dragging up between them and swirling over my throbbing clit. Electricity spikes through my core, my back arching as sharply as if I'd been shocked. I moan deeply, my fingers sliding down into his hair as he groans into my pussy.

"Such a *messy* little cunt," he growls into my thigh, making me yelp as he bites down hard on the tender skin. "Did being on your knees and being my eager little cumslut get this pussy so fucking dripping wet for me?"

My mind reels as I melt into the bed. My back arches, my hands sliding up my ribs and mauling my breasts as he devours me whole. His fingers sink into me, making me cry out when he starts to stroke two of them against my g-spot and wraps his lips around my swollen clit. He sucks on it, his tongue swirling over the aching bud as I shudder and writhe beneath him.

I shiver when I feel his thumb brush against my asshole. He strokes it teasingly in slow circles in time with his tongue on my clit, sending electric pulses through my core. He strokes his thumb higher, gathering the slickness from my dripping wet pussy before sliding it back down to my tight little hole.

My eyes roll back, my jaw going slack as I feel him slowly push into me. My ass squeezes around his thumb as it slides inside, and the feeling of being so full, of having his fingers in both of my holes as he sucks on my clit, sends me tumbling over the edge.

Oh fuck...

I can feel myself start to shake and clench all over. My back arches, my hips shamelessly pushing against his face and fingers as my thighs start to quiver.

"Kenzo..."

"Make a fucking mess for me, princess," he growls against my pussy. "I want this pretty little cunt to come all over my fucking face."

His lips wrap around my clit and suck, hard.

It's like pulling a trigger.

I cry out, my back arcing violently off the bed as the orgasm explodes through my body. Kenzo's tongue and lips and fingers stroke, suck, and tease me through the explosive release, sending electric pulses spiking through my every nerve.

He's nowhere near done with me.

I moan as he slides up between my thighs, wrapping them around his muscled hips. He centers his huge, swollen cock at my entrance as he grabs a fistful of my hair. A whimper falls from my lips as he raises me up off the bed, pulling me against his body as his swollen head sinks into me. My arms wrap around his neck as he stands. Quickly, he yanks me down onto every fucking inch of his fat cock.

"*FUCK*!" I cry out, shivering in ecstasy at the feeling of him ramming into me and taking me completely. The sheer size of him takes my breath away, and when he kisses me fiercely, I moan as I taste myself on his lips.

"You're my *wife*," he growls possessively as he turns and starts to walk across the room with me still impaled on his cock. "You're *mine*, Annika."

I gasp as my back hits the floor-length mirror. I kiss him back hungrily, my arms wrapped tight around his neck and my legs around his grooved hips as he grinds his thick cock deep inside me.

"This *mouth* is mine," he growls, sucking my tongue between his lips as he draws back and then fucks his cock deep.

I moan eagerly, rolling my hips into him as he fucks me against the mirror.

"These fucking *tits* are mine," he snarls, dropping his mouth to my neck and biting down hard before he delves to my chest. His lips wrap around a pink nipple, and when his teeth sink into the tender, pebbled nub, I cry out sharply, my back jerking and my pussy dripping around his thickness.

Without warning, he suddenly slides out of me, sets my feet back on the floor, and whirls me around to face the mirror. I moan desperately, my palms going flat to it as he positions himself behind me. I whimper, shivering as he centers his fat cock against my swollen pussy lips and sinks into me from behind.

Oh FUCK...

He pounds into me with deep, even strokes, one big hand gripping my hip tightly as the other wraps my hair in a fist. My breath fogs the glass as I stare at myself in the mirror, my moans filling the room. The view of his massive, muscled body behind me, utterly taking me as he fucks into me sends me reeling as the pleasure spreads through my core.

"Look at yourself, princess," he growls savagely. "Look at yourself taking that big dick like a good girl. Look how fucking *mine* you are."

Kenzo starts to fuck me harder—savagely, like he's possessed. Like he's leaving his mark or his claim.

Showing the whole fucking world that I belong to him.

And *fucking hell*, is that hot.

Our bodies writhe and grind together, his mouth and teeth nipping, biting, and sucking on my shoulders and my neck, leaving bruises over my skin. His fingers dig into my hip and my ass, leaving marks on me I hope don't fade soon.

Because I *like* being his.

I like being marked and claimed by him.

Dominated by him.

A sob of insane pleasure wrenches from my mouth as he rams into me hard, fucking me mercilessly against the mirror.

"Whose fucking *pussy* is this," he rasps darkly into my ear as he sinks his swollen dick deep inside me.

"*Yours*!" I cry out, rocking my hips back against his as he thrusts into me. "*All yours*!" I moan desperately, my body starting to crumple and tense as another orgasm threatens to rip me in two.

"*Yes, all mine*," he grunts, ramming his cock deep. "So be a good little slut and let me feel *MY fucking pussy* come all over this big cock."

Sweet Jesus.

My entire body spasms and clenches, the explosive release ripping through me like liquid fire. One of his big hands grips my ass as he thrusts into me. The other wraps tight around my throat from behind, squeezing as his teeth rake down my neck. My whole world comes undone, my vision blurring and turning black as every part of me squeezes around him and explodes.

Kenzo holds me as I cling desperately to him, shuddering as

the aftershocks of my orgasm tingle and ripple through my core. He turns my head and kisses me hard.

"You…" I pull back, biting my lip as my pulse races. "You haven't come yet."

Our eyes lock.

"*All of me* is yours," I murmur softly, something deviant and aching throbbing and burning inside of me.

For years, I hated that it was Valon who took my virginity. I still hate the experience, the man, the lingering shame and the feeling of indebtedness that came with it. That monster took so much from me.

But not everything.

I shiver, swallowing as I drop my mouth to Kenzo's ear.

"*I want you to have all of me*," I whisper, my voice husky. "Take it all."

An electric feeling pulses through me as I feel his steel cock throb inside me. Gingerly, I pull away, feeling his slick, swollen cock slip out. I twist and kiss him, cupping his face as I melt against him.

"*Take whatever you want*," I moan softly against his lips. "I'm all yours, every part of me."

Kenzo groans into my mouth as he kisses me. His big arms wrap around me, somehow both savagely protective and tender at the same time.

"*Don't. Move*," he growls.

He pulls away from me, turning and striding over to a chair near one of the shaded windows, pulling it over and positioning it facing the mirror before sitting in it.

"Come here, princess," he murmurs darkly, crooking his fingers at me and pointing to the spot between his legs.

Fuck. His cock is so fucking big and swollen, sticking straight up against his abs with the veins throbbing down the entire length of him.

I shiver when I step between his spread legs and he grabs me, twisting me. My breath catches as he bends me over at the hip, and when I feel his breath against my pussy, I tremble.

His tongue dives through my swollen pussy, licking and sucking at my clit before he drags his tongue back and higher. I cry out when the tip of it swirls wetly over my asshole, teasing and electrifying the raw nerve endings there. I plant my palms against the mirror, steadying myself as my eyes roll back in anticipation.

His fingers play with my pussy as he rims my ass, liquifying my whole body and making my legs shake. Just before I feel like they might give out, Kenzo slowly pulls me back into him.

He spreads my legs to either side of his as he pulls me astride his lap, my legs on either side of his.

"Look at yourself in the mirror, princess," he growls quietly.

I obey, and I flush when I see myself so lewdly spread open, with his swollen, bulging cock sticking straight up from his grooved abs.

Kenzo slowly lowers me, easing me down against his lap. I shiver, my eyes bulging wide when I see and feel the thick head of his slick cock press against my puckered back hole.

Oh fuck...

"*You're so big...*" I choke quietly.

I shiver as he kisses and nips at the back of my neck. His hands slide around me, one cupping my breasts and rolling one of the nipples, the other sliding between my thighs. I watch him stroke his fingers through my pussy lips and swirl them over my clit, making me moan.

"You control it, princess," he groans. "*You* take what you want."

Yeah, I want *it all.*

If that's possible.

I push down, gasping sharply as I feel the swollen head of his gorgeous cock press harder against my ring. The slickness from his tongue a second ago and all the sticky precum leaking from his cock smear over my asshole, lighting a fire in my core.

Seriously, he's *so* fucking big. But as I gently grind myself against him and push down gradually, breathing deeply, I can slowly start to feel myself opening for him.

The head slides inside.

Holy fuck...

My eyes go wide, my mouth falling slack as a low whine starts in my throat.

"*There you go,*" he growls against my back. His muscled arms surround me, touching me everywhere and stroking my skin as I feel myself stretch around his size. "*Such* a good girl, taking that big dick."

I whimper, sucking in air and biting down hard on my lip. I push myself down, choking as his thick cock slowly pries me open and slides deeper.

GOD, he's big.

The slight pinch of pain hurts. But it's a good hurt. A hurt that ripples deep into my core and sets my insides on fire. Kenzo's hand slips between my legs, rubbing and rolling my clit as another inch of his cock slides into my ass.

"*Good girl,*" he murmurs into my ear, nipping at the lobe. "You're doing so well, taking that big dick in that tight little hole. Look at yourself, princess," he growls thickly, spreading my thighs open as he rubs my clit. My eyes drop, hooding as my pulse throbs, watching in awe as his fat cock disappears up into me.

"*Look at what a good girl you're being,*" he groans as he rubs my clit faster. "Taking all that dick. Taking that big cock like a little slut."

My eyes roll back, my mouth hanging open as I groan a guttural, choking moan. I slide down, and down, and down, a whine bubbling up from my throat as I feel myself sink all the way down every thick inch of his swollen cock until his balls are pressed right against me.

"*All mine,*" Kenzo groans quietly against the side of my neck.

Slowly, I slide back up. My breath arrests in my chest as the sheer size of him spreads me again on the way up. But then just as slowly, I sink back down.

A deep, animalistic groan tumbles from my lips as his hands cup my breasts, teasing my nipples before sliding down to rub my clit.

"*Ride me,* princess," he groans, twisting my head to the side and viciously biting and sucking at my mouth.

I moan into him, rolling my hips and sliding up and down his shaft, my tongue dancing with his as he rolls my clit.

"Look at how fucking sexy you are," he growls, releasing my head. "Look how fucking *pretty* you are, riding that big dick, taking it up the ass like a good little cock slut. Like *my* good little slut."

My legs start to shake. The friction of him sliding in and out of me, pushing so fucking deep as he rubs my clit, is almost overwhelming. It's just this side of *too* much, and riding the bleeding edge between heaven and insanity lights a fuse inside of me.

Kenzo's mouth devours mine as he twists my head to the side again. His lips drop to my jaw and then my neck, biting and sucking and mauling my skin as he thrusts up into me. My ass slaps against his thighs, his balls hitting my pussy with every stroke as his finger rubs and rolls my clit until every single part of me is shaking.

"I can feel you squeezing so fucking tight around my cock, princess," he groans against my skin, making me cry out as his teeth sink into my flesh. "Watch yourself," he mutters, kissing the side of my mouth as he forces me to look at myself in the mirror getting fucked in the ass.

"Watch yourself come with that big dick in your ass," he growls. "Show me how my good little ass-slut comes like a good girl."

He bites the side of my mouth as he kisses me like a wild animal. My eyes are locked on us in the mirror as his big fingers roll my clit and wrap around my throat from behind.

"*Come for me, princess,*" he rasps against my mouth. "Come for me, because you're *all fucking mine.*"

When the orgasm hits me, my vision blurs and I see stars as everything goes dark. I cry out a wrenching, electric, broken sob of pleasure as my entire core tightens and explodes. Kenzo groans, driving up into me and biting my lip as his cock surges and pulses. I moan as I feel the hot jets of his cum spilling into me, pulsing deep as his arms wrap tight around me.

It feels like every single molecule of my body is trembling as I collapse back against him, utterly spent. I wince, gasping a little as Kenzo gently slides me off him and gathers me against his chest. He turns me in his lap, kissing me slowly and deeply as he lifts me in his arms and carries me to the bathroom.

He never stops kissing me as the hot water and suds fill the bathtub. Nor when he sinks down into the steam with me still in his arms.

He doesn't ever stop kissing me at all.

And I wouldn't have it any other way.

31

KENZO

For the next two weeks, life is all a hazy dream.

I spend my nights tangled up in Annika.

...I spend a lot of my *days* the same way, to be honest.

It's as if I'm addicted to the scent of her. A junkie for the taste of her. Hooked on the feeling of her lips on mine.

Sota officially announces his retirement, and sets the timeline for the Akiyama-kai to be folded into the Mori-kai. There's some grumbling here and there, but for the most part, everyone in both organizations seems excited and ready for the full strength of the new Mori-kai empire to flex its muscles.

Yes, it's all a little nerve-wracking. At the same time, I'm beyond ready to lead. I was *born* for this. It's in my blood. And with Annika by my side, I feel unstoppable.

Kir heads back to New York, but Freya ends up staying a while. She and Hana are already pals-slash-partners-in-crime, and the fact that Freya can ride seems to win Tak over, too.

Mal, meanwhile, has suddenly found himself *fully* embroiled with work and has utterly disappeared for the last week.

I have questions. Several of them. But they can wait.

For now, I'm simply enjoying the moment. I've got a throne to ascend. An empire to rule.

A wife to love, and a partner to call my equal.

Life is fucking *good*.

"How's New York?"

"The same. You miss it?" Kir chuckles over the phone.

I sigh. "Sometimes, a little. Others, not at all."

I do love New York. But it's Kyoto that feels like home—doubly so now, with Annika here too.

"So—talk to me about Yelizaveta Solovyova."

This time it's Kir's turn to sigh heavily. "My cousin is a complicated woman, Kenzo."

That's putting it mildly.

Yelizaveta Solovyova, known as The White Queen due to her albinism…and that's a nickname she gave herself, by the way…has ruled the Solovyova Bratva with an even temper and iron fist since she was twenty-three years old. She never married, never had any children, and in the *extremely* patriarchal world of the Bratva, she's *dominated* everyone.

She's not a pushover.

"Let me guess: she's mad about Valon."

He grunts. "She was bizarrely cagey about it, but yes, to say the least."

"Even though he was a piece of shit," I persist.

I know that Kir doesn't know the full history between Annika and that fuck, just that she worked for him. Annika's told me repeatedly she never wanted him to know about that dark part of her past.

"If we didn't do business with pieces of shit, Kenzo," he sighs, "then most criminal organizations wouldn't exist."

That's fair. And I can't exactly tell Kir about what really happened with Valon and Annika and let him use that to cool Yelizaveta down, because that would be a massive breach of my wife's trust.

"My cousin did a *lot* of business with Leka," Kir mutters. "I mean, he was probably a third of her export network."

Shit.

"Look, she's aware that it wasn't you who personally killed him. But..."

"But it was Annika's fight with Ulkan that led to his death. And her being my wife complicates things."

"Exactly," Kir grunts. "I've been on the phone with Yelizaveta all day. A lot of this is reading between the lines, because she's playing it extremely close to the chest for some reason. But the fact that you went after Leka's network over the last week has seriously soured things with her."

I smile smugly. With Valon dead, I *have* made sure that my people—or people we hired—have gone after that asshole's network. I had two dozen of his warehouses around Europe and the Mediterranean burned, four of his cargo ships ratted out to various international law enforcement agencies, and another two of them sunk while in port just because why the fuck not.

Yes, his brother, Besor, is in jail for life. But he expressed an interest in taking over for Valon, and *someone* with resources could very well break or bribe him out. If that happens, I've made fucking sure he has *nothing* to work with.

"I'm not apologizing for anything, Kir," I growl. "If Besor manages to pay or tunnel his way out of jail, there's not a chance he's going to take over—"

"About that," Kir growls quietly, cutting me off. "Besor was killed in prison yesterday."

My brows arch. "Really."

"Yeah."

"Typical prison violence, or…?"

"He was beaten to death in the yard. But that's not the interesting part."

"Go on."

"When the guards found him, his chest had been tattooed with a message about his brother's debt not being paid yet, and a promise to go after the extended Leka family *outside* prison if those debts were not settled quickly."

My brows knit. "Apparently whoever paid for that ink didn't get the memo that Valon is dead."

Kir is silent.

"Kir—"

"This is a delicate question, and please don't be insulted," Kir growls. "But exactly *how* in your pocket are the local Kyoto police?"

My teeth grind. "Very…I thought."

"They're the ones who found Leka's body?"

Fuck.

I'm already up and running out the door, sprinting through the house to the driveway.

"They are," I mutter as I leap behind the wheel of my black Porsche 911 and slam on the engine. "Where's this going, Kir?"

"Yelizaveta isn't so convinced that Leka is dead."

I gun the engine, screaming down the driveway. My men yank open the gate and nod as I roar through onto the open road.

"Why is *that*," I hiss.

"Because she had a video call with him this morning."

Holy fuck.

THE KYOTO PREFECTURE Takaragaike Police Station falls silent as I storm through the front doors. Most of the officers bow formally to me as I surge past them with curt nods.

They know who I am.

I'm the guy who pays their second salary. The guy who pays for vacations, cars, and schooling for their kids that a police officer could never otherwise afford.

Do I feel bad about the naked bribery in the criminal justice system?

Fuck no.

One, this is just how it's done. Two, if it wasn't me, it'd be someone else. And three, as Kir said, if we didn't do business with shitheads, criminal organizations wouldn't exist.

...And I would *not* play nicely in a corporate office.

Deputy Chief Tetsuya looks up quickly from his desk as I poke my head into his office.

"*Kenzo-san*," he growls, standing quickly and bowing. "I didn't know you were stopping by—"

"Come."

He doesn't falter at all or question me.

I like Tetsuya.

Silently, he follows me down the hall, and remains quiet as I kick in the door to his boss's office. Chief Hajime scrambles to stand from his desk as I storm in.

"*Kenzo*!" He smiles brightly, though it looks like he's suddenly started to sweat bullets. Some of that could be the way I just roared in here like a bat out of hell.

It could also be because this fuck's been lying to me, and he's just figured out that I might know it.

"Close the door, Tetsuya," I growl.

The door clicks shut behind me. Chief Hajime pales as I approach his desk.

"I want to see it."

He forces a nervous smile. "See...what?"

"The body," I growl. "And I would *highly* suggest you not ask me which body I'm talking about."

His throat bobs, his eyes darting past me to Tetsuya, pleading for backup.

Something tells me he's not going to get it. Not from a man who stands to benefit from his downfall.

"Valon Leka?" Chief Hajime blurts. "You mean—"

"*Obviously*. Well?" I gesture to the door. "Shall we?"

"Ahh, Kenzo," he stammers. "I wish you'd called ahead so that I can make sure we have access to the correct—"

"Exactly how many fucking white *gaijins* do you expect me to believe you have down in the morgue?"

"Kenzo—"

Chief Hajime blanches as I open my coat just enough for him to see the cold metal of my sword's blade glint in the light.

"I'm going to ask you this once and only once, Hajime," I growl tightly. *"Did you find Valon Leka's body."*

I want him to tell me yes. Truthfully. Because it'll mean this idea that a ghost from Annika's past is *still out there* is as ridiculous as I need it to be.

Leka is dead. Has to be. I saw him lying motionless on the ground in a *massive* puddle of his own blood. Even if he made it over that wall, there's no way he had enough blood left in his body to make it twenty feet, let alone *live*.

But I need this fuck to say it. I *need* him to tell me I'm not fucking crazy.

But that's not what Hajime says. He says nothing at all. And that's what sends a cold knife slicing up my spine.

"*Kenzo*," he chokes, his eyes widening in fear. It's as if he's remembering all the times he bragged to me about being single. About having no family or children to "weigh him down".

I'm not exactly a forgiving man. But small details like that *may* have saved him today.

"Who paid you."

He starts to sob. "*Kenzo*, please! I—"

"*Who. Fucking. Paid. You*," I snarl.

"I don't know!" he protests. "A man…a white man. He had an accent. Maybe Turkish…Greek…"

"Albanian?" I growl.

"*Yes*! Maybe!" Hajime blurts hopefully. "He came and offered me an envelope if I said we found that body. He looked not so well. Kenzo, please! I knew your father! And you and I—"

"You ready to step up?" I turn to level a look at Tetsuya.

He glances apathetically at his sobbing boss before turning back to me and nodding.

"I certainly am, Mr. Mori."

Smart man. And cold, and ambitious.

I knew there was a reason I liked Tetsuya.

"No!" Hajime screams. "No, wait—"

In one motion, I whirl, draw my sword, and slice the razor tip of it across the front of Chief Hajime's throat. A tsunami of red spills out as he clutches at the wound, his eyes bulging.

In seconds, the light goes out in them, and his body slumps to the ground.

I've paid Hajime a *fortune* for his loyalty. I will not tolerate him double-dipping, and there is certainly no place for him in my empire because of it.

I kneel and wipe my blade clean on his lapels before I stand and turn back to Tetsuya, who doesn't look remotely distraught by this turn of events.

Excellent.

"Congratulations on your promotion, Chief Tetsuya." I glance back at the body and the growing puddle on the floor. "Sorry about the mess."

"Not at all, Mr. Mori."

"I can assume I've made it clear that loyalty to me means *not* seeing other people?" I growl.

"Perfectly clear, Mr. Mori," Tetsuya says with a polite smile, bowing. "And thank you."

My foot is heavy on the accelerator as I drive home. When I call Annika and she doesn't pick up, it gets a lot heavier.

My jaw clenches as I grip the wheel tight, taking the turns up the winding roads to my house faster than I should, especially since it's dusk now.

Leka is alive.

Okay, maybe not. But he's also sure as *fuck* not "confirmed dead", as I thought. There's no body. No proof at *all.*

That...unnerves me, to say the least.

I roar up the driveway and jump out of the car.

"Annika!" I bellow as I storm into the house. "Annika!!"

"Kenzo?" I turn to see Mal stepping inside from one of the gardens. "What's up?"

"Where is she?" I snap.

His brow furrows. "Annika?" He nods with his chin in the direction of Takeshi's lair in the garage. "You just missed them."

"What?"

"The four of them just took off up the mountain road on bikes. They're headed toward Sakamoto Castle—Kenzo!"

He runs after me when I turn, bolt back outside and jump behind the wheel of the car again, revving the engine as my jaw grits tightly.

Mal opens the side door and jumps in.

"What are you doing?"

"Coming with you," he grunts.

"Buckle up."

I peel out of the driveway, roaring onto the main road.

"What the fuck is going on, Kenzo?" Mal mutters.

"Leka is going on," I say, glancing over at him. "Hajime was paid off. They never found the body after all."

"Fuck," Mal spits. "He's *alive*?!"

"Well, he's not confirmed dead," I throw back. "And that's enough for me to worry when my wife goes for a drive and doesn't answer—"

"KENZO!"

I see the skid marks on the road *just* as Mal roars my name. My foot stamps on the brakes. My hand spins the wheel to the side as we come to a screeching stop right in front of the twisted pile of wrecked motorcycles.

Holy fuck.

I'm out of the car in a millisecond, bolting for the wreckage.

"ANNIKA!" I scream. My heart almost stops when I see the black, purple, and neon pink bike twisted and wrenched in half on the side of the road. "ANNIKA!!"

"Kenzo!"

Tak is bleeding from the shoulder and limping as he emerges from the underbrush and the trees next to the mountain road. He's got his arm around a banged-up looking Hana, who's pressing a hand to a cut on her forehead.

Shit.

I rush to them along with Mal, dropping to my knees to help Hana sit on the ground.

"They took her!" Hana blurts, wincing as she looks at me, her eyes frightened. "Kenzo, they took Annika!"

"*Who?!*"

"Leka!" Takeshi grunts. He shakes his head as my eyes go wide. "He made it," he hisses quietly. "Somehow that fucker is still alive, and he's got Tengan helping him. They slammed into us with a van, wiped us all out, and then dragged Annika into the back—"

"Freya!" Hana winces, pointing across the road to the dented-up guardrail. "She went over!"

She's barely finished getting the words out before Mal is bolting, hurdling over the guardrail like he's trying to race a train before he disappears into the underbrush.

"*Which way,*" I snarl, turning back to Hana and Tak.

Takeshi points up the road. "Headed toward Sakamoto Castle. Black van, I didn't get the plate."

"Do you have your phone?" I blurt.

He nods, gritting his teeth and digging his phone out of his pocket.

It's completely smashed.

"*Shit,*" Tak swears.

Hana shakes her head. "Mine's gone—"

"Take mine," I growl, shoving it into my brother's hand. "And call our people!"

I whirl, bolting back to the car just as Mal staggers up the embankment and climbs over the guardrail.

He's carrying a body in his arms, draped with his jacket.

An anguished cry wrenches from Hana's throat, but Mal shakes his head.

"She's okay," he grunts as he lays Freya's body on the ground.

"I'm fine!" Freya's pained voice calls from under Mal's jacket. "My riding jacket tore off in the crash!"

Mal nods his chin at the sky.

It's not quite dark out yet.

My eyes drop back to Freya, lying all covered up on the ground. Shit, that's why Mal's jacket is over her: her photo-sensitivity thing.

He knew about that?

There's no time for questions. Glancing at my siblings, I yank the door open and slide behind the wheel of the Porsche.

Mal is instantly at the window. "Where the fuck are you going?"

"You know where I'm going," I growl, revving the engine and shifting into drive. "And no, you're not coming with me."

"Like fuck I'm—"

"Stay here," I say coldly, my eyes locking with Mal. "Watch them until our people get here."

He scowls. "Why Sakamoto Castle? Even at night it's gonna be crawling with tourists, and all the park staff—"

"They're not *going* to Sakamoto Castle," I growl.

"Kenzo, that's the only place this road—"

"No, it's not."

His brow furrows before it clicks. "No. No fucking *way* are you going there without any backup."

"I love you, Mal," I hiss. "But if you don't step back from the car right now, I *will* run you over."

His face is grim, but he nods. "If you find them, please, just *wait* until—"

I gun the engine and speed off just as Mal jumps back. The engine roars as I stomp down hard on the gas.

I don't have time to wait.

I don't have any time at all.

32

ANNIKA

You can tell yourself a thousand times that ghosts aren't real. But when you're faced with one, in the flesh, it doesn't matter what you've told yourself. It doesn't matter what you believe. Ghosts don't give a fuck.

At least, mine certainly doesn't.

"I've thought about you, puppet."

I shudder. The very word from his mouth makes me want to throw up until there's not even bile left. Sitting in the rusty metal chair I'm tied to, I stare unblinkingly at the stone floor. I say nothing. I don't even look at Valon, though I can feel him standing right next to me in the dank gloom.

I don't know where we are. I tried to memorize the turns we took after the bike crash, when he and Tengan dragged me into the very van that had just driven my friends off the road. But in the sheer terror of the reality unfolding around me, I lost track.

Now, I'm here.

"Here" is cold, damp, and smells of mildew. The walls are curved, moss-covered stone; the room in the shape of a cylinder. A single bulb hangs from the center of the double-height room, and a metal staircase bolted to the wall winds up to an upper level. A metal walkway rims that, with two openings that lead to dark hallways, similar to the two down here.

Somewhere in the distance, I hear a low mechanical hum that sounds like…a generator, perhaps?

I have no idea where Tengan is.

"Have *you* thought about me—"

"Never," I spit coldly, still not looking at him.

Valon chuckles a wheezing, grunting laugh.

"Still not a very good liar, are you, puppet?"

He's in bad shape. *Really* bad shape. Honestly, waiting to see if he keels over dead at any moment is one of the few things keeping me together right now.

His skin is pallid and waxy. His eyes are bloodshot, and his torn, filthy clothes are bulging over the heavy bandages around his stomach, chest, and left arm, which is in a sling.

Whatever Ulkan did to him, I wish he was still alive, so I could send him a gift basket and ask him to please do it again.

My eyes dart around the crumbling old space, taking in the rusty chairs and rotted-out desks, the old map of Imperial Japan tacked to a moldy cork board, and a few ancient metal filing cabinets tipped onto their sides.

There's also a small refrigerator and a cot, with filthy, blood-stained sheets.

I think I know where Valon's been lying low for the past week.

He winces, his face twisting in pain as he turns toward me.

"Puppet—"

"Do *not* call me that," I hiss venomously.

A small smile curls Valon's thin lips, his pale, sweaty face leering at me as he turns and walks over to a table across the room. He picks something up with his good hand, then turns and walks around behind me.

"I got you a present," he murmurs quietly.

"I don't give a *shit*—OW!"

I jerk, whipping my head to the side and staring wide-eyed at the syringe in Valon's hands.

The needle is pushed deep into the bare skin of my shoulder.

I stare at the needle and drag my horrified eyes up to his.

"*What was that?*"

He smiles coldly. "That was *insurance*. And before you threaten me with your dear husband coming for you, let me save you the trouble. I know he's coming for you." His lips twist darkly. "I'm counting on it, in fact. And you should hope that he does, too."

I stare transfixed as he slowly pulls the needle out of my skin.

"What did you just give me?!"

Valon's smile is cold.

"*Poison*, puppet."

Roiling nausea begins to surge inside me. I choke as my throat closes up, my eyes haggard as I just stare at the spot where he's stuck me.

"But don't worry. Your husband is an intelligent man. He'll figure out where I've taken you. He'll come for you. And when he does, if he's as intelligent as I think, he'll do as he's told. If he does, you'll get this."

He holds a tiny little glass bottle up in front of me.

"Antidote for what I just gave you. You've got about an hour before things start to get"...he smiles icily..."*most unpleasant*."

"You *motherfucker*." I strain against the ropes binding my wrists behind the back of the chair. "When he gets here—"

"He will do *exactly* as I tell him to do," Valon spits.

My eyes bulge as he pulls a handgun out of his jacket, wincing. The loud metallic click of it cocking echoes in the dank stone room.

"If he doesn't, he gets to watch you die."

33

KENZO

I STAND AT THE CRUMBLING, dark entrance to the bunker system, my jaw grim and set, staring into the black maw.

I wasn't entirely sure on the manic drive up here. But the black van parked behind a clump of scraggly bushes nearby tells me I was right.

This is where he took her.

Officially, these old World War Two bunkers, once occupied by the soldiers of Imperial Japan as they prepared for invasion by the allies, are closed to the public and sealed off as a safety hazard. One, who the fuck knows how the structural integrity of the hideaways has held up.

Two, what appears at first to be a single tunnel leading down through the brick archway is actually a *maze* of random pathways, caved-in barracks, and deliberate dead ends. If that wasn't confusing enough, there's been more than one occasion where would-be explorers walked into old booby-traps or happened upon deteriorating old explosives and got themselves splattered all over a wall.

For bonus points, the air down there is literally poison. Decades of old chemicals and ordinances releasing toxic fuck-knows-what means that unless you get a little air flow going, there's a good chance you'll pass out and never wake up again.

For all these reasons, the local Kyoto government has sealed the place up and posted about a hundred warning signs in four different languages to deter explorers and thrill-seekers. They've even walled the front entrance off about a dozen times. But some idiot inevitably tears it open again, ignoring every warning sign and going in anyway.

...I mean, Mal and I did *exactly that* a handful of times when we were younger.

I glance to the side again, at the barely concealed van parked at the only other place around here aside from Sakamoto Castle that the road leads to.

This is very obviously a trap. Valon wanted me to follow him here, looking for Annika.

I glare into the black murk of the tunnel entrance.

Trap or not, that motherfucker has *my wife*. The woman I love. He could be standing in front of me with an entire army, and I'd *still* be going in.

He doesn't know it yet, but he's going to die today.

I step into the darkness.

Years ago, a man named Rafe taught me something I've never forgotten: when you're hunting vermin, you can stand on the roof shooting away, hoping you hit them. Or you can lay bait and trap them.

There's only one true way to exterminate something that's taken what's yours. And tonight, as I walk into the blackness with death on my shoulder and fury pulsing through my veins...

Tonight, I'm one of Rafe's fucking *snakes.*

The darkness swallows me whole as I slip down the side of the main tunnel entrance. A first, the moonlight illuminates graffiti and street art painted and sprayed on the walls. As the light fades, so does the art.

Even the local teenagers know not to go any further.

Up ahead in the gloom, you can just see that the main tunnel curves a little to the right, around a bend. I know that from the dozens of times I explored this place when I was first in Kyoto, looking for danger and excitement.

I also know that right up ahead, just *before* the bend, there's a side passage that veers out away from the main tunnel and then doubles back into it once it makes the bend—probably a tunnel that was once camouflaged so that soldiers could more easily defend this place in the event of an attack.

Just as I get to the inky black opening to the side tunnel I freeze, my ears pricking.

Breathing.

Someone—just up ahead, right around the bend in the main tunnel—is *breathing.* Heavily.

They're waiting for me, but they're scared.

I smile coldly to myself.

They fucking should be.

Silently, I draw my sword out of its scabbard as I slip into the side tunnel and move quietly down it. At the end, I slowly peer around the corner and then tense.

My lips curl dangerously.

Sure enough, a little ways off, back toward the opening, I can make out the silhouette of a man crouched down with a gun in his hands. He's trembling, and when he reaches up to scratch his chin nervously, I get a quick glint of moonlight off his glasses.

Tengan.

I cross to him silently and quickly, surging right up behind the little fuck before my blade stabs forward in the darkness. Tengan screams, jolting and spasming as my sword stabs clean through him from behind.

"I should have done this before, when you spoke to my wife the way you did."

"*Kenzo*!" he bleats, sucking in air through both his mouth and the wet hole in his chest, which is making a wheezing, desperate sound. "Kenzo, please—"

He sobs, screaming in agony as I twist my blade a little.

"I'm not interested in your pleas for mercy," I snarl. "*Where are they.*"

"*Please—*" he gurgles. "Kenzo—"

The only thing keeping him from falling to the ground is my grip on the sword shoved right through him as he shudders and screams in agony.

"Not only is this blade against your spinal cord, Tengan," I hiss. "But it's punctured your lungs."

I give the blade another twist, eliciting a fresh cry of agony from his throat as I lean closer to him.

"Make no mistake, Tengan. You *will* die here tonight... alone...in the dark."

He chokes out a wrenching sob.

"*However*," I growl. "You can either spend the next few hours in excruciating pain, or if you prefer, you can go quickly, with some scraps of honor."

He sobs as I take a slow breath.

"I can make this *last*, Tengan," I mutter quietly. "A very, *very* long time. Or you can tell me where Valon and my wife are, who's with them, and what's waiting for me, and I will end your suffering quickly."

"*Kenzo—*"

I shove the hilt of the sword against his back, relishing the screams of agony the movement elicits.

"One level down!" he chokes, spitting blood. "Toward the back of the complex! There's a staircase at the end of this tunnel. Follow it down, take your first right, then your first *left—*"

"I know the place."

He's directing me to the old control center, where whatever captain who helmed this defensive fort at the end of the Imperial reign commanded his troops.

"Who else is there," I snarl.

"*Nobody*!" Tengan wheezes. "Just Valon and your wife!"

Behind him, I shake my head.

"*Why*, Tengan?" I snarl. "Sota treated you so well, for so long."

He starts to weep. "I…I had debts. I got in deep with the Koreans at the casino."

My lip curls. "You fucking idiot."

"*I'm sorry*," he blurts. "I was desperate, and Valon got to me." He cries out in pain when he tries to glance back at me over his shoulder. "Kenzo, Valon *needed* that deal with you and Sota. He paid me to help him push it with the two of you."

"*Why*."

Tengan shudders, coughing blood as he sags against my blade.

"He owes someone money, and they're going to start killing people to get it."

Yeah, like Valon's own fucking brother, I think, remembering that Besor Leka was just murdered in prison over his brother's debts.

I sneer at Tengan. "So—what, having you wait here in the dark and shoot me was his plan to get paid?"

Tengan whimpers as he shakes his head. "I wasn't going to shoot you."

I bark a bitter laugh, kicking away the gun he dropped a minute ago.

"*Really*," I spit.

He shakes his head again. "Over there," he chokes. "The duffel bag."

My gaze slides past him, and sure enough, my vision has

sufficiently adjusted to the dim light to spot a canvas gym bag on the ground.

"Sota already paid Valon for a test run. He brought in a shipment of electronics for Sota, like a low-pay tryout." He nods his chin at the bag. "When you came today, Valon wanted me to tell you to take the money back to Sota, *then* come back here and wire Leka a sum of money. Then he'd let Annika go."

Wait, what?

I stare at the bag.

Something smells like bullshit.

Tengan cries out, screaming and collapsing to his knees as I let go of the blade with it still through his chest. I leave him like that as I walk over to the bag and yank it open. Yep, it's filled with cash.

"What's the catch?" I hiss, turning to glare at him.

Tengan is half-slumped against the wall, his face drained of color.

"Catch?"

I dump the bag upside down, spilling the money onto the ground before peering inside. I almost miss it. But the thin strip of moonlight filtering down the tunnel glints off something in the bottom of it.

I peer closely, and my jaw tenses.

It's a wire.

I grip the little strip of black fabric over it, yanking it back.

Fuck me.

The whole underside of the bag is lined with plastic explosives, with wires leading to a remote trigger.

Valon didn't want me to deliver money to Sota.

He wanted me to deliver a fucking *bomb.*

I can see how it would play out: Tengan would give me Valon's demands, and I, blinded by my need to rescue Annika, would do as he said. When I got back here to wire whatever money Valon wanted me to, he'd trigger the bomb, killing Sota back at his house.

And then I'm guessing he'd kill *me,* too, as soon as he'd gotten his money.

Silently, my brain turning, I stuff the money back into the bag and shoulder it. Then I turn to Tengan, slumped against the wall at death's door.

"Please…" he chokes, blood dribbling down his chin. *"Please, Kenzo, forgive—"*

"No."

He wheezes wetly as I yank the sword out of him, falling forward and barely catching himself with a hand against the wall.

"But I *will* honor our deal."

With one clean stroke, Tengan's head separates from his body. I wipe the blade dry on the cuff of his pants. Then I turn and glare into the darkness.

Like a snake who's just caught the scent of its prey.

34

KENZO

RAW AND VICIOUS energy throbs through my veins as I stalk through the darkened tunnel. A section of the path leading to where Valon is holding Annika actually gets *pitch* black. But then, after the stairs and the first turn of the tunnels, a dim light ahead begins to guide me.

"VALON!" I roar.

Announcing my presence is deliberate. Obviously, the idea of sneaking up on him occurred to me. But the thought of his surprise ending in Annika getting hurt…or worse…was too much of a risk.

Besides, I *want* him to know I'm coming. I *want* him to believe I'm as blinded by rage as he wanted me to be.

Make no mistake, I *am* filled with rage. Hate. The consuming need to kill him with my bare fucking hands.

But I need to get her away from him before I do that. And what I have in mind—playing off his greed and desperation—is probably my only shot.

"That's far enough, Kenzo."

As expected, by the time I storm through the brick archway from the tunnel into the command room, Valon is waiting for me, standing right behind and a little to the side of a gagged, wide-eyed Annika. He's got a gun aimed right at me.

My gaze locks with hers, unspoken words flickering between our eyes.

"Drop your weapons," Valon growls, gesturing with his own gun. I nod, slipping my sword out from behind me and laying it down next to Tengan's gun.

Valon flinches when his gazes drops to the duffel bag in my hand. Before he can say anything, I chuck it at his feet.

"I've come to offer a trade," I hiss coldly at him. "Take your money back, for starters. I speak for Sota when I say *keep it.* I know you had a trial deal with him, and I know your intention would be to settle up with him. Your war is with me, not Sota."

I feed him the bullshit with a silver fucking spoon, looking him right in the eye as I do it.

It's critical he doesn't guess that I know what else is in the bag.

"Whatever happens here between you and me," I continue, "Sota will honor the fact that you and he are even."

Valon seems intrigued, but he nods at the bag.

"What makes you so sure that Sota *won't* want his fifty thousand back?"

"As I said," I shrug. "I have authority to speak for him. I've known the man for half of my life, and I know that settling debts is important to him. I can appreciate that your returning the money was a gesture of goodwill. But services were rendered. Sota will want to have paid for them, whether or not you do business together after today."

...Thereby planting the idea in his head that he'll be *breathing* after today.

Valon smiles smugly.

Yeah, it's working.

"I can assume since you have this bag that Tengan is...no longer with us?"

I shrug. "You can."

"Did he tell you before you killed him what else I'd requested of you, besides returning the money to Sota?"

I nod. "He did."

My eyes lock with Annika's, my lips pursing before I drag my gaze back to Valon.

"Give me Annika, and I'll wire you however much you want."

Valon barks a cold laugh. "Not a fucking chance, Kenzo. That's not how this works. You think I'm going to hand over your true love, just like that?" He snorts. "On your *word* that you'll pay me after—"

"True love?" I bark icily. I sneer, shaking my head. "You're mistaken, Valon." I jut my chin at her. "You think I give a *shit* about this little fucking thief? She's a fuck toy to me, nothing else. A plaything."

Something venomous surges in Annika's eyes, and her nostrils flare. She snarls something through her gag, but I keep my eyes fixed on Valon.

"I'm done with her. I *do* want her back, of course. That's why I'm here." I shrug. "But I can promise you, it's not for love. It's so I can kill her myself."

It takes *everything I have* to keep my eyes on Valon, and not glance at the woman I love more than I've ever loved anything in this world.

But I need to sell this.

I *have to.*

Valon looks skeptical.

"*Bullshit,*" he grunts. "You think I'm a fucking idiot?"

I shake my head. "Of course not. But you can ask anyone: this little bitch has been nothing but trouble. She's been skimming from me ever since that joke of a wedding. She's been scamming Sota, too, *and* he knows it." I frown. "Surely you know how skilled she is at what she does, and what she's capable of." I turn to spit on the floor. "Doesn't matter how much she's given, either. A thief is still a fucking *thief.*"

It's slow, but a change creeps over Valon's face, and I have to bite back my own smugness.

Yeah, that's the look of him swallowing this shit whole.

"I never should have gone near her," I spit. "You know, the first time we ever crossed paths, the bitch stole from me."

Valon frowns. "Yes… I think I've heard this story. A necklace, wasn't it?"

I shake my head. This time, I *do* look at Annika.

Right at Annika.

"A wallet," I grunt. "Bitch stole it right out of my *right jacket pocket.*"

Of all the miracles I'm hoping to pull out of my ass right now, this one's the longest shot. The bomb in that bag had a remote detonator. I've seen IEDs like that before, and I know the trigger looks something like a bare-bones cellphone.

Valon's original plan was to have me deliver the bomb to Sota, then come back here, where he'd get me to wire him money before blowing Sota to hell. If I were Valon, I'd be keeping that detonator very close, most likely *on me.*

But his left arm is in a sling. His pants pockets are a maybe. But he's not trying to cram his hand into a pants pocket for a trigger button. That's why I'm guessing it's in his jacket pocket.

The gamble is hoping Annika knows me well enough to understand what I'm saying right now.

...That I'm telling her what to do.

"Your wallet?" Valon smirks.

I shake my head angrily. "Yeah. Right out of my right-hand jacket pocket while I was buying her a fucking drink. And *not a fucking thing* has changed ever since."

And that's when I see it.

The fury and the fire in her eyes fades, and comprehension flickers to life.

She understands what I'm saying without saying it.

She *does* know me.

"Consider that money a down payment," I grunt, nodding my chin at the duffle bag by his feet. "You and I have had our quarrels. But we're both businessmen. There's no need to bring emotions or pettiness into this."

My words are meant as a distraction. It's working. I'm looking right at Valon, but at the edge of my vision, I see Annika's hand slip behind her, toward his right side.

"Let's do this, Valon," I growl. "We can both walk away from this with what we want. You get your money, and I get this bitch so I can exact my revenge. Deal?"

Annika's brows lift and lower twice. My eyes flick to her. Both her hands are now back in front of her.

She got it.

"What's your price, Valon," I growl. I pull the phone I took from Tengan out of my pocket and wave it in the air. "Name the amount, send her over, and I'll wire it to you this second. We don't need to continue this war."

Valon's eyes narrow and his mouth thins, like he's considering it. Normally, this would be an absurd offer. But it's clear he's been down here fighting off infections and trying not to bleed out. He's hunched over, and clearly in pain. Honestly, I'm amazed he's even alive, even if it looks like he's been sustaining himself down here in the tunnels on painkillers and uppers. He looks like he's being held together with duct tape, for fuck's sake.

So this might just work. And if it doesn't, I have every intention of charging him and killing him with my bare hands, even if I do get shot in the process.

"Five million," he hisses.

I resist the urge to roll my eyes.

I feign a frown, as if considering. Then I nod. "Agreed. Five million for her, and to consider our score settled like gentlemen."

Valon's lips twist.

"Wire it."

"Her first."

He doesn't move. Time stops.

Finally, he shoves her toward me. His gun is leveled at me, his finger on the trigger.

"You try anything, Kenzo..." He shakes his head.

I'm barely aware of him. All I'm focusing on is Annika as she slowly crosses the room toward me, and how hard it is not to grab her and yank her into my arms. Not to rip the gag off and kiss her until her mouth is *mine*.

When she gets to me, she stops, and our eyes lock as she looks up into my face. Her hand is between us, and when she slowly turns it over, my gaze drops to the little black fob in her palm.

My muscles coil as I take the fob, ready to spring into action.

Fuck, this is going to be tight.

I don't know how much explosive is in that bag, or how big the blast will be. It might blow this whole place to hell, who knows.

But there's no other way.

"Get back there, bitch," I snarl at Annika, forcing myself to look furious. I nod my head at the tunnel behind me. "Walk that way and keep walking until you get to the stairs. Mr. Leka and I need to finish our—"

"Stop right there."

Valon cocks the gun in his hand and throws me a look.

"The money, Kenzo," he growls. "*Now.*"

I nod, lifting Tengan's phone and pretending to thumb the screen open.

"Give me a sec…"

Quietly, I step forward, gradually moving in front of Annika.

"Okay," I murmur. "Account number?"

Valon starts to rattle off numbers, and I pretend to type them in. Slowly, I back up, pushing Annika behind me as I guide her into the tunnel.

Valon finishes giving me his bank details.

Here goes nothing.

"Okay," I nod. "Sent. A pleasure doing business, Mr. Leka. I hope this means we can both walk away—"

"Wait wait wait." He scoffs. "As if you're going to walk out of here before I check?"

I finger the fob in my hand, my pulse quickening. My muscles tensing.

The whole world holding its breath before the storm.

Valon drops his good hand to his pants pocket, reaching for his phone. As he does so, his hand brushes the side of his jacket, and he stiffens.

Fuck.

Everything slows, time itself getting sticky and sluggish as his brow furrows and his hand lifts back up and slips into his jacket pocket, feeling for the trigger fob I *know* he just realized was missing.

Still in slow motion, I whirl, shoving Annika ahead of me down the tunnel as I hear Valon roar with fury.

A gunshot echoes through the stone room. Hot fire explodes in the side of my chest.

I push the button on the fob as I dive forward to shield Annika.

All I see is bright white as heat and thundering fire slam into my back and send me over into the black abyss.

35

ANNIKA

My ears are ringing as I gradually realize I'm lying on the ground. Dust and grime choke my throat, and when I cough, gray ash wheezes from my cracked lips.

My mouth opens and closes. My vision cuts in and out as my fingertips curl against the gritty ground.

The ringing is all I hear, humming piercingly in my ears.

I cough again, breathing dust and smoke. I claw at the ground, wincing, shoving my knee up in an attempt to get to my feet.

Fuck.

The world sways, and I tip sideways against the wall. But I catch myself in time, clinging to it as the ringing whines in my ears and my legs wobble.

Kenzo.

A bolt of lightning jarring my heart, I whirl, my eyes scanning the dimness. By some insane miracle, the bulb hanging above is still lit, the shadows dancing crazily over the stone walls as the bulb swings all over the place.

My whole body tenses up as my eyes land on him.

No.

I scream his name, though I can't hear my own voice over the whining ring in my ears. I stumble toward him, almost falling twice. But I keep moving, staggering closer on unsteady legs before I drop to my knees beside him.

"Kenzo..."

My own voice comes through my ears at last, dull and muffled, sounding far away.

"Kenzo..."

He's on his back, his clothes singed and covered in rock dust, his eyes closed. Blood oozes wetly from a hole in the side of his chest.

Oh God.

"KENZO!"

When I shout his name again, I wince as the blockage in my ear cracks, the ringing melting into the background and sound filtering back into my senses.

That's when I hear it.

At first, when I raise my eyes, I'm not sure what I'm looking at. We're in the tunnel just off the main room where Valon was holding me. And as I stare through the brick archway leading back to it, the floor looks like it's...moving.

Breathing.

Melting.

There's no sign of Valon, but before I can even worry about that, the floor suddenly surges and buckles. I gasp, grabbing Kenzo to yank him back. The ground in the main room bulges, and then crumbles entirely. Black liquid surges out of the cracks before the rest of the floor caves in with a crashing splash.

...of *water*.

Holy fuck.

The rushing sound fills the room, like a dam has given way. Kenzo blinks slowly, his head lolling to the side as he swims in and out of consciousness.

The water level is rising.

"*I got you*!"

I grab him under the armpits, gritting my teeth as I try to shift his weight. Slowly I drag him away from the main room, tugging him across the floor and down the tunnel in the direction he came.

This has to be the way out. And if it takes every fucking ounce of my strength, I am *getting him* out.

I barely make it five more feet before I look up, and my heart drops.

The tunnel's caved in.

No.

I drop Kenzo's arms and run forward, clawing and yanking at the crumbled brick and rock. After I clear away the initial rubble, my hands scrape against giant, immovable chunks of concrete and metal rebar.

A choked sputter behind me whips my attention around.

"Kenzo!!"

I rush back to him as he struggles to lift his head out of the water, now ankle-deep.

It's still. Fucking. Rising.

We have to move. *Now.*

I go to grab him under the arms again. He grunts as his eyes focus a little more on me.

"Annika..."

"Come *on*!!" I scream, trying to drag him.

His arm muscles flex as he pulls away, shoving one knee underneath himself. His face twists in agony as he drags himself to his feet, turning to let his dark eyes pierce into me.

"You okay?" he grunts, his jaw clenched in pain.

"I'm fine!" I yell over the rushing water as it creeps higher and higher up our calves. I reach down to grab his sword off the ground. "Kenzo—"

"*Stairs*!" he hisses, nodding his chin at the main room that is quickly filling with water. My eyes follow his, locking on the metal staircase bolted to the wall that climbs up to the second-floor metal walkway.

"Okay!" I scream, wrapping my arm around his waist and draping his over my shoulders. Kenzo groans as he walks, leaning heavily on me as I stoop under his weight. I can feel the warm stickiness of his blood soaking into my shirt.

We're running out of time.

The water is past our knees as we exit the tunnel back into

the circular, double-height room. I take another step forward, but then shriek before I yank us back.

The floor is gone. I almost just stepped into nothingness beneath the inky black water.

Ignoring the pure terror swirling up in me, I grab him tighter, keeping us against the wall as we inch around to the stairs.

The water is up to our waists.

"Can you climb?!"

He glances at me, his face pale as he nods. "For you, I can fucking climb," he wheezes.

It's slow going, but we take them one at a time, his arm heavy on my shoulders as he grips the railing with a white-knuckle grip. The water level stays at our knees, rising in time with our ascent.

When we get to the top, we shuffle and stumble our way over to one of the two tunnels leading out, mirroring the floor below us.

"*One sec*," he groans, his knees buckling as he clings to the wall.

I stop, gritting my teeth as I help lower him to the floor, sitting up against the brick wall of the tunnel. Kenzo glances down at the hole in his side, his wet clothes soaked red as the blood continues to flow out of it.

I rip open his shirt, trying to ignore his hiss of pain as I open it wide and examine the wound.

Holy fuck, that's a bullet hole.

Without thinking, I yank my top off, pressing the fabric to his wound.

"Hold this there," I command, searching desperately for something to tie it with before I realize I can use my belt.

"When did you become a triage medic," Kenzo chuckles quietly, wincing when he tries to force a smile.

I'm not smiling. He's losing a *lot* of blood.

I wrap the belt around the shirt, cinching it tight to keep the cloth in place over the hole. It's not going to save him, but it might buy us some additional time.

"Annika."

"Hang on," I mutter, pulling the belt tighter to make sure it's in place.

"Annika. The water."

I turn my head, half-expecting a tsunami to come surging over the lip of the metal walkway. But when I look, I realize the room has gotten a lot quieter.

The water isn't rising anymore.

I get to my feet and move to the walkway. When I gaze down, the water looks to have leveled off three or four feet below us.

Thank. Fucking. God.

I go back over to Kenzo and kneel next to him. My brow worries as I push his hair out of his pale face, peering into his hooded eyes.

"How do you feel?"

He smirks quietly. "Just peachy, princess."

I smile wryly, but I can feel my heart clenching as I stroke his face and lean down to kiss him softly.

He...doesn't look good.

At all.

"Annika..." His eyes close, open, and then close again. His head falls back against the wall. "Annika, where..."

"*I'm right here*," I choke, taking his hands in mine and squeezing. I lean down and kiss him again, hating the weakness I feel in his soft lips.

We need to get out of here and get help *now*.

"*Valon*..." Kenzo rasps out. "Where..."

"He's gone—"

"*No*," Kenzo groans, shaking his head slowly. "I saw him run."

Cold, naked dread creeps up my spine.

"*What?*"

"Before..." His jaw clenches and he grunts in pain. "Before the blast... He kicked that duffel bag away and ran into the tunnel behind him."

The creeping sensation on my spine intensifies as I glance behind us, half expecting to see the monster lurking right there.

Then I swallow, staring down the dark tunnel into the abyss.

"I'm going to see where this leads—"

"Nowhere," Kenzo murmurs quietly. His eyes are closed as he slowly rocks his head back and forth against the bricks. "It leads nowhere."

"I can find a way—"

"It's a *maze*, princess," he whispers quietly. "Mal and I used to explore these old bunkers when we were younger." His head rolls side to side again. "Up here on this level, there are dozens of tunnels"…his throat bobs…"leading to empty rooms, dead ends, traps…"

His eyes flicker open and then shut again.

His breathing is getting shallower.

My pulse thuds as I glance down the tunnel again.

There's no way out. At least not through there.

"Well," I smile weakly, turning to stroke the hair out of his face. "At least the water's stopped?"

Kenzo's eyes remain closed. His head drifts side to side again.

"It's not the water," he croaks. *"It's the air…"*

I shiver. "What about the air?"

"Old chemicals...unexploded ordinances releasing toxic shit for decades..." He swallows again. "Without airflow…" His haggard, pale face swivels to mine and his eyes crack open a slit. "When—when you taste rotten eggs on your tongue," he mumbles. "That—that's when our timer starts."

It's only then that I realize the air is completely still. Before the blast, down below, you could feel it moving over you faintly, like someone left a door open.

Not anymore.

I turn to look back down the pitch-black tunnel, gaping like a demon's maw.

There *has* to be a way out. Or maybe we can escape via the caved-in floor.

Whatever it fucking takes, we *are* getting the fuck out of here.

"I'm going to find us a way out," I whisper quietly, leaning in to kiss his cheek.

His hand slips around my wrist, holding me as tightly as he can right now.

"*Valon...*" he breathes. "He might..."

I reach down and wrap my fingers around the hilt of his sword from where I've laid it on the ground next to him. It makes a smooth, metallic sound as I drag it from its sheath.

"*I'll be careful,*" I whisper as I kiss his cheek again.

I check the makeshift bandage over his wound. The blood has soaked completely through it. But it does seem to be buying us *some* time.

We're going to need it.

Standing, I turn to face the darkness, sword in hand. My heart thuds in my chest as my eyes pierce the gloom. Slowly, I make my way forward, ignoring every terrifying childhood nightmare that comes screaming out to play.

I make it fifteen steps before I come to a brick wall in front of me. The passage turns ninety degrees to the left, so I follow it. When it turns again, I keep going, trying to reach out into the blackness on either side of me to see if there are other doorways or passages.

When I hear the crunch of stone underfoot, my entire body

goes rigid and still, my heart climbing into my throat as vicious terror claws up my spine.

I'm not alone.

The crunching sound comes again. I ignore the screams in my head. I hold back the vomit that wants to hurl from my stomach as pure horror engulfs me. Instead, I shrink against the wall next to me. My fingers wrap tight around the hilt of Kenzo's sword as I try to hold my breath, listening.

A cold, wheezing chuckle floats out from somewhere in the darkness.

It's alarmingly close.

"Oh, don't go quiet yet, puppet..."

Oh God...

Valon's voice floats out of the inky dark, like an evil spirit hanging in the air.

"I know you're there..."

Keep moving. Don't get trapped.

I inch forward slowly, crouching with the sword in front of me.

"I wonder..." Valon's disembodied, ghostly voice rasps in the blackness. "Do you remember how to get back to your dear husband?"

My spine snaps up straight.

"Or will *I* get to him first. He did seem to be quite *out of sorts...*"

No.

Whirling, no longer giving a shit about stealth, I rush back the way I came, trying to remember my steps so I don't get lost in this maze. If I'm going to die in the darkness to poisoned air, I'd rather do it next to the man I—

When it hits me, all the breath leaves my body as it all comes rushing back with a vengeance.

In the terror of the explosion, and Kenzo being shot, and the water, and the climb, and the blood, a small detail slipped my mind.

But I just remembered.

One of my hands flies from the hilt of the sword to my shoulder, where Valon injected me with the poison.

My blood turns to ice.

I start to run, blindly smashing into walls and corners, bouncing off them like a ping-pong ball in the dark before suddenly, there's a faint glow of light. I round a corner and almost choke when I see Kenzo lying against the wall where I left him.

I rush to him, but just as I get there I scream when a silhouette steps into the archway from the metal walkway just past it. My throat closes around the scream, choking it off as Valon smiles cruelly and raises the gun in his hand.

"Come. Here. *Now,* puppet," he hisses, turning slightly. It's only then that I see the horror-show that is one half his face —the skin blackened and blistered, weeping pus and blood. He's missing the *ear* on that side, too.

"Now now," he growls. "Don't be frightened." His head tilts to the side, and suddenly, he's cocking the gun and jamming it down into Kenzo's face.

"COME! HERE!"

My breath is shaky as I slowly step toward him, my pulse thrumming.

"The antidote," I croak. "Valon, give me the—"

"*Of course*, puppet," he growls quietly, his lips twisting darkly. "I'll give you that *and* the way out."

His smile widens, and a cold ruthlessness I'm not sure I've ever seen in his face before creeps over it.

"But I'm going to *fuck you* first."

I flinch as though I've been struck. Recoiling, I stare at him in horror as he smiles icily back at me and every horrible memory of him bubbles to the surface.

"Oh, and I don't mean figuratively," he growls. "I mean quite literally. Right here, in front of your *dear husband*."

He turns to cast a withering look at Kenzo, who's barely conscious and scarcely breathing against the wall.

"You *disgusting* pig," I snarl, brandishing the sword as I move toward him.

"Ah-ah-ah." Valon shakes his head. He lifts something in his hand, and my heart sinks when I see it.

It's the little glass bottle of antidote.

The top is off it.

"Stop right there," Valon grunts, "or this goes into the water." His lips curl. "Besides," he smiles, "we both know you're no killer, puppet."

My eyes slide to Kenzo, willing him to get better. Wanting him to be miraculously healed so he can get up and stop this.

"Put the sword down," Valon says quietly. "And *come here.*"

My eyes stay on Kenzo. He doesn't have much time. He *needs* to get out of here, soon.

My face is grim as I turn toward the monster leering at me. "You have a way out?"

"Of course," he grunts, wincing as he clutches his abdomen, which is soaked with blood. "I don't want to die here."

"Then why did you stay?" I spit back. "Why the fuck wouldn't you just leave—"

"*Because,* puppet," Valon leers at me, "I want him to *watch.* I want your husband to see for himself what a little *whore* his wife truly is."

It feels like I'm being stabbed over and over as every horrible thing I've spent so many years burying comes rushing to the surface all at once.

"*I hate you,*" I choke as tears slip down my cheeks.

"I don't care," he hisses back. "Get over here. Eyes to the fucking wall."

"*Annika...*"

Kenzo groans as his eyes struggle to open.

"Ahhh, you can hear us, Kenzo?" Valon snarls darkly. "*Good.* Listen, you fucking prick. Listen while your whore wife *moans* for my dick."

Kenzo's arm lurches out blindly, his eyes yanking open as if by sheer will. Pure, unbridled rage explodes across his face as he lunges for Valon.

But he falls short.

I cry out and jump to go to him. But Valon's gun jammed in my face stops me.

"Face the wall, puppet," Valon hisses quietly. "Leave the sword, while you're at it."

I can't really process the sheer injustice and unimaginable horror of this moment. I know this is going to break me, but when I turn to look at Kenzo, bleeding profusely as he slumps to the floor, I also know this is the only way to save him.

If it means damning myself to hell, so be it.

If it means killing my spirit, so be it.

If it means my love is disgusted with me and never wants to look at me again...

Tears stream down my cheeks as I grit my teeth.

So. Be. It.

"Fuck you," I snarl coldly, not even able to look at Valon. I lean the sword hilt against the wall. My feet shuffle slowly, my entire body caving in on itself as I go to where Valon is pointing—the wall across from where Kenzo is slumped.

"Turn around," Valon breathes.

My eyes squeeze closed as I turn my face to the wall. Instantly he's on me, shoving me against it as his disgusting hands slide over my hips and body. Every touch feels like the slash of a blade, and I flatten my palms to the brick.

Just go somewhere else.

Shut down.

Let it happen without you knowing...

I dry heave against the wall as Valon paws at me. He grunts, yanking at his belt and zipper with one hand while he tries to shove my pants down with the other.

Suddenly, he screams.

"You *FUCKER*!" he screeches, dropping his hands from me.

I spin, staring at where Kenzo has just stabbed Valon in the calf with the buckle of my belt, which he's yanked off his makeshift bandage. Blood is flowing freely down his chest again as his eyes lock with mine and he slumps to the ground.

Valon pulls his gun out of his belt. As I look at the man I love, and then the one I hate, I know one thing with utter certainty.

This is *not* how Kenzo and I go.

This is not where we die.

Not like this.

Steeling myself, I fling my arm to the side, grab the hilt of Kenzo's sword, and then whirl, jamming the point down into Valon's foot. He screams in agony, dropping the gun as he staggers away from Kenzo, the blade sliding out of his shoe with a squelch.

"*You bitch*!" he squeals, looking at me in horror and fear. "You fucking *bitch*—"

The blade swings up in a cold, silvery slash.

Valon's left hand is severed instantly, sent flying into the wall before dropping to the ground. I stare at the stump of his wrist with as much shock as he does.

But then I feel something I've never once felt in this monster's presence.

Powerful.

I feel fucking *powerful.*

Valon lets out a high, gobbling shriek as he clutches his forearm, staring at the spurting blood in horror.

"*That*!" I roar, "is for hurting the family it took me *so long* to find!"

I swing the blade again with a fury I've never felt before. This time, I'm ready for the shock as Valon's other forearm is cleaved in two, his right hand sailing away.

"*That* is for my husband!" I scream.

Valon's eyes are wide with terror as he staggers away from me down the tunnel, splattering blood across the walls.

"And *this*?!" I rush at him, plunging the blade through his chest. Valon's entire face bulges, spittle and blood frothing from his wide mouth as he chokes violently.

"*This is for me, you motherfucker*!"

I twist the blade violently, yanking it side to side as blood pours from his chest. I pull the sword out of him, watching without blinking as he falls to his knees and then topples backward into a lifeless heap on the floor.

I drop the sword and run to Kenzo. His body's still so solid and muscled that it makes it even more surreal that he's so limp when I struggle to lift him and prop him up against the wall.

"*You got him...*" he murmurs quietly.

I'm shaking as I grab the belt and tie my blood-soaked shirt back to his wound. At this point, it almost seems useless.

Then my eyes drop to the little glass bottle on the ground with the antidote.

It's empty.

I swallow back the icy feeling inside of me, ignoring the fact that my vision is swimming a little as I sit and slide in next to Kenzo. I wrap his arm over my shoulder, pulling him close as I take his hand in mine.

"We'll rest a second," I mumble quietly. "Then we'll find a way out."

"Annika."

I swallow back the tears as I turn to him. He's looking down into my eyes with his hooded ones, a lock of dark hair splayed across his face.

"I love you," he breathes.

"I love you, too."

36

ANNIKA

It's quiet now.

I listen to the shallow, rhythmic breathing inside Kenzo's chest and the drip-drip-dripping sound of the water down over the side of the walkway.

At times, my vision swims again. Then I'll feel like something is twisting inside me. But I can't tell if it's what Valon injected me with or my mind, fucking with me.

I hold Kenzo's hand, refusing to acknowledge the truth that's staring me in the face.

We're going to die down here.

I sniff back tears. When I do, a terrible realization hits me. It's smelled dank and bad down here since I arrived. But something's different now.

Rotten eggs.

My face falls.

The air…

I tremble when Kenzo's hand finds mine and squeezes a little.

"I'm sorry," he growls quietly. "I'm so fucking sorry for pulling you into my world."

"Don't you *dare* say that," I whisper back, wiping away a tear. "Loving you has been the highlight of an otherwise pretty shitty life."

"Fantastic endorsement."

I grin through the tears as I lean up to kiss him.

"Our friends are looking for us," I whisper more urgently. "They're going to find us."

"Definitely," he grunts.

"They *will*," I repeat.

"*I know*," Kenzo smiles softly.

Drip-drip-drip.

The sound of the dripping is maddening.

Drip-drip-drip—splash.

My brows knit. The splashing sound comes again, and I stand, walking tentatively toward the rusty railing and looking down into the inky black water.

A fish breaches the surface, then dives back down.

Holy fuck.

This is *not* how this ends.

I might be a lost cause at this point. I have no idea how long it's been since Valon stuck me with that needle. I'm guessing I have…fifteen minutes or so left?

But I'm getting Kenzo the *fuck* out of here.

I'm not sad to die. I've thought for years that I've been living on borrowed or stolen time. I should have died long ago in the attack on my family. Or in a squalid alley in Athens, at the hand of a man paying to use my body.

But I didn't. I made it this far, and my reward was to have Kenzo for a little while.

He. Will. Not. Die. Here.

This was never him "dragging me into his world." This is *my* mess. *My* chaos.

And he *will not* die for that.

I stare at the rippling surface of the water, where the fish just was. That fucking fish came from somewhere. The *water* came from somewhere.

We're going to find out where.

Kenzo is barely conscious when I march back to him, lift his arm over my shoulder, and get him to his feet, groaning with the effort.

"Annika…"

"C'mon," I grunt, gritting my teeth. "Help me get you up. You're a heavy fucker, you know that?"

"Annika, stop…"

"Nope."

"Whatever you're thinking, *I can't come with you,*" he breathes raspily. "*So just leave me—*"

"Not fucking happening. Get the *fuck up,*" I spit. "Now!"

His eyes slide to mine. Whatever spark is still flickering inside of them burns a little brighter. It's not much.

But it'll do.

"*There we are,*" I grunt as he grips the wall, pushing to his feet. "Let's go, Mori."

He shoots me a doubtful look as we stumble and shuffle to the stairs dropping down into the black water. "What the fuck are—"

"Come. *On.*"

I'm running out of time.

At the stairs, I let him sit back down. Then I tug off my pants, leaving them with him as I walk down into the terrifying water.

I *hate* deep water. I hate not being able to see the bottom, not knowing what's about to come up out of the depths to grab me.

Today, that particular phobia can go fuck itself.

Without another thought, I take a deep breath and dive beneath the surface.

Fuck, it's dark. Terrifyingly so. But I force myself to kick down to the bottom of the drowned room. The massive hole in the floor is a horror all its own. But I can't let that get to me either right now. I need to push past the fear.

For him.

I scream as a shape emerges from the hole in the floor. Air bubbles cloud my vision until I realize it's just another fish. I watch as it swims up into the room, crosses the gaping hole, and then swims back down.

...And presumably *out* the opposite side.

It's not proof.

But right now, it's all I have.

I kick back over to Kenzo and climb out. I refuse to acknowledge how bad and close to death he looks. Instead, I tie one leg of my pants to each of his wrists and back up to where he's sitting on the step right above the water, looping the pants around my neck.

I turn to cup his face, looking into his hooded, shallow eyes.

"I need you to take a deep breath," I whisper quietly. "And I need you to hold it for a long time. Yeah?"

"*Yeah*," he murmurs. "Yeah, princess, I—"

I kiss him hard, searing my lips to his as I hold his face in my hands.

Time to go.

I turn, adjust the makeshift harness around my neck, and plunge forward into the water. A splash follows as Kenzo's weight tips in after me. The pants bite into my neck, and my muscles scream as I kick down, dragging us deeper into the abyss below us. Fear rips and claws into me as we near the dark hole in the floor.

But I can't stop now.

We dive into it, and I swim lower, going the same direction

as the fish, praying to whatever God or gods are listening that the fish knew what the fuck it was doing.

We're in a smooth tunnel, and as I swim forward, I realize it's some kind of sewer main or water conduit.

I have no idea what's at the other end.

But there's no turning back now.

So I swim. I swim until my legs burn and my lungs scream. I swim until my vision blurs and my body is milliseconds away from giving out, giving up, and swallowing a mouthful of death.

That's when I see the light.

There's fucking *light* ahead.

There's nothing left in my tank, but I floor it anyway. I kick and paddle, my body screaming for oxygen until, suddenly, we're falling—

And for one brief second, I can fucking *breathe*.

Then I choke on water and spray as I go plunging back into water. Kenzo's weight pulls me down, but I fight and kick, dragging us both back to the surface. When I break through, I gasp for air, sucking sweet, sweet oxygen into my lungs with a wrenching sob.

We're outside. There's moonlight glinting down on us, and air across our faces.

My eyes lock onto the shore of the runoff pond. I kick away from the gush of water surging out of the pipe behind us, swimming with everything I have left until I get to land.

Kenzo is limp as I drag him out of the water.

His chest isn't moving anymore.

"KENZO!" I scream. I turn to the side, spasming as I vomit up grimy water, wheezing before I turn back to him. "KENZO!!!" I scream in his face, slamming my fists on his chest.

Hot tears sting my eyes and roll down my cheeks.

"FUCK YOU!!" I scream, pounding his chest again.

Something else is wrong. My vision is getting darker. My breathing is slowing.

I'm getting weaker.

I raise my fist and slam it as hard as I can against his chest, screaming his name as loud as I can.

His abs clench. His throat bobs and he sputters. Sobbing, I grab his face and turn it to the side as he chokes up water, wheezing and gasping as I fall across his chest.

Smiling.

But fading.

Quickly.

"ANNIKA!"

I hear my name somewhere in the distance.

"ANNIKA!!" The voice roars. "THEY'RE OVER HERE!!"

My eyes flutter open just long enough to see flashlights bobbing and weaving towards us. They get close, and in the glow of the moon, I can make out a handful of police officers, some EMTs, and both Takeshi and Mal bolting down a hillside toward us.

My head drops to his chest, listening to his weak heartbeat and the ragged breathing of his lungs.

He's alive.

He's going to live.

"I love you," I whisper against his chest as everything fades away.

I'll take what little time we had.

That's enough for me.

37

ANNIKA

It's white when I open my eyes.

Bright.

And…

My nose wrinkles.

It smells like *bleach*.

My eyes close again. But then I open them once more. The bright white light assaults me again, just a hazy white glow, and somewhere above me, a face I can't quite make out hovers.

"Where…" my voice sounds very far away. "Where am…"

"*You're in Heaven, Annika,*" a ghostly, vaguely feminine voice whispers. "*And I am God.*"

My throat bobs.

"*Yes, motherfucker. God's a woman.*"

My brows knit. My vision begins to clear as the haze melts away.

Freya is grinning impishly down at me.

"Hellooo, Annika," she coos in that weird, ghostly voice. *"Welcome baaack."*

She yelps as I sit bolt upright, my pulse spiking wildly. Next to me, a bunch of beeps speed up, and an alarm begins to chime frantically.

"Where—" I look at her bleary-eyed and woozy, my head swimming as I try and focus. "What the *fuck…*"

Suddenly, a door bangs open. Two women and a man in white are all up in my face: prodding and poking, telling me to take a breath and calm down. They're asking me my name, what fucking month it is. If I know how I got here.

Good question. I don't even know where the fuck *here* is.

"Where is he?!" I scream, whirling. "Where's—"

Something *very* nice hits my bloodstream and instantly, I'm chilling the *fuck* out. I drop my head to the side, looking curiously at the needle one of the women has just stuck into a tube that's running into my wrist.

Neat.

Then it all fades away.

THINGS ARE LESS chaotic when I next open my eyes. I blink, frowning as I turn to the side. Freya grins sheepishly at me.

"Frey?"

"Okay, that's on me," she blurts, looking guilty. "When you were waking up before, I was trying to be funny…"

"Wellll, maybe that was NOOT so funny…" I throw at her, doing my best impression of her weird ghost voice from before.

She smirks. "Not bad."

"Not as bad as your hospital humor," I grumble. "What the hell happened?"

"I'm pretty sure I freaked you out and sent you into a panic attack," she says with another sheepish look. "So, yeah, that's my—"

"Where is he?"

She doesn't respond quickly enough for my liking.

"Where is he?!"

I sit up again. Freya is right there, taking my hand and soothing me as she looks me in the eye.

"He's *okay*, Anni. I mean, he's going to be on a bunch of antibiotics for a while—you both are. That water was *disgusting*. It's sewer run-off."

Bile rises in my stomach, but I muscle it back down.

"But he's fine. He's out of surgery for the bullet wound, and he's sleeping."

Then it all hits me at once: the kidnapping, the needle in my arm, the bomb, Kenzo, *Valon*, the swim…

I frown as I look at Freya.

"How am I alive?"

She grins. "Because you're a badass? I'm pretty sure you broke some sort of breath holding record getting you both out of there—"

"No, I mean, I was poisoned."

She shakes her head. "No… You weren't."

"By Valon, yes," I insist. "He injected me with something—"

"A slow-acting sedative."

My brow furrows. "*What?*"

"You were mumbling something about poison when they got you in the ambulance so they ran a blood test, and that's what came back. You got drugged, Anni. But with a slow-acting sedative, not poison."

The door to my room opens. I look over and smile weakly as Takeshi and Hana walk in. Hana's got a bandage wrapped around her forehead and over her eye, and Takeshi's nursing some wicked bruises, but they both grin as they walk over to me.

I wince as Hana hugs me fiercely, choking a sob into my shoulder.

"*Thank you,*" she blurts.

"For?"

"Saving our idiot brother's life," Tak growls quietly, smirking.

Hana smiles. "He's out of surgery. And it went really well. Clean shot through his side. He lost a lot of blood, and he's on some major antibiotics. But he's going to be fine. He's just sleeping—"

The door opens. Mal's brow furrows when he sees Freya, but then he looks at me and smiles one of his small, private smiles.

"Just thought you'd like to know," he growls. "Kenzo's awake."

THE FEELING when he looks at me as I'm wheeled into the room is like a high no one on Earth has ever felt, making me want to scream and cry and laugh and throw up all at the same time.

But instead of whatever all *that* craziness would look like, I just choke out a sob as Hana and Takeshi push my wheelchair over to Kenzo's hospital bed.

He doesn't just look "okay".

He looks *alive*.

The color is back in his face, as well as that fire I love so much in his eyes. When he smiles at me, it's enough to break my heart and put it back together again.

We're not even all the way at his hospital bed before I'm lurching like a drunk out of the wheelchair and climbing in with him, careful to avoid his injured side. He winces but chuckles as he wraps his arms around me, tilts his head to the side, and kisses me.

Slowly.

Madly.

Deeply.

At some point, our family and friends tire of being ignored while I kiss my husband, and they all file out of the room.

Later, a nurse comes to tell me politely I need to go back to my own room. When I ignore her, another one comes to say it less politely.

I still don't leave.

Eventually, Sota comes to visit, hugging us and grinning. He also talks to the head nurse, who apparently knows him personally. After that, people stop trying to tell me to leave.

Good. That is *not* happening.

There are no stars in hospital room ceilings, not even in Japan. So instead, it's the soft blue glow of the machines beeping quietly around us that we look up at together.

His hand finds mine. I turn to him, our eyes locking.

He tells me I'm a little thief who stole his heart.

I tell him that's beyond fucking corny, and we need to work on his lines.

He asks me if I would prefer "messy little cum slut" as a term of endearment, and I get a little wet before it occurs to me that fucking him right now would almost definitely rip his stitches out.

So I don't.

Instead, I just tell him I love him.

He says it back.

And really, what else do you need?

EPILOGUE

ANNIKA

"I'M GOING to state for the record—yet *again,* I might add—that this is a terrible idea."

I ignore the voice in my ear as I twirl the diamond blade in a perfect circle around the suction cup. With a tiny cracking sound, I'm in. Slowly, keeping pressure on the suction button, I pull my arm away.

The big circle of glass comes away clean.

I grin as I set everything aside and then use the whisper-quiet sander to dull the edges of the brand spanking new hole in the skylight.

"Hello? You heard me, yes?"

"Yes, I heard," I sigh to Freya. "Settle down. I'm in."

It's not traditional to commit felony larceny right before your own second wedding celebration. But it's not traditional to have a second wedding celebration, either.

And I don't mean a second one like you've gotten divorced and this is having another try at marriage. I mean a second celebration of the wedding you already had. With the person you've already been married to for a few months.

But when have I ever been one for tradition?

"Hey, I don't want to be late. That spread looks *nice*," Freya murmurs.

It should be. Someone spent a fortune on it. And that "some-one" is Yelizaveta Solovyova, aka the White Queen.

The woman who used Valon Leka's services for much of her "shipping logistics."

And *also* the woman to whom Valon owed a fuckload of money, Valon having tried to double dip by selling her merchandise to the Cosa Nostra.

Yelizaveta, apparently, does *not* play around. When she found out Valon owed her somewhere north of forty million dollars, she put the screws to him. That's why he was pushing so hard to work with Sota and Kenzo: he *needed* their money. Or more likely, he needed their merchandise so he could sell *that* to the Cosa Nostra and pay the White Queen off.

Considering she was ready, willing and able to have Valon's brother killed to motivate Valon to pay her?

Yeah, I might rip off the Yakuza, too.

On paper, for political reasons, it's Kir who's footing the bill for Kenzo and I's second wedding celebration, seeing as how the first was a bit of a disaster. But it's technically Yelizaveta who's paying.

I'm fine with that.

As to why Valon was trying to get rid of Kenzo and Sota? Well, that question is still unanswered. Kenzo's friend Tetsuya, who *just so happens* to be the new Kyoto chief of police—totally coincidental, I'm sure—thinks it was a move by a rival Yakuza family. There's evidence that someone within the Yakuza world was willing to pay the cash-strapped Valon to get it done, but no one's claimed responsibility yet.

Probably a good thing, given that the Mori-kai is now unquestionably the most powerful family in Kyoto, with inroads being made into Tokyo, too.

But I digress.

I test the supports of the pulley system, then clip my harness in, step over the edge of the skylight, and lower myself into the dark penthouse.

I've spent *months* trying to track this item down. I've talked to antiques dealers worldwide, bribed underground resellers on four continents, and looked into every rumor.

Turns out the fucking thing never left Kyoto at all.

Freya's already disabled the alarms, the heat sensors and the lasers. So once my feet hit the floor, I can move fast. I unclip and bolt into the bedroom. Tempting as it is to swipe the Degas on the wall over the safe, I *did* make a promise to both Kir and Kenzo: no more theft.

Okay, I'm making a small exception for the task at hand. But a thirty-million-dollar painting? That feels like...overkill.

The wealthy private collector who lives here is out of the country for the next week, but still. I'm on a time crunch. That said, the safe is *insanely* easy to crack, and I've got it open in less than a minute.

I grin as I lay eyes on the little silver necklace resting on a display block.

I've seen this necklace before. I've *held it* before.

In fact, I'm the asshole who stole it from its rightful owner and sold it to a black-market dealer here in Kyoto, who then turned around and sold it to someone else *also right here in Kyoto* for a nice markup.

It's been here ever since.

I pluck it from its resting place and set it in the nice little black velvet box I've selected for the occasion. I grin, imagining the look on Kenzo's face when I give this back to him. I even wrote him a nice card.

Needless to say, all of this comes with letting him do *whatever* he wants to me tonight, however he wants to do it. But honestly, that's more of an "us" present than a "him" present.

"You're not seriously going to—*Goddammit,* Annika Brancovich, what—"

"Mori," I correct Freya. "Annika Mori, thank you very much."

"Whatever. What the fuck happened to Annika the bad-ass thief? Because that chick wouldn't go to all the trouble of breaking into a place to steal a necklace only to *leave money for it.*"

I smirk as I set the fat roll of bills down where the necklace previously was. I've even included a little extra, for the skylight.

"Hey, I made a promise."

"Yeah yeah yeah. If you're done, we have a party to get to."

I do end up being twenty minutes late for my own party. Not because of the job, but because my dress was being an asshole and reminding me why I've historically *not worn them*.

But I don't think Kenzo minds. The second I walk in, he's pulling me into his arms, dipping me, and kissing me thoroughly in front of everyone.

He's speechless when I give him his gift. Then he's kissing me all over again and telling me he loves me.

Then he's pulling me into a side room and giving *me* a present: two shiny gold and black toys, which have me shuddering and gripping his arm as he slowly pushes them into me.

Back with our friends and family, he twirls me across the dance floor and kisses me again.

"I love you, wife," he growls quietly, holding me in his arms.

"I love you too, husband," I murmur back, my lips finding his.

The Memento Mori series continues with Mal's story in *Emperor of Rage*.

Haven't gotten enough of Kenzo and Annika?
Get their extra scene here, or type this link into your browser: https://BookHip.com/VMNXPHJ

This isn't an epilogue or continuation to *Emperor of Wrath*.

But this extra hot "follow-up" story is guaranteed to keep the spice going.

ALSO BY JAGGER COLE

Memento Mori:

Emperor of Wrath

Emperor of Rage

Venomous Gods:

Toxic Love

Devious Vow

Poisonous Kiss

Corrupted Heart

Monstrous Urges

Dark Hearts:

Deviant Hearts

Vicious Hearts

Sinful Hearts

Twisted Hearts

Stolen Hearts

Reckless Hearts

Kings & Villains:

Dark Kingdom

Burned Cinder (Cinder Duet #1)

Empire of Ash (Cinder Duet #2)

The Hunter King (Hunted Duet # 1)

The Hunted Queen (Hunted Duet #2)

Prince of Hate

Savage Heirs:

Savage Heir

Dark Prince

Brutal King

Forbidden Crown

Broken God

Defiant Queen

Bratva's Claim:

Paying The Bratva's Debt

The Bratva's Stolen Bride

Hunted By The Bratva Beast

His Captive Bratva Princess

Owned By The Bratva King

The Bratva's Locked Up Love

The Scaliami Crime Family:

The Hitman's Obsession

The Boss's Temptation

The Bodyguard's Weakness

Power:

Tyrant

Outlaw

Warlord

Standalones:

Broken Lines

Bosshole

Grumpaholic

Stalker of Mine

ABOUT THE AUTHOR

Jagger Cole

A reader first and foremost, Jagger Cole cut his romance writing teeth penning various steamy fan-fiction stories years ago. After deciding to hang up his writing boots, Jagger worked in advertising pretending to be Don Draper. It worked enough to convince a woman way out of his league to marry him, though, which is a total win.

Now, Dad to two little princesses and King to a Queen, Jagger is thrilled to be back at the keyboard.

When not writing or reading romance books, he can be found woodworking, enjoying good whiskey, and grilling outside - rain or shine.

You can find all of his books at
www.jaggercolewrites.com

Made in the USA
Middletown, DE
27 October 2024

63329902R00245